D1625192

The Marrying Season

Also by Candace Camp

A Summer Seduction
A Winter Scandal
An Affair Without End
A Gentleman Always Remembers
A Lady Never Tells

Now available from Pocket Books

CANDACE CAMP

The MARRYING SEASON

Pocket Books

New York   London   Toronto   Sydney   New Delhi

Pocket Books
A Division of Simon & Schuster, Inc.
1230 Avenue of the Americas
New York, NY 10020

This book is a work of fiction. Names, characters, places, and incidents either are products of the author's imagination or are used fictitiously. Any resemblance to actual events or locales or persons, living or dead, is entirely coincidental.

Copyright © 2013 by Candace Camp

All rights reserved, including the right to reproduce this book or portions thereof in any form whatsoever. For information, address Pocket Books Subsidiary Rights Department, 1230 Avenue of the Americas, New York, NY 10020.

POCKET and colophon are registered trademarks of Simon & Schuster, Inc.

Manufactured in the United States of America

ISBN 978-1-62490-445-5

One

Genevieve Stafford watched, smiling, as her brother led his new bride onto the floor for their first dance. "I've never seen Alec look so happy."

Her grandmother let out a small, ladylike snort. "One would think Alec could have waited a few months at least. A hasty marriage is always cause for gossip, and when it is to a nobody, people are bound to talk."

"People would talk no matter who Alec married or how long they waited," Genevieve reminded her.

"I suppose it is inevitable when one is the Earl of Rawdon. Still, there's no need poking a beehive with a stick. I had hoped Rawdon would choose a more appropriate bride, given the scandal his first engagement provoked."

"One can hardly blame Alec for Lady Jocelyn's behavior." Genevieve quickly came to her brother's defense.

"'Tis a logical consequence of Alec's considering only how a woman looks, instead of her birth or family or character."

"Alec does love beauty," Genevieve admitted. "But there is more to Damaris than that."

The countess cast her a sideways glance. "Taking up the cudgels for Alec's wife now, too? As I remember, you wanted him to marry Damaris no more than I did."

Genevieve felt a flush rising in her cheeks under her grandmother's scrutiny. The countess had a way of making her feel as if she were five years old with a stain on her skirt. "I did not want him to be hurt again. I feared Damaris was an adventuress who would leave him once she'd gotten what she wanted. He would have been devastated." Her grandmother would never know how close Alec had come to that state when he thought Damaris *had* left him. The countess had been carefully shielded from the tumultuous events at Castle Cleyre. Genevieve went on carefully, "I—I came to see that I had been wrong about her. The important thing is, Damaris adores Alec, and he loves her."

"Pfft. Love." The countess waved away the notion. "Alec has a regrettable tendency toward poetic notions." She frowned at the thought of this shortcoming in her grandson. "At least you are not given to such nonsense."

"No, of course not." Genevieve was unaware of the little sigh she uttered.

"Ah, Felicity!" Real pleasure in her voice at last, the countess turned away to greet her old friend Lady Hornbaugh. "I wondered where you had gotten to."

"Thought I'd slipped off for a nap, eh?" Lady Hornbaugh trumpeted. "I considered it, I'll tell you that. Nothing like a vicar's sermon to cure insomnia, I always say. Hallo, Genevieve."

"Lady Hornbaugh." Genevieve greeted her grandmother's friend with polite deference, though inside she groaned. Whenever Lady Hornbaugh—with a voice that could be heard across any ballroom and of an outspoken bent—was around, Genevieve lived in dread of what she might say.

"You drew a nice number of guests," Lady Hornbaugh went on, nodding and surveying the room. "Who is that with Sir Myles?"

Genevieve glanced over. Sir Myles Thorwood was making his bow to two women standing beside a well-dressed blond man. Good humor shone from Myles's dark-lashed, golden-brown eyes, almost the same shade as his sun-kissed, light brown hair. His full, expressive mouth was, as usual, curved up in a merry grin. He was impeccably dressed, his broad-shouldered form showing to best advantage in the formal black attire. He was not as handsome as some—Lord Morecombe, for instance, who had the looks of a Lucifer—but it was generally agreed that Sir Myles Thorwood was possessed of an indefinable, irresistible, and apparently unending supply of charm.

"Flirting, as always." Genevieve frowned. She was, she knew, one of the few people in the *ton* who was not beguiled by Sir Myles. The man had been one of her brother's closest friends for years, but Genevieve and Myles rarely met that they did not find something upon which they disagreed.

"That is the Earl of Dursbury. Excellent family, of course. Never a whiff of scandal."

"So that's the new earl. Knew his father, of course—

and a dull dog he was." Lady Hornbaugh raised her lorgnette and stared unabashedly. "Then the beauty beside him is his stepmother?"

"Yes. Dreadful woman." Lady Rawdon sniffed.

Genevieve studied the attractive woman now chatting with Sir Myles. Lady Dursbury's lustrous, dark hair was done up in an intricate arrangement of curls; her eyes were large and a soft, doelike brown. Diamonds winked in her earlobes, matched by the pendant around her throat. She wore a round gown of deep plum silk, her full, white bosom swelling above the lace-edged neckline. Genevieve could not help but contrast the woman's curvaceous figure to her own tall, narrow frame.

"The old earl died a year ago, as I recall, so she'll be out of her year of mourning. She's been stuck out in the country since she married Dursbury, and now, I'll wager, she intends to make a come-out of her own. Who's the young chit with them?"

"Miss Halford," Lady Rawdon said. "She was old Dursbury's ward. Lived with them since her father died a few years ago. It's said her ladyship is very fond of her."

"Harry Halford's daughter? I warrant Lady Dursbury is fond of her, then." Lady Hornbaugh let out one of her boisterous laughs. "Girl's worth a fortune. Shouldn't wonder if Dursbury has a mind to marry her."

Genevieve's grandmother shrugged. "She's a plain little thing. And I've never heard that Dursbury was cash-strapped."

"No. Still, never bad to have more. Mayhap Sir Myles

has a mind toward the heiress, as well," Lady Hornbaugh speculated.

"Myles?" Genevieve repeated, startled, then laughed. "Myles is not the marrying sort."

"He is a dreadful flirt, of course," her grandmother agreed. "I have seen him break many a foolish young girl's heart."

"You malign the young man," protested Lady Hornbaugh, who obviously had a soft spot for Sir Myles. "He's not at all unkind. Quite the opposite, I'd say."

"I did not say it was his fault. I don't suppose Sir Myles can help it if silly girls melt at his smile or think his compliments mean undying devotion. Thank goodness Genevieve had too much sense to pay attention to his blandishments."

"Sir Myles never flirted with me," Genevieve pointed out. "He was too loyal a friend to Alec. Not, of course, that I wanted him to."

"Still, no matter how much he enjoys his bachelor state, Sir Myles must marry one day," the countess remarked. "He has that whole brood of sisters, no brother to follow him or produce an heir. But I cannot imagine he would be interested in so plain a chit as Miss Halford. The widow would be more his style."

"Dursbury's stepmother?" Genevieve asked. "But she is older than Sir Myles, surely."

"Three or four years, perhaps. Married young to an old man," her grandmother summed up succinctly. "I imagine the lady's charms would outweigh that."

"It certainly doesn't seem he finds any fault in her," Genevieve said tartly.

"And Lady Dursbury returns his interest," Lady Hornbaugh responded gleefully.

Lady Dursbury's face was glowing, her eyes sparkling, as she chatted with Myles. The woman leaned forward to put her hand on his arm, smiling up into his face. Genevieve felt a twinge of annoyance, an emotion not uncommon where Sir Myles was concerned, and she turned away, looking out across the large assembly room.

"It's no wonder," Lady Hornbaugh went on. "Thorwood's a handsome young devil. Don't you agree, Genevieve?"

"What? Oh. Yes, I suppose," Genevieve said with great indifference, wafting her fan. "I have known him so long, I scarcely notice."

"Not notice!" Lady Hornbaugh hooted. "Good gracious, girl, now you have me worried about your eyesight."

"I suggest we cease discussing the man," her grandmother put in, "as he is making his way toward us right now."

Genevieve glanced over to see that Myles was, indeed, striding across the floor toward them, smiling. Her spirits rose in anticipation. Her verbal skirmishes with Myles were always invigorating, no matter how irritating the man could be. And, she was honest enough to admit, it was rather pleasant to watch him walk.

"Lady Rawdon." Myles made a perfect bow to the women. "And Lady Hornbaugh. Lady Genevieve. I cannot believe my good fortune to find three such lovely ladies unattended."

"Flatterer," Lady Hornbaugh replied without a hint of displeasure, and rapped him lightly on the arm with her fan. "As if we did not know that 'tis the presence of only one young lady that brought you over to visit us. 'Tis Genevieve who draws the young gentlemen."

"I fear you mistake Sir Myles," Genevieve said drolly. "He has no preference for me or any other particular lady. He is like a butterfly, drawn to all the flowers."

Myles's eyes gleamed gold with amusement. "Lady Genevieve! You are implying I am fickle?"

"I would not say fickle. Merely . . . indiscriminate."

He laughed. "My lady, you have a cruel tongue."

"I would say a truthful one."

"Nay, I cannot allow you to count yourself so low."

"Myself? I believe we were discussing you, sir," Genevieve shot back.

"But if I am indiscriminate in my tastes, then my desire to ask you for this dance would cast you among the vast lot of young ladies whom I admire. And you must know that you are on a level quite above them."

Genevieve could not keep from chuckling. "You are a complete hand."

"That I may be. But will you give me *your* hand for this dance?" He extended his arm to her.

Genevieve took his arm, and they started toward the center of the floor. "Rather cocksure of yourself, I must say," she told him. "Offering me your arm before I answered."

"Oh, I knew you would dance with me," Myles said with a grin. "You cannot resist."

"Indeed?" Genevieve raised an eyebrow. "You count yourself so charming?"

"No, but I know that however obstinate, haughty, and disagreeable you may be, you love to dance."

Genevieve drew in breath to shoot back a sharp retort, but instead she laughed. "You are an excellent dancer," she admitted. "Indeed, it was you who taught me to dance."

"Did I?"

"I might have known you would not remember. No doubt it is more difficult when one has danced with every young lady of the *ton*."

"One must practice, after all." Myles grinned and leaned his head toward her in that way he had perfected, as if the woman on his arm were the only woman in the room. "But 'tis always memorable to dance with you."

"Don't try to cut a wheedle with me." Genevieve rolled her eyes. "You just told me you did not recall. It was one summer when you and Gabriel came with Alec to Castle Cleyre. Grandmama had quite despaired of my learning to dance properly. My dancing tutor had left in a snit."

Myles let out a bark of laughter. "Chased off by the rough edge of your tongue, no doubt."

"He was an oily little man," Genevieve shot back indignantly. "He tried to kiss me one day—and I was only thirteen!" She stopped, realizing that Myles's teasing had led her to touch on a most indelicate subject. It was one of Myles's many annoying qualities—somehow when she was around him, she found herself blurting out the most appalling things. Fortunately, Myles rarely seemed shocked, no matter what she told him.

"I am surprised Alec didn't have his hide."

"I did not tell him, of course. I was afraid he might kill the little weasel, and I would not have wanted Alec to go to gaol, of course."

"Of course. Why didn't you get Alec to teach you to dance?"

"He wasn't as good a dancer as you. Gabriel was quite good also, but I had such a mad *tendre* for him that I stumbled all over my feet whenever he was near."

"Your girlish dreams were for Gabe and not me?" Myles raised his hand to his chest dramatically. "Lady Genevieve, you wound me."

Genevieve laughed. "Then you may take consolation in the fact that you rank well above Gabriel now." She glanced over to where Lord Morecombe and his wife, Thea, stood talking and laughing with Alec and Damaris.

"Ah, Genny . . . can you not forgive Gabe yet?" Myles asked in a more serious tone.

"He turned against my brother." Genevieve's blue eyes flashed in a way Myles had witnessed often enough in Rawdon, reminding him how close the Staffords still were to their fierce and autocratic ancestors. "The Morecombes broke Alec's heart, and it was not just Jocelyn's tossing him aside that did it. Alec believed Gabriel was his friend. You do not know how it was, growing up in the castle. There were no children of proper birth anywhere around, and a Stafford could not be friends with a servant or a tenant's child. Father would have had his hide."

"I think it was not only Alec who found it lonely at Cleyre," Myles said gently.

"Oh, well . . ." Genevieve glanced at him. Myles could be disconcertingly perceptive at times. She shrugged carelessly, erasing the heat from her voice. "I did not feel it as Alec did. When he went off to school and you and Gabriel befriended him, it meant a great deal to Alec. For Gabriel to accuse him of frightening Jocelyn into running away—even going so far as to suggest that Alec might have harmed the silly girl! It wounded Alec deeply."

"Yet Alec has forgiven him." Myles nodded toward the two men, deep in conversation.

"Yes. Well . . . Alec has a warmer heart than I." Genevieve smiled ruefully. "Mayhap he has more of our mother in him. It is enough for him that Gabriel apologized for his accusations."

"Gabriel was in a good deal of pain himself at the time," Myles reminded her. "He feared his friendship for Alec had led him to push his sister into the engagement."

"Gabriel's sister was as foolish as she was selfish, and the fact that she died as a result does not change her into a martyr. For Alec's sake I will try not to dislike Gabriel. But I shall never forgive Jocelyn." Genevieve's eyes flashed, her jaw setting.

"What a lioness you are! I can only pray that I will never be the object of your enmity."

"Don't be absurd. You would never turn your back on Alec. No one can deny your loyalty."

"Despite my many other shortcomings." Myles grinned. The music struck up behind them, and he held out his hand. "Enough talk of feuds past. Come, Genny, let us dance."

Genevieve smiled and went into his arms.

When Myles returned Genevieve to her grandmother's side, Lady Rawdon had been joined by Alec and Damaris, as well as Lord and Lady Morecombe. Morecombe bowed politely to Genevieve, though he shot her an ironic glance that said he knew full well her true feelings about him. Genevieve returned his greeting without the iciness she would normally have employed. After all, she had told Myles she would try to like him, and since his wife was Damaris's best friend, the Morecombes would clearly often be around. She smiled at Gabriel's wife with more warmth. Genevieve had been around Thea several times the past few days as the wedding preparations demanded, and somewhat to her surprise, she found herself liking the woman.

Alec was smiling, as he had been all day, and his blue eyes, even lighter than Genevieve's, were bright with happiness. Impulsively, he reached out and pulled his sister into a hug, the affectionate gesture surprising them both.

"I am very happy for you," Genevieve told him quietly.

"Thank you." Alec released Genevieve, grinning. "No doubt 'tis a great relief for everyone, given the state of my company the last few weeks."

"You were a bit of a bear," Genevieve agreed drily. With Damaris here in Chesley the past month preparing for the wedding, Alec had roamed the halls of Castle Cleyre like a ghost—albeit a testy and combative specter.

"He is *always* a bit of a bear," Damaris put in, smiling up at Alec in such a way that it turned her words into an endearment.

"I suppose I was a trifle irritable," Alec allowed, earning a derisive laugh from the others.

As the group chatted, laughing, Genevieve saw Thea draw Sir Myles aside. Thea spoke a few words to him, nodding toward the other side of the room. Genevieve looked in the direction she indicated and saw a young woman sitting stiffly beside an older lady, watching the dancers. Myles nodded, smiling down at Thea, and excused himself. Genevieve watched as he strolled across the room and bowed to the young lady, then led her out onto the floor.

"That was kind of you," Genevieve commented as Thea moved over to stand beside her.

"Oh. 'Twas little enough. I can always rely on Myles's good nature." Thea absently reached up to stuff a cinnamon-colored curl back into place. Genevieve had yet to see Lady Morecombe when at least one or two of her wildly springing tresses weren't trying to escape their moorings. "I intend to steal you away as well."

"Me?" Genevieve asked, surprised.

"Yes. We must whisk Damaris from Alec's side—no easy task, as you can see—and help her change into her traveling dress."

"Oh," Genevieve said blankly.

"That is what the friends of the bride do, isn't it?"

"Oh. Well, yes, I—I suppose so. I've never—I haven't any—" Genevieve stopped, flushing. "I mean, I have friends, of course. Just not of that sort." With every word, she was making more of a fool of herself. It was so difficult talking to people she did not know, particularly when, as Thea was apt to do, they did not follow the well-worn grooves of polite chitchat. Genevieve pulled herself straighter, retreating into the cool reserve she had always used to cover her awkwardness. "One does not, really, in the city."

"No doubt it is different here in Chesley," Thea agreed cheerfully, taking Genevieve's arm in a firm grip and pulling her toward Damaris.

Startled, Genevieve went with Thea and watched, somewhat bemused, as she slipped an arm around Damaris's waist, then, laughing and shaking her head at Alec's protests, led the new Lady Rawdon away. Thea and Damaris chattered merrily as they went up the stairs, and Genevieve followed behind them, uncomfortably aware that she should enter into their conversation, yet unable to think of anything to say.

They were talking about Damaris and Alec's upcoming honeymoon trip to the Continent. Traveling abroad was a topic on which Genevieve knew she could say something, unlike the books the two had discussed yesterday, but every sentence she came up with sounded stilted in her head, and by the time she had formed one that did not, the topic had changed to Damaris's trousseau.

"I hadn't nearly enough time to buy a full one," Damaris said with a sigh as they entered her bedroom. "But at least I managed a few new dresses."

Spread out on the bed was her carriage gown, a handsome creation of vivid blue in a high-collared, vaguely military style, accented by large frogged fastenings down the front. Genevieve sucked in her breath in a spontaneous burst of admiration.

"Oh, Damaris! It's wonderful." Genevieve went forward to examine the dress more closely. Dissimilar as the two of them were, Genevieve and her new sister-in-law found common ground when it came to fashion. She reached out to smooth her fingertips across the material. "Such a beautiful color. It will look perfect on you."

"When I return, you must borrow it sometime," Damaris told her, adding with a sparkle of humor, "After all, I wore your frocks often enough at Cleyre."

"I wish I could." Genevieve sighed. "But you have the coloring for it. I would look like a ghost walking. Years ago, when I first came out, I wanted desperately to wear something bright." She heard the wisp of longing in her voice and quickly added, "But of course Grandmama was right. Pale colors suit me best."

"You should wear it anyway," Thea told her firmly. "I have foresworn all my old dull dresses."

"I have heard love does that to people," Damaris said with a teasing glance at her friend.

Thea laughed. "Yes, I suppose it does. I recommend it for everyone."

"Well, all one has to do is move to Chesley. You met Gabriel here, and I met Alec." Damaris turned toward Genevieve. "You should look around, Genevieve; your future husband may be among the guests."

Genevieve was not certain what Damaris meant but smiled politely.

"It isn't Chesley," Thea protested. "It's Saint Dwynwen."

"Saint who?" Genevieve asked. "I've never heard of him."

"Her. She was a Welsh saint."

"The patron saint of love," Damaris added. "There is a statue of her in the church. Did you see it? In the side chapel, where the tombs are."

Genevieve vaguely remembered a rather battered wood sculpture. "It's, um, rather old?"

Thea laughed. "Older than old. We have no idea when it was carved. A local knight took it from a Welsh shrine during some campaign or other in Wales. He also brought home a Welsh bride. He was quite smitten with her, you see, and claimed that his prayers to this saint had been rewarded."

"It's a very romantic story," Damaris said. "But the local legend is about what happened after that."

"What happened?" Genevieve asked, intrigued.

"It is said that when one prays before that statue with a true and earnest heart, love will come to you," Thea explained.

Genevieve raised a skeptical eyebrow. "And do you know anyone to whom this actually happened?"

"Yes. Me," Thea said simply.

Genevieve had no idea how to respond. She turned toward Damaris. "And you did that as well?"

"Oh, no. I was doing my best to avoid love, not find it," Damaris replied drily.

"Well, I am certain it wasn't Alec who did so." Genevieve giggled at the thought of her large, fierce-visaged brother kneeling before an ancient statue to pour out his heart.

"Mm. It seems a bit unlikely," Thea agreed. "But perhaps one doesn't need to ask, only to have it in one's heart."

Alec's heart, Genevieve knew, was as romantic as anyone's, however he appeared. Her heart, on the other hand, was that of a true Stafford. She smiled faintly. "Then I fear it is quite useless for me."

It took a good deal of time and what Genevieve's grandmother termed a "raucous display" before the new bride and groom were on their way. Genevieve smiled and waved with the rest of the guests, but she could not deny the little clutch of loneliness in her chest. She had not lost her brother, of course; she knew she could always rely on Alec. But it would not be the same.

"Everything is changed now," her grandmother said, echoing Genevieve's thoughts in a manner that no longer surprised Genevieve. The countess turned and started back into Damaris's house. "We must think to your future."

"Must we?" Genevieve asked.

"Of course." The countess sat down, allowing herself the first small show of weakness since the wedding began.

"The gossip Alec's marriage will engender makes it even more imperative that you marry well."

"I? Marry?" Genevieve turned toward her grandmother in surprise.

"Yes. The family's reputation will suffer, of course, once people learn about the matter of Damaris's unfortunate birth. Your marriage to a man of excellent name would do much to counter that."

"But . . . I have no plans to marry."

"Not yet. You needn't look shocked, Genevieve. Surely you do not expect to remain a spinster?"

"Well, no, certainly not. But I had not thought of marriage . . . anytime soon."

"There has been no need to think about it until now. But you are twenty-five years old, my dear. Not on the shelf, of course, but still . . . there's the matter of children to consider."

"Children?" Genevieve responded weakly.

"Goodness, Genevieve, there's no need to parrot my words. I am simply reminding you that it is time. With Alec taking a bride, you will no longer be the hostess of Stafford House. You won't run Rawdon's household. You will scarcely enjoy giving over the reins to another woman. But, there, we don't need to discuss it now. Plenty of time later." Lady Rawdon turned away and scanned the remaining guests, and her hand went to the pocket of her elegantly simple dress. "Oh, dear. I seem to have lost my spectacles."

"Your pince-nez?" Genevieve asked in surprise. The countess wore the little glasses only for close work.

"Yes. They must have slipped out of my pocket at the church. Be a dear and fetch them for me."

"Of course."

Pausing only long enough to pick up her cloak, Genevieve walked to St. Margaret's, a squat, stone, square-towered church that lay across a small footbridge from the rest of the village. Inside the empty church lit only by the rays of the afternoon sun, Genevieve went to the front pew, where she and the countess had sat. There was no glint of the spectacles, though she ran her hand over the cushion to be sure, then squatted to search beneath the seats. Genevieve sighed and stood up. It wasn't like her grandmother to be forgetful—or wrong, for that matter. But Genevieve could not imagine why the countess would have sent her on a fool's errand, either.

Whatever the reason, Genevieve was glad to have a little time to herself to think about her grandmother's startling words. The countess was right, of course. It was time that Genevieve married. However pleasant Damaris might be, she was accustomed to running a household; she would not leave the reins of her new home in Genevieve's hands. And Genevieve was not the sort to relish living in a house under another woman's control. It was not as if Genevieve had planned never to marry. She had always expected to, presumed she would ... at some point in the future. But that point was now.

Genevieve sighed and strolled across the church into the small side chapel. Narrow, stained-glass windows cast a dim glow over the chamber, lighting the recumbent effigies on the tombs of a long-dead lord and his lady. Against one side wall stood a cracked and battered wooden statue of a saint next to a rack of votive candles and a prie-dieu. This had to be Thea's saint. She walked over to the roughly carved statue. It was even more humble than the rest of this country church. Here and there were faded traces of the paint that had once adorned it. A crack started at one shoulder and ran several inches down the figure's chest. It hardly seemed the sort of thing to inspire a legend. She wondered if, as Thea believed, true love came to those who yearned for it. Not Staffords, of course. And yet . . . she could not help but think of her brother's face as he danced with Damaris, the sharp lines softened, his eyes alight. Or the way they had looked at each other in the church today as they said their vows. Something turned in her chest, piercing and hot and cold, all at once. What must it be like to know that emotion? To lay one's heart in another's hands?

She swallowed against the choking sensation rising in her throat. Feeling faintly foolish, she picked up one of the tiny sticks beside the flickering votive candles and lit a candle from the flames of another. She knelt, carefully holding her skirt so it would not catch and tear, and clasped her hands in front of her on the padded leather bar.

Now what?

Genevieve glanced at the plain statue beside her. Crudely carved though it was, somehow the artist had made the face kind, even understanding. Genevieve turned back to the flames dancing in their small red-glass cups.

"Dear God," she whispered, "pray send me a husband. The right husband," she added hastily. But what did that mean? "A man of substance and good character."

What else should she say? Surely the Lord would know the proper qualities her husband should have. The man must come from an old family; that went without saying. While he did not need to be a Midas, a certain amount of money was necessary. Not too old. Certainly not a rattle like Lord Farnsley's son. But neither would one want a bookish man like Thea's brother, say, who always prattled on about Roman ruins and such. Someone who could ride; she could not imagine spending her life with a man who did not love horses as she did. A man who was responsible and aware of his duty. Presentable in appearance. He need not be an Adonis like Gabriel Morecombe, but she would, after all, have to see him day after day. She imagined for a fleeting, wistful moment how nice it would be to have a husband who could make her laugh like Sir Myles did or who had his charm or his grace on the dance floor—but of course those were hardly necessary qualities in a husband.

She scowled into the candles. The flames were creating little gold and black spots in her vision. It occurred to her how peculiar she would look if anyone walked in. It was altogether silly—as if one could summon up a proper husband just by kneeling and asking for one.

A door slammed, and Genevieve jumped to her feet, her heart suddenly pounding in her chest. She stepped out into the nave of the church.

A blond-haired man stood at the door, peering inside. Lord Dursbury. Presentable. Well-bred. Sober and responsible. And a lineage almost equal to her own.

"Ah, there you are," he said cheerfully and smiled. "Lady Rawdon sent me to find you. Did you find what you came for?"

Genevieve smiled back at him. "I believe I have."

Two

SEVEN MONTHS LATER

"Hallo, Myles," *a voice greeted* Sir Myles as soon as he stepped into White's.

Sir Myles glanced over at the gentlemen lounging by the fireplace and nodded politely. "Carrington. Giles. Mr. Dilworth."

"Haven't seen you in an age. Where have you been?"

"Business on the estate." Myles strolled over to them. The other men belonged to a gambling-mad set Myles rarely joined, but courtesy required that he stop to chat for a few moments.

"Thought you'd be at the Morecombes' ball tonight," Carrington went on.

"Have the invitation right here," Myles responded vaguely, patting his pocket. He saw no reason to add that he had not decided whether he would go. The social whirl had grown stale these days.

"Morecombe's a good chap. Don't know about this ball, though. Now that Lady Genevieve's engaged to

Lord Dursbury, he and his set are bound to be there. Dull dog, Dursbury."

"No doubt," Myles replied, casually picking an almost invisible piece of lint from his sleeve. "Lady Genevieve seems happy?"

"Hard to tell, with her." Mr. Dilworth chuckled. "Though the rumors are Dursbury may cry off."

"What?" Myles raised his head sharply. "Who says that? 'Twould be the act of a cad to break their engagement."

"Oh, I imagine Dursbury's too much of a gentleman to do it. But the rumors are all over. If you hadn't been ruralizing for months, you'd have heard it." Carrington gave a vague wave of his hand.

"Lady Looksby's where I saw it."

"Who?"

"You know, the column in *The Onlooker*. Lady Looksby, she calls herself."

"That scandal sheet?" Myles scoffed.

Mr. Dilworth retrieved a paper from the table in the hall. "Yes, it says right here: 'What lord is having second thoughts about his wedding? I have heard bets are being laid in Brooks's on whether Lord D___ will make it to the altar. He may be this northern lady's last hope, but with the wedding delayed yet again, Lady Looksby thinks the omens are not good.'"

Myles let out a rude snort. "Don't be a fool—as if this scribbler knows anything about either one of them."

"Smoke and fire and all that," Carrington replied archly.

"Yes, it's the devil of a thing—Lady Looksby seems

to hear it all. There are some say she's really a member of the *ton*."

"Well, gentlemen, I'll leave you to your gossip rag," Myles said, stepping away. "As you said, I have a party to attend."

"But you just arrived." The men looked at him, confused.

"Nevertheless . . ." Myles sketched them a bow and walked away.

Genevieve gazed out across the crowd as Lady Dursbury and Miss Halford assured one another that the flowers were lovely, the music was melodic, and the crowded room was quite warm. A few feet away, one of Dursbury's friends was droning on about the carriage he was considering buying.

The unfortunate fact was that Genevieve found several of her fiancé's friends and family a trifle boring. Dursbury, of course, ever the perfect gentlemen, was much too loyal and polite to seek more entertaining company. Genevieve suppressed a sigh, reminding herself that only the need for chaperonage kept her and her fiancé constantly surrounded by others. Once they were married, it would be different. They would be together alone.

A hard knot formed in Genevieve's chest. She was not sure what it was, but the constriction had made its presence known more and more often recently. She had not told her grandmother; she would not want to worry her, and it was nothing, really. Nor was it odd to be sleeping

less these days, to find it hard to fall asleep and sadly easy
to awaken.

"Ah, Lady Genevieve, look who is here," Lady Elora
said, interrupting her thoughts, and Genevieve turned to
see that Foster Langdon had joined Elora and Iona.

"Mr. Langdon." Genevieve suppressed a groan. Foster
Langdon had begun hanging about the past few weeks,
professing his admiration and bemoaning his supposedly
broken heart at the news of her engagement. Genevieve
avoided him as best she could, but Lady Elora seemed to
have a soft spot for the man and rarely turned him away.

"You put the moon to blush for shame tonight," Langdon told Genevieve now, taking her hand although she
had not offered it to him.

"Indeed, you are too kind," Genevieve said coolly as
she tried to pull her hand from his grasp, finally jerking
it free.

He leaned closer, and Genevieve edged back, wrin-
kling her nose at the strong scent of wine that rose from
him. The man was thoroughly foxed. As if to prove her
point, he swayed a trifle and reached out to steady himself. Genevieve slid a few more inches away.

"Excu—" she began, and at that moment she heard
Myles Thorwood's voice.

"Ladies," Sir Myles greeted them cheerfully. "Langdon,
I cannot allow you to keep the most beautiful women of
the *ton* to yourself."

With relief Genevieve turned to Myles as he inserted
himself between her and Mr. Langdon. On the other side

of her, Lady Dursbury preened and smiled at their new visitor, her dark, liquid eyes lambent with promise.

"Sir Myles!" she cooed. "I vow, we have not seen you in an age. You have been sorely missed. I was telling Miss Halford only yesterday that I believed you must be shunning our company."

"No, you wrong me, my lady." Myles bowed to Elora. "I have been out of the city. Pressing matters at home. Rest assured that it was out of no desire to avoid the company of such a lovely lady as yourself." He turned to Genevieve, his smile rakish. "Lady Genevieve. I trust you missed me, as well."

"La, sir, I had not realized you were gone," Genevieve replied airily.

Sir Myles grinned. "My dear lady, I know that is a plumper." When Genevieve raised her brows, he went on, "I believe you once told me I was like a small pebble lodged in one's shoe. And one is always aware when such an annoyance as that vanishes."

Genevieve's laugh trilled out at his words. Dursbury's stepmother cast her a surprised glance, but quickly said, "I am sure Lady Genevieve did not mean to insult you, sir."

"I fear Sir Myles knows me too well to believe that," Genevieve put in.

"Indeed," Myles agreed. "I have known the lady since she was in braids, and she has always been the bane of my existence."

"How unkind," Genevieve retorted, her eyes twinkling.

"If I am unkind, then perhaps you will allow me to

atone for my sins by taking a turn around the dance floor with me," Myles said.

"Of course. 'Twould be most unfeeling of me not to allow you your penance."

"Ladies." Myles bowed to the other two women and offered Genevieve his arm.

"I must thank you for taking me away," Genevieve told Myles lightly as they took to the floor.

"Langdon bothering you?"

"The man is always turning up and mouthing fulsome compliments."

"Some ladies enjoy fulsome compliments," Myles pointed out.

"Not I. And it is so difficult to get rid of him. I believe he is a trifle thick."

"I would say so if he has not realized your dislike of him. I could see it twenty feet away."

"I am glad for that." She smiled. "Did I really tell you that you were like a pebble in one's shoe?"

He laughed. "Indeed. 'Insignificant yet infinitely annoying,' I believe were your words."

"My, I must have been quite irritated. What had you done?"

"I? Why must *I* have done something?"

"Because I find that you usually do," Genevieve teased. No doubt she was grinning too broadly, but at the moment she could not find it in herself to care. It felt too sweet, too carefree, to be circling the floor in his arms.

He shook his head in mock dismay. "My lady, you wrong me . . . and after I have rescued you."

She smiled. "Very well. I shall say nothing else bad about you."

"Genevieve!" He widened his eyes. "No, think! You may do yourself harm."

Genevieve laughed. "It has been forever since we danced together. Was it at Alec's wedding? No, surely that's not right."

"I believe it was the Twelfth Night ball." He gave her a rueful grin. "But you may be excused for forgetting. I believe you had other matters on your mind that night."

"What—oh, of course." That had been the night Dursbury proposed. How foolish of her to have forgotten. "Where have you been since then? What have you been doing? Lady Dursbury is right; you have not been at any of the parties."

"I spent some time at home. I am surprised you missed me, involved as you must be in wedding plans."

"Indeed. But I believe Grandmother is enjoying it a great deal more than I." Her eyes sparkled with laughter. "It is rather fun to watch her and Lady Dursbury square off about the details."

"My money would be on your grandmother."

"You would be right. Although Elora did win on the subject of the location. She is insisting it be at the cathedral in Ely."

"No doubt Lady Rawdon wanted it to be at Durham Cathedral."

"Oh, no. She wanted it in the chapel at Cleyre."

"And what did you prefer?"

"I did not really care. The chapel was not large enough; Elora was right about that. I think that was partly why Grandmama wanted it, so they could exclude some of the Dursbury relatives—there are hundreds of them, it seems. Of course, I could not go against Grandmama."

"No, indeed."

"In the end, Alec told her he'd be damned if he'd have all those benighted people bothering him at Castle Cleyre. And Grandmother no longer likes to travel so far, anyway."

"Alec enjoys his solitary life," Myles mused. "I was surprised to hear he and Damaris were in London."

"I believe Damaris wished to shop."

"Ah." Myles smiled. "He is happy?"

"Oh, yes. He and Damaris are as mawkishly in love as ever. One hardly dares step outside one's room for fear of finding them in the hall, embracing . . . or worse."

"Spoken like the cynic that you are."

"I am not cynical!" Genevieve protested, a little stung. "I am merely . . . practical."

"Naturally." His brown eyes danced with laughter, and Genevieve, looking up into his face, had to smile. "Speaking of true love, where are Gabriel and Thea? This is their party, is it not? I haven't seen a sign of them."

"I have no idea where Gabriel is. But Thea and Damaris were talking about the baby—"

"Matthew?"

"Yes. They brought him with them. They take him with them everywhere," Genevieve added in a tone of amazement.

"Some people are oddly fond of their children."

Genevieve shot him a repressive look. "Most people leave children at home with their nurse or a governess."

"I believe I often traveled with my parents."

"Yes, and look how you turned out," she gibed with a grin.

"A fair hit, my lady."

"Thea said she was going to slip away to the nursery before Nurse put Matthew to bed, and Damaris decided to go with her, leaving me no recourse but to chat with Miss Halford and Lady Dursbury." She frowned at the memory.

"Not your favorite occupation, I gather."

"No." Genevieve sighed. "I am a vinegary wretch, am I not? No doubt I shall eventually become one of those old crones, rapping my cane on the floor and snapping at my relatives."

"I should like to see that." He chuckled. "I have an idea."

"What?"

"The waltz is about to end. I suggest we nip up to join Damaris and Thea."

"In the nursery?"

"Why not? I'll warrant 'tis livelier there. I'd lay odds we'd find Gabriel and Alec, as well."

"No doubt. They are never far from their wives. Oh, Myles, you must not tempt me."

"Mustn't I?" His golden-brown eyes lit up, and Genevieve felt an odd quiver. The music came to a halt, but Myles retained possession of her hand. "Come, leave with me."

Genevieve nodded, giving a guilty little giggle, and Myles whisked her out of the room.

Three

*M*yles led *Genevieve down the* hall and up the back staircase, both of them laughing like naughty children escaping the schoolroom.

"How do you know where to go?" Genevieve asked, a little breathless from the climb up two flights of stairs.

"You forget—I have known Gabe since we were lads. We usually gathered here or at my house."

"Yes, I remember," Genevieve replied a little wistfully. "Alec was always running off to join you. I was quite envious."

"Were you?" He glanced at her, surprised.

"Of course! You were having fun, no doubt engaging in all sorts of forbidden things, and I was stuck with my governess and my grandmother, keeping my back straight and learning how to walk appropriately."

"If only I had known that you were interested in forbidden things." His voice held an odd, husky quality, and Genevieve glanced at him sharply. His mouth was curved up in a slow, sensuous way he had never smiled at her before, and for an instant, heat flashed in his eyes. Then he dropped her hand and opened the door for her.

Maddeningly, Genevieve felt a blush forming on her cheeks, and she ducked her head to hide it from him as she slipped through the doorway. She stopped, Myles right behind her, as they took in the sight before them.

They were in the nursery wing of the town house, where the corridor was narrower and the ceiling lower. At the opposite end of the hall were Thea and Damaris. Next to his wife, Alec lounged against the wall, his pale blond hair almost brushing the low ceiling, his face relaxed and mellow. All three of them were laughing as they watched the fourth member of their group, Gabriel, Lord Morecombe, romping on the floor with a shrieking, giggling blond-haired tot.

Genevieve glanced at Myles, her eyes brimming with laughter, and they kept their silence, gazing at the handsome aristocrat, coat off and dark curls mussed, on all fours acting as "horsey" for the merry boy on his back.

After a moment, Myles murmured, "Damaris is in the family way, isn't she?"

"What?" Genevieve turned to him, startled. Damaris was not even showing yet, and she herself had had no idea until Damaris had divulged the happy news to her the day before. "How did you know?"

He shook his head. "You forget, I have five sisters— and innumerable nieces and nephews. She simply looks . . . the way they looked."

"Well, it's scarcely something you should be talking about!" Genevieve told him sharply, not sure whether she was more shocked that he had brought up such an indelicate subject or that he had so easily been able to see what she had not. "'Tis most inappropriate."

"You cannot think I would broadcast their secrets," he protested. "You are Alec's sister."

"I didn't mean you would gossip. But a gentleman shouldn't know such things."

Myles's eyebrows soared upward. "My dear girl, I am not blind nor, I hope, dull witted. After all the times that Amelia and Daphne and Meg—"

"Yes, yes, I know," Genevieve cut into his speech hastily. "You have a veritable flock of sisters. But you could at least pretend not to know such things about women."

"I hope you realize how absurd you sound."

"Oh, hush." Genevieve scowled at him.

Their argument had attracted the attention of the two couples at the opposite end of the hall, and they greeted them happily. "Genevieve! Myles!"

"Come join us."

"Yes, do." Gabriel reached back and scooped the child off his back, rising lithely to his feet. The blond boy let out a cry of protest before he spotted Myles and Genevieve. He pitched forward so suddenly and sharply that Gabriel would have dropped him if he hadn't had a firm grip on him.

Matthew waggled his hands excitedly, crowing, "Myse! Myse!"

"What is he saying?" Genevieve asked as they started toward the others.

"My name," Myles replied.

"He calls you *mice?*"

"The lad is only two; I fear that the pronunciation of *l*'s has not yet come to him." As they reached the others, Myles held out his hands to the boy, saying, "Master Matthew!"

This greeting seemed to delight the child, for he launched himself into Myles's outstretched hands with no regard for life or limb. Myles swung him upward and wiggled him about in the air. Genevieve drew in her breath in alarm and glanced at the other couples, but none of them betrayed the slightest concern, even when Myles turned the boy upside down.

Matthew apparently found it wonderfully amusing, for he erupted into giggles, and when Myles settled the boy on his hip, Matthew bounced and demanded, "More! More!"

"You young devil, you're insatiable," Myles told him, adding regretfully, "But I'd better not. Your mama will have my head if you cast up your accounts."

"Little worry of that." Thea laughed. "The boy has a stomach of iron."

"A true Morecombe," Gabriel added.

"Then I suppose he will have a head of iron, as well," Alec commented with a smile, looping his arms around Damaris from behind and nestling her against him, his chin resting on her head.

Genevieve gazed at her brother. He looked happy and contented, self-satisfied in a way she had never before seen. When he and Damaris had announced that she was pregnant, love and pride had beamed from him. Genevieve's heart clenched within her chest, filled with happiness for her brother, but also with a peculiar twinge of sorrow.

"He already has that," Thea joked, and began to recount an amusing story about Matthew's stubborn insistence on having a toy on the trip to London and the subsequent stop by the side of the road while they searched through their trunks to find it. As he listened, Gabriel wrapped his arm around Thea's shoulders.

Genevieve shifted uncomfortably as her eyes went from one couple to the other. It felt strange, standing here amid such open displays of marital affection. It simply was not done—though clearly that caused none of the others any discomfort. She felt, as she often did, different from the others. Wrong. Nonsensical, of course, for they were flouting convention, not she. Yet they seemed happy and relaxed while she hardly knew where to look.

She turned toward Myles, still holding the baby. Young Matthew had a firm grip on the lapel of Myles's coat in a way that would have horrified him had someone else done it, and with his other hand, Matthew was busily exploring Myles's tiepin and watch fob.

"Now I understand why Gabriel looked so disheveled," Genevieve murmured to Myles, and he laughed, a sound so merry that Genevieve had to join in.

"Lady Genevieve?"

Everyone turned. There, at the top of the main stairs, stood Lord Dursbury. He gazed at the group with an air of astonishment. A hush settled on the hall.

"Oh! Lord Dursbury." Genevieve was suddenly, forcefully aware of the odd picture they must present, standing about so casually, laughing—the men's arms around their wives, Myles and Gabriel rumpled from their tussles with the baby. Her color rose. "I—um—we were just—"

"I fear it is my fault, Lord Dursbury," Damaris said, stepping forward with a smile. "I so wished to see Lord and Lady Morecombe's child that I persuaded them to bring us up here. 'Tis terrible, I know, for us to sweep your betrothed away, too . . ."

To no one's surprise, Alec moved to stand by his wife, looming over everyone else, his face settling into its old arrogant lines. "I am sure Lord Dursbury understands."

Clearly Dursbury did not, but he gave them a perfunctory smile and bow. "Yes, how, um, nice. Lord Morecombe. My lady." He turned toward Genevieve. "Lady Genevieve? Shall we return to the ballroom?"

"Yes, of course." Genevieve went to take her fiancé's arm. She cast a polite smile at Thea. "Thank you, Lady Morecombe, for letting us see Matthew."

"My pleasure. You must visit us again."

Genevieve walked away with Dursbury. As they went down the stairs, she could hear the others begin to talk and laugh again.

"Odd, gathering in the nursery," Dursbury said mildly.

"Yes, I suppose it is."

"Nothing against your brother, of course."

"Of course," Genevieve agreed. "I believe they are all very fond of young Matthew."

"Rather peculiar behavior, though, for Lord and Lady Morecombe, given that they are hosting the party. Not quite the thing, I'd say." He glanced down at Genevieve. "Are you tired, Lady Genevieve?"

"What? No, I'm not at all tired."

"You sighed, that's all. I thought you might be tired."

"Did I? I wasn't aware."

"It was good of Morecombe to take in his sister's boy, especially newly married as they were. Many would not have, given the, um, circumstances of his birth. Bound to be talk."

"One cannot stop people from talking."

"Naturally. Still, one has to wonder if Lady Rawdon and Lady Morecombe are exactly the proper friends for you."

"I beg your pardon?" Genevieve's voice went icy, and she turned to him with a hauteur that would have made her grandmother proud.

"I have heard—that is, there is some question—Lady Rawdon's birth . . ."

"Lady Rawdon is my brother's wife," Genevieve said flatly.

"Of course. And they spend most of their time in Northumberland, so it's of little consequence. However, Lady Morecombe is a bluestocking, and that is not the sort of reputation you would wish to have attached to you."

"You make it sound as if she were in trade. Or worse."

"No! Not at all!" He looked shocked. "We would not have attended tonight if people thought that."

Genevieve bridled at his casual assumption that he would have made the decision for her, but before she could speak, Dursbury patted her hand and smiled at her, saying, "I would not wish even the slightest hint of any impropriety to touch you."

She swallowed the hot retort that had risen to her lips. As her grandmother frequently reminded her, she must keep a rein on her temper. Nothing was odd or wrong about a man's wanting to ensure that his betrothed's reputation was not harmed.

Dursbury apparently did not see the flash of fury in her eyes, for he was going on, quite unconcerned, "I am afraid you missed saying good-bye to the Sutterfields. That was why I went looking for you."

"That is too bad." Genevieve tried to remember what Sutterfield looked like. Was he Dursbury's third cousin or the man with the fish eyes?

"They are starting a waltz," Dursbury said as they entered the ballroom. He was fond, Genevieve had noticed, of stating the obvious. "Would you care to dance?" His expression suggested a man's facing up to a painful duty.

"No, I believe I'll just sit. Perhaps I am a little tired, after all." The thought of following Dursbury's careful steps around the dance floor lacked appeal after having floated across it a few minutes ago with Myles.

"Just as I thought." He smiled smugly. "Ah, there is Lady Rawdon."

He led her across the floor to where her grandmother sat against the wall. The countess perched ramrod straight on the edge of her chair, her hands resting on the head of her cane. She had used the cane for years, though less as a walking aid, Genevieve had long suspected, than as a convenient item with which to poke and prod or to rap on the floor to provide emphasis for her words.

Tonight, however, looking at her grandmother's gnarled hands, it struck Genevieve that her grandmother looked old. Her hair had long been white and wrinkles lined her face, but her will had overridden all hints of weakness. Now, however, Genevieve noticed that the jewel-encrusted rings that lined the countess's fingers could not distract the eye from the knobby knuckles or raised veins or brown blotches that marred her thin skin. Icy fear clutched at Genevieve's insides.

"Grandmama?" she said anxiously. "Are you all right?"

Lady Rawdon turned her piercing blue gaze on her, banishing all thoughts of fragility. "Whatever are you on about? Of course I am all right." She nodded to the man beside her granddaughter. "Dursbury. Genevieve. I wondered where you had gotten off to."

"It was perfectly all right, ma'am," Genevieve's fiancé assured her. "Lady Genevieve was in her brother's company."

The older woman frowned faintly, but she said nothing, merely nodded politely as Lord Dursbury bowed and excused himself, promising to return with drinks to refresh the ladies.

"What in the world did he mean 'it was perfectly all right'?" Lady Rawdon asked as soon as he was out of earshot. "Why shouldn't things be all right? What did it matter if you were with Alec?"

"I am sure I don't know, Grandmama. I suppose he was worried when he could not find me. I was upstairs in the nursery with Alec and Damaris."

"I find that a very odd place to be."

"Apparently so did Lord Dursbury."

"Genevieve. Did you quarrel with Lord Dursbury?"

"Of course not. There was nothing to quarrel about."

"I seem to be hearing a great deal of assurances that nothing is wrong." The countess peered at her suspiciously.

"That is because nothing is wrong." There was no point in telling her grandmother that her future husband had gotten her back up by presuming to make decisions for her. The countess would only tell her that was the way of husbands and that wise women smiled and worked their will around such obstructions.

Genevieve had always balked at the prospect of restrictions. That reluctance had underpinned her long resistance to getting married. But that was all part of the past now. She must be realistic. Her thirst for independence, her prickly nature, must soften and change a bit; that was the way when one allied herself to another. Dursbury was precisely the sort of man she should marry; she had concluded that months ago, and there was no point in doubting it now.

Her jaw hurt, and she realized that her teeth were clenched. The peculiar knot in her chest was showing itself again, too. Genevieve wished she could go home to bed. She wondered how long she must wait before they could politely leave. She wondered if Myles and Alec and the others were still up in the nursery, chatting. What did it feel like to have one's husband curl his arm about one in that way Alec and Gabriel had done—possession and protection, tenderness and desire, wrapping so openly around you? She tried to imagine Dursbury—no, Martin, surely he should be Martin to his wife—putting his arm around her that way. She could not picture it.

But what nonsense. As if she wanted that sort of husband, that sort of man. No, such behavior was what one might expect of someone like . . . like Myles, for instance. He would doubtless hover about his wife, assuring her of her beauty, his love, their happiness—and, to give him his due, he would probably mean it, at least at the time. But in a few months, he would be off chasing some light-o'-love or the other, madly in love all over again, and leaving his wife to tend to her knitting at home, alone. And filled with heartache.

"I have spent the past half hour dueling with that odious woman," Lady Rawdon said.

"Lady Dursbury?" Genevieve guessed, a smile twitching at the corner of her lips.

"Yes, of course Lady Dursbury. Do you know what scheme she has come up with now?"

"I couldn't possibly guess."

"Indeed not. No one could. She wants . . ." The countess stopped and drew a breath, as if she had to force herself to expel the rest of her statement. "She wants to release a whole horde of doves outside the church after the ceremony."

Genevieve giggled, quickly clapping a hand over her mouth.

"Yes, well, you might laugh . . . if it were *her* wedding she was proposing to turn into a circus." Her grandmother narrowed her eyes. "But this is a Stafford wedding."

"Well, to be fair, it is Dursbury's also."

"Lord Dursbury would not want it." Lady Rawdon gave an imperial flick of her wrist. "The whole thing is absurd. I will not have some great flock of birds flying about decorating all our guests, and so I told her. It got her hackles up, of course. I should have been more diplomatic, but it was a shock. The whole thing would doubtless delay the wedding even further while her gamekeeper goes out beating the bushes for doves."

Genevieve began to giggle again, and her grandmother shot her a quelling glance, though it was spoiled by the twitch of her own lips. "Do stop, Genevieve, or you will cause me to lose my high dudgeon."

"That would be disastrous." Genevieve smiled and reached out to brush her hand over her grandmother's. "Don't fret, Grandmama. I shan't mind if the wedding is later. What does it signify?"

"Nothing, of course. Everyone seems to be in such a mad rush these days to get married. I have always thought a year of betrothal was the appropriate time. Of course, your brother's was far too quick, but then, Alec never did care if everyone talked."

"If you wish us to wait a year, we easily can," Genevieve offered. "We could be wed after Twelfth Night."

"No." The countess sighed. "A January wedding can be a frightful mess. Better to leave it as it is. Besides, Lady Dursbury is all in a twitter because of that dreadful scandal sheet. She says there was another snippet about it in that last column from Lady Lackwit."

"I believe the writer goes by the name Lady Looksby," Genevieve said, smiling.

"Lady Libel is what she'll be if she isn't careful," Lady Rawdon replied sharply. "She is always dropping hints that Lord Dursbury is getting cold feet about your marriage. And she never forgoes an opportunity to add little questions about Damaris. It is enough to make one think she is targeting our family."

"She skewers everyone. That is why her tidbits are so popular."

"Well, it is fortunate that Alec never looks at such things or he would probably go down there and break their presses. I told Elora—and what sort of a foolish name is that, I ask you?—that the only way to handle such gossip is to ignore it. One must be above the common fray. But it is my opinion Lady Dursbury welcomes the chance for high drama. It seems more likely there is an actress in *her* family tree than in Damaris's," the countess added darkly.

"Speaking of libel," Genevieve teased. "Or slander, I suppose."

"I would not say so to anyone but you. One must, after all, put on a pretense of tolerating one's in-laws."

Dursbury returned with glasses of ratafia for Genevieve and her grandmother, and they spent a few slow minutes discussing the crush of people at the party and the difficulty that had created for the earl in procuring refreshments. Then Dursbury began to describe the state of his wine cellar, and Genevieve found her mind wandering. She spotted her tall brother's fair head across the room and knew that the others must have returned from the nursery. She glanced around the room and saw Sir Myles dancing with Lady Milburn.

"—don't you agree, Lady Genevieve?" she heard Dursbury say.

"What? Oh, no doubt," she replied.

"I thought as much." He nodded. "Ah, there's Fanhurst. I've been meaning to speak to him about a hunter he has for sale. If you will excuse me, ladies."

Genevieve smiled and nodded in answer to his bow. When he was out of earshot, she leaned closer to her grandmother and murmured, "What did I agree to?"

"I haven't the faintest idea. As a rule, I never listen once men start talking about horses, dogs, or liquor."

The dance had ended, and a new group began to form on the floor. The strains of a waltz struck up, and a moment later, Genevieve saw Lady Dursbury sweep by in Myles's arms. Her face was turned up to him in an expression of rapt interest. He seemed equally engrossed.

"Lady Dursbury is flirting with Myles again," Genevieve said.

"Lady Dursbury flirts with every male below the age of fifty." Her grandmother followed her gaze.

"I suspect she has a particular interest in Sir Myles," Genevieve went on.

"I shouldn't be surprised. After being married to a man almost twice her age, I imagine Elora is looking for someone more . . . virile."

Faintly shocked, Genevieve turned to her grandmother. "You can't really think she wants to marry him, can you?"

"Marriage? Goodness, no. She already has a title far higher than Myles's, and I imagine the old earl left her amply provided for. No, I think our Elora is interested only in a discreet affair. Myles would be perfect for that. He's not only good-looking and manly, he is charming and knows how to treat a woman properly. He is always discreet. All in all, Lady Dursbury could make a far worse choice."

Genevieve stared at the countess. "Grandmother! You sound as if you would countenance such an affair. After all the times you have talked to me about propriety!"

"'Tis the appearance of propriety that is paramount, my dear, and, as I pointed out, Sir Myles can be counted on not to flaunt his affairs." Lady Rawdon nodded her head approvingly. "Sir Myles is not a libertine, of course. I would not have allowed him to hang about if he were. But he is a man, so it's to be expected he would have his little conquests. He keeps his *chères amies* in good style, but he is not blatant or excessive about it. He doesn't give them a white curricle and team to tool about where all of London can see, like that dreadful Mr. Manningham. And he never pursues a married woman or a maiden, only widows such as Mrs. Bedlington, who understand such things."

"Of course." Genevieve said colorlessly. "I am not sure I know Mrs. Bedlington."

"She is here tonight." The countess surveyed the room. "There she is, that dark-haired woman talking to Mr. Jessup."

Genevieve followed her grandmother's gaze. It was easy to see why Myles would have been attracted to her. She had enviably rich, dark hair and large gray eyes, and her slender figure was encased in a lavender gown with black lace trim that, while a trifle too ornamented for Genevieve's taste, was undeniably in the first stare of fashion. Genevieve could not help but wonder if Myles had a preference for brunettes. Perhaps he found Lady Dursbury as interesting as she did him.

When Lord Dursbury's friend Mr. Colton asked her for a dance, Genevieve agreed, happy to get away from her thoughts for a few minutes. After that, Alec did his duty by taking her out on the floor, and she chatted for a few minutes with him and Damaris. As Alec swept his wife away for another waltz, Genevieve made her way back toward her grandmother.

Halfway there, a maid slipped up beside her and bobbed a curtsy. "Miss? I'm to give you this."

"What?" Genevieve glanced down in surprise at the folded piece of paper the girl extended to her. "Me? Are you certain?"

"Yes, miss. The tall lady with the pale hair."

An accurate, if vague, description. Genevieve plucked the note from her hand and opened it.

Dear Genevieve,
    Meet me in the library. Do not fail me.
                                    Myles

Surprised, Genevieve read the note again, but was no more knowledgeable than before. She looked up to ask the maid a question, but the girl had already gone.

Why would Myles ask her to meet him? What could have arisen in the past few minutes that was so urgent? She glanced around the room but did not see him. Folding and refolding the note, she tucked it into her pocket. Whatever was going on, she suspected that it was better not to tell her grandmother. Genevieve turned and slipped out the nearest door.

Four

When Genevieve stepped into the hall, she spotted Myles at the far end of the corridor, walking with Miss Halford toward a group of people that included Lady Dursbury. No doubt he was escorting the girl back to her chaperone after the dance. Genevieve thought about simply waiting for him here, but she discarded the idea. Myles obviously wanted to speak to her alone, away from prying eyes.

She wandered down the corridor until she found a long room with a door at each end. The walls on all sides were lined with shelves of books. No doubt this was Thea's favorite spot, Genevieve thought as she entered the library. Comfortable chairs were scattered about the room, as well as a small secretary. Facing away from her was a dark leather couch, and as Genevieve came farther into the room, Foster Langdon popped up and peered over the back of the couch.

"Lady Genevieve!" he exclaimed in apparent delight. "Aphrodite walks among us."

Oh, bother! She could not let Myles come in here with

Langdon hanging about. Langdon would assume she and Myles had an assignation.

"Mr. Langdon. I beg your pardon. I was looking for Lady Morecombe."

"Dear lady, no, you need not pretend." He lurched up from the sofa and came unsteadily toward her. "I am as eager as you to be alone together."

Genevieve realized she was in a worse situation than she had thought. Langdon, who appeared even more inebriated than earlier in the evening, seemed to believe she had slipped into the library to meet *him*.

"I fear you are laboring under a misapprehension, Mr. Langdon," she said, sidestepping his outstretched hand. "I was unaware you were here. Or that anyone was. Pray excuse me."

"No, my goddess, do not be shy." He grabbed her hand and began kissing it. "You are a vision! An angel, sent to me by a most kind Providence."

"Really, sir, that is quite enough!" Genevieve tried to jerk her hand away, but he clung to it like a limpet. "I am no angel, and I seriously doubt that Providence is concerned with sending you women to bedevil."

He let go but only to grab her upper arms and tug her to him. Genevieve twisted and pulled, alarmed but still doing her best to get out of the situation gracefully. "Let go of me!" she hissed. "Have you gone mad? There are people all around!"

"Yes! I feel the same! I wish them all at the devil." He wrapped his arms around her, leaning in for a kiss, and

Genevieve turned her face away so that his lips met only the side of her head.

"Let go of me or I shall scream!" Still she kept her voice low. The last thing she wanted was to make noise and attract any onlookers. She could feel her carefully pinned hair coming loose on one side, and her dress was twisted from grappling with him—the man had arms like an octopus! She must get away and put herself in order before anyone saw her.

Langdon grabbed her head between his hands, his fingers digging into her hair, and jerked her to him, planting a kiss on her mouth. Genevieve growled deep in her throat, fury seizing her, and she stamped her heel down on his instep. He let out a howl and staggered backward, his hands ripping from her hair with a painful jerk.

Genevieve whirled to run, but more quickly than she would have imagined for a man so drunk, he pounced, his hand clamping around her arm and whirling her back around. Genevieve drew her right arm back and launched her doubled-up fist straight at his face, as she had seen Alec do. She hit him square in the nose, sending a shock up her arm and blood spurting onto his white cravat.

He shrieked, his arms pinwheeling as he sought to regain his balance. He hooked a hand into the neck of her dress just as Genevieve pivoted to flee from him, and her bodice tore as Langdon crashed to the floor.

At that moment, a shocked male voice said, "Lady Genevieve!"

Genevieve turned around to see Lord Dursbury, his stepmother, Sir Myles, and several others standing in the doorway, gaping at her.

Myles had danced with Lady Dursbury, then with the shy Miss Halford. Feeling his duty done, he returned the girl to Lady Dursbury, thinking he would seek out Genevieve if she was not standing with her fiancé. Much as he enjoyed a bit of conversation with Genevieve, he refused to endure Dursbury's talking about . . . well, it didn't matter what; any topic, whether it was horses, cards, or the opera, all turned stultifying in his mouth.

However, when he and Miss Halford strolled into the outer hall, where Lady Dursbury was standing with her stepson and several of his friends, Myles could not, without rudeness, simply leave Miss Halford and walk away, so he suppressed a groan and paused to chat with the group for the smallest amount of time courtesy demanded.

Suddenly a shriek came from down the hall, and everyone turned and started for the library. The group came to a shocked halt in the doorway. Genevieve stood in the middle of the library, hair straggling down from her once-elegant coiffure, her dress twisted and the bodice torn open, revealing her chemise. Foster Langdon was half-sprawled against the back of the sofa, disheveled, blood streaming from his nose.

For a moment everyone was too shocked to speak or move. Myles took a step forward just as Lord Dursbury barked out Genevieve's name. Myles stopped, recalling that it was Lord Dursbury's place to go to his fiancée's aid, not his.

Genevieve, too, had whirled at the sound of Dursbury's voice and was staring at them all with horror. She grabbed at her bodice, pulling up the torn half to cover herself. "L-Lord Dursbury!"

"What is the meaning of all this?" Dursbury demanded. "Lady Genevieve, what is going on here? This is most irregular."

"What the devil is wrong with you, Dursbury?" Myles stared at the other man in astonishment. When Dursbury did not move, Myles strode across the room to Genevieve. Langdon, seeing him coming, scrambled away, but Myles did not bother to chase him, instead shrugging off his jacket and draping it around Genevieve's shoulders.

"Thank you, Myles," Genevieve said through bloodless lips. Her face ashen, she faced her fiancé, who had come farther into the room. "I—when I came in ... he ..." Her voice wavered.

"Good Lord, man, anyone can see what happened," Myles told Dursbury. "That blackguard obviously attacked her. And, from the looks of it, she drew his cork." He regarded Genevieve with pride. "Good girl. I always knew you would show well in a mill. Got bottom." He gave her a grin.

Genevieve smiled back somewhat tremulously. "Well, I am a Stafford."

"Are you jesting about this?" Dursbury exclaimed incredulously.

"No, of course not, Dursbury," Genevieve said a trifle

testily, her voice strengthening. "It's as Myles said: Langdon tried to kiss me, and we tussled."

There were gasps from Lady Dursbury and Miss Halford, and Lord Dursbury grew even stiffer. "Tussled? You say it as if nothing happened."

"Nothing did happen, fortunately," Genevieve answered. "I hit him before he could harm me."

Dursbury's eyebrows soared toward his hairline. "Nothing? You think this is nothing?" He swept his arm out as if to encompass the room and all the people in it. "What of your reputation? Your good name? What of mine?"

Genevieve narrowed her eyes. "*Your* name? I fail to see that this has anything to do with your name."

"You are my betrothed!" he snapped. "It has everything to do with my name. You are the future Lady Dursbury."

"I am already Genevieve Stafford." Genevieve's face was no longer ashen; bright red washed her cheekbones, and her eyes were a piercing blue. "And that is as good a name as any in this kingdom."

"Perhaps you should have thought of that before you went into the library with a man!"

"Careful, Dursbury." Myles stiffened beside Genevieve, his voice hard. "You would not want to say anything you will later regret."

"I did not go into the library with a man," Genevieve shot back. "I came in here by myself and he just happened to be here." She swung around to point at Langdon, but he was no longer in the room. The door at the other end of the room stood open, indicating where he had gone.

"Bloody hell!" Myles burst out. "I should have grabbed the cur."

"To what purpose?" Dursbury asked coldly. "To create even more of an uproar?" He gestured vaguely to the area behind him, now crowded with people avidly watching the scene. "I think this situation is bad enough already without you beating some fellow senseless."

"I think beating him senseless would do a great deal to improve things," Myles answered. "One can only wonder why Genevieve's own fiancé doesn't want to do the job himself!"

"Because, unlike you and Genevieve and her brother, I prefer to stay away from scandal." He turned to Genevieve. "Whatever happened, it is quite clear you placed yourself in this situation, my lady. You were alone with Langdon. You have caused yourself to be the subject of gossip. And you have embroiled my family in scandal, as well. It is insupportable. Your behavior is not that of the Countess of Dursbury. I regret, my lady, that I can no longer in good conscience marry you."

After an instant of stunned silence, Myles strode forward. "I didn't get a chance to give Langdon what he deserved. But I can bloody well give it to you." His right arm shot out, catching Dursbury squarely on his chin and knocking him to the ground.

Myles turned to Genevieve, offering her his arm. "Genevieve?"

She stepped up beside him, twisting her engagement ring from her finger. Dropping it on Dursbury's chest, she took Myles's arm, and they stalked out of the room.

Myles whisked Genevieve out of the house, pausing only long enough to tell a footman to inform the Earl of Rawdon that he was taking Lady Genevieve home. Genevieve, humiliatingly aware of all the eyes staring at her with avid curiosity, carefully kept her face a cool mask of hauteur. She would not give any of them the satisfaction of her breaking down . . . or even of looking as if she cared for their opinion.

Myles handed Genevieve into a hack and climbed in after her. She sank back against the seat, the shame she had refused to show the world washing over her now that she was safe from prying eyes.

"I am so sorry, Genevieve." Myles took her hand, and Genevieve surprised them both by curling her fingers tightly around his.

"Thank you." She knew he must regret sending her the note that had caused her to wind up in the library, but there was no reason. "It was my own fault for going there."

"You couldn't have known Langdon would be in there." Myles scowled. "Dursbury's a fool. Worse than a fool."

"Yes." Genevieve tightened her grasp on his hand. "Promise me, Myles, you must keep Alec from attacking Langdon. Or Dursbury. It will only make the scandal worse. Grandmama will be humiliated." Tears welled in her eyes.

"Don't worry about the countess. I am sure she is tougher than any of us. I shall shadow Alec if I have to. But my guess is Damaris will manage him."

That statement was enough to bring a faint smile to

Genevieve's lips. She was glad to go along with Myles's attempt to lighten the mood. "She does have a way with him. No one else has ever managed it."

"Love does odd things to a man, or so I'm told."

"Come, Myles. Do not tell me that you have never been in love." She cut her eyes toward him with the ghost of a roguish twinkle.

"Oh, no, a hundred times at least," he said lightly, his hand reassuringly warm and strong around hers. "The problem is I find myself out of love as quickly as I fell into it."

"No doubt leaving behind some jeweled trinket as an expression of your esteem."

"Dear girl! Wherever did you hear such shocking things?"

"I am not entirely ignorant, no matter how the world strives to keep a maiden that way. Everyone knows men have their little affairs," Genevieve said airily.

The carriage rolled to a halt, saving Myles from having to answer, and they went inside.

"Have tea and brandy brought to the drawing room," Myles told the footman, and started with Genevieve for that room.

"I am fine," Genevieve protested. "I don't need a brandy."

"Well, I do." But when the butler brought the tray of drinks, Myles poured a healthy dollop of the fiery alcohol in Genevieve's cup, as well. She took a sip, grimacing at the sharp taste, and sat down. A large, white puffball of a cat came into the room and stopped just inside the doorway, as if posing for an admiring audience.

"Xerxes!" Genevieve smiled, beckoning to the cat.

"Oh, the devil!" Myles said under his breath. The cat and Myles regarded each other balefully for a moment. Then, with a twitch of his tail, Xerxes turned, dismissing Myles, and stalked over to jump into Genevieve's lap.

Tears threatened Genevieve again, but she swallowed hard and ran her hand down Xerxes's back. The cat narrowed his eyes to slits, a low rumble rising from his chest, and Genevieve's tightly held shoulders relaxed as well, as she continued to pet him.

The front door slammed open, the noise reverberating through the house, and Alec strode through the doorway. "Genevieve? Myles? What the devil is going on? Morecombe's footman gave us your message; we thought Genevieve had taken a fall or some such thing."

Genevieve let out a snort. "I took a fall, certainly, though not the sort you mean. I am surprised no one told you."

"Everyone was buzzing, but we left without pausing to speak to anyone." Damaris came into the room behind Alec, the dowager countess beside her.

"Well?" Alec looked from Myles to his sister. "Is anyone going to bother to explain?"

"Foster Langdon made improper advances to your sister, so she planted a facer on him," Myles summarized.

"The devil you say!" Alec scowled. "That sneaking little scoundrel. I always knew he was a loose fish."

"He was in his cups," Genevieve said, "or I don't think he would have dared try to kiss me. He never has been anything but annoying before."

Damaris went over to Genevieve and knelt beside her chair, laying her hand on Genevieve's arm. "Are you all right, dear? Did he hurt you?"

"Only my pride. He was drunk as a wheelbarrow, and he assumed when I went into the library that I had come to see him. He was stretched out on the couch, and I didn't see him until he sat up or I would never have gone in. He was most importunate when I started to leave, though in fairness, I do think it was an accident that he tore my gown."

"Tore your gown!" Alec thundered.

Genevieve cast an appealing look at Myles, and he rose, going over to his friend.

"Don't erupt, Rawdon. Genevieve stopped him. She must have landed a damn fine punch, too. His blood was flowing like wine."

"Yes, I did, and no one would have known about it if the stupid man had not shrieked like a girl when I tromped on his foot."

"Ah, so you crippled him as well." Pride mingled with laughter in Myles's voice, and even Alec smiled faintly.

"Where the devil does Langdon live?" Alec turned toward Myles.

"Alec, no," all three women chorused at once, and Damaris rose, laying both her hands on his arm.

"Don't be a fool," his grandmother added sharply. "If you challenge him to a duel, it will only make the scandal worse."

"Duel? I wouldn't challenge that worm to a duel; he isn't enough of a gentleman for a challenge. I'll use my fists."

"It won't help to beat him to death, either," Damaris pointed out, fixing her lovely, large eyes on Alec's face, and she laid her palm on her abdomen, adding, "I don't want our baby's father in prison or having to flee to the Continent."

"That isn't the worst of it," Genevieve added.

"There's more?"

"Yes." Genevieve stood up, as if she must face them on her feet. "Dursbury and several others came running when Langdon screamed. And when he saw us, he— Dursbury repudiated me."

Alec and Damaris stared at Genevieve. Genevieve's grandmother made an odd noise, like air escaping from a balloon, and sat down on the nearest chair.

"I know where to find Dursbury." Alec swung around and started toward the door.

Damaris wrapped her arms around his arm and hung on. "Alec, stop. Think. You will make the scandal far worse if you go charging about beating everyone to a pulp."

"She's right," Myles agreed, positioning himself between Alec and the doorway. "It would only be harder for Genevieve."

Alec cursed, balling his fists at his sides in frustration.

"Besides, Myles already hit Dursbury," Genevieve told them.

"Good." Alec nodded at Myles.

"The important thing now is Genevieve," Damaris said, and turned toward her. "I am so sorry. I know this must be a terrible blow, but, truly, it is better you found out what sort of man Lord Dursbury is before you married him."

"Oh, Dursbury!" Genevieve said contemptuously, shrugging a shoulder. "I care not about losing him. Any more than he obviously cared about me. But my—" Her voice hitched. "My reputation is ruined now."

"Don't worry about that," Alec told her.

"Don't be a fool, Alec," his grandmother told him tartly. "We must worry. Genevieve's future is at stake."

"It will blow over," Alec said. "These things always do. The *ton* will move on to some other gossip."

"It is all very well for you to be careless about scandal," Lady Rawdon said. "For a young, unmarried girl, this is disastrous. Surely you remember what happened to Caro Godfrey after she and Mowbry were found alone in the Willhavens' garden last year."

"No." Alec looked at her blankly.

"Well, I will tell you: he would not marry her, and everyone dropped her. She'll never make a decent marriage now. And they were not even found *en flagrante*. That Nettleton girl, the one who came out when your mother did—her fiancé jilted her, and she could never show her face in the *ton* again."

"She's right," Genevieve agreed heavily. "Langdon had his arms around me; my dress was torn. You know everyone will believe that we—we were—" She stopped, her voice choked.

"No one who knows you would believe that," Damaris assured Genevieve, going over to put an arm around her comfortingly.

"Of course not," Myles agreed.

"You know better than that, Myles," Genevieve said scornfully. "Alec may not follow the rules, but you understand them."

Myles shifted uncomfortably under her gaze and said, "It could have all been smoothed over if Dursbury had not been such an imbecile."

"Yes, of course," the countess agreed. "If only Dursbury had stood by her, it would not be irreparable. There would have been a scandal, but the wedding could have been moved up, and soon the tongues would have stopped wagging."

"But he did not," Genevieve said bitterly. "No one will believe that I was innocent now. Dursbury as good as confirmed to the world that I am a trollop. Not only that, they'll say that the horrid scandal sheet was right, that he seized the first opportunity to throw me over."

"I know how to deal with anyone who spreads such rumors," Alec said grimly, his fists knotting.

"You may shut people up, my boy, but you cannot make them accept Genevieve," Lady Rawdon said flatly. "You cannot keep them from cutting her in public. You cannot make them send her invitations or come to call on us."

"Surely they would not dare offend *you* so, ma'am," Damaris protested.

"Society is unforgiving. Few would snub me, of course, but am I to go where my granddaughter is not invited? I think not." The old lady stood fiercely straight.

"I have brought scandal on the whole family." Genevieve's eyes filled with tears, and she blinked them away. "I am so sorry, Grandmama."

"I know, dear." The countess sighed. "But I fear nothing could save your reputation now but marriage."

"She has to marry that maggot Langdon?" Alec thundered.

"No!" Myles exclaimed, shocked.

"I will not," Genevieve declared. "I'd rather be a pariah the rest of my life than marry that swine. And don't say you will force Dursbury to give me his ring again, Alec. I refuse to marry him, either."

"Then the only thing for you to do is retire to Castle Cleyre," their grandmother said.

"Surely not," Damaris said in dismay.

"Lord Turnbury married a bird of paradise," Myles argued. "They didn't flee to his estate."

"Oh, him," the countess said witheringly. "It's not as if the woman was *received*. Anyway, no matter how outrageous it was, it remains that they were wed. Marriage cures a multitude of sins. It covers a woman with the cloak of a gentleman's good name. It gives one respectability, just as marrying a scoundrel colors one with his misdeeds."

"She's right," Genevieve said colorlessly as she sank back down into her chair. Silent tears spilled from her eyes and began to roll down her cheeks, but she kept her lips clamped together, refusing to break down into sobs.

"Genny, no . . ." Myles turned to Genevieve's grandmother. "It doesn't have to be Langdon or Dursbury, surely. If Genevieve marries another man, it would save her reputation, would it not?"

"Of course." Lady Rawdon nodded.

"But that is just the *point*," Genevieve burst out, dashing the tears from her cheeks and glaring at Myles. "No man will marry me now."

Myles crossed to Genevieve and went down on a knee beside her. "You're wrong, Genny. I will."

Five

"What?" Genevieve jumped to her feet, staring at him.

"I am asking you to marry me," Myles told her, annoyance tingeing his voice.

"Don't be a fool, Myles!" Scarlet flamed in Genevieve's cheeks. She was suddenly, acutely aware of how she must look—Myles's jacket thrown over her torn dress, her hair straggling down about her face like a slattern's. She was receiving her second proposal of marriage; the first one had been rather colorless, but this one was even worse. "I'm not marrying you."

Myles gaped at her. "Well, if that isn't just like you! I am trying to help you."

"I don't need your help. I don't want it."

"You were willing enough to take it before," he shot back, his own color rising.

"Of course you are going to throw that weakness up at me."

"Good gad, Genevieve—you are the most contrary creature I have ever had the misfortune to know. Are you actually lumping me in with Dursbury and Langdon?

Am I so bad that you would rather spend the rest of your days stuck away in Northumberland than be my wife?"

"Genevieve," the dowager countess said sharply, rising to her feet. "Hold your tongue. For heaven's sake, think before you speak." She went to her granddaughter and took her arm, but Genevieve twisted away.

"No! I can't. I won't." Tears started in Genevieve's eyes, and she clapped her hand over her mouth, smothering the wail that threatened to rise from her throat. Turning, she fled the room.

Behind her, she heard her grandmother say, "She is distraught, Sir Myles. Please do not take her words to heart. I will talk to her; Genevieve will come around."

Genevieve could not hold back her sobs as she ran up the stairs to her room.

His anger carried Myles all the way back to the More-combes' house before he even realized where he was walking. The lights no longer burned on the outside of the graceful white building, so the party must have ended after the drama in the library. There remained, however, a warm glow through the windows of the front room. Myles hesitated for a moment, then trotted up the steps to the front door and tapped on it lightly.

A surprised footman opened the door. "Sir!" He recovered quickly and added, "Lord and Lady Morecombe are in the anteroom, sir."

Gabriel lounged in the comfortable chair by the window, his wife sitting on his lap, her legs draped over the arm of the chair. They were deep in conversation and looked up in surprise when Myles walked in the room.

"Myles!" The couple smiled with no apparent embarrassment at being caught in such a pose, and Thea jumped up, coming toward him with outstretched hands. "What a dreadful thing! We heard what happened. Is Lady Genevieve all right?"

"It has not weakened her spine," Myles replied, taking Thea's hand and making his bow. "Nor sweetened her tongue."

"I am so sorry that it happened here. I had meant it to be a party to honor them." She sighed. "And then to have that odious man—"

"Which odious man, love?" her husband asked Thea as she took a seat on the stool beside his chair. "Langdon or her fiancé?"

"Either. Both. They deserve whatever Alec does to them . . . though it will create a worse scandal, of course."

"My wife is a bloodthirsty wench." Gabriel grinned. "No one touches her or hers, and apparently Lady Genevieve has somehow become one of her flock."

"She is Damaris's sister-in-law," Thea said simply. "Anyway, I liked Lady Genevieve when we talked at the wedding. It just takes her a bit to warm up to one. I think she is rather shy."

"Shy?" Gabriel repeated sardonically.

"Yes. Oh, don't look at me that way. You don't know what it's like—either one of you." Thea turned to include Myles in her accusation. "You're handsome and charming and everyone wants to be with you. You don't understand how lonely one can feel."

Gabriel picked up Thea's hand and kissed it, and they smiled at each other in a way that dismissed the rest of the world. Gabriel pulled his gaze away from Thea and turned back to Myles. "Sit down, Myles, sit down." Gabriel gestured toward the chair across from him. "Care for a brandy?"

"No. I'm fine. That's not why I came."

Myles's friends looked at him, waiting, he knew, for an explanation of exactly why he had come. Myles could not help but wonder the same thing himself.

"I asked Genevieve to marry me," he blurted out.

For a long moment the two continued to stare at him in silence. Then Gabriel stood up, saying, "Well, *I'm* going to have a drink." He crossed to the cabinet and filled two glasses, carrying them back and handing one to Myles without asking.

"You and Genevieve are going to be married?" Thea asked. "That's—"

"Mad," her husband stuck in.

"Unexpected," Thea corrected, shooting her husband a stern look. "But we are very happy for you."

"She turned me down," Myles continued.

"The devil!" Gabriel and Thea gaped at him. Gabriel's face turned wary. "Is this one of your jests?"

"No, I assure you. I asked her to marry me, and she jumped to her feet, looking as though I'd tossed a dead squirrel in her lap, and declared that I was a fool and she wouldn't marry me. Then she ran out of the room." Myles paused and stared down at his drink, bemused. "She'd rather be ruined, apparently."

"Myles, I'm sure that's not true," Thea protested. "She had a difficult evening, you must remember."

Gabriel chuckled. "You clearly don't know Genevieve. She is always that way. Well, the sharp words are just like her. I can't say I've ever seen her be that . . . dramatic."

"It is an effect I seem to have on her," Myles explained.

"She will feel differently when she has had time to calm down," Thea told Myles.

"That is what her grandmother said. The countess told me to return tomorrow afternoon and talk to Genevieve again. She assured me Genevieve would change her mind once she thought it over. What she meant was that she would bully and badger the poor woman until she accepts me. I have never known the countess not to have her way, so I have little doubt but that Genevieve will give in."

"Do you mean you still intend to marry her?" Gabriel asked, his eyebrows rising.

"I offered for her, Gabe. I can hardly take that back."

"You can if she refused you," Gabriel pointed out.

"Yes, I suppose I could without damaging my reputation. But I don't think I would like myself very much. Genevieve's reputation is ruined. You know what kind of a future she faces—she'll retire to that great cold pile of stones in Northumberland. Or perhaps she will live in Bath, running errands for her grandmother and her cronies. No advantageous marriage; no children. No home of her own."

"She will hate it," Thea agreed in a heartfelt voice.

"She looked so . . . shattered. I couldn't bear it." Myles grimaced and took a drink. "And then she threw my offer back in my face." He went on somewhat plaintively, "In some circles I am considered quite a catch."

"Oh, Myles . . ." Thea smiled and reached out to lay a hand on his arm. "Your pride is wounded. Of course it would be. But think how Lady Genevieve must feel. She is a very proud woman, and she was humiliated in front of the whole *ton* tonight. We all know that you are one of the most eligible bachelors in town . . . especially now that Gabriel is taken." She cast a twinkling glance at her husband. "Genevieve knows it, too; she didn't turn you down because she thought you unworthy."

"Perhaps not unworthy. But I am not the man Genevieve wants; that is clear from her original choice of a fiancé. I am no pattern card of respectability like Dursbury. No earl—indeed, not even a baron. A Stafford aims higher than a Thorwood."

"Not in this instance," Thea assured him. "Your offer hurts her pride, but not in the way you think. Some people can bear almost anything besides pity. Genevieve knew you asked her because you felt sorry for her, because you're kind. Not because you want to marry her."

"Well, I don't," Myles responded frankly. "I mean—she is not the woman I would have chosen."

"She knows you did it because you are a gentleman.

Because you're kind. And perhaps, a little, because you are her brother's friend. Not the sort of reasons a woman wants to hear."

"It would have been silly to pretend it was a love match. It isn't as if Genevieve is a romantic woman."

"Does such a woman really exist?" Thea asked lightly. "You might be surprised. The Staffords are . . . guarded, but I think it is because they know how easily they can be wounded."

"Thea has a soft spot for the Staffords," Gabriel said drily. "If Alec had eyes for anyone but his wife, I believe I would be jealous."

Thea rolled her eyes at Gabriel, but the smile on her face as she looked at him would erase even the most jealous man's doubts. "Well, that is the entirety of my lecture. I am sure the two of you would like a more private discussion, so I will retire now." She rose, saying to Myles, "Don't worry. I have every confidence it will work out exactly as it should."

The two men watched her leave, then Gabriel turned to his friend, giving him a long, considering look. "My wife, you must remember, is the daughter of a vicar. She has a tendency to view people in the best light."

"Most of the time, I share that view." Myles smiled wryly. "When it comes to Genevieve, however . . ."

"Myles." Gabriel leaned forward, setting his glass down on the table beside him. "Have a care. I know Genevieve's future is bleak. But there is no reason you should sacrifice your future in order to save hers."

"It is scarcely as if Genevieve is a horror," Myles replied, nettled. "She would do her utmost to be a good wife, and Genevieve usually succeeds at whatever she strives for. She is lovely to look at. She's witty. I am never bored around her."

"No, I imagine not." Gabriel smiled. "Don't fire up. I am not Genevieve's enemy. I understand her reasons for disliking me, and, God knows, they are justified. She is loyal to Rawdon, and I wronged him. And you are right. She is beautiful and intelligent and well brought up. The very picture of a lady. She would be a perfect wife for some man. But I cannot help but wonder if you are that man. Will she make you happy?"

"Honestly? I don't know." Myles sighed and sat back in his chair. "I have always had this vague notion that I would marry for love, as my parents did. That there would be a young lady who made me smile every time she walked into the room, the way my father did when he saw my mother. The way you look at Thea. Or Alec does Damaris. The thing is, I have never found that girl. After all these years, I have to wonder whether I ever will. Genevieve is right in saying I am not a serious man. I enjoy life; I don't suffer and brood. I cannot imagine being as Alec was about Jocelyn—either in loving her or in losing her. The way he is about Damaris; he was wild the night he thought he had lost her. I am not sure I would even wish to love like that. It seems a bloody uncomfortable way to live, frankly."

Gabriel chuckled. "I suspect it is. But love doesn't have

to strike a man the way it did Alec. It can be . . . something that slips up on you, and then one day you realize that your whole world has changed."

"Well, it has never tapped me on the shoulder." Myles smiled ruefully. "I'm not sure it ever would. Still, one has to marry."

"But Genevieve Stafford?" Gabriel burst out, but stopped short as Myles stiffened, his usually warm brown eyes icing over. "What I mean is that every time I see the two of you together, you are squabbling about something."

Myles chuckled. "I am used to squabbling. Your forget; I grew up with five sisters."

"Then why are you worried about it?" Gabriel asked. "I know you, Myles, and you didn't come here because a girl turned you down. That would only make you more determined to win her."

"You could be right." Myles's insouciant grin flashed out. "When I asked Genevieve, I did not hesitate. But when she turned me down, I told myself I must have been mad to offer for her. I don't doubt that I can talk her around. The question is, should I? What if Thea is wrong about Genevieve? What if I am? What if there is nothing deeper or warmer in her? I don't expect love; I don't even think I shall miss it. But what if—what if when you dig down underneath all that icy control, you find there really is no heart in her? That she cannot love, even in a mild way?"

"It seems a fearsome risk to take."

"I know." Myles looked down at his hands. "And yet . . . I think it is a risk I intend to take." He glanced up and grinned, and suddenly his eyes glittered dangerously. "Now . . . I believe that I shall go looking for Mr. Langdon."

Genevieve put off going down to breakfast the next morning, pinning stray hairs into place and smoothing out wrinkles only she could see, until finally, disgusted by her cowardice, she squared her shoulders and marched down the stairs. She only had to face her family, after all, not the entire *ton*. It did not matter that her eyes were swollen and her head ached from a night spent in tears and restless tossing instead of sleep.

Alec and her grandmother were seated at the breakfast table, and as Genevieve stepped into the dining room, she heard her grandmother say, "—and how in the blazes did they already know?"

"I don't know, but—" Alec glanced up and saw Genevieve. He sprang to his feet. "Ah, Genevieve, good morning."

Lady Rawdon hastily folded the sheet of newsprint, handing it to one of the footmen. "Here. Take this and throw it away."

"You are reading *The Onlooker*, I presume," Genevieve said, coming forward.

The countess's lips tightened. "It's a scurrilous rag. Someone should shut it down. I believe I shall speak to Caswell about it; the government should be good for something, I would think."

"What did they say this time?" Genevieve was pleased

that her voice was even, not betraying the nervous roiling of her stomach.

"Oh, they were crowing that they had predicted the little contretemps last night. Ridiculous, of course. But it is nothing you need worry about. Sit down and have a bite to eat. The berries are delicious."

"I am not hungry." Genevieve remained standing, her hands laced together in front of her. "I wanted to speak with both of you."

"Of course." Alec gestured to the servants to leave.

"I would like to apologize for last night," Genevieve began when the men had gone. "I bitterly regret that I embroiled our family in a scandal."

"Genny, dear girl. You did nothing wrong," Alec assured her. "Langdon is beneath contempt. And Dursbury needs a lesson in how to behave like a gentleman."

"Alec . . ." Lady Rawdon said warningly.

"No, no, Grandmother, you may rest easy. I have promised I will do nothing to him, and I won't."

"I never meant to—to besmirch the name Stafford," Genevieve went on, feeling as though she had not adequately expressed her remorse. That everyone was being nice to her only increased her sense of shame.

"Of course you didn't," Alec said. "I don't care about the scandal. And you've done nothing to taint our name."

"And, thank God, Sir Myles stepped up and asked for your hand," the countess added.

"Grandmama . . . I told Myles last night that I would not marry him."

"Sir Myles knows you were distraught. I believe he intends to call on you again this afternoon."

"Because you told him to, no doubt." Genevieve's eyes flashed.

"Of course I did. Someone had to think of your future. It was clear that you were not capable of it."

"Genevieve does not have to marry if she doesn't wish," Alec interrupted. "You know that, don't you, Genny? I will always take care of you."

"I know. Oh, Alec—" Genevieve turned away in agitation and began to pace the room.

"All that's important is for you to be happy."

Lady Rawdon gave a delicate snort. "Really, Rawdon, what pap. Genevieve, do sit down. You are making me dizzy."

Genevieve stopped, her hands balling up into fists at her sides, but she walked back to the table and sat down in her place.

"Now." Lady Rawdon turned to her granddaughter. "Listen to me. Sir Myles offered you a respectable way out of your dilemma. It is a perfect solution, and you would be foolish in the extreme if you did not take it. You said you would not take Mr. Langdon or Lord Dursbury even if Alec could force them to offer for you."

"I assure you I can," Alec stuck in.

"I understand your unwillingness to marry either of them," his grandmother went on, ignoring him. "Mr. Langdon is a cad, and Lord Dursbury is obviously as shallow as he is boring. However, Sir Myles is an entirely acceptable suitor, possessed of a good name and a respectable fortune. You are not likely to receive a better offer."

"I know that. I didn't turn him down for *my* sake. There is no reason Myles should sacrifice his whole life just because he is a kind man. It would be wicked of me to take advantage of him."

"Don't be ridiculous," Lady Rawdon said. "Sir Myles is not 'sacrificing' his life, as you put it. He is making an advantageous marriage. His family and fortune are respectable, but he would not normally aspire to marry a Stafford. While it did arise suddenly and by accident, it is still an excellent alliance for him."

"Myles is not doing this to 'improve' his social position," Alec protested. "Which, by the way, is good enough for anyone but you, Grandmother. He is a true gentleman and a good friend. That is why he offered, not because it was advantageous for him."

The countess gave her grandson a long, cool look. "I am fully aware that Sir Myles is a gentleman. Do you think I would advocate Genevieve marry him if that were not true? That does not mean he was unaware of the value of the marriage for him, as well. I am not one to disdain a decision to align oneself with a name like Stafford. And the fact remains that this is an excellent marriage for him. Genevieve has no need to worry about 'trapping' him or some such nonsense."

"It would not be right." Genevieve set her jaw, not looking at her grandmother. Neither her grandmother's nor her brother's arguments left her feeling particularly happy.

Lady Rawdon released a weary sigh. "Well, I can see there is no reasoning with you at the moment. Perhaps Sir Myles will have more luck with you this afternoon." She turned to her grandson. "Alec, dear, don't you think you should check on Damaris? You said she was unwell this morning."

"Is Damaris ill?" Genevieve turned to Alec, who was frowning now, his eyes clouded with worry. "Did what happened upset her so? She is not—"

"'Tis merely the sort of thing one can expect when one is in an 'interesting condition,'" the countess said coolly. "I am sure she will be fine. However, Alec, a bit of tea and toast would not be amiss."

"Yes, of course." He rose, then stopped and fixed his gaze on his grandmother. "Don't think I don't know why you're sending me away. You are not to bully Genevieve just because I am absent."

"Really, Rawdon," the countess said in a glacial tone. "You have a most peculiar opinion of me. I would never do anything to harm Genevieve."

"I know your interest is for Genevieve's welfare," her grandson told her drily. "It is the means you use to ensure that outcome that worry me." Giving his sister a comforting pat on the shoulder, Alec left the room.

Genevieve's grandmother waited until she heard the sound of his footsteps on the stairs, then turned to Genevieve. "Now—no, do not protest. I am only going to tell you this once, and then, if you choose to continue along this ruinous, headstrong path, I shall not bother you further. I do not ask you to consider what this additional scandal will mean for your brother and his wife, whose position in the *ton* is already precarious enough. Nor should you think of how it will affect me. If you are not accepted in society, I shall simply retire to Bath, and no doubt it will be much pleasanter there, anyway."

"Grandmama . . ." Genevieve said wretchedly.

"No." Lady Rawdon held up her hand in a regal gesture. "It does not signify. But what does matter, what I want you to think about long and hard, is how you want to live the rest of your days. Do not think that this is a trifling matter, that you can spend a few months at the castle and then return to London as if nothing had happened. It is dire. The cloud of scandal will follow you the rest of your life."

"I know," Genevieve said in a low voice.

"No, my dear, I doubt you do. I do not think you can imagine the extent of the regret you will feel for the rest of your life if you toss this opportunity away. You cannot expect an eligible gentleman like Sir Myles to hang about after you have rejected him."

"I am not rejecting him. I am trying to save him from himself."

"I understand precisely how you feel." Lady Rawdon sent her granddaughter a pointed glance. "However, I doubt Sir Myles would view your refusal in that light. He offered you the most precious thing a man could give a woman."

"Myles does not love me," Genevieve retorted.

"I am not talking about his heart. You are becoming just like Alec." Her grandmother grimaced. "Myles offered you his name. His honor. 'Tis no small thing, my girl. And you turned him down flat. You told him, in effect, that the name, the home, the life, he is willing to give you are not things you value."

Genevieve gaped at her. "I never said that."

"Not in so many words." The older woman shrugged. "I fail to understand your reluctance. It is not as if you were some silly chit who must have 'love' in her marriage."

"No, of course not. It—it is much the same arrangement I had with Lord Dursbury."

"Precisely. Why is it different with Sir Myles?"

"I don't know," Genevieve said miserably.

"I would think it would be easier. After all, you have known Myles for years. I am sure Myles will be a perfectly amiable husband, and you will find him a great deal more entertaining to live with than Dursbury. After you have done your duty and produced an heir or two, you will be able to go your separate ways and enjoy your lives. He will have his mistresses, of course, but you can trust Sir Myles to be discreet."

"Yes, you told me he always had been," Genevieve agreed hollowly.

"You will have the household to manage and children to raise. You will be able to enjoy your usual place in society—once the scandal has died down, that is. Now—" The countess patted Genevieve's hand again and released it, turning away with a satisfied look. "It must be a quick marriage, I think. Normally I would not advocate haste, but in this instance, I think it is necessary to quiet the scandal. Myles can obtain a special license. You could be married tomorrow. I have a cousin who is a vicar here in London."

Genevieve sat back, hardly listening as her grandmother continued to happily make plans for her future. She could not, she thought. She simply could not enter into this bloodless marriage with Myles. But what else was she to do?

Six

Vultures. *Well, at least your* butler has turned them away." Damaris turned from her post at the edge of the draperies, letting the heavy cloth fall back into place. "He is quite good at it."

"He has had ample practice with Grandmama," Genevieve replied, doing her best to ignore the ice growing larger by the moment in the pit of her stomach.

"No doubt." Damaris chuckled.

"The gossips are the only ones who called on us today." Genevieve realized her comment must sound self-pitying, and she quickly added, "It is what I expected, of course."

Her sister-in-law kept her eyes on her needlework as she said carefully, "There are many things to enjoy outside the boundaries of the *ton*."

"Yes, of course. It is much more enjoyable to ride at Cleyre. And parties can be such a crush." Genevieve stuck her needle into the cloth determinedly.

"Indeed. We will have much more comfortable parties at Cleyre. And Thea and Gabriel will come to visit. We can go to Chesley."

"Yes, of course." Genevieve thought of spending her days with the two happy couples. "Ouch." She pulled back her finger and sucked at the blood that welled out where she had stabbed herself. Tears pooled in her eyes and she tried to blink them away, but she could not prevent a few from sliding down her cheeks. "Oh, bother." She reached into her pocket and pulled out her handkerchief to dab them away.

"Oh, Genevieve." Damaris set aside her needlework and came over to sit on the sofa beside her, taking her hand between hers. "I am so dreadfully sorry you have been placed in such a position. Dursbury is a coward and a fool."

"I know. I shan't regret not marrying him." Her smile was brittle. "There is no need for you to feel bad for me. I should have known better than to go into the library. I did know better. If it had been anyone but Myles, I would not have considered it."

"If what had been anyone but Myles?" Damaris looked puzzled. "What do you mean? What does Myles have to do with it?"

Genevieve's eyes widened. "Nothing. I mean—"

"It isn't nothing. What are you talking about?"

"Please, you must not tell Alec. I will not have him angry with Myles."

"Tell Alec what? Why would he be angry at Myles?"

"He shouldn't be. Oh, blast! Myles asked me to meet him in the library; that is why I went there. I would not have done so if it had been anyone else. But I knew there was no danger with Myles. But then Foster Langdon was there before Myles could arrive! It was the worst luck."

"But why did Myles ask you to meet him?" Damaris asked.

"I don't know. I didn't ask him after . . . after everything happened. It hardly matters now. But I think that is the reason behind Myles's offer. He feels responsible. But it was not his fault. I shouldn't have gone there to meet any man."

"It is perfectly understandable. Why shouldn't you be able to meet a friend, even if he is a man? It's ridiculous. You couldn't have known that you would run into Langdon."

"No. But that is why there are rules of propriety—so that one avoids situations where such things can happen. I have always been so careful." Genevieve realized her hand had curled up into a fist, and she relaxed it. "Well, it does not matter now. 'Tis done."

"Genevieve . . . would it be so terrible to accept Myles's offer? I know you do not love him, but—"

Genevieve narrowed her eyes at Damaris. "Did Grandmama send you here to talk me?"

"No, oh, no, you must not think that," Damaris said hastily. "I mean, well, yes, she did talk to me, but only to make sure I understood that I was to vanish the moment Sir Myles arrived. I would never urge you to marry against your wishes. But I do hate for you to be unhappy, and I cannot help but think your life would be much more to your satisfaction were you to marry Myles."

"Yes, it is an excellent solution for me. If I did not realize that, Grandmama made it exceedingly clear." Genevieve jumped up and began to pace the room. "I feel—I feel so wild and torn!" She raised her hands to her temples, as if she could hold her turmoil down. "I cannot bear for my scandal to fall on Grandmama. She will not let anyone see it, of course, but her pride will be so wounded. And she has spent her life taking care of me. She could have gone on living in London, attending parties and visiting with her friends, but she came back to the castle after my mother died because she felt she had to raise me. She—my father was not an easy man. Perhaps Alec has told you."

"He was a brute!" Damaris's eyes flashed. "Do not tell me that he hurt you as he did Alec? Or your grandmother?"

"No, oh, no," Genevieve said bitterly. "It was always Alec on whom our father took out his rages—even when it was I who had done it. Sometimes I wished he *would* hit me. I think it would have been easier than standing outside his study and hearing him punish Alec and knowing . . . knowing Alec never ran away because he feared Father would turn to me." She stopped, reining in her emotions, pulling up the cool mask that had always served her so well. "Father did not, however, hit me. And he would never have dared touch Grandmama." A faint smile curved her lips. "I think she was the only person my father feared. Or perhaps the only one he loved. It was difficult to tell. But she disliked living at Cleyre. It is lonely and wild and cold. It made her bones ache. She enjoys company. Lights. Dancing. The theater. It was a tremendous sacrifice for her to bury herself at the castle all those years for my sake."

"She loves you. I am sure she was glad to do it."

"Yes, no doubt. But I have repaid her badly. I meant to soften the scandal, and instead I made it worse."

"The scandal of Alec marrying me?" Damaris asked softly.

Genevieve glanced at her guiltily. "No. I mean, well, there was also the whole affair of Jocelyn jilting him." She smiled wryly. "We Staffords seem to have a problem keeping hold of our betrotheds. Everyone blamed Alec; there were even whispers that he had murdered her."

"I know. And his then marrying a woman with a past did not help." Damaris softened her words with a smile. "Do not worry. I have always known that. But I could not sacrifice our love for the sake of the Stafford name. Nor should you have to pay for it by marrying anyone you don't want to marry. There is no need for you to accept Myles for Alec's sake; you know Alec cares not what others say of him. Nor for your grandmother, either. She will not lose her position in the *ton*, not for any real length of time. I suspect that most of them fear her as much as your father did."

Genevieve laughed, relaxing a little. "You may be right."

"It is you I was thinking of. I think you like Cleyre little more than your grandmother does."

Genevieve shrugged. "I do not love it there."

"If it were some man other than Myles, I would not urge you. But he would be a good husband. He is kind and so easy in his ways."

"I know. I know. Myles has many virtues. I am not the

one who would suffer. It would be Myles. How can I let him do such a thing?"

"But, Genevieve, he asked you. Myles is very kind, but in my experience men usually do things because they want to—even if they may not realize why they want it."

"Myles does not think before he acts." Genevieve set her jaw. "And he is generous to a fault. It is exactly the sort of rash thing he would do. But we would not suit. Anyone can see that. We never agree. He loves the world and I—I love hardly anyone. He should marry someone sweet and happy, a woman who could love him as he deserves. Not me. Not a woman with the heart of a Stafford!"

"You should not disparage the Stafford heart." Damaris smiled. "I have found it to be quite large. And consider this: Myles did not propose to any of those women you described. He asked *you*."

As Genevieve started to reply, she heard the knocker on the front door rap sharply. She looked at Damaris, the cold knot in her stomach suddenly expanding to fill her entire torso. Damaris went to the bow window once again and lifted the side of the drape to peer out.

"It is Myles." Damaris picked up her needlework.

Genevieve had risen to her feet at Damaris's words, her hands unconsciously going to her stomach. "You needn't go."

"I have clear instructions from your grandmother." Damaris gave the other woman an encouraging smile. "'Twill be better if the two of you talk alone."

"Sir Myles Thorwood, my lady," the butler intoned from the doorway, stepping aside to allow Myles to enter.

"Sir Myles," Damaris said, going forward to offer him her hand, and the two of them exchanged the usual greetings and pleasantries while Genevieve remained stock-still and silent as a statue. "Well . . ." Damaris cast a glance toward Genevieve. "Forgive me, but I was just about to go upstairs. I am sure you and Genevieve have much to discuss."

"Indeed." Myles turned to Genevieve after Damaris left the room, his warm smile lighting his eyes. "Come, Genny, you need not look at me as if am a snake about to strike. I intend you no harm."

"Of course not. Don't be silly." It was ridiculous the way her heart was pounding. This was *Myles*. She gestured toward the chair at right angles to the sofa. "Pray, sit down. May I offer you some refreshment?"

He shook his head. "You know why I have come."

"Indeed I do, and it was wrong of my grandmother to persuade you to do so. I cannot—"

"No, wait." He looked at her earnestly. "Pray extend me another chance. I handled it so ill last night one would think I am a raw lad from the country."

"It was not your manner, I assure you."

"You are saying, then, that is my entire being that you find unacceptable?" Myles lifted his brows. "Some might take offense at that."

"What?" Genevieve blinked. "Of course not. Myles, really, don't twist things around."

"I assure you, my desire is only to be as clear as I can about my ardent desire to marry you."

"Myles! You know you—"

He raised a finger and laid it against her lips. "Shh, now. You must not interrupt me every other breath, or we shall never be done here." He took both her hands in his. "I realized that last night, in my haste to make my suit, I did not offer you in the proper way. So I came here today to woo you." He went down on one knee, pulling her down to sit in her chair. "Lady Genevieve, would you do me the honor, the very great honor, of accepting my hand in marriage?"

"Myles!" Genevieve tried to tug her hands from his grasp, but he would not let her go. Absurdly, tears threatened her eyes, and she had to swallow hard. "Myles, you cannot wish to marry me."

"Can I not?" He smiled at her in that crooked way he had that invited one to join him, then raised her hand to his lips, velvety soft. "Genevieve, come . . . am I so bad? Really?"

"Of course you are not bad." She tried again to discreetly tug her hand away, to no avail.

"Even your grandmother says I am acceptable. Surely that must count for something. We all know how high Lady Rawdon's standards are."

"My grandmother is desperate to find me a husband."

"You mean she approves me only as a last resort? Genevieve, you wound me."

"Don't be nonsensical." Why did Myles have to act in this gentle, gallant manner? It was so difficult to be sensible. Honorable.

He kissed her hand again, and though he was only

teasing, her skin tingled at the brush of his lips, the touch of his breath. "Myles . . ." she whispered.

"Genevieve," he murmured back, and looked at her with those laughing amber eyes. "Surely you cannot intend to dash all my hopes?"

"You do not need to do this. You owe me nothing. Rawdon would never ask it of you."

"Rawdon? What does your brother have to do with this? I am not asking to marry him."

"You are a good friend. A kind man."

"Then surely you cannot reject so sterling a gentleman."

"Will you stop teasing? I am trying to save you from yourself."

"I am perfectly serious. Genevieve . . . I don't ask for your love. I am offering you my name, my home, my honor. I know that there is no woman to whom it is safer to entrust them. And I look forward with hope to the day when you will be able to return the respect and affection I feel for you. Genevieve, please, say you will become my wife."

Genevieve's throat swelled so that she could hardly speak, and this time she could not hold back the tears that welled in her eyes. She should not accept him. It was wrong and selfish of her. She should try again to convince him that he would come to regret his decision.

She took a long, shaky breath. "Yes. I will."

Once committed, Genevieve made no effort to delay the moment, and the two of them were married by special license the next day, attended only by her family and Lord and Lady Morecombe. Genevieve noticed with some irritation that, even though her own nerves were thrumming like the strings of a violin, Myles seemed perfectly at ease.

But she was grateful for the warmth of his hand curled around hers, as he bent to murmur in her ear, "Courage, Genny. We are almost through it."

When it was done, Myles turned to her, tilting her chin up, and bent to lightly kiss her. His lips were warm and soft as silk, and the scent of him teased at her nostrils. It was strange to be this close to him, to have him touch her like this in front of other people. Her stomach quivered. Dursbury had given her a peck on the cheek a time or two, and even once on the lips in parting. But it had not been the same; it had never felt like this to look into Dursbury's eyes.

Damaris and Thea took her upstairs to change into her carriage dress for traveling, and Genevieve could not help but remember the three of them doing the same thing only a few months ago at Damaris's wedding. How different her own wedding was from that joyous celebration. Determinedly she fixed a smile on her face and tried to enter into the other women's conversation; they were trying hard to make this whole peculiar situation seem normal.

"Genevieve." She turned to see her grandmother standing in the doorway.

"Grandmama." Her throat tightened. Beside her Damaris cast a significant glance at Thea, and the two women slipped out of the room, leaving her alone with the woman who had raised her.

"How lovely you look," the countess said, coming forward. "Exactly as you should." She reached out to smooth a wrinkle from one of the long sleeves of the gown.

"Thank you." Genevieve cast a look around them. Her bedroom seemed empty without her familiar brushes and bottles of perfume and lotion on the vanity. She twisted Myles's signet ring around her finger, thinking of the abashed glance Myles had sent her as he slipped it on her finger. "I must put some ribbon around this ring," she said, striving for a light tone. "It will fall off if I'm not careful."

"No doubt Myles will get you a suitable one soon," her grandmother said, and let out a little sigh. "It was very little like the wedding we had planned, was it?"

"No. No cathedral . . . no harp, no bouquet. Only five guests, and three of them are related to me." Genevieve's smile wobbled a bit, but she managed to keep it on her face as she added, "But at least there was no Elora—or her doves."

A chuckle escaped the countess's lips. "Yes, we must be grateful for that." She grasped Genevieve's shoulders and leaned forward to kiss her on the cheek in an unaccustomedly affectionate gesture. "I wish you very happy, my dear. I was so proud of you today. You were a Stafford through and through. No one would have known that the wedding was . . . not what you would have wished."

"And they will not." Genevieve set her jaw. No one, least of all Myles, could be allowed to glimpse the ache in her.

"Do not—" The countess cleared her throat and turned away from Genevieve as she went on, "There is no need for you to be frightened."

"Of Myles?" Genevieve looked at her blankly.

"Of your wedding night, dear." Her grandmother sent her a straight, flat look.

"Oh." Genevieve felt her cheeks heat. "I—I had not even thought of it." She had always done her best not to think of it when she was engaged to Dursbury. She could scarcely imagine the embarrassment of climbing into bed with a man she scarcely knew. Of course, she knew Myles, but that made it embarrassing in an entirely different way. She flushed even more deeply.

"It is not the most pleasant thing, of course," the countess went on. "But you have the fortitude of a Stafford, and I know you will do your duty. Myles is not a green lad; he will, I am sure, take care with you. It won't be so painful once you become accustomed to it."

"Painful?" Genevieve's stomach dropped. She had not thought past the embarrassment. Now her grandmother's words conjured up an even worse possibility.

"Yes, dear, but you need not worry. I am certain Myles will be a gentleman. There are other sorts of women to satisfy the lower appetites."

"Yes, no doubt," Genevieve responded faintly.

"Good. There." Lady Rawdon nodded and turned away. "Myles is waiting downstairs. I am sure you need to get away soon."

Her stomach curling in on itself, Genevieve watched her grandmother walk out the door. She turned away and found herself gazing into the mirror of her vanity table. She resembled a ghost, she realized, her light blond hair and pale skin in stark contrast to the dark-rust-colored traveling dress. Behind her she heard the plaintive mew of her cat, and she whirled around, her heart lifting a little. "Xerxes!"

The fluffy white cat sprang lightly onto the bed and let out another irritated meow. Genevieve scooped him up and hugged him to her, tears choking her throat. He stretched up, butting his head gently underneath her chin, then rubbing it against her shoulder.

"I wish I could take you with me," she told the cat. Her grandmother had insisted that it was not appropriate to take a cat on one's honeymoon, and finally, reluctantly, Genevieve had agreed to leave Xerxes behind. As the countess had pointed out, the animal actually belonged to her, not Genevieve. "But it will only be for a while. I will return before you know it." She tucked him into the crook of her arm, her heart aching, knowing that it would in fact be weeks, if not months, before she returned. With a final glance around her bedroom, she walked out.

Myles was waiting at the foot of the stairs, chatting with her brother and Gabriel. They laughed together, a deep, warm, masculine sound. The sconce behind them glinted on Myles's light brown hair, turning the strands a deep gold. He pivoted at the sound of Genevieve's step, and the full force of his smile caught her. She almost missed a stair, and her hand tightened on the banister.

Myles reached out his hand to her as she reached him, and Xerxes narrowed his eyes to slits, hissing and swiping his paw through the air. Myles looked at the cat, and his expression turned decidedly less warm. "Don't tell me you mean to bring that blasted animal?"

"No. I am leaving him here," Genevieve replied coolly and set Xerxes down, running her hand one last time along his spine. Then she straightened, squaring her shoulders. "I am ready."

Strolling beside her toward the door, Myles leaned down and murmured, "We aren't really walking to the gallows, you know."

"I don't know what you mean." Genevieve's reply was as light and unrevealing as her face.

It was gray and drizzling outside, and the footman held an umbrella over their heads as they hurried out to the post chaise, a chorus of well wishes following them. Myles handed Genevieve up into the vehicle, then paused and went back to Alec and Damaris to say a few words before returning. Genevieve's heart seemed to swell inside her chest as the carriage started to roll away from her home. It was all she could do to keep her face calm and smooth, not giving away the panic that gripped her. She was leaving everything she knew. She turned her face away, fighting her tears.

Myles tried to start up a conversation a time or two, but Genevieve could not reply for fear she might start to cry in front of him. The silence continued as they drove out of London and emerged into the countryside.

"You must speak to me sometime, you know," Myles said finally, amusement underlying his tone. "It would make our marriage a trifle uncomfortable, don't you think, if we never spoke?"

"I am happy I provide you with so much amusement," Genevieve snapped, a little relieved to feel irritation pushing back her sorrow.

"So am I," he answered candidly. "Else our squabbles might come to wear on me."

"When was it decided that we were going to retire to your manor house?" Genevieve asked, goaded by his flippant manner. Obviously the man viewed this whole miserable situation as some sort of jest. "I suppose you and Grandmother came up with the notion, as you have everything else. After all, why should I have anything to say in the matter?"

"It seemed the best course," Myles said mildly. "There was no time to arrange a proper honeymoon, and we need to let the gossip die down in London. Besides, I thought it proper to inform my mother in person. She will be most sorry that she was not able to attend the ceremony."

"Oh. I had not thought of that." Genevieve unbent a little. "No doubt you are right." His mother should, of course, be told before other people knew about the marriage. But Genevieve dreaded meeting the woman. She would be bound to despise Genevieve for this hasty wedding.

"If you wish to go somewhere else afterward, you have only to let me know," Myles went on. "Italy, perhaps? Switzerland is lovely."

"No. There is nowhere I want to go." Genevieve took a steadying breath, keeping her eyes on her hands. "I apologize. I am being beastly—and after all you've done for me. Pray do not think that—that I am not grateful to you."

"Hush. I don't ask for your gratitude," Myles said softly. "Ah, Genevieve, things so rarely go to plan, do they?" He smiled at her and reached out to untie the ribbons of her bonnet.

"Myles, what are you doing?"

"I think what you and I both need is some rest. A hat is not conducive to sleeping." He set the straw concoction on the seat and pulled her snugly up against his side, leaning back into the corner of the carriage.

"I could not sleep," Genevieve told him, holding herself stiffly upright.

"Well, I could. I rose far too early this morning and have been running about all day." He pressed her head gently down against his shoulder, where, Genevieve discovered, it seemed to fit surprisingly well. "Just relax. I promise you, we can argue all you want later."

It was so odd to lean against him like this, yet it was inviting as well. His body was soothingly warm against her, and he smelled pleasantly like, well, like Myles. It was almost impossible to keep her muscles tense, and she gradually let go, sinking into his side.

Genevieve woke up in darkness. The chaise jounced over a rut, sending her body rolling forward, but Myles's arm tightened around her, holding her in place. She blinked, pulling her hazy mind back into focus. She lay against Myles's chest, her face buried in his coat. She pulled herself upright and found Myles watching her.

"I have rumpled your coat. I am sorry."

"You have apologized to me yet again. I am beginning to fear that I have mistakenly married someone other than Genevieve Stafford."

She pulled a face at him. "Must you always play the fool, Myles?"

"Ah, good, it *is* you, after all." He, too, sat up and straightened his coat.

Genevieve slid over on the seat, putting several inches between them. The coach slowed and turned, the sound of the road changing beneath its wheels. There were shouts and lights outside, and Myles flicked the window curtain aside to look out.

"We've reached an inn. Hopefully it will be able to at least provide us with a meal."

Rain was pouring down as they stepped down from the coach, and even with her cloak thrown over her, Genevieve was soaked by the time they reached the door. Myles acquired a private room for them to dine in, though the fare proved ordinary—rough bread and over-cooked roast beef. Though the maid built up the fire, the room took time to heat up, and Genevieve found herself shivering as she ate. Her wet cloak did little to keep her warm, and she wound up spreading it and Myles's jacket on a chair in front of the fire to dry.

The sense of comfort she had felt earlier in the chaise with Myles had vanished the moment they stepped inside the inn. Nothing was natural about being here, nothing was normal in sitting down to eat alone with Myles in his shirtsleeves. Genevieve could not think of anything to say, and she wished, as she often had, for the ease of conversation that other women possessed. Sadly, the only sort of speech that seemed to spring without difficulty from her lips was sharp. Even Myles was quiet, and his silence deepened her gloom. She wondered if he was regretting his actions.

"The rain doesn't appear to be letting up," Myles said finally. It lashed the window as the wind gusted.

"Yes." Genevieve forced a smile. "Not good weather for traveling, I'm afraid."

"Shall we get a room here?"

Genevieve's stomach danced. "I—is that what you prefer?"

"It is not where I hoped we would stop. There are nicer inns on the road home, but unfortunately the rain held us up. And you are cold and tired and wet."

"I will be fine," she assured him quickly.

"I know." The corner of his mouth quirked up. "You are a Stafford and forged from iron. But I fear I am not made of such stern stuff. It will doubtless prove a grave disappointment to you."

"Don't be nonsensical." She sighed. "Very well. I suppose it does not matter." His eyebrows rose slightly, and she realized belatedly that her lack of enthusiasm was less than tactful. "I mean, well, you know." She began to blush.

"Yes, I know." He saved her from continuing to flounder by rising and pulling on his jacket. "Why don't you sit here by the fire? I shall speak to the innkeeper."

Genevieve was glad to leave her plate and huddle on a footstool in front of the fire, but its heat could not take away the chill inside her. Tonight was her wedding night. Her hands tightened on her knees as she thought about her grandmother's words, and it occurred to her that she had been foolish to agree to this marriage without thinking it through.

Myles returned, candle in hand, and led her up the stairs and down a narrow, dark hall, into a room that was equally dark and cramped. Genevieve's heart dropped even lower as she glanced about, taking in the single rickety chair and the small washstand that were the only other objects in the room besides the bed. Someone, the innkeeper she presumed, had brought up their bags and lit an oil lamp, but the small glow did little to alleviate the gloom of the chamber.

"I am sorry," Myles told her, surveying the unprepossessing place. "I fear this is all they had. The rain has driven several people to stop here."

"I am sure it will be fine." Genevieve managed to keep her voice even. "It looks, um, clean." Her eyes skittered over the bed. It was hard to look anyplace else in so small a room.

"I'll step out for a moment. Give you a chance to, um . . ." Myles, too, glanced around vaguely, and Genevieve realized that he must feel awkward as well.

Somehow this thought bolstered her courage, and she was able to smile at him almost normally. "Thank you."

As soon as he left, she dug out a nightgown from her bag and hurriedly undressed. Her fingers, clumsy with cold, fumbled at the buttons of her dress, and she dreaded the thought of being caught half-dressed when Myles returned. Once she was in her nightgown, her clothes neatly folded and stuck back into her traveling bag, she hesitated, unsure what to do. It was awkward to just stand about, and it made her blush to think of Myles seeing her in her nightgown. It was no more revealing than a number of evening dresses she had seen, but that she wore nothing beneath it—and that Myles would know that—made it seem indecent.

Finally, she crawled into bed. It might be forward of her, she supposed, but she was chilled and quite worn-out from a combination of nerves and misery. She curled up on her side, pulling the covers up over her shoulders, and waited for Myles to come. She thought of closing her eyes and pretending to be asleep, but that was a coward's way out.

Her heart beat faster at the thought of Myles's disrobing and getting into bed with her. What would he expect her to do? To say? She could not help but think she would displease him. She had never known how to attract men. Some had told her she was beautiful, but that, she suspected, had more to do with who she was and how large a dowry she possessed than with herself. Indeed, she was apt to turn men away with her sharp tongue.

Certainly Myles was not attracted to her. In all the years she had known him, he had never made any attempt to court her. Oh, he had flirted with her, but Myles would have flirted with a statue if that was all that was around. Genevieve had seen his mistress, a small, curvaceous brunette, completely unlike herself.

Myles would come to regret marrying her. Perhaps he already did. The tears she had been struggling to suppress throughout this whole miserable day suddenly came flooding forth, too many, too strong, to deny. And, of course, that was the moment Myles chose to come back into the room.

Genevieve hastily turned away, struggling to gulp back her sobs. She listened to the sounds of Myles moving about the minuscule room, pulling off his boots and removing his jacket. Genevieve buried her face in the pillow. Perversely, the harder she tried to conceal her sobs, the more they pushed out of her.

"Genevieve?" Myles stopped in the midst of taking off his waistcoat and turned toward the bed. "Are you—" He lifted the candle. "Genny! Are you crying?"

He set down the candle and crossed the room. Genevieve moaned and rolled away from him. "No! Don't look at me."

"Dear girl." The sympathy in his voice was almost too much for her to bear. "I can hardly spend our married life not looking at you." Myles sat on the edge of the bed and took her by the shoulders, turning her toward him. "Don't cry. 'Tis not so bad as it seems."

She tried to pull away, but he would not let her, wrapping his arms around her. His warmth and strength surrounded her, and she could not hold back any longer. Genevieve flung her arms around him, burying her face in his chest. "Oh, Myles! I am so ashamed!"

Genevieve broke into sobs, clinging to him, and Myles

lay down on the bed beside her, cradling her against him. "Ah, Genny, I know I am not the sort of man you envisioned marrying. But I'm not a bad sort, really. We'll rub along together well enough. You'll see."

His words reminded Genevieve of her grandmother's vision of their marriage. Somehow this image, which she had once viewed with equanimity with Lord Dursbury, now, with Myles, seemed bleak and barren. Her tears came even harder. Myles kissed the top of her head, his hand stroking soothingly up and down her back. He held her while she cried out all her misery. Then, finally, she fell asleep, cradled in his arms.

Seven

Myles opened his eyes. His cheek rested against Genevieve's head, her fine, blond hair tickling his nose. His arm underneath her body had gone numb. But that inconvenience was the least of what filled his consciousness. What he was acutely aware of was her lithe, long body inside the circle of his arms, snuggled up tight against him, her round, firm bottom fitting perfectly into the cup of his pelvis. Their legs were tangled together, one of his knees between hers. One of his hands might be asleep, but the other one was quite awake as it rested upon the sweet curve of her hip.

Genevieve sighed in her sleep and wriggled back into him, and his body leaped in response. She was a warm, soft, desirable armful. And she was his.

He slid his free hand over her hip and down onto her leg. Her innocent and unrevealing nightgown had worked its way up during the night, so that her legs were bare from the knee down. He thought of exploring farther, of inching up the gown to show more of her long legs, and once again his body pulsed in response, hard and eager.

But that would be foolish in the extreme. It took no particular genius to know that Genevieve was an innocent when it came to the marital act. She was, after all, the daughter of a proud, aristocratic family, sheltered and chaperoned, kept not only inviolate but as unknowing as possible until the day she married. As brother to five sisters, he was aware just how well young girls were shielded from reality. Genevieve, he suspected, was more skittish than most. It would be cruel, not to mention unwise, to give free rein to the desire coursing through him. Myles was not a man to rush his fences. He must woo her.

He stroked his fingers lazily over the point of her shoulder and down her arm, then on to the dip of her waist, the swell of her hip. A sensual smile hovered on his lips. It might take some strength of will to hold back from making love to her now, but it would be worth the wait.

Genevieve had always drawn him. He had denied it, sometimes even to himself, pulling his mind away whenever it moved in that direction, knowing he would never have her. He could admit now how many times his thoughts had strayed to her over the years, imagining her in his bed, her long legs wrapped around his back, her voice breathy and yearning in his ear. Something in her distant, even cold, demeanor made him ache to turn that frost to heat, that reticence to hunger.

If he could awaken her desire, if he could find that spark that leapt between them in their quarrels and turn it into passion, then perhaps he could turn their marriage into something real. And if he did not?

Well, in that case, he had made a ruinous decision. Myles sighed and eased his arm out from beneath Genevieve. He rose to his feet and slipped silently across the room to recover his boots and jacket. It would be better to slip out and get himself under control lest he awaken Genevieve in a way he might later regret. A brisk morning walk would be just the thing to get his brain working better than certain other parts of his anatomy. When he came back, he would be more ready to begin the daunting task of winning Genevieve.

Something tickled along Genevieve's neck. She floated toward consciousness, aware of a vague, eager feeling, something pleasant, no, something *pleasurable* that teased her, pulled at her. Her eyelids floated open, taking in an entirely strange room—and the heretofore unknown sensation of a man's lips kissing their way up the side of her neck.

A quiver ran through her, ending in a rush of warmth deep in her belly. "Myles."

"Ah, you are awake." He pressed his lips to her neck again, and his hand moved a swath of her hair aside to open up her neck to further exploration. He kissed the bony edge of her skull just beneath her ear, then his lips hovered over her ear itself, sending little shivers down her.

"What are you doing?" Genevieve strove for a cross tone, but she feared it came out more of a quaver.

"Why, kissing my wife awake." He pressed his lips to her ear.

"I am awake now." When he didn't respond other than to brush his lips against the tender skin of her temple, she added, "You may stop."

"I could." He took her earlobe gently between his teeth, eliciting a little gasp from her. "But what would be the fun in that?"

Genevieve dug her fingers into the mattress beside her. She didn't know what to do. She had never felt anything like the bright sensations rippling through her at the touch of his lips and teeth and—oh, my, his tongue, as well. It seemed likely that what he was doing was not at all the thing and she ought to pull away from him. But it was too delicious, like the taste of chocolate melting on one's tongue.

He circled the shell-like whorls of her ear with the tip of his tongue, then dipped inside, startling her almost as much as did the way her insides softened. Her eyes drifted closed and her breath caught in her throat. His lips moved onto her cheek, sliding along her jaw. He cupped the side of her face, turning it toward him, and Genevieve found herself rolling onto her back and gazing up at him.

Her mind was scattered, and all she could think was how handsome he was. Genevieve was aware of a strange desire to run her thumb across the lines of his eyebrows and cheeks, to test the plumpness of his bottom lip. A host of new feelings were coursing through her, tingling and warm and unsettling.

He bent and brushed his lips over hers, and everything hovering inside her burst into frantic life. His mouth touched hers again, soft as a feather, fleeting as a breath, then returned again for a longer taste, and his tongue traced the line where her lips met.

Genevieve was so startled that she jumped and slid away from him. She stared at him, her lips parting in surprise. "I—we should be on our way." Her voice came out as breathless as if she had been running.

He smiled lazily. "No doubt you are right." He rolled onto his side, propped up on his elbow, and looked at her, his eyes sliding down her body, almost as tangible as a touch.

Heat rose in Genevieve's throat. She was conscious of how little she wore and how her night shift had ridden up, exposing her knees. She tensed, waiting in a curious combination of apprehension and anticipation, but Myles only stood up, extending a hand to help her.

Vaguely disappointed, Genevieve put her hand in his and slipped out of bed. It was useless to be embarrassed now about his seeing her in her nightgown since he had already done so, but she simply could not get dressed in front of him. She cast about for some diplomatic way to get him to leave.

"I shall wait for you downstairs; they're laying out a breakfast for us," Myles said, resolving her dilemma.

Genevieve could not decide whether she should be grateful for his social acumen or irritated that he could so easily discern her thoughts. He chuckled, obviously reading that latest idea on her face as readily as he had the others. She frowned; she had long prided herself on concealing her emotions from the world.

Myles sketched a bow and started to leave, but he turned back, pulled her to him, and kissed her. This was not one of the light kisses he had rained on her a few minutes ago, but a full, deep claiming of her mouth. Genevieve trembled, and her heart slammed in her chest as his lips explored hers, his tongue delving in to taste and touch and tantalize.

Then, just as abruptly, his mouth left hers. His arm remained around her, holding her to him, and Genevieve leaned her head against his chest, unwilling to look up and reveal the wild tumult of feelings inside her. She felt his lips press against her hair.

"What I wouldn't give for an hour and a pleasant room," he murmured, sending Genevieve's pulse racing even harder. Then he released her and was out the door, leaving Genevieve staring after him in stunned dismay.

It took Genevieve a moment to collect her wits. She started toward the dress she had folded on the chair last night. She was unused to being without the services of her maid, who had remained behind to pack the rest of Genevieve's clothes and bring them to Thorwood Park. Fortunately the carriage dress was easy enough to put on, buttoning as it did up the front, and for traveling, a simple hairstyle was more proper anyway than the more elaborate style her maid had curled and crimped it into yesterday afternoon for the wedding.

She glanced down at her hand, where Myles's gold signet ring sat on her ring finger, a ribbon wound around it several times in the back to ensure it would not slide off her much slenderer finger. She was Lady Thorwood now. Myles's wife. It seemed most peculiar, yet something about the idea was exciting, too. When her grandmother talked about the duty of marrying and producing heirs, Genevieve had not envisioned anything like the way Myles had just kissed her. She closed her eyes, remembering again the tingling of her skin, the rush of blood in her veins, the way her entire body had seemed to open up when he slipped his tongue into her mouth. Surely that wasn't usual. Something that thrilling and outrageous was bound to be improper.

She wondered if he would do it again. And when. Was it that sort of thing that made Damaris smile at Alec in that secret, sensual way? Did kisses like that make up for the pain the countess had warned her of? She felt so strange inside, so jangly and uncertain and wanting . . . something.

She was like a boat tossed about upon a vast sea. However pleasant—well, more than pleasant—however stirring those sensations were, they were completely out of her control. And that was not the way she wanted to live her life. She drew in a breath. This simply would not do. She needed to regain her calm. Her control. She could not allow Myles to send her off course.

The inn was not as terrible as it had seemed last night, she decided as she went downstairs. Though small and low-ceilinged, it appeared brighter with the sun coming in through the thick, leaded-glass window at the end of the corridor. It was almost quaint. Everything appeared much better this morning.

The door was open to the private room, and Myles was standing by the window, sipping a cup of tea. She paused for a moment, watching him. The sun coming in the window turned his hair almost golden. His jacket hung perfectly on him, and his breeches were well fitted to his long, muscular legs. He had, she thought, exactly the form most pleasing in a man—not that such things were important.

She must have made a noise, for he turned and smiled. "Genevieve. How lovely you look."

He set down his cup and crossed the room to her, bending slightly to kiss her cheek and lightly stroking his hand down her arm. A shiver ran through her, setting up the tangle of nerves in her stomach that she had so carefully smoothed away. He escorted her to the table, seating her, then began to dish up a choice piece of meat for her, urging her to try this dish or that.

"Really, Myles, what are you doing?" Genevieve asked sharply. "Why are you fluttering around me?"

"Genevieve! Are you criticizing my attempts to spoil my bride? I am devastated."

"You are ridiculous," Genevieve corrected.

He laughed and sat down. "My love, will you not let me play the attentive groom? I think I have a calling for it." He tore off a piece of buttered bread and popped it into her mouth, then ran his thumb along her lip to remove a dot of butter.

A flutter started in her stomach, and Genevieve hastily turned her attention to her plate. Normally she would have tossed back a tart response, but her mind had gone blank. Her eyes strayed to Myles's hands, efficiently spreading the pale butter on another bite of bread. His fingers were long and agile. She thought of them sliding down her arm, bringing all the nerves beneath her skin to life.

Genevieve cleared her throat and set about making wifely conversation as they ate. "I know very little about you, I fear. I have not met any of your family."

"No reason for you to," he said with a careless smile. "My mother has never liked London overmuch, and since my father's death, she never comes to the city. You may have met my sister Meg; she is the next one down from me. She married Lord Devonbrook and spends most of the Season in the city, though no doubt in different circles. But the eldest, Amelia, married the local squire's son, and she rarely leaves the area, for how else could she manage the lives of everyone around her? Daphne married a clergyman with a living in Devon. Amelia and Daphne each have four children, and I shall not bother you with their names, for there are too many to remember."

"Oh, my. You do have a number of nieces and nephews."

"That is only the beginning. The next sister down, Phoebe, married a military man, and she has three little ones, whom you will meet. While her husband is with his brigade in Portugal, she has brought her brood home to the Park to live. There is another on the way, you see, and she wants to be close to our mother." He laughed. "No, you need not look alarmed. It will not be such a crowd. Thorwood Park is no Castle Cleyre, but it is a rambling old house with plenty of room for everyone. The company is nice for my mother."

"I believe Grandmama said your mother was related to Lord Aylesworth?"

"She is his sister. Their father was not well pleased when she told him she would marry the son of a lowly baronet and no other."

"What did he do?" Genevieve asked.

"What could he do? He made them wait for a year before he finally gave his permission, but in the end, of course, he gave in."

Genevieve thought that her own father would have found a great number of things that could be done to impose his will on a recalcitrant child, but she did not say so. She glanced down at her plate, a little surprised to see that she had eaten everything on it. She took a sip of her tea. "Your parents were a love match, then?"

"Very much so." He nodded, setting his plate aside. "My father adored her, and she him. He had a rose arbor built for her, all white roses, so that, he said, they would form a perfect backdrop for her beauty. When they are in season, she always puts a bouquet of the roses at his grave."

"That's very romantic."

"It is." He gave her a bittersweet smile. "But 'tis sad, as

well. She has never been the same since his death. She enjoys life; I don't mean to imply that she does not, or that she does not love her children and grandchildren. But she has been . . . incomplete, I suppose. I think she will not be whole again until she joins him."

"I cannot imagine that."

"And here I thought you would greatly mourn my passing," he replied lightly.

"Don't be nonsensical." She frowned at him. "You know I would be quite sorry if you died. But it is hardly as if we are a love match."

"It's true. Still . . . we have time." He linked his hand with hers, bringing it up to his mouth to press a kiss upon the back.

She wondered if he was teasing her again. Surely he did not expect them to fall in love. She shifted a little uncomfortably. "Myles, I do not think—I mean, I am not the sort of woman to—oh, you know what I am!" she finished crossly.

"My dear girl, what do you mean?" His brows rose slightly.

"Don't put on that expression with me. You are quite aware what I mean." She straightened, and her expression became one of a person taking her medicine. "Myles, I promise you I will be as good a wife as I can be. I will manage your household and visit your sick tenants and call on the vicar's wife. I will make needlepoint pillows and plan any sort of party you wish. I will be polite to your friends, even that frivolous Alan Carmichael, and I shall not fuss about you going off with them to your club or to watch men beat each other about the head or to tramp about the moors shooting things, for I am well accustomed to that with Alec."

"Ah, Genny." He chuckled. "What an interesting view you have of a wife's duties. However, I must tell you that I have no need for needlepoint cushions, though I shall appreciate your effort to be civil to poor Alan. And, alas, the vicar does not have a wife, only a daughter of rather youthful years."

"Myles, be serious for once." She leaned forward, her eyes fixed earnestly on his face. "If you expect me to be a . . . a frilly sort of wife or someone who hangs on you and never says a sharp word to you, I fear you will be doomed to disappointment. I have the heart of a Stafford, not that of a loving woman. You know what I am like, and I don't think I can be changed into another sort of person. I should have explained all this; I was wrong to accept your offer without your truly understanding that I am lacking in such attributes. Perhaps, if you wish it, well, perhaps we might be able to get an annulment, not having . . . you know . . ."

"Consummated the marriage?" Genevieve nodded, not looking at him. He leaned closer to her, planting his elbows on the table and tilting up her chin so that she had to look into his face. "My dearest Genevieve, you are right. I do know you, and I knew your nature when I offered for you. I have seen ample evidence over the years of the heart you carry inside you, and while I think you wrong yourself, I would not try to make you into something you are not. I have no interest in frills nor any need for you to have only sweet words for me—though I will admit that one or two now and then would not displease me." He smiled into her eyes and bent to press his lips gently against hers. "I have no desire for an annulment. I confess that I am looking forward to consummating our marriage."

Genevieve felt as if every nerve in her body had awakened and was waiting, tingling, for what he would do next. His breath was warm, its touch like a feather against her skin. His mouth was only an inch from hers, and she could think of nothing except the way it had felt upon her a few minutes ago in their bedchamber. He raised his hand and slowly drifted the tips of his fingers down her cheek and onto her throat, curving around to cup her neck.

Then, with a sigh, he released her. "Unfortunately, 'tis hardly the time or place to continue." He rose to his feet and extended his hand to her. "I fear that we must be on our way."

They set out again for Thorwood Park, traveling at a better pace than the day before. With the curtain open to the soft summer day, Genevieve watched the landscape roll by while Myles described the people and places around Thorwood Park. He painted the nearby village of Hutchins Gate in comic tones, but his affection for the place and the people who lived there was clear in his voice. And when he spoke of the lands and tenants that his estate comprised, it was just as evident that he understood and enjoyed both the people and the business.

"I am surprised you know so much about it," Genevieve told him.

"About what? The people who live where I grew up?" He looked puzzled.

"No. Well, yes. I mean, that you know so much about the details. What your tenants raise, who their families are."

"Does not Alec?"

"Yes, but he is not like other young men that way. Not many gentlemen regard their tenants as 'their people,' as Alec does. Most see their estate as merely a well of money for gambling and drinking and clothes."

"Mm. I confess I am not as proprietary as Alec. My family was never their 'liege lord' in the way of the earls of Rawdon. But still . . . it makes little sense to ignore the details of what enables one to live as we do. That 'well,' as you say, can run dry. I should hate to wake up one morning and find myself destitute because I had not paid enough attention to my tenants."

"I am very impressed," Genevieve told him honestly.

"That I am not completely frivolous?" His smile took the sting from his words, but Genevieve blushed, fully aware that she had misjudged him.

She started to protest, then stopped herself. "Yes. You are right. I am sorry."

Now it was his turn to look surprised. "Genevieve . . . I don't know what to say."

"Oh, hush. You would think I had never apologized to anyone. Anyway," she added rather crossly, "it isn't as if you've ever talked of such things before."

"True. I am not inclined to mention crops and rents and such at a gala or the opera."

"Or to a woman."

"I admit, 'tis not the first thing that crosses my mind." He smiled. "Had I but known it was the way to your heart . . ."

"Don't be foolish," she told him severely, but honesty impelled her to add, "At least you were willing to tell me instead of warning me to mind my knitting."

"My dear, I would never tell you that. I have seen the scarf you made for Alec."

Her eyes widened, and a hot retort came to her lips, but instead laughter tumbled out. The time passed far more quickly than Genevieve would have imagined possible. Their conversation roamed far from the subjects she was accustomed to—and she felt sure that some of it was not in the least appropriate for him to discuss with a lady. But she could not deny that it made conversation with him far more interesting.

Late in the afternoon their chaise rolled into the yard of a prosperous-looking inn. They were clearly in a more substantial town than any they had passed before. Genevieve could see the spire of a cathedral over the treetops and roofs, and the road had turned into a cobblestoned street.

"Are we stopping here for the night?" Genevieve

asked, and the nerves in her stomach, which had been quiet during the ride, began to set up a jangle once again.

"Yes, it is too far to reach the Park tonight," Myles said. "I think you will find the Three Swans much more inviting than the accommodations last night."

As they entered the large stone inn, the innkeeper hurried forward to greet Myles, who was obviously an honored guest. Within moments a maid had whisked Genevieve up to a large, well-appointed bedchamber. The girl completed Genevieve's pleasure in the room by saying, "Shall I light the fire and bring up the slipper tub, ma'am?"

"A bath?" Genevieve smiled at the thought of washing away the grime of travel. "That would be delightful."

Within minutes, two maids had brought in a small slipper tub and placed it in front of the fireplace. As the girls bustled in and out, filling the tub, Genevieve pulled the pins from her hair and began to brush it out.

Myles strolled through the open doorway and stopped short. His eyes went to her hair, tumbling over her shoulders, then flickered over to the tub. His eyes darkened, his face changing subtly. He started toward her, and Genevieve jumped to her feet, setting the brush aside, her heart suddenly hammering in her chest. Of course. How could she have forgotten? Her room was no longer her own.

"Myles! I, um, was about to . . ." She glanced toward the tub, irritated that she could not keep the blush from rising up her throat. She looked away, and her gaze fell on the bed, and the heat under her skin increased.

"Yes, I see." He raised his hand to trail it down her hair to her shoulders.

Genevieve swallowed, and her eyes came back to his face. His mouth had a soft sensuality. She remembered the pressure of his lips against hers, the teasing of his tongue.

"Perhaps I should stay to help you bathe," he murmured.

"Myles!" Genevieve glanced over at the tub, where the maid was pouring water from a steaming kettle. "The maid . . ." She kept her voice low.

He grinned, following her gaze, and his eyes danced. Leaning closer, his lips inches from her ear, he whispered, "She cannot hear us."

His breath drifted across her skin, igniting little shivers, and Genevieve had to brace herself not to show it, taking a hasty step back. The maid turned and bobbed a curtsy toward Genevieve, her eyes going to Myles with obvious interest.

"Just call if you need my help, ma'am," the girl said as she left the room.

Genevieve turned back to Myles, who was grinning in an annoying way.

"No need for a maid," he told her lightly. "I am quite able to unfasten the buttons of your dress."

"No doubt you are," Genevieve retorted tartly. "I am sure you have had ample experience."

"Genevieve! What a shocking thing to say." His eyes gleamed gold as he idly toyed with a strand of her hair.

"Do stop being nonsensical and go away. I must get ready for dinner." Did he actually mean what he'd said? Did he intend to undo her clothes, to watch as she stepped into the tub? Her breath hitched in her throat as embarrassment flooded her, carrying with it the oddest twist of heat deep inside her.

No. He would not do something so . . . so indecorous. Myles had always been the soul of courtesy, despite his frequently odd sense of humor. But a look was now on his face she had never before seen there, with a fierce intensity in his eyes, a hint of something almost predatory in the set of his mouth.

"Are you sure? I can be very helpful." He lifted her hair and bent to lay a soft kiss upon her collarbone. "Washing your back." His mouth drifted upward teasingly onto her throat. "And other things."

"Myles!" Her voice came out far shakier than she liked, and Genevieve moved back.

"No? Some other time, perhaps." He took her chin between his fingers and bent to place a light kiss on her forehead, then turned and left the room.

Genevieve dropped onto the chair, air rushing out of her. She felt shaken, on uncertain ground. Myles her brother's friend was not necessarily the same man as Myles her husband, and she was not quite sure how to deal with him. What to say. What to think.

She did not call the maid back to help her out of her clothes. All she wanted right now was to be alone. She was relieved to find that the door had a key in the lock. It was a bit unnerving to think Myles might pop into the room again. She peeled out of her clothes and stepped into the tub, sinking down into the warm water with a contented sigh. For the moment at least, she was determined to luxuriate in the pleasure, and she refused to think any more about her hasty marriage or her husband . . . or the wedding night that loomed before her.

Eight

Revived by the bath, Genevieve dressed for dinner with
the help of the accommodating maid. The wide neckline
of the dress seemed to call for some sort of adornment,
and she was contemplating the small amount of jewelry
she had included in her valise when after a knock on the
door Myles came into the room.

"Ah," he said, looking down at the two simple necklaces. "I
see that I have arrived at just the right time." He was dressed
for dinner, elegant in a dark wine jacket and snowy-white
shirt and neckcloth. He carried a small box in his hand.

"Myles." Genevieve could not help but think of the
last time he was in the room with her; she hoped a blush
would not betray her. Her stomach tightened as he
walked toward her. "What are you doing?"

"Do not look at me so warily." He laughed. "I come
bearing gifts."

Genevieve looked at him blankly. "Gifts? What? From
whom?"

"From me to you, of course. 'Tis customary, is it not, for
a groom to give his bride an engagement present? I realize

it is a bit late for that, but . . . well, our engagement was a tad short."

"But when—how—"

"I could not give you the wedding ring that was intended for my bride, as I keep it at the estate. Clearly a lack of foresight on my part." He took her left hand in his, stroking his thumb across the heavy signet ring on her slender finger. "'Twas my grandmother's, and she gave it to me for my bride. I apologize for this clumsy substitute."

"It does not matter." Warmth bloomed in Genevieve's chest as she realized that her lack of a wedding ring had not been from disinterest on his part, that he wanted her to have the family heirloom.

"Indeed, I would hope my ring does matter to you," he replied with a smile. "But I am grateful for your forbearance. I did manage to find you a small token of my esteem, however. I would have given it to you yesterday, but there never seemed to be an appropriate moment." He extended the flat box toward her.

Genevieve opened the lid and drew in a sharp breath. Inside, lying on a bed of velvet, glittered a necklace and earrings in icy splendor. The necklace was a simple design, a chain of diamonds and jewels so pale a blue they were almost clear, with matching earrings of the same clear blue stones, surrounded by tiny diamonds.

"Myles! They're beautiful!"

"They are only aquamarines. I meant to buy you sapphires, but these were so much the color of your eyes I could not resist."

"Thank you." Genevieve smiled up into his eyes, her throat closing with emotion.

"For that look in your eyes, I would have given you twenty necklaces." He raised her hand to press his lips gently against her fingertips.

"I think that I might find it difficult to wear so many." Genevieve strove to keep her manner light.

Myles took the necklace and stepped behind her to drape it around her neck. Fastening the clasp, he bent and pressed his lips to the fragile ledge of her collarbone. A shiver ran through Genevieve at the soft touch of his lips on her skin, the warmth of his breath. He straightened, and their eyes met in the mirror.

"It looks just as I thought it would," he murmured.

His eyes held hers in the mirror as he ran his forefinger lightly across her skin, just below the necklace. She trembled at the sensations his feathery touch roused in her. She could not look away from his gaze. The gold-brown glint of his eyes darkened, and he slipped his arms around her from behind, his hands gliding over her stomach. The sight of his hands spread out against her body sparked something deep inside her, a lush warmth that bloomed and throbbed in a way she had never imagined.

Myles pressed his lips again to her soft, exposed skin, making his way across her collarbone and up the side of her neck. Genevieve let her head fall to the side, baring her neck to his exploration. She felt strangely limp, almost unable to move, and she closed her eyes, though she was not sure whether it was to hide from herself or to luxuriate in these new sensations, both exciting and vaguely frightening.

His hands glided over her front, roaming down over her abdomen and up until they brushed the undersides of her breasts. He caught her earlobe delicately between his teeth. She was grateful for the strength of his hands, pressing her back into him, holding her up, for she was not sure but what her knees would give way. His hot breath drifted across her ear, and his tongue teased around the edges, making her gasp. Myles let out a pleased little chuckle, and she felt something move against her from behind.

"There." He raised his head, and his arms tightened around her for a moment. "I had best stop or else I will not be presentable for supper." He released her, his fingertips drifting light as a feather across her breasts.

Myles turned away, going to the window to look out as Genevieve struggled to compose herself. Her body was a stranger to her suddenly, pulsing and unaccustomedly warm. Her breasts felt fuller and faintly aching, and her nipples were puckered into tight buds. She looked at her reflection, amazed by the flush of pink in her cheeks, the lambent warmth of her eyes, the soft fullness of her mouth.

This was not, she thought, a little panicky, the way a lady should feel. She dared not even glance at Myles, wondering in embarrassment if he had sensed how she responded inside. Was this how gentlemen treated their wives? Or was this something peculiar to Myles, some licentious, tempting ability to make a woman feel eager and hungry and breathless?

Genevieve sneaked a glance at Myles. His back was to her, his arms crossed, as he stared out at the gardens. She wondered what he was thinking. It occurred to her that his posture was that of a man holding his temper in check. What if she had displeased him? Perhaps she had been too eager . . . or perhaps she had been too cold. It was so difficult when one did not know what was expected of one. She sighed softly and turned away.

"I suppose we should go down to supper."

"Yes, of course." Myles returned to her, and though she scanned his face, she could read nothing in his expression, as genial as ever. She was beginning to realize that a pleasant manner could be as effective a mask as the iciest of demeanors.

Genevieve sat on the chair beside the bed, waiting for Myles. Her back was as straight as that of the chair, her hands lying still in her lap, her feet together, demurely peeping out from beneath her dressing gown. Nothing in her correct posture or smooth face betrayed that her stomach was knotted inside her or that fear iced her veins. She had been all right through supper, where she and Myles had carried on the sort of light, meaningless small talk that made life run in an even, predictable course.

When the meal was through, however, and she had left Myles to enjoy his port, her nerves had started to fray.

The moment she had been dreading for the past two days was rushing down upon her. Myles had been kind and patient last night, demanding nothing from her; he had even held her as she cried. But that would not be the case tonight. His words and actions this afternoon had made clear his intentions. It was what any groom would expect from his bride.

With the maid's help, it took her little time to dress for bed and comb out her hair. Then Genevieve sat down to wait. The longer she sat, the more knotted her nerves grew. She could not help but think of what her grandmother had told her. Or how embarrassing it would be when she removed her dressing gown in front of Myles and he would see her clad in only the thin lawn nightgown. She had never before thought about how the dark circles of her nipples showed through the material or how the outline of her entire body was visible if she chanced to stand in front of the lamp.

Why was Myles waiting so long to come to bed? Perhaps he was sitting in the dining room alone, drinking, trying to work himself into coming to her. There was, after all, little to recommend her. She was as tall and thin as a stick, pale as a ghost. Myles had seemed to desire her earlier, but perhaps he had merely forced himself into a pretense so that she would not feel unwanted, the same way he could be counted on to ask a wallflower to dance.

A nervous giggle escaped her at the thought of courtesy in this context. She told herself it was absurd to worry whether she appealed to Myles. It made no difference, for they were irrevocably bound together now. And wouldn't it be preferable if he found her undesirable? Then he would leave her to her own devices. She would not have to go through this anxiety and worry each night.

A soft rap at the door struck her as if it had been a shot. She jumped up and whirled toward the door, her heart slamming in her chest. Her voice came out a whisper, and she had to clear her throat and repeat, "Come in."

Myles entered the room and started toward her. Genevieve curled her fingers into her palms, forcing herself to leave her hands at her sides, to face Myles as if her pulse were not racing through her veins. She wished she could see his face better than the candlelight permitted. His face, usually so open, revealed nothing to her now.

"Myles." She was relieved to find that her voice did not betray the tangle of nerves inside her.

"Genevieve." He walked toward her. The faint smile that graced his lips was familiar to her, but the look in his eyes was not. Something dark was in them, some depth of purpose that made her feel even shakier.

She waited breathlessly as he stopped in front of her, gazing down into her face. Reaching down, he took her hand, and surprise flitted across his face.

"Your hands are like ice."

"Oh. I'm sorry."

"No need to apologize." He looked at her quizzically as he took her hands between both of his, warming them.

"Is the room not warm enough?" He glanced toward the fireplace. "Shall I light the fire?"

"No. No need." Genevieve feared he would feel her shakiness in her hands. He was only inches from her, so warm, so close, so overwhelmingly masculine that Genevieve's nerves fairly vibrated with tension. He reached up to touch her cheek, and she stiffened involuntarily.

"Genevieve?" He frowned, gazing at her for a long moment. She saw his eyes fill with amazement as he said, "Are you frightened? Of me?"

"No! Of course not." She pulled away, turning her face from him. "Why would I be frightened of you? You are only—"

"Only Myles," he finished sardonically.

Her eyes flew to him then. "I did not mean—" When he quirked an eyebrow, she finished lamely, "Well, I did not mean anything bad. You are Alec's friend, and I have known you forever. I know you are not a . . . a rough or cruel man. It is just that I—well, I have never—I know that you expect—oh, the devil!" She glared, setting her jaw.

Myles chuckled as he reached out to take her chin in his hand and turn her face up to his. His eyes were warm with sympathy. "My poor girl. Did you think I was going to force myself upon you tonight? That I would pull you into bed and ravish you?"

She scowled. "Do not laugh at me. What am I supposed to think? We're married; you are my husband. Grandmama said—"

"Ah. I see." His face cleared. "Your grandmother is a

lady of the highest birth and the utmost dignity. She is the model of propriety. But she does not know me—nor, I suspect, men in general. Let me guess: she spoke to you of duty. Obligation. What else?" He paused in thought.

"Pain."

"Oh, Genny." He bent to press his lips against her forehead. "I am sorry. The countess would have done better to have remained silent." He sighed, his breath tickling her skin. He gathered her to him, holding her loosely. "I have no interest in your duty or obligation. Most of all, I have no desire to bring you pain."

"I know." Genevieve relaxed, lulled by the warmth and strength of his arms about her. "I know that is just the way of it."

"I shall do my best to make it very little of the way of it." He stroked his hand down her arm. "Genevieve, I realize full well that I am not the groom of your choice. I know you expected your wedding bed to have a different man in it." His fingers moved back up her arm, making languid circles over her skin. "Your heart was set on Dursbury."

"No, it wasn't," Genevieve replied so quickly that Myles released a little chuff of a laugh.

"Then that is all to the good." He continued to trail his fingertips up and down her arm, awakening a network of nerves that Genevieve scarcely realized she had. She could not hide the shiver that ran through her. He kissed the top of her head again before he went on, "I am aware how dearly protected a young girl is from men and the passions that drive us. I know that you 'have never . . .' And however long we have known each other, I am still in many ways a stranger to you. You may rest easy. I do not intend to take you to my bed tonight."

"Truly?" Genevieve pulled back and looked up into his face.

"Yes, truly. I plan to sleep in another room. Will that put you more at your ease?"

"Yes." Genevieve studied him for a moment. "But then what do you intend? Are we—will we have a marriage in name only?" Curiously, that thought made her feel a trifle deflated.

"No," he said with some finality. "That is not what I had in mind."

"What did you have in mind?"

He smiled in a slow, secret way, his eyes lighting. "What I have in mind"—he leaned down to brush his lips against her cheek—"is to woo my wife." He kissed her other cheek.

Her nostrils were filled with the scent of him; his body warmed her. His lips brushing her skin made her tremble. "Woo me?" she murmured, just to keep him talking.

"Yes. Woo you. Court you." Each statement was accompanied by the stroke of his lips over her skin, touching her so lightly, so softly, that her senses hummed. "Seduce you."

His mouth settled on hers. He kissed her slowly, tempting and pleasing and tasting. Genevieve's entire body quivered under the sensual assault. Warmth flooded her, making her feel oddly loose and languid, and her fingers tingled so that she had to curl them into his shirtfront to keep them still. His kiss went on and on, his tongue teasing her lips open, then exploring her mouth in a way that was shocking—but not as shocking as the response that welled up inside her at his touch. She clenched her hands more tightly in his shirt, bombarded by new and startling sensations.

She wanted to press herself against him, to move her hands over him, to meet his questing tongue with her own. Tentatively she touched her tongue to his and felt the shudder that ran through him. His arms tightened around her, pulling her up into him, and his body molded to hers in just the way she wanted. And now, she realized, she wanted more. Exactly what that more was, she wasn't sure. Then his hands slid down the length of her back and curved over her buttocks, and she knew that was what her body craved.

Genevieve slid her arms around him, holding on tightly, and an odd, low noise rose in her throat as his fingers dug into the fleshy mounds of her buttocks, squeezing and lifting. He raised his head, but only to change the angle of their kiss, then buried his lips in hers again. He kissed her over and over while heat flooded her.

His hand curved around her breast, and she gasped at the surprise of it even as her nipples tightened in response. His lips trailed across her cheek to her ear, and he toyed with the lobe as he had this afternoon, teasing bright shivers of pleasure through her. All the while, his hand cupped her breast, his thumb drifting over the tight bud of her nipple in lazy strokes, so that pleasure washed through her from both sources. Genevieve had never dreamed of feeling such things, and it was all she could do to hold back the noises that threatened to bubble up in her throat.

Myles was no more indifferent than she, for she felt the sudden surge of heat in his hand as he caressed her, heard the involuntary catch in his breath. It seemed somehow amazing that these things he did to arouse her incited pleasure in him as well. His arm still encircled her, and she was glad for that, for her knees seemed too weak now to hold her up. And when his mouth began to move down the side of her neck, her legs gave way entirely, and she sagged against him.

She felt languid and warm and entirely given over to pleasure. She suspected that the way she felt was probably quite wrong, even sinful, but at the moment she did not care. It was too delicious. When Myles raised his head, she had to bite her lip to keep from protesting the loss. He looked down at her, his face loose with desire, his chest rising and falling in rapid pants. Genevieve could not look away from his lips, reddened and lush from their kisses; desire coiled deep inside her, and she wanted to pull his face down and take his mouth all over again. The need was so fierce, so urgent, that it frightened her.

Myles let out a long, shaky breath and straightened, his arms falling away from her. Genevieve sank back down in her chair, not sure if she could stay upright. She dropped her face to her open hands, afraid of what might show there.

"I should go now," he told her huskily. His hand came out to stroke across her hair. "Else I shall move beyond mere wooing." He bent and kissed the top of her head. "Good night, Genny. Sleep well."

Nine

"Are we there already?" Genevieve glanced out the window of the post chaise, her heart sinking. It was only midday, and she had thought she would have a few more hours at least before she had to meet Myles's mother. It would have been a bit unnerving at any time, for Genevieve knew she was not at her best when meeting someone, but the circumstances of their wedding made the prospect daunting.

"Not yet." Myles was looking out the other window, a faint smile on his lips. "This is the village."

"Hutchins Gate?" Genevieve peered out the window. "Oh! There is the church. It is just as you described it."

The vehicle pulled up into the yard of a small stone inn, and Genevieve looked over at Myles, puzzled. "But why are we stopping?"

He smiled. "It's a surprise. You'll see. Suffice it to say that we are going to continue on horseback."

"Really?" Genevieve's brow lifted in surprise, but a smile immediately followed. "Myles! How lovely!"

"I thought that would please you. It helps to have

known you since you were ten." He paused, then added belatedly, "I trust you brought your riding habit."

"Of course. But if I had not, I would make do. I haven't had a chance to ride for weeks, and then it was just along Rotten Row. Oh!" She turned back to him. "I just realized: Sapphire—"

"—will arrive with your maid and the rest of your things next week. I spoke to Rawdon about it." Myles went on as they got out of the carriage, "It will mean going into the inn to change, so you will have to endure a number of stares. I am sure it is all around the village by now that I am bringing home my bride."

Myles was certainly right in that regard, Genevieve found. The innkeeper's wife, who whisked her into their best room to change, as well as the woman's two daughters, peeping over the stair railing from above, not to mention the maid, slowly sweeping the hall, all gawked at her, but with no enmity, only an awed and eager curiosity. Besides, Genevieve was too happy at the prospect of getting on horseback again to care if others stared.

When she returned to the yard a few minutes later, she found Myles standing chatting with the innkeeper and a groom who held the reins of two horses. Myles turned and smiled at her, and she could see the flash of unfeigned pleasure in his eyes. Her tall, spare figure, Genevieve knew, showed off best in a riding habit, its close-fitting, military jacket accentuating her slender form and straight shoulders.

"Myles, she's lovely." Genevieve went at once to the

dainty gray mare, running her gloved hand down the horse's neck.

"Not as fine a mount as your Sapphire," Myles said, coming over to stand beside her. "But I think you'll find her acceptable. I had them sent over from the Park."

"More than acceptable." Genevieve turned to him, her eyes sparkling.

"I should have known the way to your heart was a horse, not a necklace."

They rode out of the yard and down the street, Genevieve spending the first few minutes of the ride becoming accustomed to her mount, but then Myles kicked his horse into a gallop, and Genevieve was quick to follow. They raced down the road, Genevieve's heart lifting within her.

The land on either side of the road was rolling and green, separated by low, thick hedges, far different from the wide, desolate moors and stone-walled fields around Castle Cleyre. The innkeeper had sent a hamper of lunch with them, and they ate it beside a rushing brook. Afterward they followed the rocky stream as it wound its way deeper and deeper into a narrow valley until the cliffs rose steeply on either side of them. Beside the stream ferns and foxglove grew in profusion.

They rounded a curve and the valley widened slightly, forming a small cul-de-sac. At the far end of the semicircular valley, the stream rushed down the side of the cliff in a rainbowed waterfall, splashing into a pool at the bottom before it rushed out in a rocky stream. Genevieve drew in her breath sharply. "Oh, Myles, it's beautiful!" She turned to find him watching her, smiling.

"Do you like it?"

"Yes! How could I not? It's—it looks like the sort of place where fairies and sprites live." She gave a slightly embarrassed smile. "If one were being fanciful, of course."

"We definitely should be fanciful."

She looked back at the scene. For a moment all her attention was on the waterfall, but then she noticed a little cottage nestled against the cliff wall. Built of stone, it was half-covered in ivy and sheltered by several trees, and though it boasted no garden, a wild rosebush climbed up its front, heavy with red roses.

"Who lives here?"

"No one. This is part of Thorwood land. We call it Madge's Cottage, but no one is sure who the original Madge was. The most popular story is that it was built by some long-ago Thorwood as a love nest for his mistress so that he could slip away to join her from time to time. My mother likes to think that his parents would not allow their marriage because of Madge's low station, so he did his filial duty by marrying another, but built this charming spot for the woman he truly loved. A romantic tale."

"Mm. Rather less romantic for his wife, I imagine."

Myles laughed. "That's my Genny."

She cut her eyes at him. "I realize I am stodgy and unromantic, but I cannot help but think how the wife in such tales must have felt, tied to a man but never able to win his affection. It seems to me it would have been better for him to show some spine and marry Madge to begin with and leave the other poor woman out of it."

Her answer made him laugh again. "Come, let me show it to you." He urged his horse forward. Beside the house was a large pen, built from the trunks of saplings, but it seemed sturdy enough. Myles unsaddled their horses and let them loose inside it.

"Are we staying awhile?" Genevieve asked.

"I hope so, unless, of course, you mislike the place."

"It's lovely." Genevieve glanced around the peaceful scene. "But shouldn't we go on to the Park? We must not keep your mother waiting."

"Don't worry about that. She won't expect us yet." Myles took her hand as they walked up the beaten-dirt path to the low door. "We used to come here often as children, either with our parents or with our governess and servants. It's a wonderful spot for swimming." He gestured toward the pool beneath the waterfall. "In truth, I think my parents sneaked up here sometimes to get away from all of us, as well."

He opened the door, and she walked inside, going to the center of the room and turning all around to look at it. The cottage consisted of only one large room, with a small alcove to one side where a cabinet and a small table stood. The bed was neatly made, and wood was laid in the small fireplace, ready to be lit. A simple vase on the table held a bouquet of summer flowers.

"But, Myles—it looks prepared." She turned to him in puzzlement.

"When I wrote my mother to tell her of our marriage, I asked her to have the cottage cleaned and stocked with provisions." He came over to her, taking her hands. "Since there wasn't time to plan a proper honeymoon, I thought it would be nice to stay here for a while, away from everyone else. Of course, if you do not wish to, we can ride on to the manor house."

"No. I mean, yes." Genevieve smiled. "It is a cunning little place; I like it indeed." She surveyed the room again, her muscles relaxing. She had not realized until that moment, she thought, how taut she had been. It would be so comfortable here, without anyone else around. She would not have to worry about whether his family liked her or what she should say or do. "Thank you for thinking of it."

She had to swallow the lump in her throat to speak. It struck her all anew how kind and thoughtful Myles had been to her. Impulsively she took his hand and stretched up to kiss his cheek. She saw the spark of surprise in his eyes, but he did not speak, merely looped his arm around her shoulders, nestling her against his side. It felt quite good there, Genevieve thought, and that was another surprise.

"A swim might be nice after our ride," Myles suggested.

"I don't know how to swim," Genevieve protested.

"I could teach you. But you needn't learn right now. 'Tis shallow enough where it narrows into the stream. You can easily stand in it."

Genevieve looked out the window at the tranquil pool. The ride had been warm, and the thought of slipping into the cool water was inviting. A smile hovered on her lips.

"But what would I wear?"

"You need wear nothing." He chuckled at her alarmed expression. "But I think it would be easy enough to wear your shift."

"Only my underclothes?" Genevieve felt something sizzle through her, as much thrill as shock.

"There is no one about to see you."

"Except for you."

"Ah, but I am your husband." He grinned as he reached up to her hat, sliding the long pin from it and taking it off. Skewering it once again with the pin, he tossed it on the bed. "We are one body now, are we not?"

"So looking at me would be no different than viewing yourself?" Genevieve arched one eyebrow skeptically, crossing her arms.

"No, I think it will be vastly different. And infinitely more enjoyable." He bent to kiss her quirked eyebrow, his soft lips tickling her skin. "It is my opinion that one's shift shows little more than a nightgown. And I saw you last night in that."

"I had my dressing gown over it," Genevieve reminded him drily.

"Indeed, but if I remember correctly, it somehow came open." His fingers went to the neck of her riding habit, opening the top hook.

"I cannot imagine how." Genevieve's voice was a trifle unsteady.

"It is a mystery," he agreed gravely, sliding down to the next closure. His eyes were steady on hers as his fingers worked the hook and eye open.

"Myles . . . I thought you said that we would—"

"Move slowly?" His lips curved up in a way that was more sensual than humorous. "Oh, I shall move as slowly as you wish." He inched down the bodice. "This is a lesson on which I am prepared to spend a long, long time."

The bottom fastening opened, but his fingers still clutched her riding jacket as he leaned down and kissed her lips. He kissed her with infinite patience, taking his time to open her lips to him and steal inside, rousing her with slow strokes, his lips moving gently on hers. This time he did not slide his arms around her, and Genevieve found herself waiting for the moment he would, wanting it. Her heart picked up its beat as his mouth continued to explore hers. A throbbing set up deep inside her, aching and sweet, and her breasts turned heavy and full, anticipating his caress.

As he lifted his mouth from hers, his hands moved apart, sliding the bodice of her habit back and down her arms. With a flick of his wrist, it joined her hat on the bed. His hands on her hips, he tugged her down into the chair. Kneeling before her, he grasped one of her riding boots and pulled it off. Something about his position at her feet was strangely titillating—his bowed head, his care as he slid the boot from her leg. One hand cupped her calf, separated from her skin by only her thin stocking, and his other hand caressed her foot, ending by running his thumbnail up the center of her sole. Genevieve's insides clenched at the touch, and she was suddenly hot and damp between her legs, the vague ache turning to a throbbing.

Myles repeated his actions on her other leg, then slipped his hands up one leg past her knee. Genevieve drew in a sharp breath of surprise, but before she could even move, he hooked his fingers into the garter and rolled her stocking down. Though it was not a surprise when he went on the same foray up her other leg, the sensations it evoked were even stronger. She could not help but think of how she had been tempted to press her own hand between her legs last night to ease that yearning ache. The image of Myles's hand going there instead made the yearning even stronger. She blushed at her wayward thoughts.

Myles stood, taking her hands and pulling her up with him, and he unfastened the button at the waist of her skirt. The heavy fabric fell to the floor. His eyes roamed down her, his lids heavy, and his face changed subtly, his mouth softer and somehow fuller. Genevieve knew he could see the dark circles of her nipples through the material, the taut peaks pressing against it. The simple scoop neck revealed her arms and upper chest, and without the usual overlying petticoats the shape of her legs was obvious. Genevieve's cheeks flamed, but she did not move to cover herself or turn away.

"You are lovely," he murmured, crooking two fingers over the neckline of her chemise. "Your skin is like porcelain." His fingers drifted slowly along the edge of the garment, his nails gliding over her flesh.

Genevieve's breath caught in her throat as heat coursed from his fingertips all through her. She wasn't sure how he could make her feel this way with so little effort. His touch turned her hot and liquid, making her tingle and pulse in ways she had never imagined. And she knew she wanted him to glide his hands over every inch of her skin until the heat completely engulfed her.

He pulled his hand away and turned aside, and Genevieve clenched her teeth in frustration. As Myles shrugged out of his own jacket, she pivoted away to hide what she was sure must be in her face. It was alarming how she felt—the way her hands itched to touch him and her mouth hungered for his lips. She could not remember when she had ever felt so little in control of a situation or herself.

She looked back at Myles. He had divested himself of his jacket and boots, and his hands were busy loosening the intricate folds of his neckcloth. He glanced at her and smiled. Genevieve realized that she would like to unfasten the buttons of his waistcoat as he had undone her clothes, and she clasped her hands together behind her back, like a child refraining from grabbing a sweet. Not until she saw the swift darkening of his eyes, drawn to her bosom, did she notice how her movement had thrust her breasts forward, the hard buttons of her nipples pressing against the fabric.

She dropped her hands, embarrassed, and crossed her arms, once again turning away. She wandered over to the window and gazed out, trying to keep her mind off the sounds of Myles's undressing. After a moment, she began to wonder exactly how many garments he intended to take off.

Genevieve sneaked a glance back toward him, relieved to see that he was walking toward her still clad in his breeches, his shirt hanging loose and open outside his pants. Her gaze went to the strip of skin revealed by the unfastened ties of his lawn shirt. She could see the hard center line of his chest, the light V of hair running down that line, the bands of muscle that crossed his stomach, and the sight of him did peculiar things to her insides. She thought of sliding her hands beneath the edges of his shirt and moving them over his skin, such an extraordinary thing to consider that it made the blood wash up her face.

Again he took her hand, his fingers entwining through hers as he led her outside and down to the pool. When they reached the water's edge, he stripped off his shirt and tossed it aside. His fingers went to the buttons of his breeches.

"Myles!"

A grin lit up his face. "Best turn your eyes, love. I fear I am a most immodest man."

Genevieve colored and swung away, but she could not resist peeking back just a bit as he stepped into the water. She caught sight of his legs, muscled and sprinkled with curling hair, and the pale curve of his buttocks. Immediately she ducked her head again, her pulse pounding, aware of an urge as immodest as Myles was, to stroke her hand over that rounded flesh.

"Come in; 'tis safe."

Genevieve turned. He was standing waist deep in water, which did provide the most basic of covering to his nakedness, but his upper torso was completely bare, revealing the chest that the open strip of his shirt had only hinted at. His wide shoulders tapered down to a narrow waist; muscles rounded his arms and padded his chest. He ducked under the water and came up, pushing his hair back from his face, and water sluiced down his body.

She swallowed, then stepped into the pool and walked toward him, taking the hand he held out to her. The water rose around her, deliciously cool in the heat of the afternoon, gliding around her body as she moved forward. Her eyes kept straying to Myles's chest, slick with water. She tore her gaze away, shielding her eyes to look at the waterfall at the opposite end of the pool. The water tumbled down the cliffside, falling the last few feet in a graceful, clear curtain.

"It's beautiful."

"See the ledge behind the falls?" Myles pointed to a shelf of rock jutting out from the cliff wall just above the level of the pool. "If you swim to the other end and climb out onto the ledge, you can look out through the water. It's amazing. You can dive in; the water's deeper there." He gave her an inquiring glance. "Want to learn to swim?"

Genevieve nodded. She had never been one to back away from a challenge, especially a physical one. Her attire was not ladylike, but no one was here to see it beside Myles. "Shall we start?"

"Of course." He grinned. "First you need to learn how to float, which is simple, really. Here, I'll support you." His arm went around her, and he gently pushed her shoulders back. "Just lie down."

"But I'll sink."

"I won't let you. Don't worry. Relax and lie back." His other arm slid beneath her hips, raising the lower half of her body.

Genevieve did as he said, leaning back and extending her legs. It sent a little thrill of fear through her to lie back in the water, but Myles's arms were strong beneath her, holding her up.

"Loosen up a bit; go a little limp," he instructed. "There, that's the way."

The water lapped around her in a soothing way, and Genevieve closed her eyes. It was pleasant to lie here, rocking a bit, the water holding her up. Myles's arms were only lightly holding her now, and he slid the lower one away. She opened her eyes to look up at him. His eyes were a clear golden brown in the sunlight, and they looked down at her with a fierce heat. A breeze touched her damp skin, setting up a little shiver, and she realized how her damp shift clung to her, transparent now, delineating every line and curve of her body.

She should stand up, she thought, and turn away, yet she continued to lie there as his gaze roamed over her. The warmth, now becoming familiar, began to burn deep within her, and she had to consciously refrain from letting her legs slide apart. She was being brazen, she knew, but it was exciting, tempting, so she let her eyes drift closed again, as if by cutting off her sight, she could deny her willing participation.

With his arm under her, supporting her, Myles spread his other hand out flat on her stomach and moved over her front, caressing her breasts and sliding down onto her abdomen, then back up. Genevieve's lips parted, her breath coming faster, as his fingers moved back up to circle her nipples, teasing them into tautness. Moist heat flooded between her legs, startling her, and it only increased as his hand slid downward, moving into the V of her legs.

Genevieve jerked in surprise then, her legs coming down, and she stood up. Myles's face was heavy with desire, his mouth full, his eyelids drooping over his heated gaze. They stood that way for an instant, then his hands went to her hips, and he pulled her against him and kissed her.

His hands went down her back, molding her to him. She could feel the naked thrust of his desire against her, pulsing and eager, and that, too, excited her. Genevieve linked her arms around his neck, holding on as a firestorm of sensations rushed through her. His mouth was hungry, his kiss no longer a gentle coaxing but a fierce predatory taking. She met him eagerly, pressing up against him.

With a low growl, he broke their kiss and, sweeping her up in his arms, stalked into the house.

Ten

Myles *set her down inside* the cabin, and his hands went to her wet shift, pulling it up and off and dropping it on the floor with a sodden splat. His eyes swept down her, making her blood heat. Curious, Genevieve let her own eyes drop down the length of him, taking in the powerful masculine beauty of his form. Her eyes widened and she could not hold back a gasp when her gaze fell on the engorged length of his maleness.

"Myles!" Her gaze flew up to his, astonishment and a touch of fear in her eyes. "You are so—I mean, it will never—" She broke off, a fiery blush sweeping over her cheeks.

"Don't fret, my love." His hands went to her arms, stroking up and down soothingly. "It's all right, I promise you. And we will go no further than you wish." He brushed a kiss across her forehead. "I promise. For now, just let me look at you." His voice dropped huskily.

Genevieve gave an almost imperceptible nod, and he scooped her up, carrying her to the bed and laying her down with care. Stretching out beside her, he propped himself up on one elbow and let his eyes rove over her. He trailed his forefinger down her body and traced the slope of her breast. She twitched, tensing, as he slid over her stomach and dipped into the shallow well of her navel, then moved lower until his fingers tangled in the hair at the apex of her legs.

She let out a choked cry, and he moved away, tracing the crease between her torso and leg, first one side and then the other. He leaned forward to place a light kiss on her nipple, and Genevieve's breath shuddered out.

"Too much?" he asked softly, and she shook her head. She could picture his smile as he bent to kiss her again, this time tracing his tongue around the button of flesh. "Is this all right?" At her nod, his mouth closed around her. His tongue stroked and teased as he gently suckled her. As his mouth continued to work its glory on her, Genevieve could not hold back a low moan. She bit her lower lip, embarrassed by the sound. Myles only applied himself more ardently to the task.

Moisture flooded between her legs, and she moved restlessly against the bed. Finally he released the reddened, thrusting bud. He blew gently upon it, causing it to pebble even more. Myles bent close to her ear, his breath teasing new shivers in her as he whispered. "More?" She nodded, and he kissed her ear. His tongue traced the whorls as he murmured, "Say it."

"Myles . . ."

He took her earlobe between his teeth and worried it. "What, love?" He bent and pressed his lips to her other breast. "Would you like this?" His tongue flicked over her nipple. "Or this?" He placed light kisses in a line up the underside of her breast. "Or perhaps this?"

"Yes." The word shuddered out of her. "All."

The noise he made was half laugh, half groan as his mouth closed around the nipple. As he brought it to tight, throbbing life, his hand slid down her torso as it had before, but this time when he reached the V of her legs, Genevieve moved her legs apart, wordlessly inviting him. He lifted his head, his eyes glittering, and claimed her lips. He kissed her deeply, possessively, as his finger delved into the soft mysteries of her femininity.

Genevieve froze, suddenly afraid that he would be repelled by the moisture that had pooled there, but he seemed to revel in it, for he made a low noise and his lips dug into hers even harder. He stroked the slick folds, delicately exploring. Genevieve moved against his fingers, astonished at her boldness. She had never felt such aching, eager pleasure. She yearned for something, and the feeling grew more desperate with each touch, each kiss. She dug her fingers into his shoulders, her mouth melding with his.

Myles pulled away and stared down into Genevieve's face, his eyes almost feverish in their intensity. His forefinger settled gently on the fleshy nub between her nether lips, and Genevieve could not hold back a groan of pleasure. He stroked her, his eyes drinking in the emotions running over Genevieve's features. She pressed up against him, seeking more, and he clenched his jaw, the strain evident in his face.

"Shall I go on?" he whispered, looking into her eyes.

"Yes," she breathed.

A primitive male satisfaction flared in his eyes. His fingers moved down, slipping into her, and Genevieve's eyes widened in surprise. He slid in and out, gently stretching her. Then he moved between her legs, lifting her hips, and his maleness probed her tender flesh. She tightened at the touch and he stopped, stretching out above her and pressing his mouth to hers. He kissed her sweetly, seductively, making her whole body flame with passion. She relaxed, her legs falling apart, and he entered her.

There was a slash of pain, and then he was sliding into her, filling her. She had never imagined this, the deep fundamental satisfaction of having him inside her, a part of her. For a long moment he remained still, then he began to move within her. This, too, was a new wonder, she realized, as he thrust into her again and again. The pleasure that had danced through her body began to coalesce, tightening into a knot deep inside her.

He surged inside her, a low cry issuing from his lips. Genevieve felt as if she teetered on the edge of something marvelous, but then it was gone as Myles sank down on top of her. His breath rasped against her neck; his body was like a furnace. And those things, too, increased the heat that teased within her. She had never felt so wonderful, so alive and sparkling, yet something gnawed at her, some lack that she could not even name.

Myles raised his head and looked down at her. "Ah, sweet Genny. Not quite there yet, are you?"

She had no idea what he meant, but he rolled from her, and she sighed at the loss of his fullness. His hand slid down to find her again, and she blinked in surprise.

"Myles, what are—" A little moan of pleasure cut her off, and her eyes fluttered closed. "Myles . . ."

"You'll see," he told her huskily, his touch slow and insistent.

The powerful tension was building in her again, taking her over. Her breath was almost a sob as she arched up against his hand, her body tensing.

"There now, sweet girl," he murmured, kissing the point of her shoulder. "Patience. I won't leave you wanting."

His hand tightened on her, firm and demanding. Suddenly the teasing promise exploded within her. Genevieve clenched her teeth as she convulsed beneath his touch, pleasure rippling out through every part of her body. She went limp, her breath sighing out of her.

Myles wrapped his arms around her, rolling onto his back with her cradled to him. Genevieve slipped her arm around him, luxuriating in the feel of his warm, damp skin beneath her. What, she wondered as she slid effortlessly into sleep, had her grandmother been warning her about?

In late afternoon they awakened and returned to the pool. Genevieve protested walking outside unclothed, but Myles picked her up and slung her over his shoulder. She shrieked, but found the view of his backside from this position too interesting to keep up her complaints. They splashed about in the water, teasing and laughing, and this time she managed to float on her own—at least until he bent down to kiss the ruby tips of her breasts peeking up above the water, which sent her immediately sinking to the bottom in surprise. But it did not matter, for he scooped her up to kiss her. As he held her there, hard against him, she did what she had been thinking about ever since the night before and wrapped her legs around him.

Myles gave a little grunt of satisfaction, and hands on her hips, he ground her against him. Genevieve leaned her head on his shoulder, marveling at the response of her body to the feel of his hard length against her most intimate flesh. Did all wives feel like this? She could not help but wonder whether she was more wanton than most. Yet, she could not but think of Damaris's obvious happiness—and Thea's, as well. Of course, neither of them were models of propriety.

"Ah, Genevieve," Myles murmured, trailing slow kisses down her neck. "You tempt me past all my good intentions." He kissed her lightly on the lips and set her from him.

"Oh." Genevieve was distinctly disappointed. "Of course. You would not wish to . . . to continue in that vein after, um, it's over." She had taken a misstep. She turned aside, very conscious now of her nakedness. "I fear that I am not conversant with the proper—"

His hand wrapped around her wrist, pulling her back around. "It's no question of propriety." He took her chin, tilting it up until she looked into his face. "And it certainly is no question of what I want. There is nothing I would like more than to make love to you again right now. Right here." He pulled her to him again, smiling down at her. "Cannot you feel what I desire?"

"Yes." Genevieve colored a little and leaned her head against his chest to hide her face. "I do indeed." Her hand slipped down between them as if to touch him before she jerked it back guiltily.

"Go ahead," he said in a low voice, and his hand covered hers, sliding it back down his body.

She curled her fingers around him, glad that he could not see her face, and slid it down the length of the shaft, intrigued by the satin-smooth texture, the pulsing hardness pressing beneath it. He made a sound, muffled in her hair, and she paused, uncertain.

"No, don't stop." His voice was laced with amusement and hunger. "Feel free to do with me as you will." He kissed her hair.

Genevieve glided her hand back up and between his legs, cupping the heavy sac, and this movement pulled a low groan from him. She was coming to understand that such sounds were of pleasure, not pain. She looked up into his face, curiosity outgrowing her embarrassment now. His eyes were closed, his lips slightly parted. She experimented, watching the play of emotions across his face. Something in seeing how she could affect him was deeply thrilling.

"Then why did you stop?" she asked, teasing her thumbnail back up the length of him.

"For you." He stroked his hand down her hair. "I feared it was too soon—I do not wish to hurt you."

Genevieve raised her head, startled. "Does it always hurt?"

"No. Oh, no." He cupped her face in his hands and bent to kiss her. "I thought only that you might be a trifle sore. The truth is, I am not accustomed to untried maidens." He smiled faintly. "I would use care with you."

"Oh." Genevieve leaned her head against him, smiling to herself. "I am not so very delicate, you know."

"No?" He slid his hand over her shoulder and down her back.

"No." It was tempting standing this close to him, touching him. Her fingers itched to touch him in other places. He did not seem to mind her boldness, and on that thought she slipped her hands up across his abdomen and over the jutting points of his hip bones, curving back to smooth over his rounded buttocks. She felt him prodding her, and she knew her touch had pleased him.

So she did not cease her explorations, but continued down onto his thighs and back, digging her fingertips into the fleshy mounds as he had done with her. Her mind went to the other things he had done, the tormenting, arousing way his mouth had teased her. Without stopping to think, she pressed her lips against his chest. He was wet from the pool and faintly salty, his skin warm. She wanted to taste him more.

She went to one flat, masculine nipple, circling it with her tongue before clamping her mouth around it.

A groan escaped him, and he dug his hands into her hair. Genevieve lifted her head, and her voice was teasing as she said, "But perhaps we should wait."

"Waiting be damned." His grin flashed.

He lifted her again, sliding into her as she wrapped her legs around him. A sharp, deep surge of satisfaction went through her as he buried himself deep within her. Bracing her against the bank of the pool, he kissed her, taking her mouth as surely, as deeply, as he took her body. Genevieve clung to him, her fingers digging into his shoulders as he sent the desire inside her ratcheting up, higher and higher, until she was aware of nothing but him and the roaring hunger inside her. He shuddered, his seed pouring into her, and at that moment, the tension in her broke and washed through her. She buried her face in his neck to stifle the groan of pleasure that erupted from her.

He sagged against her, and for a long moment there was nothing but the sound of their ragged breathing. Genevieve struggled to pull her scattered thoughts together—to pull her very self together, it seemed.

"Ah, Genevieve, it seems you are death to my good intentions," he murmured, and nuzzled against her hair. The rich satisfaction in his voice signaled his evident pleasure in that fact. "'Tis your fault, you know."

"Mine? I like that," Genevieve retorted in mock indignation.

"Did you?" He kissed her neck. "Like it?" He raised his head, looking down into her eyes. "I am sorry if it was too soon."

"Yes, I liked it." Genevieve felt a blush spreading across her cheeks, and she ducked her head to hide it, resting against his shoulder. A bubble of contented laughter rose from her. "I liked it very much."

Evening was rapidly falling, and they retreated to the cottage, where Myles lit the fireplace already laid for them. Genevieve put back on the dress she had worn earlier, though her undergarments were too soaked to wear.

Myles professed disappointment in her dressing at all, but he smiled, his eyes drifting down her. "Still, this will do well enough."

"I don't know why you should look so," Genevieve replied tartly. "You cannot see that I have anything less on."

"Ah, but I know it." He brushed the back of his hand across her breast, his eyes darkening at the involuntary response of her body. She gave him a severe frown, but he only laughed, turning away to pull on his breeches. "However, if you look in the drawers, you will find some of my sister's clothes that I had brought over."

"I hope you had them bring food." Genevieve went over to open the drawer of the small chest. "I am starving."

"We must keep you fortified." He opened the cabinet and pulled out a loaf of bread and a sack of apples. "There's a cold cellar out back; there should be something there."

He returned a few minutes later, bearing a meat pie and a healthy slab of roast, and they sat down to their feast. They talked and laughed as they ate, with the ease of those who had known each other for years, yet freed by their new intimacy from the constraints that had always lain on their conversations. Myles recounted tales from his younger days with Alec and Gabriel, making Genevieve laugh so hard she had to hold her sides.

Later, hunger sated, Genevieve sat down in front of the fire to untangle her still-damp hair, happy to discover that the servants had also brought a comb and a brush.

Myles settled down behind her, taking the brush from her hand. "Here, let me."

"It's tiresome," Genevieve warned, leaning back on her hands.

"Mm. Perhaps to you." He dragged the brush through her silver-gilt hair with long, smooth strokes, releasing each strand slowly to float back down to her shoulders. "I, on the other hand, have wanted for years to see it down."

"I can't imagine why."

"Can't you?" He smiled faintly and smoothed his hand over her tresses. "Unbound hair whispers of a lady's boudoir. 'Tis the prerogative of the man who shares your bed." He twined a lock around his hand, bringing it up to press it to his lips. "And your hair is beautiful. Like spun silver."

Genevieve looked at him in surprise. "It's so pale."

"Like moonlight." He began to brush it again.

"Like ice." She gazed at him steadily. "I know that men call me the Ice Princess. Cold and—"

"Perfect." His grin was a trifle cocky. "It takes a brave man to approach such perfection." He leaned forward to brush his lips against her forehead. "To dare to bring a blush to those cheeks. A sparkle to your eyes." His lips followed his words, touching each cheek. "To kiss your lips into rosiness."

He hooked an arm around her waist, pulling her flush against his body. His hand spread out across her stomach, moving possessively over her. "Your mouth looks well kissed now, my lady." His deft fingers found the tight button of her nipple, squeezing it gently. "It is not ice in you, Genny, but pale fire."

Genevieve's breath shuddered out. "Myles . . ."

"Mm?" He nuzzled her neck with velvet-soft lips.

"You are a terrible flatterer."

"I protest. I am an excellent flatterer." His hand slipped down the front of her dress, cupping her breast as his mouth teased at her ear, sending heat slithering through her. "But it isn't flattery, is it, if one speaks the truth?"

"You cannot want to again," she said, but her voice caught on the words, spoiling the scolding tone she had intended.

"Can I not?" His breathy laugh at her ear increased the shivers running through her. He nibbled her earlobe gently. "I fear you are too enticing for me to be moderate in my appetite. I should like to lay you down and cover your body in kisses."

"Myles! You are utterly indecorous."

He laughed unrepentantly, his fingers working downward into the V of her legs. "I am. And so should you be." He kissed a trail down her neck, saying coaxingly, "Come, Genevieve, take off that frock and let me show you." He reached down on either side, bunching up the material of her gown.

"Stop that!" Genevieve laughed, slapping his hand lightly, and she pulled away from him, twisting around to look at him. "I cannot imagine why you are so eager to see me naked. One would think you would have had quite enough of that already."

"Not nearly enough." He grinned, reaching for her hands to pull her back to him.

"You just want to embarrass me."

"I do enjoy that a bit." He leaned in to kiss her thoroughly. "But far more than that, I enjoy looking at you."

"Why? I am tall and gawky and—"

"Genevieve!" He looked at her in genuine surprise. "Do you really not know how beautiful you are?"

"Oh, I know my face is well enough, though I have been told that I lack . . . vivacity."

"That could have been said only by someone who had not angered you as I have."

Genevieve grimaced. "But I am not girlish or dainty or pleasantly curved as a woman should be." She looked away. "Oh, what a nonsensical thing to be talking about."

"Come here," Myles told her sternly, pulling her up onto her knees. He reached down and grasped her gown, whisking it off over her head.

"Myles!" Instinctively, her hands moved to cover herself.

"No, none of that." He put his arm around her and eased her back onto the rug. Reclining on his elbow beside her, he took her chin in his hand and looked down into her eyes. "Now . . . we have discussed the beauty of your hair, how it flows like the palest, finest gold, like pure sunlight."

He took a lock, rubbing it between his fingers and letting it drift down slowly, catching the glow of the fire. He curved his forefinger over her brows and cheeks and nose. "And we've touched on the perfection of your face, the porcelain beauty of your skin, the pale rose of your cheeks." His finger traced the lines of her lips. "The sweet curve of your lips." Myles kissed her lips lightly. "Matched only by the sweetness inside." His mouth returned in a deeper kiss, his tongue teasing her lips open. "And that chin." He kissed the part in question. "A very Stafford chin, always leading the way. Your neck." He stroked his finger over her chin and down the line of her throat. "Long and elegant."

"Like a giraffe."

"Like Nefertiti," he corrected. "It is an invitation to a man's mouth, a delicate pathway down to what he most desires." He laid feathery kisses down her neck, his fingers gliding down to drift across her breast.

Genevieve clapped her hands over her breasts, saying. "I am flat, like a boy." She turned her head away, her jaw setting mulishly.

"Like no boy I have ever seen," Myles retorted with a grin. He slid his hand across her chest, slipping beneath Genevieve's hand and cupping her breast. "Your breasts are perfect, exactly right to fit into my palm, firm and round, like the most succulent fruit, and tasting of heaven." He bent over her, kissing her breasts, pulling the nipple into his mouth with a languid suction, his tongue working on it, so that when at last he pulled away, the bud thrust up hard and red and glistening. "With the most delicious raspberry on top." He gave the same treatment to her other nipple, and the movement of his mouth seemed to pull at a chord in her that tugged all the way down through her, inciting the damp heat between her legs.

He leaned back on his elbow, surveying her body like a man studying a treasure. Genevieve watched him, torn between embarrassment and pride, and vying with both, hot desire thrummed in her, stroked into being by the caress in his gaze. He ran his hand slowly over her breasts and stomach, curving over the bony ridges of her pelvis and onto the long line of her thighs.

"Your body is lithe and lovely, your legs so long, so firm, that a man could drive himself mad thinking of them wrapping around him." His eyes flashed gold as he looked into her face. "As they did to me only hours ago."

Genevieve gazed back at him, unable to tear her eyes away. Her breath came shallowly in her throat. His words made desire coil in her abdomen as surely as his touch. She realized that she was waiting, every nerve alive, her pulse throbbing, aching for him take her.

"I have imagined you naked for years now."

"Myles!" Her eyes widened. "Really? But you never said anything—"

"Tell my friend's sister that I desired her?" He quirked an eyebrow at her. "'Tis not the sort of thing one reveals to a gently reared young girl. But still, I thought of you. Whenever I held you in my arms during a waltz. When I saw you standing across the room at a gala. Or even just sitting in your drawing room. I thought of how you would look beneath your frock, peeling your garments from you piece by piece. I imagined the curve of your breasts, your hips, the shallow dip of your belly. And I wondered whether your hair was the same silver gilt below as it was above."

His fingers crept down, tangling in the curls at the apex of her legs. Genevieve drew in a shaky breath at the touch of his hand on the soft flesh, separating and exploring the slick folds. Without her thinking, her legs moved apart, giving him access to her innermost secrets. He propped his head on his hand, leaning on his elbow, his eyes intent on her face, as his fingers aroused her, teasing and tormenting the spiral of hunger inside her into ever tighter and tighter coils. Genevieve could not hold back a whimper as passion shimmered in her, stretching achingly close to that peak of release. She pushed up against his hand, her hips circling.

"No, not just yet." His finger slid away from the hot center of her desire. He bent to kiss her mouth while his fingers again stoked the flames in her, bringing her nearer and nearer to the edge. He raised his head. "Almost there, love. I want to watch it take you. To see you melt into pleasure."

"Myles . . ." Her head turned restlessly against the rug, the movement of her hips urging him on.

Then it struck her, pleasure so hard and intense she groaned, convulsing helplessly. As the tide of pleasure rushed through her, her body relaxed, turning so limp and liquid she felt as if she could melt into the floor. She gazed up at Myles, her eyes lambent and faintly dazed. His features were taut with desire, his whiskey-brown eyes alight with golden depths.

Genevieve reached up, putting her hand on his chest. His flesh burned as hot as his eyes. She moved her hand across him lazily. "Don't you want—"

"Oh, I want." He grinned and bent and kissed the corner of her mouth. "If you are ready?"

"I'm not sure I can move."

He shucked off his breeches, revealing exactly how ready he was. Taking her hips in his hands, he tugged her up and over to straddle him, making Genevieve's eyes widen in surprise. He guided her as she sank slowly onto him, delighting in the way she fit around him.

"What do I do?" she asked, though instinctively her hips began to circle slowly.

Pleasure flickered across his face. "Whatever you wish. Lead the way."

"Whatever I wish?" Her eyes lit up with devilry. She ran a fingernail down the center line of his chest.

"Indeed. I am sure you will enjoy tormenting me."

"Myles . . ." she said in a playfully scolding tone, lifting up, then gliding back down in a slow dance that turned his breath ragged. "One would think I were quite wicked, the way you talk."

He slid his hands up and down her thighs, his movements growing ever more restless as Genevieve experimented with this newfound pleasure. She knew now what he had meant earlier, for it excited her to watch his face change with each new sensation, holding out against the driving hunger until it built to almost unbearable heights. Then the pleasure took him, and he jerked against her, holding her hips in place as he thrust hard and fast, and Genevieve found that, amazingly, she, too, was swept with passion all over again, tumbling with him into the same dark abyss of pleasure.

She collapsed upon him, her breath rasping in her throat, and he wrapped his arms around her. They held each other, spent and at peace.

Eleven

Myles stood at the window, watching Genevieve stroll toward the cottage. They had found a wild plum bush not far from the falls, and while he was bringing in the food from the cold cellar, she had gone there to pick plums for dessert. She was wearing a simple cotton frock, and her feet were bare. Her silvery hair tumbled around her shoulders, shimmering in the sun. She carried the plums in her skirts, gathered up in front, and her long legs were bare from the knees down. The lack of any sign of a petticoat or undergarment told him that she had thrown on only her dress after their swim.

His groin tightened at the sight of her, as seemed to be the case so often this week. He had known that Genevieve stirred his senses, and their verbal sparring was exhilarating, so he had hoped that theirs would be a marriage that carried far more than convenience in its wake. However, he had not been prepared for how thoroughly she aroused him in almost every way. They had spent a week here at the cottage, and during that time they had explored the mysteries of the marital bed, making love whenever and however the fancy struck them. And Genevieve, despite her initial shyness, had been a willing and adventurous partner, even if she often protested in shock before she plunged ahead into some new delight.

She had awakened sensually during their days together, and the cool correctness of her demeanor had melted away. She laughed and teased, giving as good as she got. This morning he had been astonished—and delighted—when she had awakened him with caresses, initiating their lovemaking. Looking at her now, he had to wonder when, if ever, she had walked like this down a country path, hatless and disheveled. She looked, he thought, more like a mistress going to her love nest than the daughter of an earl.

Genevieve saw him watching and waved saucily. Myles went to meet her and greeted her with a kiss. She chuckled, shoving at him with her shoulder.

"Stop. You shall make me drop my hard-won plums. I had to climb that little tree to get the best of them."

"I am sure they are worth it." He peered down into the basket formed by her skirt and selected one of the deep purple fruits. He bit into the warm, sweet flesh, the juices trickling over his tongue. "Mm. Almost as sweet as you, Lady Thorwood." He bent to kiss her again.

"Delicious." Genevieve ran her tongue over her lip, and desire pinched at him again.

"The kiss or the plum?"

Genevieve rolled her eyes. "Enough of that. What about the rest of our supper?"

"Cheese, bread, and wine to go along with our plums, as well as a bit of sausage."

"It's rather like having the fairies flit in and take care of you, isn't it?" She smiled and bit into one of the plums, and the sight of her white teeth piercing the plump flesh sent lust corkscrewing through him.

Myles wrapped his hand around her wrist and pulled her into him, burying his lips in hers. When at last he raised his head, Genevieve's face was flushed, her eyes a pale blue flame.

"Would that we could stay another week," he murmured, then sighed and stepped back. "However, we are almost out of supplies. I fear that we must go on to the manor house tomorrow."

"Oh." Genevieve's face fell.

"'Twill not be so bad," he assured her as he opened the door for her. "You will, I think, like having a maid and your own clothes. The house is not as grand as Cleyre, of course." His eyes twinkled at her as he went on, "But neither is it so drafty."

"I am sure Thorwood Park is lovely." Genevieve set the plums down on the table.

"Then what is it, love?" Myles took her hand, leading her over to the chair and sitting down, pulling her down into his lap. Genevieve leaned against him, her head nestling on his shoulder. He had come to realize that it was a most enjoyable sensation.

Genevieve hesitated, then said softly, "I dread meeting your mother."

"My mother?" Myles's voice vaulted upward in amazement. "Good heavens, why?"

Genevieve sat up and fixed him with a sardonic gaze. "Because I have ensnared her son in a scandalously hasty marriage, that is why."

"There is no need to worry. Lady Julia is the most amiable of women."

"I am sure she is. And I am sure you have no need to worry. Mothers do not blame their *sons* for such things. She will regard it as entirely my fault . . . and the worst of it is that she will be right."

"My mother is well used to my fits and starts; she will put any unseemly rush down to my own impulsiveness. She wants me to be happy, and she has been hinting for at least five years now that it is time I marry. She will like you. I promise." He kissed her lightly on the lips, and his eyes darkened. "Now, I suggest that we make the most of the time which is left to us. . . ." His arms went around her as he pulled her in for a deeper kiss.

Genevieve knew that Myles believed his assurances that his mother would like Genevieve, but privately she had her doubts. The woman would be bound to resent Genevieve for pulling her beloved only son into this scandal. Throughout the ride to the house, the nerves in her stomach tangled into ever-worse knots. It had been so sweet in their little cottage, but now life would go back to normal.

There would be no more lazy, intimate evenings sitting about in a shockingly disheveled manner, no rambles through the trees or dips into the pool. They would again have to take their places, both in the household and in society. What had pleased Myles on their secluded honeymoon would not do for his wife and the lady of the manor. Though it was the role for which she had been groomed all her life, Genevieve could not help but feel vaguely downcast at the idea of assuming it.

They left the sheltered valley and made their way through the fields and meadows, coming at last through a pleasant stand of trees and out onto a wide expanse of grass. Across the wide lawn stood a rambling house in a hodgepodge of styles and materials—Tudor timber-framed plaster, red brick, and even stone, much of it covered in crawling ivy, all jutting off in different directions—all of it, amazingly, somehow fitting together into a warm and welcoming whole. It was a far cry from the looming stone fortifications of Castle Cleyre, and had Genevieve been more at ease, she might well have found it charming. As it was, Genevieve's chest tightened so that she could only hope that she did not embarrass herself by fainting.

Myles dismounted and helped Genevieve down, turning their mounts over to the groom who had come running. As they started toward the house, a jumble of people poured out of the front door. Genevieve's steps faltered for an instant, and Myles gave her hand a comforting squeeze. The crowd at the door resolved itself into a group of children, with a plainly dressed woman hurrying after them, calling out cautions.

"Uncle Myles! Uncle Myles!" all of them were shouting, interspersed with squeals and whoops of joy. It seemed impossible that only three of them could make so much noise.

The two smaller children, a girl and a boy, outstripped the older girl, whose sense of dignity (or the stern admonitions of the governess) apparently kept her from racing. The boy launched himself straight at Myles. Genevieve froze, but Myles let go of her hand and stepped forward nimbly, reaching down to catch the child and lift him high in the air.

"Master Nigel!" Myles cried, as he had with the baby Matthew the other night, and like Matthew, the small boy dissolved into giggles.

In the meanwhile, the girl, a bit larger than the boy, slammed into Myles's legs and wrapped her arms around them.

"April, my little love." Myles squatted down, setting the boy on the ground beside her and curving an arm around each of them. "Have you been good while I've been gone? Obeyed Miss Wilson? Eaten your vegetables?"

His questions were all answered with shouted affirmatives, but the older girl, joining them, told him scornfully, "Nigel never eats his peas. He drops them on the floor for the cat to chase."

Myles laughed. "Most inventive, Nigel." Myles stood up and swept the taller girl into a hug. "Blanche, I swear you have grown since I was last here."

"Uncle Myles!" she protested, her smile belying the indignation of her tone. "You've only been gone a few weeks."

"Is that the lady?" Nigel asked, curiously craning his neck to see past Myles to Genevieve.

"It is indeed. The Lady Genevieve Thorwood." Myles turned to Genevieve, his hands on the children's shoulders. The three children gazed at Genevieve with wide eyes.

"Ooh," April breathed. "You're beautiful."

"Are you the Snow Fairy?" Nigel asked reverently.

"No, you goose," April told him in disgust. "That's a picture."

"I'm sorry," the oldest girl said. "Nigel loves that drawing in the nursery." She smiled shyly. "You do look like her; you're awfully pretty."

"My dear," Myles said, "these young scamps are my sister Phoebe's children, Blanche, April, and Nigel. Children, this is my wife, your new aunt Genevieve. Say hello to her."

"Hello, Aunt Genevieve," the three chorused obediently.

"Now, children, give her a chance to breathe," a woman's voice said, and Genevieve looked up to see a middle-aged woman walking toward them. Her hair was dark golden, with wings of white sweeping back from her temples. Her simple dress of muslin was sprigged with tiny blue flowers, and her only jewelry besides a ring was a cameo brooch pinned to her dress. She smiled as she went on, "Miss Wilson, now that they have greeted their aunt and uncle, why don't you take them back to the nursery. And, children, remember to be quiet so you won't disturb your mother."

The governess met with some resistance from her

charges, but a kiss on the cheek and a pat from their grandmother helped to speed them on their way. Lady Thorwood moved on to take her son's hands and kiss him on the cheek as well.

"Myles, you naughty child. What am I to do with you? Sweeping this poor young girl off her feet without even giving me a chance to witness the wedding!" Her words were scolding, but her tone held only love. She turned toward Genevieve, a certain watchfulness in her eyes, Genevieve thought, but she said sweetly, "My dear, I am Lady Julia, Myles's mother. Welcome to your new home."

"Thank you, my lady. It is an honor to meet you." Genevieve bobbed her a little curtsy.

"None of that," Lady Julia said, taking Genevieve's shoulders and kissing her on the cheek. "You are my daughter now."

Genevieve blinked in surprise, but managed to murmur a polite response. Lady Julia linked an arm through Genevieve's and took her son's arm with the other hand, leading the two of them up the walkway to the front door.

"I hope you will excuse my daughter Phoebe for not coming to greet you. She is in an interesting condition and is feeling rather tired in the afternoons. But you shall meet her another time. We are all agog to meet Myles's bride."

"Do not frighten her, Mama," Myles teased. "Genevieve is not used to such a crowd."

"Nonsense, Myles," Genevieve protested. "I am most happy to meet your family. Thank you, ma'am, for welcoming me."

"Of course, my dear."

At that moment a girl came tearing out of the house, skirts lifted to her knees. Her hair was the same light brown as Myles's, streaked with blond from the summer sun; one of the bows that tied her braids had come unknotted and hung down like streamers. Her heart-shaped face was alive with joy.

"Myles! Myles!" Like Nigel, she threw herself at him.

Myles let out an exaggerated "Oof" as he caught her. "Nell, you wild hoyden." Any criticism in his words was belied by the affection in his voice. "Where have you been? Wading in the stream again or climbing trees?"

"Neither!" She laughed. "I was up watching for you."

"Nell!" Lady Julia's hand went to her heart. "I have told you—"

"Never to go out on the roof again," Nell finished, smiling over at her mother. "But I didn't. I had Myles's old spying glass, and I was at the gable window in the attic."

"Ah, that explains the state of your clothes," Myles said, and they both looked down at the torn ruffle and streaks of dirt at the bottom of her dress.

"It scarcely matters," Lady Julia said with a sigh. "There's no more hem to be let down. She has outgrown all her clothes."

"We are being rude," Myles said, turning toward Genevieve. "I have not introduced you to my bride. Genevieve, this example of perpetual mischief is my youngest sister, Nell. Nell, please welcome my wife, Lady Genevieve."

Nell turned to Genevieve and gave her a creditable

curtsy, saying politely, "I beg pardon, ma'am. Welcome to Thorwood Park." She grinned, her formal demeanor vanishing in an instant. "Xerxes will be so happy to see you!"

"Xerxes?" Genevieve repeated blankly. At that moment a large, fluffy white cat strolled out the front door and stopped, surveying the scene before him with an icy blue gaze. Genevieve stared. "Xerxes!"

The animal padded toward them in a supremely indifferent way, but as Genevieve leaned forward, reaching for him, he leapt into her arms. His head butted her jaw and he began to mew in a long series of what were clearly complaints and recriminations.

"How did you get here?" Genevieve laughed, rubbing her face against the cat's. She turned toward her husband, who was regarding her with a smile. "Myles? How did you—"

He shrugged. "I suggested to Damaris that they might wish to rid themselves of that devil by sending him with your maid when she brought the rest of your clothes here."

"Oh, Myles!" Genevieve's throat was suddenly clogged with tears, and she bent to hide her face against Xerxes's soft hair. "Thank you." She raised her head to smile at Myles.

"'Twas nothing. You should probably thank my mother and Nell, who have doubtless been the subjects of Xerxes's attacks."

"Oh, you!" Nell gave her brother's arm a push and turned to Genevieve. "Myles never had a way with cats. He is a dog person, and cats sense it."

"More like Xerxes senses my deep and abject terror whenever he's around."

"Don't be silly," Myles's mother told him, smiling. "He has been quite good. He and Nell took to one another right away."

"Really?" Genevieve regarded Lady Julia, then Nell, in astonishment.

"Oh, yes." Nell nodded. "Although he has rather startled the upstairs maids once or twice."

Myles muffled a snort of laughter. "There were bound to be a few skirmishes before Xerxes established his supremacy over the household."

Nell turned to Myles. "You must come see what I have done to my dollhouse."

"Indeed, I should like to, but Genevieve has only just arrived." Myles looked toward Genevieve a trifle questioningly.

"Oh." The lively girl looked abashed. "Indeed, I am sorry, Lady Genevieve. I did not think."

"Oh, no, pray, do go with Nell. I am sure Lady Julia will take good care of me," Genevieve assured Myles. She liked the girl, and she knew well how it felt to have a much-loved older brother return.

"Of course," Lady Julia agreed. "I should enjoy having a few minutes getting to know my new daughter-in-law."

Genevieve smiled at the woman with more confidence than she felt. However pleasant Myles's mother had seemed, Genevieve suspected Lady Julia would present a less welcoming demeanor once away from Myles's company. But Genevieve could hardly keep Myles with her always to deflect his mother's criticism. It was usually best to simply get an unpleasant task done.

Genevieve was rewarded with a grateful smile from Nell as she turned and bounded up the stairs. Xerxes watched her leave with great interest, but when he jumped down, he made no move to follow her, instead circling Genevieve's ankles.

"Such a sweet boy." Lady Julia smiled after her son. "But then, I am sure I need not tell you that."

"No, ma'am. I am very conscious of Sir Myles's kindness."

"Please, call me Julia. I hope we shall be friends."

"Of course. I hope so as well." Genevieve waited somewhat warily for what else the woman had to say.

They started up the stairs, and Xerxes darted up the steps in front of them. Genevieve cast about for something to say.

"Nell seems very proud of her dollhouse," she began, then realized that perhaps that sounded disapproving. Myles had told her the girl was fifteen, which seemed a mite old to still be playing with dolls. Genevieve was relieved when Julia smiled with pride.

"Indeed. She started building it when she was ten. Of course, that first version has long since been consigned to the scrap heap."

"She is building it?" Genevieve asked in astonishment. "You mean with hammer and saw?"

Julia nodded. "Old Godfrey helps her with the finer

carpentry. I think what she enjoys most is the planning of it, but she puts it together, as well. She is creating a veritable village up in the nursery. Of course, since Phoebe arrived, her children have enjoyed it tremendously."

"I can imagine. I should like to see it myself."

"Nothing would make her happier. Amelia tells me I spoil her, and perhaps I do. But she will have to be a lady soon enough; I prefer to let her enjoy what remains of her childhood."

"Indeed." Genevieve thought she did not have to look far to understand Myles's easygoing personality. She tried to imagine what her own grandmother would have said if Genevieve had decided to construct a dollhouse.

"Myles tells me that you are Alec's sister," Lady Julia went on as she led Genevieve down the hall on the next floor.

"Yes. You know Alec?"

"Dear me, yes, the boy has been here many times. The man, I should say. They are all still boys to me. But now they are all married, even Myles. It seems so odd to think of it. I believe I would have guessed who you were, just from seeing you. Your hair and eyes are very like Lord Rawdon's."

"Yes, we have the family coloring."

"And the height, as well." Lady Julia gave a little sigh. "I always yearned to be tall. I am the shortest in my family; it was always a trial to me. Thank heavens Myles turned out like his dear father." She stopped in front of a door. "Here we are."

Genevieve turned to face her mother-in-law, determined to swallow her medicine and get it over with. "Ma'am . . . Julia . . . I must apologize to you for the haste of our wedding. I am sure you must wonder, and you have every right to."

"My dear, there is no need to apologize." Myles's mother smiled. "I am quite used to Myles's impetuous ways. I am sorry I missed his wedding, but I was not surprised that Myles should tumble head over heels and want to marry without a moment to waste. The only thing that is important is that Myles is happy. I have hoped for years he would find a woman whom he could love the way his father and I loved each other. And now he has. If you are the woman Myles wants, how can I be upset?"

"Oh, but Myles—" Genevieve started to protest that Myles did not love her any more than she loved him, but she caught her tongue before she could blurt it out.

Myles must have presented it as a love match in his note to his mother. Perhaps he had thought the idea would make his mother more accepting of their haste. Or maybe it was simply that he knew it would please the romantically inclined Lady Julia to think her son had found real happiness and love. In either case, it would be wrong of Genevieve to spoil this woman's pleasant delusion.

"Myles and I should have waited long enough for you to join us," Genevieve amended her statement.

"That is very sweet of you, dear, but I understand young love." Lady Julia linked her arm through Genevieve's and led her into a large, pleasant chamber overlooking the gardens. "I hope you will find this room to your liking."

"It is lovely," Genevieve answered honestly, glancing about at the mahogany furniture and blue-patterned brocade curtains and bed hangings.

"Much better, I thought, than Myles's old room, which is too small, of course, and still too much the same as it was when he was a boy. Not the sort of room for a married couple. But, of course, if you should prefer the master bedchamber, I would be happy to move. I offered it to him after his father's death, but he would not take it. But now that he is married—"

It took Genevieve a moment to realize what Myles's mother was saying. Lady Julia expected Genevieve to share a bedroom with Myles. Genevieve had never known a married couple who did not each have his or her own chamber—at least, not people of their class. Admittedly, she was not privy to the sleeping arrangements of all her acquaintances, but she was certain that her mother had slept in the bedroom adjoining the earl's. And if her grandmother had, by some odd circumstance, occupied the earl's chamber, she would not have dreamed of remaining there when Alec succeeded to the title, no matter what Alec wanted. Things were simply done a certain way.

However, Genevieve could hardly be so rude to Myles's sweet and accommodating mother as to protest the arrangements. "Oh, no, you must not consider moving. This is a beautiful room, and I shall be quite happy here."

She sincerely hoped that her words would prove true,

Genevieve thought after Lady Julia politely left her alone to rest. The room was indeed lovely, with a restful view of the gardens, but her chest tightened at the thought of having no room of her own. She had never shared a room with anyone—well, except for the past few days in the cottage with Myles, of course. But that had been out of the ordinary, a singular event. To live with someone else each and every day was something else entirely. She could not retreat into solitude when she was tired or worried. She could not send her husband away if she was irritated with him. What was she to do, where was she to go, when emotions swelled in her, threatening to explode?

At a noise in the hallway, Genevieve turned. Her maid, Penelope, was standing in the doorway, and she bobbed a curtsy. "My lady. Welcome home."

"Penelope." A smile broke across Genevieve's face, a larger one, she supposed, than was warranted. But alone in this unfamiliar house, surrounded by strangers, however nice they might be, Genevieve was relieved to see her abigail's familiar face.

"I'm very happy to see you, ma'am." Penelope came forward, smiling. "Shall I help you out of your things? Perhaps you'd like to lie down for a bit. A nice cool cloth on your forehead would be just the thing. A drop or two of lavender, perhaps?"

"That sounds delightful."

Penelope started toward the door to close it, but before she reached it, Myles stepped into the room. The maid curtsied to him, then turned back tentatively toward Genevieve. "Shall I come back later, then, ma'am? With the lavender?"

"Yes. That would be good." Genevieve hid the little twinge of disappointment at the delay.

Myles strolled over to her, a faint frown forming between his eyes. "Is everything all right? Is the room to your liking?"

"Oh, yes, 'tis most pleasant. Your mother was very kind and . . . and pleasant."

His lips twitched into a smile as he took her hand. "Good. I am glad that everything is so"—he raised her hand and kissed her fingertips—"*pleasant.*"

"You needn't make fun of me," Genevieve said coolly, and started to turn away, but Myles held on to her hand, stopping her, and his hands dropped to her waist, gently tugging her forward until she was flush against his body.

"Myles!" she said, shocked, and glanced toward the door. "Someone might see us."

"I am sure they would be scandalized to see a husband holding his wife." He grinned. "Now tell me, Genevieve, what is bothering you?"

"Nothing. I told you." She scowled at him. "This morning I was wondering why I once found you so annoying. But now I recall."

Myles chuckled and hooked his arms around her loosely, bending to nuzzle the crook of her neck. "Ah, Genevieve . . . I was beginning to wonder what had happened to my astringent girl. I feared I might have lost her entirely."

"Don't be nonsensical." Genevieve strove for a severe tone, but somehow her voice came out more soft and affectionate than scolding. The feathery brush of his lips on her skin sent little shivers through her, as they always did. She raised her hands, resting them on his arms, her fingers digging into the material as the now-familiar desire washed through her. "Do stop," she said without conviction.

"Not until you tell me what has made you stiff and prickly."

"I—your mother put us both in this room," she blurted out. As soon as the words were out, she wished she could call them back. She sounded petty and ungracious. She jerked away, and Myles dropped his arms, letting her go.

"I see." He paused for a moment, then said carefully, "And you would prefer to sleep alone."

"No," she replied, startled, thinking of sleeping in an empty bed without Myles's warm, hard body against hers. Without his arms around her. "That's not what I—I mean, it isn't done." When he continued to simply look at her, she went on hastily, "You understand, don't you? Husbands and wives have their own rooms. It's the way of things. Not everyone, I suppose, but, well—" She stumbled to a halt and burst out, exasperated, "Oh, Myles, you know what I'm talking about."

"Do you?" he retorted quickly, his eyes flaring golden for an instant. He started to speak, then stopped, pressing his lips tightly together before he went on calmly, "I am sorry. I am sure Mother did not intend to distress you."

"It doesn't distress me," Genevieve said quickly, wishing more and more by the second that she had never brought up the topic. "It's simply . . ."

"You want to be alone," he finished evenly.

"I—I am not accustomed to . . . living with someone," she finished lamely. She could not expect Myles to understand, she knew. Men always had places that were theirs alone—the study, a smoking room, their club; indeed, the whole estate belonged to a man, when one came down to it.

The stiffness in his posture eased, and Myles said in a warmer, gentler tone, "I think we managed it well enough this week." He tipped up her chin, smiling down at her, and Genevieve could not help but smile back.

"Yes, of course."

He bent and pressed his lips to hers lightly. "There are moments that you found enjoyable."

Genevieve blushed faintly. "Myles . . . we cannot always be . . . like that."

"Can we not?" he asked lightly, and kissed her again.

"We're back to normal life. That was different. Special."

"How special?" His lips teased at her earlobe.

"Myles, stop." She giggled. "You make it difficult to think."

"Good." She felt his lips curve up in a smile against her skin. "Ah, Genevieve . . ." He let out a sigh, then, with a final little nip to her earlobe, he lifted his head and said lightly, "'Tis no problem. My old room is down the hall." He smiled and turned away.

"Myles!" A coldness clutched her chest. "No, wait."

He turned back, his brows lifting in inquiry.

"Your childhood bedroom isn't suitable for the master of the house. Your mother was right. This room is much more appropriate."

He shrugged. "I have slept well enough there for years."

"Yes, but . . . I do not want your mother to think that I am ungrateful. She has been so kind."

"Genevieve, what are you saying?" Myles regarded her quizzically.

"I—well, maybe it would be better, while we are here at the manor, at least, if we were to, you know, keep this arrangement."

Myles smiled faintly and strolled back toward her. "You want me to stay here with you?"

Genevieve felt her cheeks warm. "Well, yes. I mean"— she shrugged—"I do not want to offend your mother."

"No, we would not want that." He pulled her into his arms.

Twelve

Genevieve came slowly awake. She shifted, feeling the sheets slide across her bare skin. A familiar sensation was between her legs, too satisfying to be called an ache, more a lingering awareness of the pleasure she had known the night before. But the warmth she was accustomed to feeling beside her was gone. She rolled onto her back, her eyes going around the room and settling on Myles, who was standing in front of the shaving stand, sliding a razor up the underside of his jaw.

She had witnessed his performing this male ritual before—every morning at the cottage. But she had yet to tire of it. She wasn't sure why she enjoyed it, although she suspected that it had something to do with the sight of Myles's bare back and the play of muscles beneath his skin.

He cast a sideways glance at her and smiled. "Good morning, my love. Did I wake you?"

"I don't think so. I don't mind. I like to watch you shave." She had not meant to say so; the words had simply tumbled out of her. It was, no doubt, an entirely foolish thing to feel, let alone express. To avoid his eyes, she stretched, and the sheet slid down perilously close to the pink tips of her breasts.

Myles's eyes followed the movement of the covering; she could see the flash of desire in his eyes, the softening of his lips, and the signs of his arousal stirred her own passion. Genevieve thought of lifting her arms again until the sheet slipped off her engorged nipples, imagining how his gaze would darken then. She wondered what he would do, whether he would wait, watching her, or if he would cross the room and pull the sheet farther down, exposing her to his gaze.

"What are you thinking?" he asked, his voice low and sensual. He wiped the remainder of the shaving soap from his face and walked over to sit down on the bed beside her. "I could see the mischief in your eyes from across the room."

"I'm sure I don't know what you're talking about," Genevieve replied loftily.

"Naturally." The corner of his mouth quirked up, and he hooked a finger beneath the hem of the sheet, edging the cloth down over the peaks of her breasts. "I believe you are thinking of seducing me, my lady."

"Only thinking?" Genevieve retorted with a smile, and crossed her arms behind her head, gazing back at him boldly as the movement sent the covering sliding even farther.

He chuckled and bent to lightly kiss each rosy tip. "You are a wicked woman. It is fortunate that I am a man of such willpower." He rose to his feet. "I have a great many things to do this morning. I fear I cannot satisfy you right now."

Genevieve swept out her hand and grabbed the pillow next to her, flinging it at his retreating back.

Myles let out a laugh as he continued to the dresser and picked up an object. "Now, now. You should not attack the man who is about to give you a present."

"A present?" Genevieve sat up, intrigued, and pulled the sheet up to cover her.

He turned around and made a face. "How unkind of you to spoil my view."

"You rejected me, sir," she retorted. "Now show me the present."

He grinned and came back to her, hiding his hand behind his back until he reached her, then holding out his palm in a flourish. A diamond ring lay in his hand, flashing its brilliance as a ray of sun hit it.

"Myles!" Genevieve let the sheet go as she leaned forward to look at the ring. "It's exquisite. Is this—" She looked up at him.

"Your wedding ring. Yes. I meant to give it to you last night, but, um, as you remember, we were rather busy after supper." He cast her a roguish glance. "Do you like it? If you do not, I will get you another; you need not wear my grandmother's ring."

"Don't you dare. It is beautiful." Genevieve held out her hand so that he could slide the elegant band onto her finger. "And I like that it was your grandmother's." She tilted her hand one way, then the other, admiring the square-cut diamond, flanked on either side by two smaller diamonds. Her throat felt oddly full, as if she might cry, which was absurd. There was no reason to wax weepy over a ring, no matter how lovely it was. She went up on her knees on the bed, wrapping her arms around his neck, and kissed him. "Thank you."

He returned her kiss with fervor, his hands gliding down her back and pressing her against him. "I think," he said, breaking their kiss, "that I have a little time to spare before breakfast."

A good deal later, the two of them made their way downstairs to the breakfast room. A babble of voices came from the chamber at the end of the hall, and Genevieve glanced up at Myles apprehensively.

"You may have been spared meeting the onslaught of our family last night, but I fear that Amelia and her brood must have stormed the walls today at dawn," Myles said sardonically.

"Oh." Genevieve's nerves began to dance. It had been far easier than she had expected last night, with only Lady Julia and Nell at the dining table with them, for Phoebe had felt too tired to join them.

"Courage," Myles murmured. "I promise they will not bite."

"Don't be nonsensical. I am sure it will be quite pleasant." But she could not keep from gripping his arm more tightly as they continued down the hall. "It is just—I am not adept at making conversation."

"You needn't worry about that. The difficulty with my family is managing to get a word in."

When they stepped into the breakfast room, everyone

turned to look at them, all sound dying instantly. For a frozen moment, it seemed to Genevieve as if the small room were stuffed with people. Myles began to introduce her around, and the crowd resolved itself into Nell, Lady Julia, and Myles's sisters Amelia and Phoebe, as well as Amelia's two adolescent sons, who had ridden over with her this morning. Amelia looked a much younger version of her mother, but Phoebe, heavy with pregnancy, seemed a faded copy of the other two women, lines of discontent forming grooves that ran down from her mouth.

"Genevieve, my dear, come sit here beside me," Lady Julia said, rising to take Genevieve's arm and slip her into the empty chair situated between her and her son's seat at the head of the table.

Across the table from Genevieve sat Amelia and Phoebe, in whose eyes Genevieve saw the looks of curiosity and wariness that she had expected from all Myles's family. These two, she thought, were not ready to take her to their bosom as his mother had. She braced herself for a subtle probing of the circumstances surrounding Genevieve's whirlwind courtship and marriage to their brother, but to her surprise, it did not come. Though she could feel them studying her covertly now and then, there were no subtle barbs, no penetrating questions.

Indeed, as Myles had predicted, Genevieve discovered little need to worry about talking. The Thorwoods were a lively group, and there were no lulls. They chattered and laughed, conversations darting every which way across the table. Genevieve relaxed into her chair, listening with some amazement as Nell and Amelia's sons chattered right along with all the adults. Genevieve's grandmother had allowed Genevieve to join her and Aunt Willa in the dining room when Genevieve was fourteen, but only if no guests were present. Genevieve had known better than to speak unless one of the adults had directed the discussion her way.

She glanced at Lady Julia when Nell asked her mother to let her go riding with Amelia's sons, expecting a reprimand, but Lady Julia only said in a mild tone, "But what about your schoolwork, dear? Miss Wilson said you were behind in Latin."

Nell groaned. "I hate Latin. And Adam and William are allowed to ride this morning."

"They are home from school on holiday," Lady Julia pointed out.

"And they will be here for only two more weeks," Nell reminded her, neatly slipping into a new argument. "I can do my Latin after they are gone." Her mother looked uncertain, and Nell pressed on, "Myles can come with us to supervise. You know Putnam said I was taking my fences wrong. Myles could help."

"Genevieve is who you should ask," Myles said, nodding toward his wife. "She is an excellent horsewoman, not to mention more adept at riding sidesaddle than I, I'm sure."

"Yes! Would you?" Nell's eyes lit up and she turned to Genevieve. "It'd be ever so much fun."

Genevieve glanced toward Lady Julia. "Certainly, I'd be happy to, if your mother does not object."

"Wonderful! Then we can all go." Nell turned her gaze back to Myles. "Say yes, do."

He smiled at her. "I think it sounds like a grand idea. But, much as I would enjoy it, I have a number of tasks I must see to this morning. And there is still the matter of your schoolwork. You do your Latin today, and tomorrow morning we shall all go. I am sure the boys would be happy to return."

Myles's response surprised Genevieve, who would have expected him to be less strict about the rules. But Nell's expression, while disappointed, held little surprise.

"I can help you with your Latin, if you'd like, Nell," Genevieve offered. "I was never bookish, but I rather enjoyed Latin." She grinned. "It was like having a secret language because Grandmama's Latin was atrocious, but she was too proud to admit that she didn't know what Alec and I were saying."

"Would you?" Nell brightened considerably.

"Of course."

So immediately after breakfast, while Myles headed to the estate office, Nell and Genevieve went up to Nell's bedroom. "Phoebe's children are studying in the nursery," she explained to Genevieve. "It's impossible to get anything done there. And, anyway, Miss Wilson will be cross if we disturb them." She handed her Latin text over to Genevieve with a resigned expression.

They worked for over an hour, and Genevieve could see that Nell was more bored than unable to do the work. "Perhaps you would enjoy reading Virgil more than Pliny the Elder," Genevieve suggested. "We could try that tomorrow, if you'd like."

"Oh, yes, anything besides this. Though it is much more fun with you than with Miss Wilson. Would you mind helping me again?"

"No. Not at all." Genevieve was faintly surprised to realize that her words were true. "Now . . . let's work for a bit longer, and then I think we can safely say you've done enough to warrant a ride tomorrow."

Almost an hour later, Nell closed her book with a satisfied thump. "There! Miss Wilson will be amazed. Thank you."

"You are most welcome." Genevieve smiled and rose to her feet. "Perhaps—I wondered if you might show me the dollhouse you were working on. Lady Julia said it was quite remarkable."

Nell's eyes lit up, and she jumped to her feet. "Of course! If you really want to. Myles said I must not bother you."

"I should like to see it. Very much."

Nell led her up the back stairs to the nursery above. Down the hallway, they could hear April reading haltingly to her governess, but Nell ducked into another chamber several doors down from the schoolroom.

"Nell!" Genevieve exclaimed, following Myles's sister into the room. "It's amazing." She turned around, taking in the whole room. "You mother said it was more a village now, but still I did not realize."

Genevieve walked around, looking at the houses, rang-ing from a thatched-roof cottage to a tall, narrow town house to a sprawling medieval castle. The level of artistry varied from one to another, revealing Nell's growth in skills.

"Here is the church I am working on, and I've already done the inn."

"It is all wonderful. I cannot imagine doing something like this." Genevieve could, however, imagine her grandmother's reaction to her doing so. "Your mother is very proud of you."

"She's awfully good. Phoebe thinks it is the most useless thing ever. But Mama has never complained. She tells me I will be the new Bess of Hardwick—though I would not want to marry four men, of course."

"You must come with me to Castle Cleyre sometime. It is still much the way it was built, though the wall to the south has been taken down."

"Really? I would like that." Nell's eyes sparkled.

"Nell!" They heard a boy's shout from down the hall, followed by the sound of running feet and the governess's exasperated cry.

Nell and Genevieve turned as Nigel pelted into the room.

"I knew it was you!" he told Nell triumphantly. "We finished and Miss Wilson said we can play." He looked over at Genevieve and offered generously, "You can play, too."

"Oh. Well." Genevieve looked at him, nonplussed. What did one say to a child? "Thank you."

"You're welcome."

"Nigel! You aren't to bother Lady Genevieve," his oldest sister said severely, coming to the doorway behind him. "Miss Wilson said."

"He's no bother," Genevieve hastened to assure her, though from the way the young boy set his jaw and turned to glare at his sister, Genevieve suspected he had little trouble standing up for himself.

"She wants to play with us," he told Blanche. "I asked her. Don't you, Lady Genevee?" He stumbled over her name.

"Lady Genevieve," April corrected in a quiet voice, leaning shyly around Blanche's side to peer at Genevieve. "Nigel sometimes gets his words mixed up."

"Well, 'tis a difficult name to say," Genevieve admitted. "Not as nice a name as April." The little girl giggled and hid behind her sister's skirts once again. "Perhaps you could just call me Genny."

Nigel, unwilling to be distracted from his purpose, went on, "Do you want to be a goat or the troll?"

"I beg your pardon?" Genevieve looked at him.

Nell laughed. "It's a game the children play in the other wing of the house. Mama has it closed off unless there are lots of guests. There are sheets over the furniture and the draperies are shut. It makes for nice hiding places."

"Nell's a good troll. She stomps and growls," Nigel explained, adding magnanimously, "But you could be the troll if you wanted. Couldn't she, Nell?"

"She could be the fairy," April suggested, leaning around her sister again.

"There's a fairy, as well?"

"There's whoever you want," Blanche explained. "Nigel

likes to be a goat so he can jump about from chair to chair. I'm a princess. April's my lady-in-waiting." Blanche looked down at her younger sister assessingly. "Or sometimes a cat."

"I like your kitty." April came up to stand beside her sister.

"You can be a goat, too," Nigel assured Genevieve, and held out his hand to her. "I'll show you the best places to hide."

"That's very generous of you," Genevieve told him gravely. "You know, I have never played goats and trolls before."

"Never?" Nigel looked at her with a mingling of astonishment and pity.

"Never." Genevieve reached down a little awkwardly to take his hand. "So you can see that I shall certainly need your help."

"Don't worry." He squeezed her hand as he led her from the room. "I'm very brave."

Sir Myles walked briskly through the rear door and started down the corridor. It had taken longer than he'd expected with the estate manager, and he wondered how Genevieve had fared. He suspected that between Nell's Latin, Phoebe's complaints, and Amelia's managing ways, Genevieve had probably fled to her room by now. He went first to the small sitting room, where his mother most liked to spend her time, and stuck his head inside the door.

"Myles, dear." Lady Julia looked up from her crocheting and smiled. "Done with the estate manager?"

"Yes. Finally." He came farther into the room. "Where is everyone?"

"Phoebe is napping again, and Amelia and her boys have gone home. Haven't they grown tremendously?" She patted the sofa beside her. "Here, come sit with me and chat awhile. I've hardly talked to you."

Myles smiled and joined her on the couch, taking the hand she held out to him.

"But I suspect that it is Genevieve whose location you are most interested in. She and Nell are upstairs with the children, I believe."

"The children?" His eyebrows rose. "Are you sure?"

"Hodgings said they were taking their luncheon up in the nursery." His mother smiled serenely. "It's nice, isn't it, that she and Nell are getting along so splendidly? Nell needs a younger woman to guide her. It is much easier to take advice from someone other than your mother."

"Well, Genevieve knows all the rules."

"Of course. One would expect nothing else from the Countess of Rawdon's granddaughter. I remember that woman when I made my come-out; we were all terrified of her."

"I believe she has that effect on everyone."

"It is good to see you settled." Lady Julia smiled. "And your bride is lovely."

"I agree. And you are a jewel to be so welcoming to her."

"My dear, she is your wife. What else would I be? One thing I have never been, I hope, is a mother who demands that her children marry as she wishes."

"No, you have not. But many mothers would feel somewhat . . . aggrieved by our lack of a grand ceremony."

"I was surprised at the suddenness, but I knew there could be nothing unseemly about Lady Rawdon's granddaughter. And as long as you are happy, I am well contented. To be frank, I was just as glad not to have to travel to London for an enormous ceremony. Even worse—ride to the wilds of Northumberland."

"Indeed. One might run into blue-painted savages."

"Oh, you." She tapped his arm playfully. "Do not tease your poor old mother." With another loving pat on his arm, she went on, "Now, go on. Go look for your girl, as I know you are eager to do."

"You are the best of all mothers." Myles grinned at her and started away, but at the door, he turned back, his expression serious. "It's not a love match, you know."

"Ah, but I know you, my dear." Lady Julia smiled. "It will be."

Myles glanced in the music room as he passed it, then trotted up the stairs to their bedroom, fully expecting to find it closed and Genevieve inside. However, the door stood open and the room was empty. A look out the window revealed no sign of his wife in the garden. He continued to Nell's room, then, frowning, started up the stairs toward the nursery. It was empty as well, but he heard a laugh and a shriek coming from the old wing. The laugh had sounded like Nell's. Perhaps she knew where Genevieve had gone. A faint, unaccustomed tug of concern pulled at him.

He walked down the hall and stopped. Hearing the whisper of voices, he eased open the door beside him. The corner of the sheet that covered a chair lifted and a small face appeared.

"Uncle Myles!" Nigel leapt out of the chair and hurled himself across the room. "Look, Aunt Genny, it's Uncle Myles."

"Aunt Genny?" Myles repeated in astonishment.

"She's hiding," Nigel confided. "She's really good at it—except when she sneezed that time." He took his uncle's hand and pulled him across the room, reaching down to yank up the coverlet on the bed. Genevieve peered out at him from under the bed.

"Genevieve!"

Her cheek was smudged with dirt, with several streaks down the front of her dimity gown. A hank of hair had come down and straggled down the side of her neck. Myles stared at her in shock for a moment, then let out a whoop of laughter. Genevieve wriggled out from under the bed and stood up, and Myles laughed even harder, clutching his stomach.

Genevieve lifted her chin, looking down her nose at him in her best imitation of her grandmother, and said icily, "And just what is the matter?"

"Oh, Genny." Myles swallowed his laughter and reached out to pull her into his arms. "My dearest girl. Nothing is the matter. Absolutely nothing."

Thirteen

As the days passed, Genevieve found herself falling into a comfortable routine. She had often found herself bored during the months at home at Castle Cleyre, but it was altogether different here. Myles took her with him on his rides about the estate, introducing her to his tenants and their families. She visited the poor and ailing with his mother or Amelia, and even, she told Myles with a twinkle, made her duty calls to the vicar's daughter. She helped Nell with her Latin as well as—more entertaining for both of them—instructing Nell on her form in the saddle. If she wished a quieter pastime, she could sit with Myles's mother, sewing the fine stitches on baby gowns for Phoebe's upcoming child. And always, there was the underlying little hum of anticipation, knowing that that night Myles would be in her bed.

Of course, Genevieve reminded herself as one week eased into another, these halcyon days were only temporary. Eventually things would return to normal. They would go back to London and the social whirl. She would grow bored with rural entertainments. Even, at some point, the sensual delights to which Myles had awakened her would begin to pall. That was simply the way things were. However pleasant something might be, it did not last forever. Things changed.

As if to prove her point, one morning as she and Myles lingered over a late breakfast, the butler brought in the morning's mail. Genevieve recognized her brother's handwriting and asked, with a smile, "What does Alec say? How is Damaris feeling?"

"I'm not sure. He has not mentioned it." Myles stopped halfway down the page and went back to read it again, more carefully, his brows rising higher and higher as he read.

"What is it?" Anxiety clutched at Genevieve's stomach. "Is there something wrong? Grandmama—"

"No; your grandmother is fine, I think. Genevieve . . ." He lifted his head and looked at her, puzzlement mingling with exasperation in his face. "Would you care to explain to me why your brother believes I had something to do with your running into Langdon that night in the library?"

"She told Alec?" Genevieve exclaimed. "Damaris said she would not reveal it!"

"Then it's true?" He gaped at her, stunned. "You told Damaris I asked you to meet me in the library?"

"I'm sorry, Myles, I know I shouldn't, but it just—"

"I should say you should not!" Myles jumped to his feet. "Why would you tell her such a thing?"

"I didn't start out to tell her, but we were talking, you know, and I, well, I was worried that you felt guilty because of what had happened. That you offered because of that, and it really was not your fault."

"Well, of course it was not my fault! I cannot imagine—" Genevieve stiffened, her own temper flaring up. "I would not say that, precisely! I should never have gone to meet you, I know, but you were the one who wrote me the note."

"Note!" Myles stared at her as if she'd taken leave of her senses. "What the devil are you talking about? What note?"

Ice began to form inside Genevieve, and she rose slowly to face him. "The note you sent me that night. The one asking me to meet you in the library."

"Genevieve. I did not send you a note."

They stared at each other in silence. Genevieve dropped back down into her chair, as if her legs would no longer hold her.

"You asked me to meet you in the library," she said, barely above a whisper.

"I did not." Myles half-turned away, his hand going up to comb through his hair. He swung back to her abruptly. "Why in the world did you think it was from me? Was it in my hand?"

"I—I don't know."

Myles seized her wrist, pulling her from the dining room and down the hall to his study. He shoved an account book aside and dug into a stack of papers, hauling one out and thrusting it in front of her face. "*This* is my handwriting. Did it look like this?"

"Stop waving it about like that!" Genevieve snapped, and grabbed the paper from him. "No," she admitted.

"Well, honestly, Myles, how was I to know it wasn't your hand? It isn't as if you'd ever written me before."

"Of course I hadn't! I wouldn't have been penning you secret notes, now, would I?"

"I don't know why you are bullying me about this. It isn't as if I made it up!"

"No, you just believed the worst of me," he shot back. "Good God, Genevieve! You really don't know me at all, do you? How could you think that I would have asked you to meet me in such a clandestine way? That I would be so careless about your reputation—or any young lady's, for that matter?"

"It had your name on it!" Genevieve set her chin, feeling beleaguered. "You're being unreasonable. How was I to know you would not do such a thing? You have always been rash, jumping into things without thinking."

"Oh, have I? Like asking you to marry me, I suppose."

Genevieve stiffened. "Are you throwing that up to me now?"

Myles bit back a retort. He took a breath and stepped back. "No, of course not. That was entirely my decision."

And from his tone, one he now regretted, Genevieve thought, with a sharp pang in her chest. She turned away and walked over to the window to look out, saying carefully, "I beg pardon for misjudging you."

Myles let out a sigh. "Genevieve . . ."

"The note said something like, 'G—I must talk to you. Library. Myles.' I thought it must be important—well, clearly I did not think or I would not have gone."

"I should have thrashed that blackguard then and there!" Myles growled.

"You think it was Mr. Langdon who sent it?"

"Who else could it have been? He was in the library, waiting for you." Myles began to pace. "Why didn't you tell me before?"

"I thought you knew! I wondered why you had sent it, but . . ." She shrugged, unwilling to say that she had avoided the topic because she had not wanted him to feel that she blamed him for her predicament.

"I knew Langdon was a cad, but I would not have thought he would stoop to such a level." Myles stopped his restless pacing. "I am going to London. I intend to pay Mr. Langdon a visit." He started toward the door.

"I'm going with you." Genevieve moved to intercept him.

"What? No."

"No?" Genevieve said in a dangerous tone. "You think to leave me immured out here in the country? Absolutely not."

Myles sighed. "Genevieve, think. It hasn't been even a month yet. The gossip won't have died down, and it will start up harder when we return."

"No doubt. But the gossip will reignite whenever I return. I have to face them sometime; I won't let a bunch of rumormongers scare me away. This is my fight, Myles. It was my reputation that suffered. And I intend to find out why. I am going."

Myles crossed his arms over his chest, and Genevieve was certain he was about to argue the point.

"If you do not take me with you, I shall only go on my own."

"Devil take it! You would, too," Myles said, aggrieved. "Oh, very well." He dropped his arms and strode toward the door, tossing back over his shoulder, "But I warn you—I'm not waiting for you to pack your trunks. We leave in an hour."

They arrived in London two days later. The servant who opened the door at Rawdon's house gaped at Genevieve and Myles in surprise, and Genevieve's grandmother appeared equally astonished. However, the countess quickly pulled her face under control and rose to her feet.

"Genevieve, child, what a surprise." Her blue eyes were sharp on Genevieve's face, and she sent Myles a quick, suspicious glance. "Sir Myles. I did not expect you for some time."

"Business called me back to the city, Lady Rawdon, And Genevieve was kind enough to keep me company. I am having Thorwood Place set up for us to live there, but I am not sure it is in a proper condition yet."

"You must stay here, of course, until your house is quite ready. I fear Rawdon and his wife are not home just yet; they went to the theater with Lord and Lady More-combe. Pray, sit down. Have you had anything to eat this evening? I am sure that Cook could whip up something."

Genevieve demurred. It was rather strange to be treated like a guest here in the home that had been hers for so long.

"Sir Myles, no doubt you would enjoy a glass of brandy in Alec's study after your long journey," Lady Rawdon went on. "I shall see Genevieve up to your rooms." The countess's courteous offer was clearly also a dismissal. Myles took it with his usual good grace, casting a humorous glance at Genevieve before he bowed and took his leave. Lady Rawdon turned to her granddaughter. "You must be tired. You are slouching." She laid a light hand on Genevieve's back, and instinctively Genevieve straightened her shoulders.

Genevieve followed her grandmother's perfectly erect back out the door and up the stairs, keeping to herself the thought that she could find the room in which she had slept for years perfectly well by herself. She knew that her grandmother's intent was to talk to her in a place free from the prying eyes and ears of servants.

"Is everything all right, Genevieve?" Her grandmother turned to Genevieve as soon as she shut the bedroom door behind them. "This is a terribly swift return from your honeymoon." She narrowed her eyes, studying her granddaughter.

"Yes, of course. Myles and I are—well, we have gotten along quite well." Genevieve faltered, aware that she was probably blushing.

The countess's expression eased. "Good. I am pleased to hear that you are not unhappy. But you must see, dear, that it looks a trifle odd for the two of you to come rushing back to London from your honeymoon."

"Myles had something he needed to attend to." Genevieve hesitated. "The fact is, we learned that my running into Mr. Langdon in the library was not by accident." She explained their discovery regarding the note.

"Really, Genevieve, why did you go to the library to meet Sir Myles?" Lady Rawdon asked crossly. "Surely you must have realized the impropriety."

"Yes, of course, but . . . well, it was Myles," Genevieve said, realizing how weak her excuse sounded.

"I should hope that Sir Myles would not have been so foolish as to put you in a compromising situation," the countess retorted. "I cannot imagine why you did not know that."

"Apparently you know him better than I," Genevieve replied somewhat resentfully.

"You must be careful to keep this to yourself. It would sound even worse if the *ton* learned you had intended to meet a man secretly, especially since you were engaged to another. Accidentally running into a man whom everyone knows is a rake is far less damaging than arranging trysts."

"It wasn't a tryst." Genevieve's eyes flashed.

"Of course not, dear, but that is not the point. Everyone would assume it was a tryst, and that is what matters. The gossip has died down for the most part, but if this was known, it would flare up all over again."

Genevieve started to retort, but she held her tongue. She had learned long ago that it was of no use to argue with her grandmother, especially over something that she had no plans of doing, anyway. Instead she said mildly, "I suspect the talk will revive as soon as I make an appearance."

"Yes, of course, but there's no need to add wood to the fire." Lady Rawdon paused, thinking. "I don't see why this news brought the two of you back to town."

"Mr. Langdon obviously must have arranged the whole thing. He is even more culpable than we thought. Myles was furious, and he means to find him."

"Oh, bother." Lady Rawdon grimaced. "I would have thought Sir Myles would have more sense. As it is, I have managed to keep Alec from doing something outrageous, but once he hears this . . ." She shook her head. "I do hope Sir Myles will keep his head enough that this isn't made public."

"He doesn't intend to have a duel at dawn with the man, if that is what you mean. But I think we deserve to confront the man who threw me into a very public scandal."

"The fact that you may 'deserve' it does not make it an intelligent course of action." Lady Rawdon waved a hand, dismissing the subject. "Well, there's no need to talk about that now. I shall leave you to get some rest. Hopefully Mr. Langdon will be bright enough not to show his face in London until Sir Myles has calmed down." Her grandmother hesitated, then came forward to lay her hand on Genevieve's cheek. "I am glad you are finding married life acceptable."

"Thank you, Grandmama." Impulsively Genevieve leaned forward to give her grandmother a peck on the cheek. "I am . . . quite comfortable."

"Very good. I told the butler to put Sir Myles in the yellow room. It is not the best view, but I thought it the likelier choice since it is next door."

"Oh." Genevieve was aware of a curious sense of disappointment. She had grown accustomed the past few days to Sir Myles's presence in her bed. But that had been the product of the circumstances. They were back in the world again, taking up their normal routines. "Of course."

After her grandmother left the room, Genevieve sank down on the chair before the fireplace. Xerxes padded over to leap up into her lap. Oddly, here in this familiar room, she felt lonelier than she had in days.

Throughout their drive to London, the atmosphere between Genevieve and Myles had been strained. They had not brought up the issue of the note that had precipitated their trip, instead discussing setting up their household in the Thorwood home in London, which the family had not used for several years. But through all the discussions of ongoing renovations and such things as decorating, hiring servants, and setting up a town carriage, Genevieve could not help but brood over their argument. Now she wondered whether, with Myles having a separate bedroom, he would even come into her room tonight.

She busied herself with getting ready for bed, but finally, wrapped in her dressing gown, her hair down, she could find nothing else to do, and she sat down in the chair by the window. It would be foolish to stay up. Myles might decide to wait up to speak with Alec when he got back. He might be tired and go straight to bed. She sat for a few more minutes. The sound of the front door's closing roused her from her reverie, and she stood up to look out the window.

Myles was walking down the street away from her.

Doubtless he was heading for White's or some other club to see his friends. To drink and gamble and . . . do all those things a gentleman of the *ton* did. It was no surprise. They were back in London; it was only natural that Myles was returning to his usual routine.

Genevieve turned away, her throat tightening. Slipping out of her dressing gown, she snuffed out her candle and went to bed.

When Genevieve went downstairs for breakfast the next morning, she found Sir Myles and her grandmother already seated at the table. Myles popped up from his seat with a look of relief. "Genevieve."

"Sir Myles and I were just discussing the renovations to his house," Lady Rawdon said as Genevieve sat down in the chair Myles pulled out for her.

"Yes, and I fear the countess found me sadly lacking in knowledge," Myles added. "I told her you were taking over all the arrangements with the house."

"Yes, of course." Genevieve gave him a tight smile. She wondered when he had come in the night before; he certainly did not look like a man who had spent half the night out carousing. She turned toward her grandmother. "I thought I would look at the house this morning, Grandmama. Why don't you and Damaris come with me?"

"Certainly, dear."

"Genevieve. Myles." They all turned as Alec strode into the room. He came over to kiss his sister's cheek.

"Good to see you, Genny. I was surprised to find Myles here when we returned last night." He sat down, adding with a frown, "You must excuse Damaris. She does not feel well enough for breakfast these days."

"I am sure she will be fine, Alec." Genevieve glanced at her grandmother, who gave her a sardonic look. "'Tis only to be expected. She feels well the rest of the day, does she not?"

"She says she does," Alec replied doubtfully, picking up a piece of toast and beginning to butter it. "I'm not sure we should have gone to that play last night."

"Every one of my sisters has gone through it, Alec," Myles put in. "All of them did perfectly well. You'll see."

"But none of them were Damaris," Alec pointed out unarguably.

"I never realized Damaris was so frail," Genevieve mused.

"She's not." Alec shot his sister a dark glance. "It's all very well for you to laugh, Genny. You, too, Myles." He waggled his butter knife at Myles. "Just wait until you go through it. You'll find it's an entirely different thing."

Genevieve glanced over at Myles and found him regarding her thoughtfully. She felt a flush begin to rise up her throat, and she hastily returned her attention to her plate.

The countess cleared her throat delicately. "Be that as it may, Alec, I think you will agree that this is hardly a fit topic for the breakfast table."

"Of course, ma'am." Alec tucked into his breakfast.

Alec waited until their grandmother excused herself to get ready for their morning excursion, then turned to his sister. "Myles told me what happened. That bastard Langdon. I should have taken care of him that night. I don't know why I let Damaris dissuade me."

"Perhaps because you were being sensible for once," Genevieve suggested. "I hope the two of you will consider that before you charge off to do something to him now."

"The man has to be taught that he cannot treat my sister that way," Alec told her sharply.

"My wife," Myles corrected in a calm but firm tone. When Alec turned toward him, somewhat surprised, Myles continued, "I respect your sentiments, Alec, but Genevieve is my wife now. And it is my place to take care of her."

Alec looked as if he might argue, but then he gave a short nod. "You are right, of course. How can I help?" He looked to Myles.

Genevieve crossed her arms, irritation rising in her at the way the two of them were claiming ownership of the issue. Of her.

"I want the name of your Bow Street runner," Myles told Alec. "I went out last night to see if I could find out anything about Langdon, but no one has seen him since that night."

"You went looking for him?" Genevieve asked. "You didn't tell me you were going to."

Myles glanced at her, startled. "Well, not the sort of thing one talks about to a lady."

"I'll be glad to give you my runner's name," Alec put in. "In fact, I'll take you to meet him this evening and we'll set him to finding Langdon."

"Excellent. Do you think we—"

"And I, I suppose, have nothing to say about the matter?" Genevieve asked in an icy voice. "Of course, why should I? I am only the one whose reputation was damaged."

Her brother and her husband turned to look at her in some surprise.

"But, Genevieve, surely you can't expect us to ignore this," Myles said. "We shan't be indiscreet, I promise you."

"Of course not," Alec agreed. "Parker knows how to keep his mouth shut; I have used him before."

"I don't expect you to ignore it," Genevieve said. "But has it occurred to you that I might like to confront this man myself? I want to go with you to meet the runner. Oh, do stop gaping at me, both of you. Why shouldn't I be involved?"

"Genevieve, I meet him at a tavern by the docks," Alec said. "It's not the sort of place for you."

"Oh, I see, it's not appropriate—unlike all those places you took Damaris last year when those men were chasing you."

"That was different."

"In what way?"

"Well, um, Damaris is not—I mean, she was—we were—" Alec stumbled to a halt and turned to Myles.

"Genevieve, it just isn't done," Myles protested. "What would your grandmother say?"

"My grandmother? I am a grown woman. Married, in

case you have forgotten. Am I still required to live by my grandmother's dictates? Oh, and yours, of course."

"But it's hardly something that you would wish to do." Myles looked puzzled.

"No doubt you would know that better than I. Just as you knew last night I would not want to be told you were going out to search for Langdon. And I would have no interest, of course, in hearing what the results of that search were. It has long been my preference to sit in ignorance, waiting for someone else to take care of my worries."

"You sat up waiting for me?" Myles asked, surprised. "My dear, I am sor—"

"I did *not* sit up waiting for you!" Genevieve snapped, slapping her napkin down on the table and shoving her chair back sharply.

"You would probably prefer to discuss this between yourselves," Alec began, rising hastily to his feet.

"Coward," Myles muttered.

"Oh, no, Alec, pray do not bother," Genevieve told him with exaggerated sweetness. "You and Myles should continue to decide my life for me. I shall just go tend to my little 'women's business.'" She stalked to the door and turned. "I hope it is appropriate if I look at your house this morning, Myles. Since my grandmother will be along, it should not be too scandalous. But you might want to send word to your man of business, giving me permission to look at it. I should not want to step out of line." She closed the door behind her with a snap.

Fourteen

I did warn you she had the Stafford temper," Genevieve heard her brother say before she strode off down the hall. She thought of turning back to give Alec a piece of her mind, too, but she decided that would only reinforce the idea that her temper was at fault. She stalked down the hall and up the stairs. At the top she ran into Damaris, who looked lovely and rosy-cheeked and not at all in the fragile state Alec had drawn of her.

"Genevieve!" Damaris's smile fell away as she took in Genevieve's scowl. "Oh, dear. Should I not go down?"

"Not unless you enjoy eating your meal with two of the most obtuse, irritating men in the city."

"Ah. Well." Damaris turned and fell into step beside her. "I wasn't interested in eating anyway. I was going there to see you."

"I fear I am not very good company, either."

"What happened? Are they arguing? I'm terribly sorry; I did not mean to break your confidence. It's most irritating; Alec knows me all too well. I find it's difficult to hide anything from him. But I thought

Myles had explained everything, and Alec was not angry with him."

"Oh, no, they are not angry with each other. The two of them are quite happily making plans for dealing with my life. There's no need to apologize. *You* are not at fault."

"Ah. I see." Damaris nodded wisely. "They are 'protecting' you."

Genevieve snorted inelegantly. "They are plotting revenge on Mr. Langdon. *I* am the one who was wronged! But apparently I am too delicate and refined to confront the man myself." She stopped and swung around to face Damaris. "He had the nerve to tell me that it just wasn't done. Myles! Lecturing to me on what is proper and what isn't!"

"Men can be most aggravating," Damaris agreed, and took Genevieve's arm, leading her down the hallway to the upstairs sitting room.

"Of course, it's all part and parcel of the rest of it. Myles has been in a mood since he heard about the note."

"I am sure he is angry at Langdon for playing such a trick on you."

"He is looking for Langdon to take it out on, but it is me at whom he's angry."

"You? But why?"

"I don't know!" Genevieve cried, pleased to find someone who understood her side of the matter. "He says I should have known he wouldn't have sent me the note. But it isn't as if I thought he had some wicked intent by doing it. I presumed he needed to tell me something in a more private way than the dance floor allowed. Is that wrong?"

"No, of course not," Damaris agreed soothingly.

"What would he have had me do? Ignore an urgent missive from him? How was I to know it wasn't in his hand? It isn't as if I'd had any letters from him. And when I pointed that out, all he could say was of course he wouldn't have written me any letters, he wouldn't set out to damage a girl's reputation—as if I had suggested he had!"

"It sounds as if he was being most unreasonable."

"Exactly." Genevieve nodded emphatically. "Then he was upset because I had not told him about the note. But why would I have told him? I thought he was the one who sent it to me. I was careful *not* to say anything about it because I didn't want him to think I blamed him for what happened. I was trying to be fair. To be nice." She grimaced. "For all the good it did me."

"I have found that men are . . . imperfect when it comes to telling you how they feel. Or even being aware of it themselves. I suspect Myles was upset because of what happened to you and because he was not there to prevent it. Worse, it was the use of his name that lured you into it. I think Alec often flares into anger because he is frightened."

"Alec? Frightened?" Genevieve asked dubiously.

"He has little fear for himself. But when he thinks of something happening to me, it scares him, especially when it is something he cannot control. That is why he is in such a twitter about my 'condition.' He cannot protect me from harm, so he fusses until it's enough to drive me mad." Damaris smiled fondly. "He is furious that he cannot convince the best doctor in London to spend the next six months in Northumberland looking after my lying-in. But I know his anger is because he feels helpless. I am sure Myles must feel that way, too, about not keeping you from harm."

"But Alec loves you. Myles and I are not like that."

"Oh, Genevieve . . ." Damaris took both Genevieve's hands in hers. "I am sure Myles cares for you."

"I am sure he does, as I care for him, of course." Genevieve turned away, going over to the window. "We have known each other these many years past. We are friends, but it is not the same as you and Alec." She thought with a pang of Myles's leaving the house the previous night. "He went out looking for Mr. Langdon yesterday," she went on, her words following her thoughts. "There is nothing wrong with that, of course. I don't expect Myles to sit in my pocket. But he did not tell me where he was going or what he planned. He did not ask me even one question about what I wanted to do about Mr. Langdon."

"Even though you are the person who was injured by Mr. Langdon."

"Exactly." Genevieve swung back around. "Myles wanted to come to London all by himself! I had to insist on accompanying him. Now he and Alec are going to meet with that Bow Street runner to set him to finding Langdon. But of course I cannot go with them; it would be indecent. Do you know Myles had the effrontery to ask me what my grandmother would say about my behaving that way?"

"Oh, my." Damaris shook her head. She thought for a moment. "You know, there might be other ways to go about finding out what happened and where Mr. Langdon is. Things women might be handier at discovering."

"What do you mean?" Intrigued, Genevieve came over to sit down beside her sister-in-law.

"Mr. Langdon couldn't have just given the note to you himself, so there must be someone else involved."

"Just a maid." Genevieve straightened. "But of course. It's possible she might have known more about it. Perhaps she even knew him. I cannot remember exactly what she said when she handed it to me."

"It must have been one of Thea's servants," Damaris pointed out. "We can visit Thea and talk to the girl."

"Of course!" Genevieve popped to her feet. "We'll go—no, wait, I told Grandmama we would go look at the Thorwood house today. Myles set his man of business to having it made ready for us to live in—Myles's mother never came to London after his father died, so Myles didn't bother to open up the place just for himself. The countess was quizzing Myles about it this morning at breakfast." The memory of Myles's harried expression brought a smile to her lips. "So I told her she and I would inspect it—you will come, too, I hope. But I can't change my plans."

"No, that won't do. It will keep. We shall call on Thea tomorrow."

Genevieve's grin widened. "I would like to see Myles's expression if we manage to find out something he can't."

Impulsively she reached out and took Damaris's hand. "Thank you."

"Of course. Now . . . let's go inspect your new home."

Tompkins, Myles's man of business, met the ladies at Thorwood Place, smiling and eager to please. Genevieve could see that he had been not only fast, but competent as well. The house had obviously been scrubbed top to bottom, and he had already hired a skeleton staff of servants. The butler, Bouldin, was a lean, young-looking man with a sparkle in his eyes that betokened a sense of humor. The housekeeper, Mrs. Aycott, on the other hand, was thoroughly no-nonsense.

"I did not change anything, only retouched things here and there," Tompkins assured Genevieve. "If there is anything you should like done a different way, ma'am, you need only tell me. Sir Myles instructed me to implement whatever you requested."

"It is lovely," Genevieve replied. "I am tempted to move in immediately."

Mr. Tompkins appeared faintly surprised at her statement, but said only, "Certainly, if you wish it."

Genevieve started to explain that she had not been serious, but stopped. Actually, now that she thought about it, she realized that it was exactly what she would like to do. She cast a questioning look at the butler. "Would that be possible?"

"Of course, madam. Shall I tell Henri to prepare a supper menu for your approval?" Bouldin replied calmly.

"Yes, that would be excellent." Genevieve smiled and turned toward Damaris. "It is not that I am unmindful of your generosity, but—"

Damaris laughed. "No, indeed, I understand. Of course you would wish to set up household as soon as you can."

Genevieve's grandmother looked less certain, but she said nothing. As Bouldin went off to confer with the chef, Mrs. Aycott escorted them upstairs to show off her domain. The dustcovers had been taken off the furniture, and the bedrooms gleamed just as much as had the ground floor. One or two of the chambers were somewhat bare of furniture, but the master's bedroom at the back of the house was fully furnished and ready for occupancy.

"A very nice bedroom for Sir Myles," Genevieve's grandmother pronounced as she surveyed the room, partially paneled with a dark, rich wood and the rest painted a deep hunter green. A wingback chair of matching green leather stood near the window, which overlooked the small garden behind the house.

"Yes. Quite elegant." Genevieve idly opened one door to reveal a dressing room. The door on the opposite wall proved to lead into another bedroom. Almost as large as the first room, it was tastefully decorated in blues and creams.

"Oh, your chamber is lovely, Genevieve!" her grandmother said with delight, coming up beside her.

It was silly, Genevieve thought, to be taken aback at

the thought of her bedroom. Of course, she and Myles would have separate rooms here, as they had at Alec's house. They had shared a bedroom at Thorwood Park only because Genevieve had not wanted to offend Lady Julia. She had always intended to have her own bedroom in this house. She looked forward to it.

"Yes. It is most attractive." Genevieve walked farther into the room. If her bedroom was a mite remote and cool also, well, that was the style she preferred, wasn't it?

It was nonsensical to feel this pang at the thought of no longer sharing a bedroom with Myles. One wouldn't want his boots and shaving equipment and such cluttering up one's room. And it would be a dreadful nuisance for him to come in after a long night of being out with his friends, bumbling about and waking her up.

"It will do splendidly," Genevieve said, turning to her grandmother with a determined smile. "We shall send our things over this afternoon."

Myles trotted up the front steps of his house, humming a tune under his breath. He had been taken aback when he'd returned to Rawdon's house a few minutes ago and was told that Lady Genevieve was already moving into Thorwood Place, but, as he thought about it, his surprise had turned to delight.

He had feared that once Genevieve was back under her family's roof, she would be content to stay in the familiar place, taking her time with decorating the house. And the thought of making love to her right down the hall from her grandmother—not to mention her brother—felt deuced peculiar. When he had come back from looking for Langdon the night before and had seen that her room was dark, he had decided not to even go in. But it had been equally wrong to sleep in his bed alone. After only a few weeks of being with Genevieve, the bed had seemed uncomfortable and large and . . . lonely.

Clearly Genevieve was as eager as he to be alone together in their own home—why else would she have rushed to move into their house? They had had a bit of discord this morning, but Genevieve had always had a temper. She had just learned to govern it better and was no longer apt to chase one down the hall, wielding her hairbrush like a club, as she had when she was twelve. But she was apt to cool down quickly, too. And he could not imagine that she truly wanted to go meet the runner this evening. Genevieve was not the sort to flout convention.

Still, it was a relief to find that she was now happily engaged in setting up their home. She must be over her odd humor of this morning. It would be as it had been at the manor house. No, even better, it would be like their time in the cottage, the two of them alone, sharing their meals, sitting and talking after supper, sleeping with her warm and soft in his arms. The thought of Genevieve lying in his bed sent a ripple of primitive male lust through him, and Myles took the stairs two at a time and went down the hall toward the master bedroom, following Genevieve's voice.

Before he reached it, he found her not in his bedroom,

but in the elegant bedchamber adjoining his. He stopped, watching her direct her maid as she put away Genevieve's clothes, and disappointment settled in his chest like a rock.

Apparently this was not going to be just like their time in the cottage.

"Well, my dear, let it never be said you are not efficient," Myles said, putting on a pleasant voice with an effort.

Genevieve gave a little start at the sound of his voice and turned to him. "Hello, Myles." She held herself a little stiffly, and her voice had a formality that he had not heard in weeks. "There seemed little point in delaying."

"No doubt." Myles advanced into the room. Genevieve cast a look at her maid, and the woman bobbed a curtsy and left. Myles leaned against the footboard of her bed, his legs stretched out in front of him in a pose that looked more relaxed than he felt. Xerxes, who was lying on the end of the bed, shot Myles a look of contempt and sprang down, stalking off with his tail in the air. "I hope you warned the servants about your cat. No doubt we'll soon have maids leaving our employment."

"Don't be nonsensical."

"Ah, but that's part of my charm." He glanced around the room. "I see that you have established your separate bedrooms." To his dismay, he realized his light remark wasn't entirely devoid of bitterness.

"Yes, of course." Genevieve raised her chin fractionally. "That is what is done, isn't it?"

He heard the echo of his own words to her this morning, and he wondered if she was still in a dudgeon about that. He tried a smile. "I suppose so. Still, I confess I will miss the way it was."

"Yes. Well." Genevieve turned away and began to straighten the bottles on the vanity. "We are in the city now. Life will return to normal. We need not be in each other's pocket all the time."

"Not if you do not wish it." He stood up, faintly surprised at the disappointment he felt. He knew Genevieve well; she was not the sort to be a clinging wife. A few weeks in the country, no matter how sweet it had been, were not going to change her into a woman who would hang on his every word. He would not want her to be. Her spine was one of the things he had always admired about her. But, somehow, he wished she were standing there smiling at him, her hair a silvery curtain, her eyes full of sensual promise, as she had been a few days ago.

"Grandmama invited us to their box at the theater tomorrow," Genevieve went on. "She thought it would be a good place for us—for me—to make an appearance. People will talk, of course, but they will whenever I go out the first time. And I will not have to mingle as I would at a party. I suppose I should get it over with."

"I bow, as always, to Lady Rawdon's knowledge," Myles agreed, striving once again to hit the right note. Why did it suddenly seem awkward with Genevieve, when only a few days ago they had lain tangled together, her breath warm against his bare skin? "I shall be happy to take you to the theater."

"You do not have to come," she said in an airy tone, returning once again to nudging the perfumes and lotions about. "I do not expect you to shield me everywhere I go. No doubt you have interests of your own to attend to."

"Do you not wish me to accompany you?" He was unprepared for the twist of hurt, but he kept his voice even.

"No, I didn't mean that." Her eyes flew to his, startled. "I was just saying, you do not need to tie yourself to . . . to defending my reputation. I will have Grandmama, and Damaris said she and Alec will go as well."

"And so will your husband." Myles grasped her wrist, turning her toward him. "Genevieve, stop fidgeting with those bottles and look at me. What are you playing at?"

"I am not playing at anything!" she fired back. "I am only saying—"

"What? That you have no need of me?" He felt his temper rising, matching the ache in his chest. "I am well aware of that and always have been. But I think it will look somewhat better if your husband of less than a month is actually with you."

"Yes, of course, that is very important to you, how it looks."

Myles stared at her. "You are accusing *me* of being concerned about how things look?"

"You certainly seemed so today." She lifted her chin.

"You *are* still angry about this morning." Myles had to smile. This was not so bad, then. Feminine annoyance was something he knew how to handle.

"I don't know what you're talking about."

"What a bag of moonshine. Try that with someone who doesn't know you." He took her chin between his thumb and forefinger, giving it the tiniest shake. "I see that tilt of your chin. Are you really up in the boughs over my wanting to find Langdon?"

"I never said I didn't want you to find him."

"Do you really wish to go to some dockside tavern with us to talk to this runner?" His voice rose in surprise. "That hardly sounds like you."

"Yes, no doubt I am far too poor-spirited to do such a thing."

"I would never call you poor-spirited." He grinned again. "Conscious of the proprieties, let us say."

"You are right. I am." She twisted her chin from his grasp. "I am glad to find that you, too, have some sense of what is acceptable. I will admit it surprises me."

His hands went to her waist, and he pulled her closer. "I love it when you scold." He bent to nuzzle her neck.

"Really, Myles, is that your answer for everything?" Genevieve twisted her head away, but it only exposed a longer line of her neck and shoulder for his lips to explore.

"I find it suffices for a number of things." He slid his hands down over the curve of her buttocks, desire spearing inside him.

"It is almost time for supper," she protested. "I must dress."

He huffed out a little laugh against her skin as he kissed his way down her chest to the neckline of her gown. "Ah, then first you must undress. I can help you with that." He cupped her breast in one hand, kissing the trembling top of it above the lace of her dress.

"Stop. Do you think I am that easy? That all it takes to fob me off is a few kisses? That I can be soothed by your skillful lovemaking into doing whatever you want?"

"You seemed to enjoy it well enough last week." He smiled sensually and ran a teasing finger along the neckline of her dress.

"I said, stop it!" Genevieve twisted away, planting her hands on her hips, and glared at him. "Honestly, Myles, you cannot be this obtuse."

"Apparently I can," he shot back, her words rankling. "Obviously I am once again a great disappointment to you."

"Don't be absurd. I didn't say that."

"You didn't have to." He could feel the heat of resentment spurting up inside him. "It is clear; it has always been. In the past, I was too loose, too lax, too uninterested in the rules or propriety. Now am I too concerned with what people might think. You need not look for excuses, Genevieve; I understand wherein the fault lies. It is not whether I am proper, whether I ignore the rules or follow them too well. It is me. I am what is wrong in your eyes."

"What!" Genevieve stared. "No! Myles . . . I never said that!"

"But it is what you think." He could feel his calm slipping, knew that he was revealing too much. But he could not seem to hold it back. "I am 'just Myles,' the handy friend of your brother, the man with whom one wants to dance but not the sort one takes seriously. I am the man you would never have stooped to marry if you had not been forced into it. Even though I am the one who helped you when you needed it, who offered you his name to save you from social ruin."

Genevieve drew in a sharp breath. "You are throwing that up to me?"

Myles felt a pang of remorse, he could not hold back the words. They welled up from him like blood from a wound. "I tried in every way to make it easier for you. I cajoled and smiled and turned away your anger. I held my tongue because I knew you suffered. I did my best to awaken you gently, to give you pleasure. I held back until I thought I would explode because I did not want to hurt or frighten you."

"Do you want another apology from me? Am I supposed to spend the rest of our marriage thanking you? Yes, I know you sacrificed your life so my reputation would not suffer. I am sorry, so dreadfully sorry for it! But I cannot pay you back by—by pretending that I am something I am not."

"I am not asking you to!" He could feel his pulse pounding in his head, and he took a breath, struggling to control his voice. "I just wish that any of that meant something to you. Dursbury suited you. It didn't matter that he was more shell than substance. He was high enough for you; his family was old enough; his pride matched yours. You cannot bear the thought of being only my wife. Not Genevieve Stafford, the daughter of an earl, but just Genevieve Thorwood."

"I will always be Genevieve Stafford!" Color blazed in Genevieve's cheeks. "Marrying you doesn't change me!"

"That's obvious," he shot back. "You are still the same cold woman you have always been!"

Genevieve stiffened, looking as if he had slapped her. The anger drained out of Myles as suddenly as it had flared up, leaving behind only an icy hollow.

"Of course I am the one who is at fault. I am cold." The words fell from Genevieve's lips, as hard and unforgiving as her eyes. "Well, you are right. I don't share your . . . your egregious appetites. I think there is more to life than carnal pleasures." She waved her hand toward the bed.

"I see. So it's all very well to enjoy your conjugal pleasures in the country, where there is not much to do. But here you are not swayed by lust. There are better ways to occupy your time."

Genevieve faced him defiantly, her arms crossed over her chest. "I am sorry I don't meet your expectations. I am sorry that you expended so much time and effort trying to imbue me with warmth and turn me sweet. Anyone could have told you that it was an impossible task." She looked away. "I will not apologize for my pride in being a Stafford. And I cannot live the rest of my life begging your forgiveness. I warned you not to do it, Myles!" Her voice caught, and she stopped for a second, then went on in a low voice, "I have to be more than your wife. I am not meant for honeyed words or sweet kisses. There is no need for you to 'hold back' or try to 'awaken' me. I will manage just fine without your conjugal pleasures."

"I don't believe you," Myles said flatly.

"I beg your pardon?" Genevieve sent him a look down her nose that would have done justice to her ancestors.

"I said, you're lying. I'm just not sure whether it's to me or to yourself." Myles strode away, turning back at the door. "I will, of course, respect your wishes and not bother you with my unwanted attentions. But you forget; I have made love to you these past few weeks. You want me in your bed. And sooner or later you will admit it."

Fifteen

Genevieve stared at her reflection in the mirror without seeing it. Behind her Penelope said, "Ma'am? Is there something wrong? Do you wish me to change the style?"

"What?" Genevieve realized that she had been sitting there silently for far too long. "Oh, no, everything is fine. You did an excellent job, as always. I am afraid I was woolgathering."

Her maid stepped back, still watching her somewhat uncertainly. Genevieve knew she had to stand up and start down to supper. She could not delay it any longer or Penelope would know something was wrong. She could not give the servants cause for gossip. Genevieve stood up, clutching her skirts in her icy hands, and turned toward the door. Her breath caught in her throat and for an instant she could not go forward.

She could not go down there and face Myles. Not after the scene this afternoon. How could she talk to him as if everything were perfectly all right? How could she sit there and eat when her stomach revolted at the very idea of food? He would see the puffiness in her eyes, no matter how she had tried to soothe it away with a cool, wet rag; he would know that she had cried over him.

She wanted desperately to hide up here like a coward and claim illness. Put off facing him until the next day. But she could not allow herself to do that. However much his harsh words had hurt her, she had to hold her head up. She had to act like a lady. Like a Stafford.

So, drawing a shaky breath, she wrapped herself in her breeding like an armor and left the room.

Stomach jittering, she went down the stairs and into the dining room. Myles was standing at the window, and he turned at her entrance. Genevieve forced herself to meet his gaze, though she could not bring up a smile. His face was unusually grave, and the look in his eyes—but, no, she would not think about his eyes. Or his lean, strong hands. Or the way his smile crooked up higher on one side than the other.

"Genevieve." He started toward her.

"Sir Myles." She gave him a polite nod and looked over at the sideboard where the butler stood, as if her only concern were the quality of their supper. Going to her seat, she managed not to look at Myles as he pulled out her chair, grateful that the length of the table lay between them. It was easier to look at him without really seeing him this way.

"Tompkins did quite well with the house, I thought," she began stiffly.

"Good. Then it was all to your liking?"

"Yes. Quite nice."

They continued to talk in this manner through the first three courses, as polite and awkward as strangers. They discussed the weather and the long summer evenings, the wall covering of Moroccan leather in the study, and the beauty of the dark-wood, Jacobite paneling that had been moved into this library from the old Thorwood residence on the Thames. As they talked, Genevieve pushed her food around on her plate in the hopes of appearing to eat it, though the few mouthfuls she forced down could have been gruel for all she tasted them. After a time, they lapsed into silence, and Genevieve congratulated herself that she had gotten through over half the meal.

Myles cleared his throat, shifting a little in his chair. "Genevieve . . ."

She lifted her head and looked at him with cool inquiry, her eyes flicking away to Bouldin, standing at the sideboard. Myles followed her gaze and let out an impatient sigh.

"This evening, with Alec and the runner," he began, then stopped.

Genevieve concentrated on her small cup of palate-refreshing sorbet.

"I do not intend to stay out long," Myles started again. "Perhaps, when I return—"

"Oh, pray, you need not return early on my account. I am rather tired, I confess, and doubtless I shall retire early. You and Rawdon enjoy your evening with Mr. Parker."

"It isn't a question of enjoying it," he said irritably.

"Indeed? Well, I would hope you will, nevertheless. It is so rare that Rawdon joins you on your gentlemanly excursions."

"Our gentlemanly excursions?" Myles's voice took on its familiar bantering tone, but Genevieve ignored it. She did not have Myles's apparent ability to fall back into their old manner. She could not pretend that she did not know how he really felt, how much he resented . . . and regretted . . .

She pulled herself back sharply from her thoughts. "Yes, your clubs and such. I am sure you have missed them in the country." She turned toward the butler. "Bouldin, please give my compliments to the chef. The food is delightful."

Myles stabbed his fork into his meat and sawed away at it. After a moment or two of grimly eating, he laid his knife and fork down. "Bouldin, I think we can manage the rest on our own. As you can tell, my lady's appetite is rather slight this evening."

"Sir." The butler bowed and started from the room.

Genevieve laid her napkin on the table. "If you'll excuse me, Myles, I shall leave you to your port."

Bouldin stopped and swiveled back.

"I don't care for port," Myles said, scowling at Bouldin, and the butler quickly turned and slipped out the door. "Genevieve, wait."

She was already out of her seat, but she stopped and turned to him. "Yes?"

He rose, too, looking unaccustomedly awkward.

"About this afternoon. I want to beg your pardon for what I said. I did not mean—"

"La, Myles . . ." Genevieve managed an unconcerned wave of her hand. "There is no need to pretend between the two of us. We have always, I think, been truthful with one another. We made a mistake, and now we simply must make the best of a bad situation." She smiled brightly in his general direction, then whirled and hurried toward the door.

"Blast it, Genevieve—"

She did not look back, though she heard him take a few steps after her, then stop. By the time she reached the stairs, she was almost running. She made it to her room and closed the door, turning the key just in case Myles should take it into his head to come after her and argue. She knew she would never be able to hold back the tears if she had to face him again. As it was, she had to pull in great gulps of air, shoving the tears back down inside her. She would not cry. She would *not*.

Genevieve awakened and looked up groggily at the tester above her bed, unsure for a moment where she was or why a heavy ache was inside her. Then she remembered. She was in her new bedroom at Myles's house. And the brief happiness of her marriage had come to a crashing halt the day before.

She rolled over on her side, hoping that she might go back to sleep and this would all go away, but, however muzzy-headed she might feel, she was obviously awake for the day. She did not want to go downstairs. Most of all, she did not want to see Myles again.

Last night she had gone to bed early, having nothing else to do, but once there, she had been unable to sleep and had lain awake for what seemed hours, listening to the ticking of the ormolu clock on the mantel. Finally, long after all the sounds of the servants in the house had ceased, she had heard the front door open and Myles's footsteps coming down the hall. The steps had stopped outside her door, and Genevieve closed her eyes, feigning sleep, as she waited, every nerve alert, for Myles to open the door and come in. She thought she heard the sound of the knob turning, but the door did not open, and the steps began again, walking past her door and into Myles's room.

For a time she heard the faint sounds of his moving about inside his room, and it occurred to her that perhaps he would come through their connecting door. Then the light disappeared from beneath the door, and there were no more sounds. It had been hours before she fell asleep.

She was glad, of course, that he had not come into the room. She had not relocked it after Penelope left, but that hadn't been because she expected him to come to her. Not really. She did not, after all, want him to take her into his arms as if nothing had happened. Knowing how he really felt, what he thought about her, it would have been unbearable to have him kiss her and caress her.

A hot tear trickled from the corner of her eye and across her cheek into the mass of her hair. Why had she worn it down last night? It was far easier to put it into a braid so it would not tangle. She had grown accustomed to leaving it loose because Myles liked it that way. But that did not signify anymore.

In the silence of the room, she heard the small sound of the knob of the connecting door turning, and she closed her eyes, pretending sleep. She waited, keeping her breathing slow and even and wishing she knew whether he was still standing there. Finally she heard the snick of the latch catching, and she relaxed and opened her eyes, aware of a curious blend of relief and sorrow when she found herself alone.

She stayed in bed, pretending to sleep each time the door from the hall opened, though the next two times she felt rather sure it was Penelope who peeked in on her. She was hiding, she knew, and she chastised herself for it, but still she did not get up. Finally, when she heard the sound of the front door closing, she got out of bed. The next time Penelope peered in, Genevieve was up, sitting by the window.

"Oh, miss! You're up." Penelope smiled and hurried toward her. "Are you unwell?"

"What? Oh, no." It occurred to her that her behavior would look less peculiar if she were ill, so she hastily amended her words. "I mean, well, perhaps I am feeling a bit under the weather."

"Here, best put on your dressing gown, then, or you'll get worse." Penelope wrapped her in her brocade dressing gown and opened the heavy draperies. "There, maybe you'd like to look out on the garden. Shall I bring you some tea and toast?"

"I'm not really hungry."

"Just a bite, maybe," Penelope urged. "Tea always makes you better."

Genevieve nodded. It was easier than arguing. Perhaps she really was sick. She could not remember ever feeling like this. A tiff with one's husband should not do this to one. She had heard Alec and Damaris go at it hammer and tongs a few times, and Damaris did not wilt like a flower left in the sun. Surely Genevieve should not be so weak.

Penelope brought her tea and toast, and Genevieve sipped at the tea and idly shredded one of the pieces of toast. But she was still sitting in her dressing gown an hour later when Damaris appeared at her door.

"Genevieve? The butler said you were unwell. Do you have a fever?" Damaris went over to her and bent down to lay her hand against Genevieve's forehead.

"No. I'm fine." Genevieve straightened, embarrassed. "Really. I am just a trifle lazy this morning."

"Oh." Damaris looked down at her, frowning slightly. "I—well—we had plans to see Thea today. To talk to her servant."

"Oh!" Genevieve stood up. "I am so sorry. I forgot."

"It's perfectly all right. I am early anyway. I can wait for you to dress."

"I don't know. Perhaps I shouldn't." The prospect of getting dressed and going to talk to someone seemed too taxing. "It was probably a foolish idea. What would the maid know? No doubt Langdon simply gave the note to her and handed her a shilling to deliver it to me."

"Are you sure you're feeling all right?" Damaris stared at her.

"I'm sorry. I am being very poor-spirited."

"Genevieve . . . what is wrong? You scarcely seem yourself." Suddenly Damaris's eyes lit up and she leaned closer. "Are you—do you think you are enceinte already?"

"What!" Genevieve blushed. "No. No. I am sure not. Please, I don't know why I am being so foolish." She stood up, squaring her shoulders. "Just let me change, and we'll go to Lady Morecombe's."

Genevieve dressed quickly and joined Damaris downstairs, doing her best to appear her usual self. But she could not quite succeed at playing the role, and she was aware of Damaris's concerned gaze on her as the carriage took them to Thea's house. It was too early, really, for paying a call, but clearly Thea thought nothing about the oddity of their arriving on her doorstep before noon.

"Genevieve! Damaris. Do come in. Matthew is upstairs with Nurse, having his lunch, and I finished my book, so I was casting about for something to do. I did not realize you were in town again, Genevieve."

"I only arrived recently. I, um, Myles has come back to find Langdon."

"What? Now?"

Between them, Damaris and Genevieve told Thea the whole story of the note, including Myles's male stubbornness in not letting Genevieve join him in the search for the man who had tricked her.

"That is so like a man," Thea said, shaking her head. "And the worst part of it is, they always say they're doing it to protect you."

"I thought if I could talk to the maid who gave me the note, she might know something more about Mr. Langdon," Genevieve went on. "Perhaps he said something to her that might help me."

"And you might find him before Myles!" Thea finished, apparently seeing nothing odd about this desire. "Of course. That's a splendid idea. Let's talk to the servants." Thea popped up and started toward the door.

"We are going to the servants' quarters?" Genevieve asked, surprised, as she and Damaris followed Thea. She had assumed that Thea would summon the butler and he would bring the maids in to be interviewed.

"Oh, yes," Thea tossed back over her shoulder. "The servants are becoming quite accustomed to my oddities."

Indeed, though everyone in the kitchen area suddenly attacked his or her task with more energy when the three women walked in, none of them seemed in the least surprised.

"My lady." The butler hurried out of his pantry, bowing. "How may I help you?"

"We wish to see the maids who were serving the night of the ball."

"Of course, madam." The man betrayed no surprise at this peculiar request, and soon all the maids were lined up in the kitchen. Genevieve looked up and down the line, and she slumped a little in disappointment.

"I don't recognize any of them."

"Well, you only saw her briefly." Thea turned to the maids. "Did any of you give Lady Thorwood a note that night? It is all right if you did. We just wish to know something about who gave it to you."

The women gazed at her blankly, then at each other, and began a chorus of "No, ma'am."

"But someone did," Genevieve protested. "She was a maid, not one of the guests."

"My lady, it could have been someone else," the butler offered. "We hired several extra girls that evening to help with the serving. If you wish, I can check with the agency."

"Of course!" Thea's face brightened. "It was doubtless one of them. That's an excellent idea, Reynolds."

When the three of them returned to the drawing room, Thea said, "Reynolds is very efficient, and he will soon have their names."

"I can send for them, I suppose, and question them," Genevieve said.

"Oh, no, Damaris and I are not about to be left out of the mystery," Thea protested. "We shall gather here again when I have the names."

"If they can describe them, I think I could tell which one it was, so we would not have to bring them all here to interview."

"Why don't we just go where she lives?" Damaris suggested. "After all, she might not come if you send for her.

Especially if she knows something about that reprobate Langdon."

It would be entirely inappropriate, Genevieve was sure, for a lady—or three—to go tromping about looking for a servant, but she could not deny the tug of interest. Myles, of course, would disapprove. Her mouth tightened. "You are right. We should track her down and talk to her."

They chatted for a few more minutes about the ins and outs of their plan, but Genevieve found her thoughts wandering to the more immediate prospect of what she would do tonight. There would be another meal to sit through. Myles had said he would accompany her to the theater, so she would have to sit through that, too. Worst of all, her grandmother would be there. The countess would immediately know that something was wrong; she always did. Unconsciously, Genevieve let out a little sigh.

"Genevieve?" Damaris asked, frowning. "Are you sure you're all right?"

"Yes, of course." Then, to everyone's surprise, including Genevieve's, a tear escaped from the corner of her eye.

"Genevieve!" Damaris slid over from her seat at the other end of the sofa and curled her arm around Genevieve's shoulders, leaning in solicitously. "What is wrong?"

"Nothing, really. I don't know—" Her throat was suddenly choked with tears and she had to swallow hard. She swiped at her eyes. "I am sorry. I don't know what's the matter with me."

Thea slid forward on her chair, reaching out to take her hand. "Is it Myles?"

"He regrets marrying me," Genevieve burst out, and now the tears began to flow in earnest.

"No! Did he say that?"

"Yes. No. I'm not sure." Genevieve drew a little hiccuping breath. "But it was obvious! He said I was—" Her stomach clutched. She could not say it, could not reveal that Myles, too, found her cold. She jumped up, feeling somehow defenseless in the face of their comfort. She wrapped her arms around her stomach. "He says I am too proud. He wishes I were—other than I am."

"But what happened? Why did he say all this?" Damaris frowned. "He always seems so . . . pleasant."

"He is!" The words came out in a wail, and Genevieve stopped, struggling to control her voice. Finally she went on, low and swift, "Myles is the most easygoing of men. I tried to tell him. I tried to tell everyone. I knew it would turn out badly. But I was too . . . too much a coward. I could not keep from snatching at his offer." She swiped at her tears again, then began to fiddle with the button of her glove. "Everything was too easy. I see that now."

"I don't understand. If it was too easy, why is Myles suddenly saying these things?"

"It was easy because he was hiding it!" Genevieve turned and faced Thea and Damaris, her expression bleak. "He is so accommodating; you know how he is. The one you can always count upon to ask a wallflower to dance or to talk to your great-aunt who bores everyone to tears. He is a very *kind* man. He said—he said he tried to turn aside his anger because he knew I was suffering. That he cajoled me and made jests. And he did, you see. I knew at the time that he was being good to me. But eventually, he could not bear it anymore, I suppose. I—well, I tried to be nicer, too. Really, I did. I was grateful to him; I tried to tell him I was. But, well . . . you know how I am," she finished with a miserable glance at Damaris.

"Oh, Genevieve . . ." Damaris said, melting in sympathy. "I am so sorry. You were rushed into it, I know. It was not what you wanted; surely he did not expect you to be happy."

"But I was." Genevieve sighed. "I was such a goose. I thought everything was going well until all this came up about the note. But now I see that Myles was not happy from the beginning, no matter how hard he tried to be. One cannot will these things. He . . ." Her voice caught a little but she went on, "He said I looked down on him, that I wanted a man like Dursbury, that I preferred Dursbury's name and title and lineage."

"Dursbury? Ah." Thea nodded wisely and shared a smile with Damaris. "He is jealous."

"Of Dursbury?" Genevieve stared in such astonishment that the other two women burst out laughing. "No. That couldn't be right. I told him I did not care for Dursbury. He knows I hold the man in contempt."

"But Myles is a man," Thea said firmly. "They are very sensitive about this sort of thing, I've discovered."

"That's true. Alec starts to scowl whenever any man pays me a compliment."

"Yes, but Alec is mad for you," Genevieve argued.

"Myles is your husband, and he cares for you. He would not have offered for you otherwise," Damaris told her. "A man doesn't just throw away his future happiness because he wants to be a gentleman. It isn't like offering you his coat."

"And Dursbury is the man you *chose* to marry," Thea said. "That is quite different from agreeing to Myles's offer because you had no other choice."

Genevieve looked at them. Her chest felt suddenly lighter, less restricted. But after a moment, she sighed and shook her head. "No. I don't think that could be it. He wasn't upset with Dursbury, the way Alec is about some man who flirts with you. He was angry at *me*. If you could have heard him, you would know. He holds such resentment! He says I am ungrateful. I'm not, truly, but . . . I cannot be what he wants me to be."

"But what does he want?" Thea asked.

"I'm not sure. That is how far I am from his ideal. We are so different. It was sheer folly to think we could get along. He wants me to be nicer. Sweeter. He would be happier with someone more like him. Someone sweet and biddable. A woman who just wanted to be his wife, you see, and love him. Someone who would be happy to have him protect her. Not a woman who is prickly and sharp and has a temper. A woman who is . . . not warm."

"But he knew you for years before he offered for you," Damaris pointed out.

"He knew what I was like, yes. But I think he did not realize how little he would like being married to such a woman. I should be the way he wants. Anyone would tell you I am the one who is wrong, not he. But"—Genevieve shook her head, her eyes sad—"I cannot be sweet and kind. I am as I am. It is all I know how to be." She lifted her chin. "I am a Stafford."

"So is Alec," Damaris reminded her gently.

"Yes." Genevieve smiled faintly. "But an odd sort of Stafford, one with a heart. They do not come along very often. Well, 'tis pointless to talk about it. We are tied together now. And this is the way marriage is." She glanced at the other two. "Usually, anyway. I must stay here in London for a time, of course, or else it will seem to the *ton* that I am afraid to face them. But then perhaps I'll keep Grandmama company when she travels to Bath." Genevieve seemed to develop an interest again in the pearl button of her glove. "I beg your pardon for turning into such a watering pot. I should go now." She raised her head, forcing a smile. "Thank you for letting me speak to your servants."

"I shall tell you when we have the names from the agency," Thea promised, her forehead still creased in concern.

"Yes, thank you." Genevieve looked at Damaris. "You need not go. Stay and visit with Thea. I can walk home from here."

"No, I'll go with you," Damaris insisted. "Alec always frets if I don't lie down for a bit in the afternoon." She made a droll face. "And you know how biddable *I* am."

The two of them took their leave of Thea, who stood for a moment, staring thoughtfully out the window, before she strolled down the hallway to her husband's study. Gabriel was sitting hunched over the large, dark walnut desk, his elbows resting on the desk and his head in his hands as he studied the large flat book before him. He looked up at the sound of Thea's footsteps and smiled, pushing his chair back and smiling.

"Thea, my love, have you come to save me?" His cravat was askew, and his hair stuck out in several different directions.

Thea chuckled as she crossed the room to him and slipped her hand in his. "It looks as though Matthew must have been in here wrestling with you."

He tugged her down onto his lap, his arm curving in a familiar way around her back. "If only that were so. No, I have been wrestling with the accounts for the estate." His dark eyes lit up as he went on hopefully, "Perhaps you would like to take a look at them?"

"Thank you, I think not. Your estate manager has an utterly illegible hand." Thea snuggled into him, resting her head against his.

"I heard Damaris's voice," he said, idly wrapping one of Thea's springing cinnamon-colored curls around his finger.

"Yes, she and Genevieve came by. Genevieve and Myles have returned to town."

"So soon?" His brows lifted. "Surely they have not run aground already?"

"Mm." Thea sighed. "I fear they have entered some rocky waters, to further your analogy."

"I am a little surprised, actually. I would have said Myles could get along with any woman—though Lady Genevieve would certainly put him to the test."

Thea dug her elbow gently into his stomach. "Don't be unkind. I like Genevieve. And it always seemed to me that Myles had a certain fondness for her."

"You are probably right." He laid a soft kiss on the point of her shoulder. "You generally are."

"Genevieve was most unhappy. She started to cry."

"You're jesting, surely. Genevieve?"

Thea nodded. "I could tell she was unhappy, and I could see Damaris thought so, too, and then she began to cry and just poured out her heart to us."

"You have the oddest effect on the Staffords. First Rawdon and now Genevieve. I don't believe I've ever heard her express a word about her emotions."

"She is convinced Myles regrets marrying her." Thea lifted her head to look in Gabriel's eyes. "Do you think he rues his offer?"

"I don't know. I haven't seen him." He looked thoughtful. "But I cannot imagine Myles giving up this quickly. I've seen him spar, and he is deadly patient. On the other hand, Genevieve is a woman who could try any man's patience."

"I wonder if he really feels as she thinks. She believes he wishes she were sweeter. Someone more like he is."

"Doesn't sound like Myles. I would have said that he preferred a bit of spice. He and Genevieve have always fussed at each other, but, truthfully, he seemed to enjoy it more than not. After all, where is the fun in marrying yourself?"

"That is what I thought. But she seems quite hopeless. She was talking of traveling to Bath with her grandmother."

"Perhaps it would help if they spent some time apart."

Thea gave him a level look. "Do you think it would have improved our marriage if after one of our rows, we had gone to live in separate places?"

"No." He narrowed his eyes suspiciously. "Why do I have the feeling that you are about to suggest something I won't like?"

"I haven't the least notion," Thea said airily. "But it did occur to me that Myles might not know that Genevieve was . . . feeling so beset. It could be that he views it as nothing but a trifling spat. He is, well, rather more experienced than Genevieve in matters of the heart."

"You want me to talk to Myles," Gabriel said flatly. "Thea, my love, I don't think Myles would want me delving into his love life."

"You needn't be *obvious* about it. But I thought that since you are friends, you might run into one another at your club one day. And you might sit down to talk."

"And I might just steer the conversation in the direction of his marriage?"

"Exactly."

He heaved a sigh. "You know, it is not as if Genevieve regards me as a friend."

"But Myles is your friend, and you cannot wish him

to have an unhappy marriage." Thea smiled at him. "Besides, I am not asking you to do a favor for Genevieve." She leaned closer, gazing into his eyes. "I am asking you to do a favor for me."

"You are trying to manipulate me." His voice teased, but she could see the sudden leap of light in his dark eyes.

"Am I succeeding?" Thea grinned and leaned closer to press her lips lightly against his.

He let out a breathy little laugh. "It is possible I might be persuaded to bring up the matter with Myles."

"That would be wonderful." She brushed her lips against his cheek.

"But I am not going to pry into his personal life."

"Naturally." She kissed the tender skin beside his eye. "And of course"—she kissed his ear—"since it would take up some of your time, I might be persuaded to take a look at the accounts for you." She nipped his earlobe lightly.

"To hell with the accounts," he muttered and pulled her into him for a kiss.

Sixteen

Genevieve *went down to supper* in a cooler, calmer frame of mind. Embarrassing as it had been to break down as she had at Thea's, she had returned home feeling better. It had been somehow a comfort just to have Thea and Damaris sympathize with her, to know that they did not blame her for the awful tangle she had made of her life.

She met Myles coming down the hall from his study toward the dining room, and her heart skipped a little. Could Thea have been right? Could Myles's words have sprung from jealousy? She scanned his handsome face, now tight in a way she had never before seen on him, the usual merriment gone from his eyes. No. His was not the face of jealousy. He looked . . . stiff and uncomfortable. His expression was more that of someone facing an unpleasant duty.

A saving spurt of resentment surged up in her, piercing the blanket of misery. If Myles found being her husband so onerous, he shouldn't have offered for her. He had known her for years, after all; it was not as if she had concealed her true nature from him. She lifted her chin a little and laid her hand lightly on the arm he offered her, as she would have done with a stranger. She would be all right; she knew how to behave, how to get through difficult situations. She knew how to put on a polite face and save her tears for her pillow at night.

"I hope you had a pleasant day," Myles said formally as they entered the dining room and he seated her.

"Yes, thank you. And you?"

"I, um, went to White's."

"How nice." Genevieve nodded to Bouldin to begin serving.

A heavy silence fell on the table, broken only by the clink of silverware. At last Myles began again. "What did you do today?"

"Damaris and I called on Lady Morecombe."

"Thea?" His smile was surprised and more natural this time. "I am glad you like her."

"Yes. She is quite pleasant."

That topic seemingly exhausted, silence once more reigned. After a time, Myles said, "I spoke with Alec's runner last night."

"Indeed? Have you tasted the turbot? I believe your estate manager found a jewel in our chef."

"Blast it, Genevieve. You wanted to know about this."

"Did I?" Genevieve turned her icy blue gaze full on him, grateful for the flash of anger that stiffened her spine. "Then I must beg your pardon. It is quite your affair, of course. I am more concerned with finding another chair or two for the drawing room. It seems a mite bare as it is."

His cheeks reddened and she thought for a moment

that he was about to flare up as he had yesterday afternoon. She straightened, waiting—even perhaps anticipating—his outburst. But he pulled himself back under control. "Of course. If that is what you wish."

After that, nothing passed their lips but the most ordinary and stilted of comments.

By the time supper was over, Genevieve's stomach was in knots and a headache was forming behind her eyes. It was a huge relief to end the meal, but the even more awful prospect of attending the theater awaited her. She wished that she had taken Myles up on his suggestion that she stay at the Park instead of coming to London with him. Of course, now she realized that he had suggested it because he had been eager to be away from her—and that thought was another sharp little stab to her heart.

The theater was ablaze with lights when they arrived. Every eye in the crowded lobby seemed to be on her, but Genevieve did not look to either side, keeping her chin high. Much to her annoyance, her hand trembled a little on Myles's arm. He laid his other hand over it, and Genevieve glanced at him, surprised. He looked for a moment like the old Myles, his eyes alight in a blend of mischief, defiance, and warmth. She could not help but smile at him a little in gratitude.

He took her free hand and raised it to his lips.

"Myles, we are in public," she protested, her heart suddenly fluttering inside her chest.

"I know. That is exactly why."

"Oh. Of course." He was putting on a show for those

who watched them, playing the part of a devoted husband. Genevieve looked away, afraid of the disappointment he might read in her face. It turned her stomach to ice to see all the faces staring at her, then glancing hastily away. It seemed as if the buzz of voices grew louder.

They started toward Alec's box at an unhurried pace. Myles paused to greet a friend here and there, introducing his new wife with great pride. Genevieve could only marvel at his deft social touch. His calm imbued her with the same quality, and she greeted each person with a smile, her way eased by Myles's confidence and geniality.

"Sir Myles. And Lady Genevieve," Lady Hemphurst greeted them. She was one of the women who hung about Genevieve's grandmother, hoping to be counted as her confidante. But Genevieve could see the greedy interest in the woman's eyes, and she knew that the woman's greeting was prompted less by loyalty to Lady Rawdon and more by a desire to see the proud Lady Genevieve Stafford brought low by scandal. "What a surprise to run into you here in London. I would have thought you would find a more . . . entertaining way to spend the time." Lady Hemphurst tittered behind her fan, casting a sly look at Myles.

"My lady, I confess I could not stay away from you." Myles took Lady Hemphurst's hand and bowed charmingly over it, flooding the woman with compliments.

Lady Hemphurst bridled and giggled. "Sir Myles, you are such a flirt. It has sent all of London into a dither to learn that its most eligible bachelor has been snapped up. We were all agog to hear that Lady Genevieve had caught you."

"Lady Genevieve was the catch, I assure you, not I." Myles favored his wife with a tender look. "I only hurried to secure her hand before someone else could steal a march on me."

Lady Hemphurst beamed at Myles. "You have my sincerest congratulations, sir. Lady Genevieve's grandmother is a woman of the greatest consequence."

"Indeed she is," Myles agreed affably.

"I do hope you and Lady Genevieve will be able to attend my little party next week. Just a trifling thing, you understand, nothing to compare to the countess's balls at Stafford House, but I promise we shall have dancing. Everyone would love to see the two of you take the floor as husband and wife for the first time."

"Indeed. You can count on us," Myles said smoothly.

"Genevieve." Lady Rawdon strode toward them, Alec and Damaris trailing in her wake. "Lady Hemphurst. So good to see you. I hope you will excuse us; I have not had a chance for a good coze with my granddaughter yet."

The countess slipped her arm through Genevieve's, and with a gracious nod to the beaming Lady Hemphurst, she swept Genevieve away to their box, the others all falling in around them, effectively separating Genevieve from the rest of the crowd. "What a ghastly crush," the countess said as they went inside the box. "Here, Genevieve, come sit beside me in front. Let them get out all their staring straightaway. Alec, close the door at once before someone wants to join us."

Alec obeyed, then seated Damaris on Genevieve's other side as carefully as if his wife were made of glass. The three women cast a glance at each other and began to laugh.

"Yes, yes, I know," Alec said good-humoredly. "I am an old woman." He nodded toward Myles warningly. "Just you wait until it happens to you. Then you'll see."

Genevieve looked down at her gloved hands to hide the pang that struck her at his words. Myles would want an heir, of course, but how was she to bear him coming to her bed now, knowing what he thought of her? Cold. She had melted in his hands, but he found her cold. Her grandmother's conversation flowed around her, but Genevieve heard not a word.

"Genevieve, hold your head up." Her grandmother tapped Genevieve on the leg with her fan. "You cannot droop in front of everyone."

"Yes, Grandmama." Genevieve obediently lifted her head. "I'm sorry. I was lost in thought."

"What is playing tonight?" Damaris asked, drawing the countess's attention.

"Goodness, child, I don't know. What does it matter? Ah, there is Lady Somerdale; I knew the rumors of her demise were false. It would take more than a fall down the stairs to carry her off." The countess gave a regal nod of her head to the old lady in the box across from them. "Genevieve, smile at them. Lord Somerdale hasn't the slightest idea who you are, of course—or anyone else, for that matter."

The countess continued in this vein, nodding, now and then giving a smile to someone, other times staring down some upstart or other with her opera glasses, all the while chatting away as if she and Genevieve were carrying on a lively conversation. Genevieve did her best to keep her mind on what her grandmother was saying, but found it a relief when the curtain opened and she was able to sit back and pretend to watch the play.

When the first act ended, Genevieve and the others left the box. It would be better, as Lady Rawdon pointed out, to face the curious masses in the lobby, where they could walk away, rather than risk being trapped in their theater box by some gossip who hadn't the courtesy to leave. Alec and Myles set off to get refreshments for the ladies, and Genevieve strolled down the corridor with Damaris and her grandmother, schooling her face into a look of polite unconcern.

"I believe that you have made a far better match than your original one," her grandmother said, watching Myles as he walked away.

"That is faint praise," Genevieve retorted.

"True. Lord Dursbury was a disappointment. However, what I meant was that Sir Myles will make you a better husband than I *hoped* Dursbury would be. I used to think Sir Myles a bit of a peacock, but I am beginning to believe I underestimated him. I could not have orchestrated your entrance tonight any better myself."

"Yes, he is very adept." Genevieve saw that Myles had paused to speak to a group of people, one of whom was the attractive dark-haired woman her grandmother had identified as Myles's most recent mistress. The woman greeted Myles with a smile, and a sharp pain twisted in Genevieve's chest. She wasn't jealous, of course. It would be absurd to expect a man such as Myles not to have had lovers.

But, if she was honest, she knew that it galled her to think that Myles had once done the same things with this woman that he had done with her. Worse, she could not help but wonder if he had enjoyed it more with Mrs. Bedlington. She was, after all, a widow, accustomed to being with a man. She would not have been anxious or clumsy or uncertain or any of the things Genevieve had been. She would not have been *cold*.

Nor could she help but think how easy it would be for him to find some attractive, agreeable widow or courtesan who would shower him with affection, never saying a cross word. She jerked her gaze away, irritated with herself, and when she looked back, Myles had left the group and she could no longer see him.

Beside her, Damaris said in a low voice, "Lord Dursbury is here."

"What?" Genevieve stiffened. Of all the terrible luck! "Where?"

"Yes, I saw them," her grandmother said, her face revealing none of the irritation that sounded in her voice. "They are standing near the staircase."

Genevieve casually surveyed the room until her gaze fell upon her former fiancé, talking with one of his friends and Iona Halford, who was hanging on Dursbury's every word. "Why did I ever decide to marry that man?" Genevieve murmured, and Damaris chuckled.

"He was a most eligible bachelor, however lacking he turned out to be. He is still much sought after. I have heard that the little mouse has made great inroads in that regard."

"Miss Halford? She is welcome to him." Genevieve was faintly surprised by the indifference she felt at seeing Dursbury.

Alec returned and handed Damaris a glass, saying in a warning voice, "Have a care; you're about to receive a visitor." He took up his place beside his wife and stood stoically.

"What?" The countess glanced up. "Oh, blast! It's that dreadful woman."

Genevieve followed her gaze and saw Myles walking back toward them, Lady Dursbury clinging to his arm, her face turned up to him admiringly. Genevieve could not help but notice that not only was the neckline of Lady Dursbury's dress far lower than her own, she also had a great deal more to reveal. As she watched, Elora playfully rapped Myles's arm with her fan before opening it to flirt with him over the top of it.

"Countess. My dear." Myles disengaged from Elora as he handed Genevieve and her grandmother their glasses of ratafia.

"Countess!" Elora swept forward to take Lady Rawdon's hand between both of hers. Anyone who knew her grandmother would have recognized irritation in the twitch of her lips.

"Lady Dursbury," Lady Rawdon replied with a great deal less enthusiasm. "How very . . . unexpected to see you."

"Indeed. Had I known you would be here, of course, I would have been even more eager to attend . . . though I would not, of course, have encouraged Dursbury to come, as well. Lady Rawdon." She gave Damaris a cursory nod before turning to Genevieve. "I had no idea that we would see you here, Genevieve. I was so surprised when Sir Myles came up to me. I had assumed, of course, that you were still on your honeymoon. Is that not just like a man to cut one's honeymoon short so he can return to the city?"

"Lady Dursbury." Genevieve gave the woman a carefully measured smile.

"You must not be so formal with me!" Elora reached out and patted Genevieve's arm. "We know each other far too well for that. I hope you will not think that I hold any animosity toward you. Whatever anyone else said, I was certain that you did nothing wrong. I told my stepson that very night that it was bound to be just a misunderstanding." Elora shrugged. "But, of course, Dursbury is a very proud man. And people love to talk. That dreadful Lady Looksby simply would not keep silent about it. Well, it sold an enormous number of *The Onlooker*, and one cannot expect such people to have any honor, after all. Thank heavens you were not here so you did not have to read all the articles."

Genevieve murmured some response, though Elora clearly needed none to keep her conversation going. Elora turned to cast a coy look at Myles and laid her hand on his sleeve, saying, "Sir Myles is such a knight, in both truth and spirit, coming to your rescue in that way."

Genevieve's eyes followed Elora's hand, something hot and fierce sparking in her chest. The smile she turned on the other woman made Elora's eyes widen in surprise.

"It was Lady Genevieve who did me the honor," Myles said pleasantly, stepping into the awkward gap.

Elora let out a romantic sigh, her eyes shining up at Myles. "Such a jewel of a man, is he not?" She turned back to Genevieve. "There is no need to wish you happy, for I know that must be the result of your union. I am sure Sir Myles's mother must have been extremely eager to meet you. Such a shame that you were married too quickly for her to attend."

"Yes. Lady Julia is a lovely woman," Genevieve countered.

"I hope that you and I will remain friends, despite the . . . incident." Elora stepped closer to Genevieve, turning back to face Myles, positioning herself, Genevieve suspected, so that Elora's lush, dark beauty would contrast favorably to Genevieve's pale, angular appearance. "Indeed, I hope you will all come to my musicale next week. I would have sent you an invitation already had I realized you would rush back from your honeymoon so quickly."

"That is most kind of you, but I don't think we should," Genevieve began her refusal.

"No, you must not refuse me. I shall be devastated if you will not come. And if you are worried about any awkwardness, let me assure you that my stepson will not be there. He despises musicales. So like a man, isn't it?'

Genevieve did not believe in the woman's pretense of friendship any more than she wanted to accept it. It was ludicrous that Elora was talking to the woman her stepson had jilted only a month earlier, and Genevieve suspected that her sole reason in doing so was to seize an opportunity to flirt with Myles. She opened her mouth again to decline, but Elora waved her words away.

"No, no, do not answer me yet. Think about it first. I am sure Lady Rawdon will agree with me that our being seen together at my little gathering will do much to repair this silly puff of a scandal." Elora smiled at Genevieve and the countess, then looked up at Myles, her lips curving sensually. "Do tell me that you will accompany them, Sir Myles."

"I fear you are quite right that men do not like musicales," Genevieve put in lightly. "Myles is quite opposed to them."

Myles smiled, "Indeed, my wife is correct, as always. Ah, I believe the second act is about to start. We must take our leave."

He extended his arm to Genevieve, and she was quick

to take it. Elora, Genevieve was pleased to note, looked decidedly petulant as they walked away from her.

The remainder of the evening passed with excruciating slowness. Afterward Genevieve could not remember anything about the play they had seen, but she managed to get through the ordeal, telling herself that it was bound to be easier after this. Myles chatted with her as they left the theater, still playing the role of devoted husband. It was, she knew, the best way to handle the gossip, but she found it hard to bear having him smile at her as he had before they came to London, his eyes warm, his smile fond. Looking at him still made her heart leap in her chest, just as it had a few days ago, but now she knew that it was all pretense.

Once they were inside the carriage, Myles's conversation wound down, and as they drove closer and closer to their home, the atmosphere between them became more tense. When they reached the house, Genevieve expected him to take his leave of her, going to his study or even leaving the house again. But to her surprise, he remained with her, escorting her up the stairs.

Genevieve's insides danced with tension, very aware of Myles's presence at her elbow. She could not help but think of the way they had walked to their bedroom when they were at the manor house, the heat and anticipation building. Now she could only dread reaching her door with him beside her. It would be bad enough to enter her empty room; it would be even worse to have him come in with her, feeling as he did about her but thinking he must do his duty to produce an heir.

She opened her door and turned toward him, her hand on the doorknob and cool dismissal in her voice. She had learned this talent long ago to ward off unpleasant situations. "Thank you for accompanying me to the theater tonight. Hopefully the worst is over now." She started to go inside.

"Genevieve . . ." Myles said quickly. "Wait. I must apologize for yesterday."

"There is no need." Genevieve forced herself to face him unflinchingly, as if it did not affect her to look into his clear, golden-brown eyes, as if she had not traced the tiny scar on his chin as they lay together, sated and drowsy, or felt him surge into ecstasy inside her. She would not think of that. "You have every right to feel as you do. I see no reason to speak of it again. We are both—"

"No," he said firmly, wrapping his hand around her wrist. "I was angry. I said things I should not have said. I hurt you, and I—"

"Nonsense." She lifted her chin. "It takes a great deal more than words to hurt me." She jerked her arm from his grasp and slipped into the room, closing the door sharply behind her.

"Genevieve! Blast it, will you let me explain?"

She saw the doorknob turn and she whipped out her hand, turning the key in its lock with a click.

"Genevieve." She heard the astonishment in his voice, then the annoyance crowding it out. "Open this door. I want to talk to you."

"No. This is my room." She sounded childish, she knew, but she didn't care.

He let out a curse and slammed his hand hard against the door, then walked away. Genevieve turned and leaned back against the door, her heart pounding, tears pushing at her eyes. She heard Myles's door close furiously, and her eyes flew open, remembering the connecting door between their rooms. She started toward it, but long before she reached it, she saw its lock had no key, and she stopped, waiting, torn between dread and a strange anticipation.

The doorknob turned as she watched, and Myles opened the door. He stood in its frame, his eyes stormy. "There is no need to lock your door against me. I have no intention of coming in here. You are right; it is your room and yours alone. Pray enjoy your solitude."

He turned, slamming the door shut behind him.

Seventeen

$\mathscr{S}$ir Myles strode into White's, frowning. He had left the house early, as he had for the past two mornings, feeling as if he were sneaking out of his own home like a schoolboy escaping punishment, but he had not been able to face another breakfast sitting in lonely splendor at the opposite end of the long table from his wife, exchanging iced small talk. He had gone down to Cribb's to work out some of his frustration in sparring, but it had barely taken off the edge. He was beginning to wonder if anything would.

"Thorwood."

Myles turned and saw Lord Morecombe, sitting at a table by the fireplace, a newspaper in his hand. Myles started toward his friend.

"By the scowl on your face, I presume you've been reading *The Onlooker*," Gabriel said, folding up the newspaper.

"What? No." Myles dropped into the chair beside him. "That bloody Lady Looksby again? About Genevieve? What could she possibly have to say now?"

"'What notorious lady is already back from her honeymoon and frolicking in London?'" Gabriel began to read.

"'Frolicking in London'? What the devil is that supposed to mean?"

"I don't know, but it sounds faintly immoral, doesn't it?" Gabriel took up the story again. "'The recent bride is looking a bit wan—could it be because the groom's eye is wandering to a new prospect?'"

"What?" Myles half rose out of his chair, as if to launch himself at something, but sat back down and lowered his voice. "What the devil is she talking about?"

Gabriel regarded his friend over the top of the scandal sheet. "I would imagine you have more of an idea of that than I."

"You believe that—that tripe?" Myles grabbed the sheet and crushed it in his hand.

"Calm yourself, Myles, everyone is watching."

Myles glanced around and let go of the wadded-up paper, settling back into his chair.

"Well." Gabriel shrugged. "I had to wonder. Thea seemed to think that the, um, bloom was off the rose, so to speak."

"Thea thought—what does Thea know about this?" Myles frowned.

"I presume whatever Genevieve told her." Gabriel smoothed out the paper and refolded it, keeping his eyes on his hands. "They are apparently becoming thick as thieves."

"Genevieve went running to Thea? Bloody hell . . ."

"I take that to mean that Thea was right? You have become disenchanted with your bargain?"

"I—why is it that *I* have become disenchanted? Is all this my fault now?"

"My dear Myles, since I haven't the slightest notion what 'all this' is, I cannot say. However, as a man who is married, I can assure you that whatever happened, it will be your fault."

Myles groaned and sat forward, leaning his elbows on the table and propping his head on his hands.

"So who is the new light-o'-love toward which your eye is wandering?" Gabriel went on cheerfully.

Myles turned a baleful gaze at him. "There *is* no new woman. Trust me, Genevieve is more than I can deal with; I cannot imagine trying to juggle two of them."

"Mm. Well, I am sure it must be a terrible matter to realize you've married the wrong woman."

"I never said I'd married the wrong woman!" Myles sat up. "That's a hell of a thing to say."

"Oh. I beg your pardon. My mistake; I thought you were saying you were unhappy with Genevieve."

"No!"

"Ah." Gabriel's brows rose lazily. "I see. This is how you look when you are happy."

"Oh, God. Of course not." Myles raked his hand back through his hair. "Genevieve is the most stubborn, most maddening female that ever walked. We have not spoken the past three days except in a stilted, commonplace way. 'How is your dinner?' 'I believe I'll have that armchair upholstered.' 'It was quite warm today, wasn't it?'"

Gabriel smothered a laugh.

"Oh, yes, very funny for you. You are not the one who has to sit there with that freezing blue gaze on you every night, trying to pierce the armor of her meticulous courtesy, and knowing that you haven't a chance in hell of taking her to bed tonight."

"So that is where the problem lies." Gabriel nodded sagely. "I feared as much."

Myles glowered at him. "I don't know why you'd think that."

"Well, Genevieve has never been a *warm* sort of woman. If you'll remember, I warned you that you'd likely spend your nights alone."

"I remember," Myles said shortly. "You were as wrong then as you are now. Genevieve is . . ." He stopped short. "She is not cold."

"Indeed? My mistake."

"She is anything but cold."

"I see. So it must be her arrogance? Her contempt for others? That waspish tongue?"

"She is not arrogant. A little proud, perhaps, but that is scarcely the worst fault. Her standards are a bit high. But she holds herself to the strictest test. She does not carp or belittle or—oh, the devil! I've made a muddle of it." Myles's face was a study in misery. "Me! After all these years, the only time it is important, and I have been the most ham-handed, bumbling, misspoken fool."

"What did you do?"

"I'm not sure. Everything was fine; it was better than fine. We were happy. And then suddenly, it all began to fall to pieces. I suppose Thea told you about the note Langdon sent her, purporting to be from me. How could Genevieve have thought that I would have put her in a compromising position? That I would play fast and loose with her reputation? She acted as if I was foolish to be offended by that. And then . . ." Myles's face fell into aggrieved lines. "Then she got angry because I wanted to come back here and take care of that scoundrel."

"She was concerned for Langdon?" Gabriel's brows rose.

"No, of course not. She was just offended because—well, I'm not sure why. One would think she could trust me to not create a scandal. I wasn't going to challenge him to a duel, for pity's sake."

"So it was the scandal that bothered her."

"No. It was—well, she seemed furious with me because I wouldn't take her to meet Rawdon's runner. As if I would take a lady to some dockside tavern to meet a runner. I could scarce believe my ears. Genevieve! Who's never stepped a foot off the path of propriety. Who has rung a peal over my head more than once for paying too little attention to the rules. I told her it would be most improper."

"You didn't."

"Yes. I did. I asked her what the countess would think of it."

Gabriel let out a snort and dropped his head, his shoulders shaking.

"What are you doing?" Myles sent him a sour look. "Are you *laughing?*"

Finally Gabriel raised his head, mirth shining from his dark eyes. "Oh, Myles. I beg your pardon. I feel a great deal of sympathy for you. But I must say, for a man who has always known just what to say and how to say it, you made a dreadful shambles of it."

"Because I wanted to protect my wife? Would you not have done the same thing?"

"Of course I would. And Thea would have scalded my ears for it." He shrugged his shoulders. "When there was all that trouble concerning Matthew, I did my best to keep Thea out of it. But she was determined to be involved. She was not about to let anybody take Matthew away from her."

"Yes, but that was Thea. Genevieve's not at all like that."

Gabriel arched an eyebrow. "Not stubborn? Not independent? Not capable?"

"Well, no, of course she's all those, but she's different from Thea."

"Naturally. However, I'd guess if you thought about it, you might realize they are far more alike than you'd think. And I would also guess that Genevieve is no more biddable or self-effacing than my wife."

"Lord, no," Myles agreed, struck.

"I don't think you would like it if someone had harmed you and then getting your satisfaction from him was taken out of your hands."

"Of course not. But this is Genevieve; she doesn't step outside the boundaries."

"No? Then why did she go to the library when she thought you needed her?"

Myles stared at him for a long moment. "No. It's not like that. You make it sound as if she—no. She does not have feelings for me. She married me for the sake of her reputation. She and I are both aware of that; there is no need to sugarcoat it or pretend."

"Mm. No doubt that is why the two of you are so angry with each other." Gabriel paused. "That night, after you proposed to her, when you came to see Thea and me, you said you were worried that Genevieve might truly be the cold woman people supposed her. That she might not be capable of feeling. Is that what you have learned about her? Does she have no heart?"

"No, I am sure Genevieve has a heart. And one that is easily bruised, moreover. What I fear is that I cannot win it."

"You?" Gabriel looked at him skeptically. "The man who always knows what to say? And how to say it? Think, Myles. You may have made a mull of it now, but who could better find his way out of that?"

Myles looked at Gabriel for a long moment, then smiled suddenly, his eyes lighting up. "You are right. If there is one thing I can do, it is coax a woman into something she has no intention of doing." With a nod to Gabriel, Myles stood up and strode out of the club.

When Genevieve walked into the dining room for breakfast, she was brought up short by the sight of Sir Myles sitting at the table. She had become accustomed to his being gone in the mornings, and she had not braced herself to see him. He looked up and smiled at her in so much the same way as he had done in the past that she was momentarily startled into smiling back.

"My dear. How lovely you look." He stood up and pulled out the chair on his left, and for the first time Genevieve noticed that her place setting was not at the end where it was wont to be but at right angles to Myles's place at the head of the table. "I told Bouldin to put you here beside me. It seems most absurd for us to sit shouting down the table at one another when there is no one but us."

She could do or say nothing without looking most peculiar in front of the servants, so Genevieve took the chair he offered. Myles pushed her chair in, then turned away, his hand gliding softly across her shoulder. Her eyes flew to his, but he seemed not to notice, merely sitting down and taking a sip of his tea.

"What plans do you have in mind for today?" Myles asked pleasantly. "Perhaps shopping with your grandmother?"

"I—I'm not sure. I hadn't really thought." Flustered, Genevieve picked up the cup of tea the butler had poured for her. "I mean, I intended to call on Thea later."

"Again? The two of you are becoming quite friendly."

"Yes. I suppose so."

Her hand was resting on the table beside her teacup, and Myles reached out, lightly stroking his fingertip down the line of her fingers. "I was thinking of going to Tattersall's."

"Indeed?" Genevieve struggled to concentrate, intensely aware of the feel of his skin on hers. A low, steady heat began to build deep within her. She shifted away, pulling her hand away and putting it back in her lap.

What was the matter with Myles? He was acting as if everything were all right between them, as if their quarrel had never happened. He glanced over at her and smiled, his eyes darkening in that familiar way, and desire coiled inside her in response.

He continued to talk, straying from the subject of a new set of grays for the town carriage to the suggestion that she have the hassock in his study replaced to a discussion of which invitation they should accept for the following evening. Genevieve picked at her food as she struggled to answer. She found it difficult to concentrate on anything, for he kept reaching out to touch her arm or brush a curl back from her face or leaning over to offer a spoonful of his blueberries and cream.

"Do you ever think of our cottage?" he asked.

"What?" Genevieve glanced at him, her pulse picking up.

He smiled, his eyes a dark, rich gold, the color of honey, and a certain softness to his lips tugged at her viscerally. "I would like to go there when we return to the manor."

"You would?" She sounded like an idiot, she realized, but she was having difficulty pulling her thoughts back from the images his words had brought flooding back to her.

"Yes." He leaned forward, taking her wrist lightly in his hand, his fingertips stroking, slow and feather light, up and down the tender skin inside her arm. "I enjoyed it. The pool. The waterfall. Teaching you to swim."

Genevieve swallowed, unable to look away from his gaze, thinking of his hands on her skin. His lips. His firm, naked flesh against hers.

"You enjoyed it too, didn't you?" he asked.

"I, ah, of course. I mean, 'twas most . . . pleasant."

His grin was slow and meaningful. "I remember."

"I . . . uh . . ." Genevieve shoved her chair back suddenly and stood up. "The time." She gestured vaguely in the direction of the clock. "I should get going. I must get dressed to go to Thea's."

"I was unaware you were not dressed." He cast a look down the length of her and back up.

"No. Of course I am. But, um, I should change. Into something more appropriate. Pray excuse me." Genevieve turned and rushed out of the room, pelting up the stairs to the safety of her own bedchamber.

Once there, she paced about the room, wondering if she had gone mad or if Myles had. He had not touched her in days, had not looked at her in that scorching way. He had called her cold and selfish and—and—well, she could not at the moment remember what, but all of it had been bad. Clearly he had wanted as little to do with her as possible, avoiding her on every occasion he could, spending their brief time together in short, impersonal chatter. And now here he was acting just as he had at the cottage.

Genevieve stopped and took a deep breath, willing herself to regain some semblance of calm. Whatever had prompted Myles to act this way, she was certain it was merely a performance. His contempt for her the other afternoon had been clear. She must rid her mind of Myles's behavior and get on with her day, instead of jittering about up here like a madwoman. With a sigh, she sent for Penelope. After what she'd said to him, now she would have to change into a different dress.

Her maid gave her an odd look when Genevieve told her she had decided to change into one of her other day dresses, but Penelope helped Genevieve change into another of sprig muslin with sunny yellow ribbons for decoration.

"Just let me get a yellow ribbon for your hair," Penelope said, and left the room. Genevieve sat down at her vanity to dab on her perfume.

At a sound at the door, Genevieve turned. Myles stood in the doorway, leaning his shoulder against the frame. "You are an equally enchanting picture in that dress, as well." He strolled into the room, and Genevieve rose to face him. Grasping her gently by the shoulders, he bent and pressed his lips to the crook of her neck. "Mm. You smell delicious."

He straightened, his hands sliding down to her hips, and smiled down into her eyes. Genevieve's heart slammed in her chest. He was going to kiss her. Then this whole awful quarrel would be over. He would unbutton her dress and pull her into bed. Myles leaned closer, and her eyes fluttered closed. She felt him press his lips against her forehead.

"Have a pleasant day, my dear," he said.

Her eyes flew open as he straightened and walked away from her. Genevieve stared after him in astonishment. Then she finally realized what Myles had been playing at today. Her husband was seducing her.

When he accused her of coldness, she had tried to save face by telling him she did not need him in her bed. Now Myles intended to make her admit that she did. He wanted to show her how much she craved his touch, how easily he could control her. Hurt and fury flooded her. She would never have believed that Myles could be so unkind, that he could want to bring her low like this, to humiliate her. Coolly, calculatingly, he had set out to use her lust for him against her, to bring her to heel like an obedient little pet, no longer Genevieve, but only Myles's wife.

Well, let him try. Genevieve set her jaw. She might be embarrassingly eager for his touch, but she was stronger than her desire. Myles would soon find that he could not bend her to his will.

Damaris and Thea were waiting for Genevieve when she arrived at Thea's home, and Thea triumphantly handed her a list of the employees sent by the agency to the Morecombe ball.

"This one is blond, according to the housekeeper." Thea pointed to one of the names.

"Then it isn't she. I am certain she was a brunette."

"These two no one could remember, and the butler was quite definite that the woman named Joanie was graying, because he had asked them to send only young women and he was most put out with them."

"The girl who gave it to me was young." Genevieve pointed to the remaining names. "So it was one of these two."

"Are we going to track them down?" Damaris asked.

"Of course." Thea's gray eyes were sparkling. "I am sure that our coachman would dig in his heels at driving us to such an address, but we shall go for a stroll and catch a hack a couple of streets over."

"I feel sure we should not go to either of these areas," Genevieve hedged, frowning. "Alec will flay me alive if anything happens to you, Damaris."

"But how is he to know?" Damaris grinned. "I certainly won't tell him. I am tired of being treated as if I'm made of glass."

"He is afraid of losing you."

"I know. And I don't argue with him . . . much. But I should really hate to pass up an adventure."

"What can happen?" Thea pointed out. "There are three of us, after all, and I shall take my parasol." She lifted her parasol from the stand and brandished it like a sword.

"You are right." Genevieve laughed, feeling lighter and more carefree than she had since she returned to London. "Let's go find her."

The three women strolled out of the house and down the street, and as soon as they turned the corner, Damaris hailed the first hackney that approached. The first address yielded no information, as no one was home when they knocked, and, hopes somewhat dimmed, they set out for the second one. As they drove deeper into the East End, the houses became more ramshackle, and the lane they sought turned out to be little more than a walkway. The carriage rolled to a stop, and the women got out, looking dubiously down the lane.

"'Ere now," the driver said, jumping down and holding out his hand. "Yer not goin' 'fore I get me coin."

"Very well, but you wait for us," Thea told him firmly, but she dug into her reticule and handed the man the fare, with a tip above that to encourage him to do as she bid.

As there were no house numbers, it took some time and a few inquiries to determine the right building. They climbed two flights of narrow stairs and knocked at the door. A young woman answered and stared at them in amazement.

"You served at a party at Lord Morecombe's house a few weeks ago." Genevieve had recognized the girl as soon as she saw her. She checked the paper in her hand. "Your name is Hattie Withers?"

"I did." The girl eyed Genevieve warily.

"You gave me a note."

"I didn't." The girl stepped back, but Genevieve followed her, bracing herself against the door so the girl could not close it on them.

"Yes, I think you did."

"I don't know nothin'," the girl said in a surly voice.

"We mean you no harm," Thea told her, but the girl, her eyes on Genevieve's face, did not seem reassured.

"Who gave you the note? That is all I want to know. I shall be happy to pa—" Before Genevieve finished her sentence, the girl lunged forward, shoved Genevieve roughly aside, and darted out the door.

Genevieve tore out after her, with the other two women on her heels. When Genevieve reached the street, she could see Hattie turning the corner at the far end of the lane. She ran after her, not looking back to see if her friends followed. She could hear them running behind her, though she was outstripping them. Turning onto the street the girl had taken, she slowed down, looking around her. She saw a flash of blue skirt as the girl ducked into another lane, and Genevieve took off again. She cast a look back toward her friends before she turned up the narrow street after the maid. Thea and Damaris were doggedly following her.

It occurred to her that this was not perhaps the best thing for Damaris. Genevieve should stop. With a sigh, she came to a halt as Hattie swung left onto the street ahead, and Genevieve walked back to meet her friends.

"Did she get away?" Thea asked.

"Yes." Genevieve looked at her sister-in-law. "Are you all right? I think maybe you shouldn't be running."

"I'm fine." Damaris grimaced. "Don't worry about me."

"I fear we have lost her, anyway." The three of them started back the way they had come.

"Clearly she must know something that would get her in trouble," Genevieve mused. "Or else she wouldn't have run."

"She could have just been frightened by us appearing at her door. She probably thought she would get blamed for something," Damaris pointed out. "Any girl in her position would be anxious, I think."

"I suppose so," Thea agreed.

"But I told her I would pay her," Genevieve protested. "It seems to me that she must have been very frightened to have run from that offer."

"She might not have believed you," Damaris said. "Oh, blast!" She stared down the street ahead of them.

"What?" The others followed her gaze.

"The hackney!" Thea exclaimed. "He's gone."

They hurried to the end of the narrow lane. The hackney was nowhere in sight. Looking around her, Genevieve knew a touch of anxiety. The houses loomed on either side of the narrow street, dark and unkempt. It was not a good place for three women in their finery to be walking. Still, there was nothing for it but to go forward.

"This is the direction we came from," Genevieve said. "If we go back, we're bound to come upon a larger street where we can find another hackney."

They started out, ignoring the looks that were sent their way, though Genevieve noticed that Thea took a firm grip on the handle of her furled parasol. Genevieve wished she had something more substantial than a reticule in her own hand. Behind them, she heard a call and a laugh, but she did not look around. A larger street lay ahead, and there would be stores and people there, and, hopefully, a vehicle they could hire.

But as they turned onto the street, the first thing Genevieve saw was Hattie Withers walking quickly toward them, glancing back over her shoulder. Genevieve started forward, and at that moment the other woman glanced up and saw her. An almost comical expression of dismay came over her features, and she whirled around, taking off in the opposite direction. Genevieve gave chase.

Ahead of them the street ran at an angle into another one, spreading out into a market. Stalls full of flowers and fruits and vegetables lined the street on either side. A girl with a pushcart of apples stood gaping at the women running toward her. Hattie grabbed her cart and yanked it around, tilting it over and sending the apples rolling into Genevieve's path. Genevieve dodged around them, felt something catch at her skirt, and heard it rip. She paid no attention, but ran forward.

Hattie had vanished, but Genevieve caught a flash of something out of the corner of her eye and turned to see the woman disappearing down a narrow alleyway. She changed her course sharply and caught the edge of one of the stalls. Flailing for balance, she grabbed one post of the stall, and it broke in her hand. The shade above the stall fell, and the woman beside it shrieked and grabbed at Genevieve.

"'Ere! Wot do you think you're doin'?" Genevieve's sleeve tore off in her hand.

As Genevieve lurched away, Thea tried to make the turn as well and skidded, falling into Genevieve and sending her sprawling forward. She crashed into the stall-keeper, and the woman reeled backward, knocking the stand—nothing but a small table stacked with fruits—into the stand beside it. All of them went down, women, stands, baskets, fruits, and awning, ending up in a tangled heap.

Eighteen

By the time Genevieve and Thea picked themselves up from the ground, with the help of Damaris, who, luckily, had not fallen, they were surrounded by the vendors of the produce stalls. The women had offered the angry group all the coins in their reticules, but the sellers had declared it not enough. One stocky man in particular, regarding them with angry suspicion, declared that they were nothing but light-skirts out on a lark.

"No lady would be actin' this way, chasin' about, knockin' over decent folks' stands," he told Genevieve darkly.

Genevieve had a strong desire to slap him, but she held herself in check, saying, "I am Lady Thorwood, and I will pay you the rest of it as soon as I return home."

The man laughed. "And I'm the Prince of Wales, I am."

"You have my word," Genevieve said in her frostiest tones and lifted her chin, gazing contemptuously down her nose at him.

Her manner seemed to convince the man to some extent, for he scowled and said, "Aye, well, we'll see about that. " He clamped his hand around Genevieve's arm. "Let's go there right now."

Though only three stalls had been wrecked, all of the sellers apparently found it necessary to accompany them. They closed down their stands and carts and marched along behind the women as they walked back home. Genevieve thought it entirely humiliating, especially given her thoroughly disheveled appearance, and she regretted ever setting out on this mad chase. Still, she could not deny that it had been exhilarating while it lasted.

The Morecombe house lay farther from them, and bringing Damaris to her own door like this was out of the question, so Genevieve took the ragtag band to Myles's home. When she stopped in front of the house, the cart-keeper looked over at Genevieve suspiciously. "This is your 'ouse?"

"Of course it is," Genevieve snapped, pushing back a strand of hair that had come loose and kept falling into her face. Her hat had come off and wound up under a melon, beyond repair. "I did not walk here with you for the amusement of it."

At the man's heavy knock on the front door, the footman opened it and goggled at the sight of them.

"This swell mort says she lives 'ere," the man beside Genevieve growled. The servant seemed to be able to do no more than stare at them, mouth open.

"Oh, botheration!" Genevieve exclaimed. "Where is my husband?"

"I—ah—in the study, ma'am," the footman managed

to stammer out and scurried down the hallway in front of them.

Genevieve started after him, trying to pull her arm from her captor's grasp, but he would have none of it. They straggled down the corridor behind the footman, the vendors gazing all around them with awe.

"Lady Thorwood, sir, and, uh, her companions," the footman announced in the door of the study, and quickly stepped back to allow Genevieve into the room.

Myles was sitting at his desk, reading a letter, and he looked up in puzzlement at the servant's announcement. His eyebrows shot up as Genevieve stepped into the room, all the others crowding in behind her.

"My dear, what an unexpected surprise." Myles rose from his seat. His eyes went to the man's hand wrapped around Genevieve's arm, and his expression turned to ice. "If you wish to retain use of your hand, I would suggest you release my wife's arm."

The man's hand dropped. "Sorry, sir. I had no way of knowin'. I wouldn't 'ave thought she was any gentleman's missus."

"Mm." Myles's gaze, brimming with laughter, ran down Genevieve. "One would not, I suppose."

Genevieve was acutely aware of her appearance. She was carrying her crushed hat. Her skirt had a tear, as well as a rather large red stain where she had fallen on a to-mato. One of the cap sleeves of the dimity frock had been torn entirely off. Her hair was straggling down around her face, and she was fairly certain that her cheek was smudged with dirt. She looked, in short, disreputable, and she could hardly blame the street vendor for taking her for some sort of low person.

The cart-keeper began to explain what had happened and wrongs done him, and Genevieve and her friends hotly protested. Myles, struggling not to laugh, quieted them all with a wave of his hand.

"No, no," he said, biting his lip, "there is no need to explain. I am sure we can all agree that some sort of peculiar misunderstanding has occurred here." Myles opened the top drawer of his desk and pulled out a small leather bag of coins. "I assume there was some damage done to, um, your property?"

It took only a few minutes of Myles's charm, as well as a goodly portion of the coins, to send all the stall-keepers on their way. He turned to Thea and Damaris with great courtesy. "Ladies? Would you care to stay for tea?"

Thea chuckled. "No, I should get home; Gabriel and I always try to have tea with Matthew." She took off her spectacles, which had become smeared with dust, and began to clean them with her handkerchief.

"I am terribly sorry," Genevieve told her friends, her body rigid with humiliation. "I should not have pulled the two of you into my misadventure."

"Nonsense. Life has been rather dull lately," Thea said brightly. "Though Gabriel will doubtless be sorry he missed out on the excitement."

"I know Alec will not take it that well." Genevieve turned to Damaris. "I am sure he will want my head for this."

"He will be fine." Damaris waved the matter away. Her lips curved up into a smile. "He's very sweet when he fusses. It may make him come down in favor of our returning to Cleyre instead of staying here for a London doctor, which will suit me just fine. I rather miss the country."

Myles sent a footman to fetch a hackney for the ladies and handed them up into it with care and courtesy. Genevieve gave a last wave to her friends and walked back to the study, her stomach knotting. She turned as Myles stepped inside and closed the door behind them, bracing herself for his anger. Instead, he burst into laughter.

"You're laughing?" Genevieve asked. "Your wife has been running through the streets and knocking over vegetable carts and all you do is laugh?"

"I'm sorry." He did his best to rein in his amusement. "It was just—I had to keep it all inside when that chap was telling me how you'd—you'd leapt over the curbing and—and—" He dissolved into laughter again.

"I might have known. I should not be surprised that you find your wife being dragged home like a common thief amusing."

"I beg your pardon." He managed to still his laughter and pull his face into a more serious expression. "I am sure I am utterly frivolous. Would it be better if I scowled?" He demonstrated. "Should I play the stern husband?" He strolled toward her, his eyes suddenly bright and intent. He did not stop until he was only a few inches from her. "I should scold you, no doubt." He laid his forefinger on her shoulder and traced it down over her shoulder and onto her bare arm.

The touch of his skin upon hers made her shiver. Genevieve knew she should toss back a retort, but she found herself suddenly wordless. His eyes—so bright with promise, so knowing—held her still, made her nerves start to jangle.

"I should probably tell you how naughty you have been." His eyes followed the path of his finger as it came back to her shoulder and drifted down, skimming over her breast. "What sort of punishment do you think would be appropriate?" He bent and brushed his lips against her ear. "What would change you into an obedient wife?" He caught her earlobe between his teeth, worrying it gently. "What, I wonder, would turn you soft and willing?"

He nuzzled her neck, his hand coming up to cup her breast. Genevieve felt the rush of heat in him as his lips moved over her skin, velvet and slow. The now-familiar ache blossomed between her legs, swelling and throbbing. It galled her that she should want him this much, that the merest touch of his hand or mouth could send lust flooding through her. He knew how she would react; he enjoyed seeing her respond to him, while he was obviously immune to her.

Genevieve stiffened and stepped back from him. "I must change into something more appropriate. Pray excuse me."

His eyes flared with heat. "I could help you with that. As you know, I make an excellent ladies' maid."

His words brought back to her their time in the cottage by the waterfall, when Myles would button up the back of her dress—and half the time let the frock tumble to the floor as his hands strayed to her body instead. The memory choked her, and Genevieve could not answer. She could only turn and flee the room.

"Genevieve!" Startled, Genevieve glanced up to see her grandmother striding into the drawing room, her blue eyes blazing, Bouldin trailing along ineffectually after her. Waiting only until the butler had left the room, the countess shook the rolled-up paper in her hand at Genevieve. "Whatever in the world possessed you?"

"Grandmother?" Genevieve looked at her blankly. "What are you talking about?"

"Don't play the innocent with me, my girl. I've known you since you first drew breath. You think I didn't notice that little row between my grandson and his wife two days ago? I knew they were hiding something from me. And now it's all over the scandal sheets." The countess slapped the newspaper down on the table beside Genevieve's chair.

"Oh, dear." Wrapped in her own private misery the past few days, Genevieve had almost forgotten the chase after the maid. She looked down at the newssheet, carefully folded back to show the Lady Looksby column.

"Yes, I should say, 'Oh, dear.'" Her grandmother began to recite Lady Looksby's gossip, "'What bride was seen dashing through the streets of the East End on Monday?

It seems Sir M. cannot control his new wife's headstrong behavior.' Whom do you suppose she is talking about?" Lady Rawdon finished acidly.

"I can't imagine how she could know!" Genevieve shot back.

"How do these people know anything?" The countess threw up her hands. "They pay for information. Servants, cartmen, those hawking their wares on the streets. They're all happy to make a few pennies for a juicy bit of information like this. How could you, Genevieve? Have you no sense?"

"I didn't set out to go running through the streets," Genevieve said defensively. "I just went to talk to her, and she ran from us."

"You did not have to give chase, did you? Who was she, anyway? Who could you possibly visit in the East End?"

"It was a maid who served at Lady Morecombe's party." Her grandmother stared. "Why on earth would you want to talk to her?"

"Because of the note from Mr. Langdon. I told you about it, Grandmama."

"Yes, I know, but what did you hope to achieve by talking to this girl? The scandal is old news."

"You say that, but *The Onlooker* began to snipe at me as soon as we returned—and all I did was go to the theater with my family!"

"Yes, but without fuel, it would be short-lived. All you had to do was be circumspect. Why can you not let it die?"

"It matters to me. I want to find out if Langdon did indeed give me the note. Perhaps she knows more about him, such as where he is."

"You can't possibly mean to find him! Genevieve!"

"Yes, I do mean that. I want to know for sure that it was he. I want to know why he did it."

"I think it's quite obvious why he did it," Lady Rawdon retorted scathingly. "Men like him have only one thing on their mind, and it is not anything a lady would care to hear. You are behaving most unlike yourself, Genevieve. A Stafford should set an example. And given the present situation, you must be especially careful."

"I've done nothing wrong. It's scarcely a crime to run down a street. Why should I have to be so careful all the time? None of those things are important; none of them change who I am."

"Genevieve!" Her grandmother stared at her, shocked. "You cannot be serious. Really, I am beginning to think Damaris and Lady Morecombe are not good influences on you. You should spend less time with them. In fact, it might be best if you returned to the Thorwood estate for a while. You should rest; I can see that you are not feeling yourself."

"I am feeling very much myself!" Genevieve's eyes flashed. "In fact, I am feeling more myself than I ever have."

"Dear, that's absurd."

"I don't care. I can be absurd if I want to."

Her grandmother looked at her for a long moment.

"Well. I am not sure how I am to answer that." She stood up. "I shall take my leave of you."

"Oh, Grandmama, I am sorry." Genevieve rose, too, and went to the older woman, taking her hand. "I should not be short with you. I am on edge. Sometimes it all seems so . . . so constricting."

"All what, Genevieve?"

"I don't know. The parties and calls, the way everyone stares and whispers." She could hardly tell her grandmother the real reason her nerves were so frazzled these days was because her husband seemed intent on teasing and tempting her until she was driven mad by lust. "Lady Hemphurst's ball is tonight, and we are bound to see Lady Dursbury there. I wish I had not agreed to go."

"She *is* dreadful." Lady Rawdon was happy to seize on a mutual dislike. "But one must learn to ignore her sort."

"She spent the entire intermission the other night flirting with Myles."

"Pffft!" The countess waved away this trifling concern. "Myles has far better taste than to take up with Lady Dursbury."

"Yes, I know." Genevieve did not point out that the countess's statement was not exactly reassuring, leaving open the possibility that Myles could be lured by someone else.

"Perhaps you should stay home this evening."

Genevieve considered spending the whole evening alone with Myles, engaged in their contest of wills, and she sighed. "No, I must go. Otherwise I will seem to be hiding because of that tidbit in that scandal sheet." She shook her head and forced herself to smile brightly. "But enough of such nonsense. Sit down and take tea with me. It seems an age since you and I have had a chance to talk."

Genevieve was seated in front of her dressing table, Penelope putting the finishing touches to her hair, when she heard Myles's steps upon the stairs. She turned toward the door, unconsciously tightening the sash of her dressing gown. But, no, that would look as if she were waiting for him, she realized, so she turned back to her mirror. Myles stopped in the doorway, and Genevieve turned to him with a practiced casualness. She hoped her expression hid her dancing nerves. Once she had known exactly how to act in every situation; nowadays it seemed to her that she was always uncertain, especially with Myles.

He smiled and came into the room. Penelope bobbed a curtsy and left—though not, Genevieve noticed, without a curious glance back. Her maid knew, of course, of the cold chasm between Genevieve and her husband. One could not keep such things from one's servants.

Penelope was well aware that when she came into Genevieve's bedroom each morning, Genevieve lay in her bed alone. Penelope would have heard the gossip in the servants' dining room of the awkward conversations between the Thorwoods each night at supper or the way Myles had for a time rushed out of the house each morning to avoid breakfasting with his wife. Did they talk, too, of the more recent days, when Myles had taken up flirting and teasing her?

Had they seen the shockingly intimate manner in which he sometimes stroked her arm or shoulder or the way he would look at her while they talked, his gaze a heated caress?

"You look lovely tonight, my dear," Myles said now, strolling over to stand behind her. Putting his hand on her shoulder, he met her eyes in the mirror. His mouth softened and his eyes darkened as he moved his hand across her shoulder and slid it ever so slowly down, edging under the lapel of her dressing gown. His skin was hot against hers, awakening each nerve as he glided over her. He held her gaze in the mirror as his fingertips curved over the soft top of her breast, and he smiled faintly, as if he knew how she was suddenly damp and throbbing, swelling in a fevered hunger for his touch.

Genevieve popped to her feet, turning away from him. "I can hardly look anything. I haven't even dressed yet."

His chuckle was low and breathy. "I noticed."

Genevieve's cheeks colored. "Oh, Myles, do go away. I have to get ready for the party."

"Whatever you say, my dear." His eyes danced as he bent to plant a soft kiss on her forehead. "I must get ready as well."

He brushed another kiss on her lips. Suddenly his mouth returned, seeking and hot, his hands digging into her shoulders. Genevieve melted into him, letting the sweet taste of his lips overtake her, pulling her into that honeyed, shadowy world where nothing existed but him and the thrum of desire. He kissed her until she was trembling, desire pulsing deep inside her.

Myles lifted his head, gazing down into her face, his eyes dark and hungry. For an instant, they hung there, poised on the razor's edge of desire. Then he tore his gaze away and stepped back and said hoarsely, "I had best go change or we shall be late."

He strode out of the room, and Genevieve sank back onto her chair, her knees too weak for her to stand.

The Hemphursts' home was ablaze with lights as Genevieve and Myles stepped down from their carriage. Genevieve's breath hitched a little as they started forward. It had never been easy for her to walk into a room full of people, but it had lately become an ordeal. Her marriage might not be smooth, but she was grateful to have Myles by her side, as he had been each time they went out. It was easier to brave the curious stares with his arm firm beneath her hand.

She was not surprised to find the whispers and stares more plentiful tonight. No doubt most of them had read about her scandalous run through the streets of the city the other day, and even if they had not, someone who had read it would have spread the word to them. It was too delicious a bit of gossip to pass up.

Genevieve kept her head high as they greeted their hostess, then made their way across the room, pausing now and then to chat so they would not appear to be doing exactly what they were: escaping to the dance floor. They moved out onto the floor as the strains of a waltz started, and Genevieve relaxed in the familiar circle of

Myles's arms. She smiled, recalling exactly why she had always loved to dance with him. The strain between them vanished as they swept around the room, and when the dance ended, Genevieve scarcely noticed the whispers that followed them as they made their way through the crowd to where Genevieve's grandmother and Damaris sat, Alec standing like a watchdog beside his wife.

Damaris popped up to greet them warmly, though Alec frowned pointedly at Genevieve.

"Damaris. Alec." Genevieve nodded hello and launched into her rehearsed speech. "I apologize for my thoughtless behavior the other day. I should have thought before I pulled Damaris into such a venture."

Damaris immediately began to protest, and even Alec relaxed into a smile. "No doubt, but if I know my wife, it was more likely she who pulled you into the venture, not the other way around."

"Actually, I think we should put all the blame on Thea, as she is not here to contradict us," Damaris said, grinning.

"You are all three very naughty young women," their grandmother said, settling the matter. "But there is no irreparable harm. Now sit down, Genevieve, I am tired of craning my neck to speak to you."

Genevieve obediently sat beside her grandmother as Alec took his wife out onto the dance floor. "Oh, drat!" Lady Rawdon muttered. "Here she is again. I vow, she must have been watching for you."

Genevieve looked up and saw Lady Dursbury bearing

down upon them, smiling, towing an obviously reluctant Miss Halford with her.

"I cannot understand that woman's obsession with you. I never saw any evidence of her peculiar affection for you when you were engaged to her stepson."

"Her obsession is on another, I suspect," Genevieve said caustically as Elora smiled dazzlingly at Myles.

"That neckline is perilously low," the countess went on. "Though I have to admit the gold is lovely with her hair."

"Yes," Genevieve agreed. Elora's full breasts swelled above her gown, quivering with every step she took, drawing the eye of every man she passed. "She has excellent taste."

In both clothes and men.

Elora swooped up, bending down to greet the seated countess. Genevieve noted cynically that she stayed in that position far longer than necessary, allowing Myles an excellent view down the front of her dress. Genevieve could not bring herself to look over to see whether he was taking advantage of the pose.

"Dear Countess," Elora was effusing. "You remember my ward and friend, Miss Halford, don't you? Say hello to the countess, Iona."

The young woman made a creditable curtsy to Genevieve's grandmother. With her mouse-brown hair and gray eyes, she was not the sort to ever draw the eye, but next to Elora's colorful good looks, she faded almost into invisibility. Genevieve felt a pang of pity for the girl until Iona sent Genevieve a distinctly hostile glance.

"And Lady Genevieve." Elora sat down on the other side of Genevieve, edging herself into the space between Genevieve and Myles so that he had to move over to allow her to sit. "Everyone is making such a to-do over that article in *The Onlooker*. As if that scandal sheet were of any importance. When Lady Hoddington told me it said you had been running through the streets, I told her straight out that it was utter nonsense. Didn't I, Iona?"

"Yes, ma'am," Iona responded coolly.

"I could not persuade her, of course." Elora waved her hand as if casting that memory aside. "People will believe what they want to. So many seem to love to gloat over one's mistakes. But it will pass, you needn't worry, Genevieve."

"I am not worried," Genevieve replied calmly.

"I hope you were not bothered by the article, Sir Myles." Elora looked up coquettishly at him.

"I pay no attention to such things," Myles said. "I have complete confidence in my wife's character."

"How charming!" Elora clasped her hands together at her bosom, a movement that shoved her breasts together and up so that they seemed in imminent danger of spilling out. "That is so like you, sir. I vow, Genevieve, you are the envy of every lady in London."

"No doubt," Genevieve responded drily.

Elora went on, "I was so pleased when I saw you. I had been afraid you would let the rumors keep you away."

"Why would I? Like my husband, I pay no attention to the scandal sheets."

"You are so advanced in your thinking," Elora marveled. "I fear most ladies do not possess your . . . courage."

"Is it cowardice to have a care for one's good name?" Iona asked.

"Iona, dear, be a love and fetch my wrap, would you?" Elora watched her companion leave, then turned back to Genevieve with a smile. "You must not mind Iona, dear. I fear the poor thing always had a bit of a *tendre* for Lord Dursbury, and of course her hopes were dashed when he proposed to you. Oh, dear." Elora made a little shocked face, pressing her hand to her lips. "I should not speak of such things in front of Sir Myles." She cast a sly glance up at Myles.

When she got no response from that quarter, Lady Dursbury went on without missing a beat. She launched into how excellent the orchestra played and how much she loved to dance, sighing over Sir Myles's skill as a dance partner and giving other such broad hints until at last Myles succumbed to the pressure and asked Elora to dance.

"She is even worse than I remember," Genevieve's grandmother said. "I would have thought that was impossible."

"I suppose she felt she had to be more polite because I was engaged to her stepson," Genevieve said, watching as Myles guided the attractive woman around the floor. His face was attentive, his smile charming, and Genevieve could not help but wonder if he looked any different when he danced with her. Did every woman who danced with him feel he gave her his undivided attention? Did his eyes light with warmth and laughter, his smile quirk up at whatever amusing thing she said? Worse, did he enjoy holding Elora in his arms more than he enjoyed Genevieve?

A cold fist clutched her heart. She tried to look at them objectively. They made a lovely couple, Genevieve had to admit. And Elora would be a soft, desirable armful—all curves and admiring smiles. Myles had never seemed particularly interested in the woman, but Genevieve knew she was no expert in such matters. She had, after all, believed that Myles had desired her as much as she desired him, that he, too, had been swept away when they made love.

But then it turned out that he found her cold, selfish, and proud.

Genevieve turned to talk to her grandmother, ignoring the dancers. But when the music stopped, she could not keep from sneaking a glance back at the floor. Bright pain shot through her as she watched Myles walking with Lady Dursbury in the opposite direction.

"Thank goodness," her grandmother said in heartfelt relief. "Sir Myles has the good sense to escort that woman to some other spot than here. I think I would have had to leave if he brought her back to us."

Perhaps that really was what he was doing—making sure that Elora would not again intrude on Genevieve and her grandmother. Still, Genevieve could not help but wonder if his real reason had simply been that he preferred the other woman's company to his wife's. And though she did her best not to acknowledge it, relief rippled through her a few moments later when she saw Myles strolling back toward her.

At the beginning of the next waltz, he took her out on the floor again. Genevieve protested, "Really, Myles, this isn't necessary. We have already waltzed."

"It may surprise you to learn that I don't dance with you out of necessity," he retorted, taking her into his arms. "And I can waltz with you as often as I like now that I am your husband." He looked down at her quizzically. "Do you not enjoy it?"

"I always enjoy dancing."

"Ah, but do you enjoy dancing with me?"

"Are you fishing for compliments? You know you are an excellent dancer."

"The question was not how well I danced, but whether you liked to dance with me."

"Don't be absurd. Of course I do."

"Good." His hand tightened on her waist, pulling her a little closer. "Because I like to dance with you." He gazed down into her eyes warmly and intently. "I like holding you in my arms, warm and soft and yielding. Looking at you, so elegant and beautiful, knowing every man in the room envies me."

"Really, Myles . . ." She glanced around, as if someone in the whirling crowd might overhear his words.

"I remember how it feels to remove your dress," he went on, ignoring her protest. "Revealing you inch by inch. How sweet it is to untie your ribbons and peel off your stockings, anticipating the moment when you are finally naked before me."

"Myles!" Treacherous longing stirred in her. She was suddenly breathless and far warmer than she should be, and she suspected that her face was flaming. "This is hardly appropriate conversation for the dance floor."

"I know." He grinned. "I like that, as well. And I love knowing exactly how you look beneath that dress. The white perfection of your skin, the dark rose of your nipples. Those long, luscious legs and the treasure that waits for me between them." The heat in his eyes made her tremble. "I think about the way you close your eyes in pleasure when I thrust into you, the little moan that you cannot quite hold back. The pink flush that blooms on your chest when you reach your peak."

If her face had not been red before, she was certain it was now, though she was not entirely sure whether it was from embarrassment or arousal. A sweet ache was deep within her, a hunger brought to pulsing life by his words.

He leaned closer, murmuring, "And I also enjoying watching the blush that comes to your cheeks when I talk of making love to you."

No adequate response came to Genevieve's mind. The only thought she had, it seemed, was a lustful desire to pull him into some secluded room and wrap herself around him. How could he talk this way? Look at her as if he hungered for her, when just the other afternoon he had stormed at her for her cold nature? She knew she could not trust his words. He was toying with her, using her desire to bring her to heel. The awful thing was, she was afraid he might succeed.

They did not stay long after that, and as they rode home, Genevieve struggled to bring her wayward nerves back under control, a difficult task with Myles's eyes on her the whole trip. She could not read his expression in the dim light of the hackney, but it wasn't difficult to guess that he was thinking the same sort of thoughts he had expressed during the dance. She had an ache within her that could be eased only by him. Lowering as it was to admit, she felt an almost desperate yearning for his touch. His kiss. His powerful body surging within her.

He took her hand to help her down from the carriage, and he kept it, lacing his fingers through hers as they walked up the steps into the house. When the footman opened the door, he let go of her hand, but only to slide his arm about her waist. It was inappropriate in front of the servants, but Genevieve made no protest. His hand was light against her side, drifting slowly upward as they climbed the stairs, until his fingers were almost touching the underside of her breast.

Myles was talking about something, but she had no idea what. All she could think of was his hand hovering near her breast and whether he would move that last bit of space to touch her. When they reached her room, he walked in after her, and Genevieve's heart hammered harder in her chest. It took her a moment to realize that her maid was not there waiting for her. She started toward the bellpull, but Myles took her wrist.

"Never mind. I told Penelope not to wait up. I shall be your maid tonight."

She should have scolded him for his high-handedness, but she did not. She clasped her hands in front of her to hide their trembling as his hands went to her hair, carefully picking out her hairpins one by one until her hair fell around her shoulders. He wound his fingers through her hair, separating the strands and combing through it, massaging her scalp. Genevieve sighed in pleasure, relaxing beneath his ministrations.

Next he went to the buttons down the back of her dress, undoing them slowly, and her dress sagged open, sliding downward. Myles grasped the sides and pulled it slowly down, letting it drop at her feet. He put his hand on her shoulders, gliding down her arms, and he bent to kiss the line of her collarbone. She could feel him, hard and urgent, behind her, and she moved a fraction backward, pressing against him. His hands flamed suddenly hotter on her skin, and his breath turned ragged.

Genevieve smiled to herself. He *did* want her. The fire he stoked in her raged in him as well. He was going to make love to her again, and then these last few horrid days would be over. They could return to the way it had been. She relaxed against his hard body, anticipating his arms going around her, his mouth roaming over her shoulders and neck.

His hands dropped away and he stepped back, and though his voice was a bit uneven, he said, "I believe you can manage from here."

Genevieve turned to him, too stunned to hide her response. "What?" She stared. "Why are you doing this? What do you want?"

He took her chin in his hand. "I want you to come to me. That is what I want. You. In my bed."

For an instant Genevieve could only stare, and then a saving anger rushed up through her. "Then go!" She drew herself up, flinging her arm out toward the door, her eyes blazing a blue fury and her voice drenched in scorn. "You think you can reduce me to begging? I will never be your slave. Your obedient, adoring wife. You were a fool to marry me, and I was an even greater one to agree to it. Get out of my room!"

Heat flared in his face. "Gladly!"

He whirled and strode out of the room, and Genevieve rushed over to the door behind him and slammed it shut with a resounding crash.

Nineteen

Genevieve saw Myles stop at her door, but she ignored him, as she had done her best to do the past few days. She had remained polite but cool ever since the night of Lady Hemphurst's ball, answering his questions and responding to his conversational gambits, but she refused to rise to his remarks, no matter what the provocation, and she kept herself away from him as much as possible. She took breakfast in her room, not coming out until after he left, and in the evenings, she did not come down to supper until the last moment.

The future, she knew, was impossible if they continued in this manner. But she refused to give in to him. She would not give up her very self. For the moment, in the midst of her anger and pain and loneliness, this was the best she could manage. It was not a marriage. Not even a life. But she could get through the day without bursting into tears.

"I am going to meet Rawdon now," Myles said, and she turned to look at him. He was wearing the expression she was growing accustomed to: his jaw set, his eyes murky, the carefree Myles grin missing.

She had ruined his life, she thought, just as surely as she had ruined her own. Emotion clogged her voice, and she had to swallow hard before she could reply in a neutral voice, "Say hello to my brother. And to Lord Morecombe, too, of course."

"I will." He paused. "I do not have to go, you know. I could accompany you to Mrs. Parminter's gala, if you wish." He frowned faintly. "Without your grandmother or Damaris there . . ."

"No, I am fine by myself." She turned away, casually lifting a bottle of lotion from her dresser and pouring a dab in her palm. Keeping her gaze on her hands as she rubbed in the lotion, she went on, "You have been planning to attend this fight for days. There is no reason for you to give it up to take me to a gala. I have been doing it for years. After all," she added lightly, "it has been three days or more since Lady Looksby has put my name in a column."

"Very well." He continued to stand there. "Genevieve . . ."

She gave him a bright, remote smile. "Go on and enjoy yourself. I will do the same."

His mouth tightened. "No doubt."

And he was gone. Genevieve sank down on the stool in front of her vanity, resting her head on her hands. She would not cry. She would not. Penelope came into the room, and Genevieve quickly raised her head. "Ah, Penelope. I believe I shall wear the blue gown with the silver tissue wrap tonight."

Even with Penelope's help, it seemed to take a long time to get dressed. But Genevieve had little desire to reach the party early. Whatever she had said to Myles, she dreaded entering the party alone. But, of course, she must become accustomed to that.

As soon as Genevieve walked through the door of the Parminter house, she realized that something was wrong. The hall did not precisely fall into a hush when she entered, but there was a definite lessening of the hum of conversation, and she noticed that several heads turned her way. Mrs. Parminter's smile as she greeted Genevieve was tight, though her husband, the colonel, cast a decidedly roguish glance in Genevieve's direction.

Whatever was the matter?

Genevieve strolled across the wide entry hall into the assembly room beyond. Was it her imagination, or was the crowd actually parting before her, edging away as she approached? Her stomach suddenly felt as if she had swallowed a block of ice. With all the nonchalance she could muster, she glanced around, hoping to see someone she knew. Indeed, at this moment, she would have welcomed the appearance of her grandmother's friend Lady Hornbaugh.

Heads swiveled toward her; she felt the avid heat of their eyes, but when she turned, the gazes slid hastily away. Heads were put together in hushed whispering, punctuated by curious glances in Genevieve's direction. Genevieve caught the eye of Lady Carstairs, and Genevieve nodded to her. After a second of hesitation, the woman nodded back, though she immediately pivoted and began to talk to her neighbor.

Something was dreadfully wrong. Genevieve had no idea what was being said, but it was obvious that many of the people here knew something she did not—and they were busily informing everyone else of their knowledge. She could feel a blush rising up her throat, and she cursed her fair skin for being so revealing. Genevieve strolled to the side door of the large room and stepped out into the broad hall.

A number of people were scattered around the hall, and they behaved in the same peculiar fashion. Genevieve looked across the corridor into the room beyond. She would have liked to turn and run for the front door, but she could not play the coward. A Stafford never ran, she reminded herself as she strolled across the hallway and into the music room. She glanced around. The room seemed full of people, all staring and whispering, and she stopped, panic clutching at her chest. Out of the corner of her eye, she saw an empty chair. It was awkwardly placed, one of a pair from which the mate had been removed to another cluster of seats. Somewhat behind the piano, it was both isolated and too noisy for conversation, and that made it perfect for Genevieve.

It was hard not to run to it, but she managed to keep her pace even. Sitting down, she placed her hands on her knees, her back straight, and her legs demurely crossed at the ankle. She would not hang her head, she thought, and lifted her chin. But she could not bring herself to look at anyone, so she fixed her gaze on a small statue sitting on a shelf straight across the room from her. Her mouth was like cotton, and her ears burned with shame. Why was everyone acting this way? Surely it could not be just because she did not have Myles or her family as a buffer tonight.

And how long would she have to endure it before she could escape? On the other hand, she realized, she was not sure she could stand up and leave this little island of safety. Now that she was here, she could almost feel as if she were hidden—so long as she did not look at anyone. It would take an effort of will to once again traverse the gauntlet of stares and whispers.

Suddenly a familiar voice met her ears, and she looked toward the door. Was that Myles's voice? Genevieve sagged in relief, on the verge of tears. Myles was here. She would be all right now. She heard him again, too far away to be distinct. The sound moved away, and her heart began to thud. What if he left? What if he glanced around and did not see her and thought she was not here?

Genevieve jumped to her feet and slipped through the crowd, not caring if people turned to look at her. She reached the corridor just as Myles stepped out of the room opposite her. He was smiling and nodding to someone, but Genevieve could see the hint of tension in his expression, and his eyes were sharp and purposeful. His gaze fell upon Genevieve, and his face eased. He smiled, starting toward her.

Genevieve had to rein herself in to keep from running

to meet him. With what she hoped seemed only pleased surprise and not the sense of deliverance she felt, Genevieve moved forward.

"My love." He took her outstretched hand and bowed over it, touching his lips to her fingers. She knew he must feel the iciness of her hand, the faint tremor.

"Myles. This is a surprise. What happened to your plans with Gabriel and Alec?"

"I deserted them. They will doubtless mock me for weeks for being hopelessly domesticated, but I would rather be here with you."

"I am glad you did." He had kept her hand in his, and the warmth spread through her, supporting her.

"Is there anyone else here we know?" he asked, casually tucking her hand into his arm as he started toward the music room. It was the last thing Genevieve wanted to do, but she knew he was right. Whatever was going on, the only way to combat gossip was to face it down. It might not dispel a rumor, but it established that one considered it unimportant.

"Yes, of course." Genevieve cast about trying to remember any of the faces she had seen in her frozen walk. "Lady Carstairs. And, um, I believe Mr. Sanderson."

Myles spotted someone he knew and stopped to chat, keeping Genevieve close to his side. A certain wariness was in the eyes of the woman with his friend, but like most women, she was susceptible to Myles's charm and was soon chatting more warmly. After a few moments, Genevieve and Myles strolled on, stopping again and again to chat. Myles was making the rounds purposefully, engaging first this person, then that, in casual conversation, forcing people to greet them or to be openly rude to him.

He was also, Genevieve noticed, most affectionate. He did not cross the boundaries of polite behavior, of course, but he kept her close by his side, leaning over now and then to whisper in her ear and gazing into her face with rapt attention when she spoke. In short, he appeared to be a man enamored of his wife. Since Genevieve knew he was anything but that, he had to be playing the role for some purpose. She didn't know what it was, but she had too much faith in Myles's social acumen not to play along. She smiled back at him and flirted, gazing up at him with lambent eyes, doing everything but bat her eyelashes at him.

It was excessively tiring, Genevieve found, and she was glad when Myles finally settled on a corner of the music room where one of his acquaintances stood and launched into a protracted conversation about the exhibition of fisticuffs that he had just left. Genevieve was not expected to join their chat, and no woman was there with whom she would have to make polite conversation, so she was able to relax and let her mind wander as one girl after another showed off her skills at the piano. Myles had neatly positioned them so that the three of them formed a tight, closed-off triangle in the corner of the room, making it difficult for anyone to casually join their conversation.

After a time they left to partake of some refreshments, though Genevieve had even less interest in eating than she did in sitting and listening to a variety of young women slog through pieces on the piano. Finally Myles gave her a slight nod, and she knew he had decided that they had stayed long enough to leave without the appearance of running away. They strolled to the front door, stopping to assure their hostess with utmost mendacity that they had enjoyed the evening. Myles whisked Genevieve down the steps and along the sidewalk.

"Let's walk. It's a short distance, and I don't want to wait for the carriage to return."

"Of course." Genevieve preferred to take some exercise to rid herself of some of the tension fizzing in her. "What is wrong? What happened? Why was everyone acting like that? Why did you race over to the gala?"

"I had a note from your grandmother. She thought to catch you before you left, and the chap delivering the note was so distressed that you had gone that Bouldin sent him on to me. Apparently there was another comment in that wretched scandal sheet today."

"*The Onlooker?* But what could they have said that would have caused everyone to—to react that way? Lady Carstairs all but gave me a direct cut." Genevieve could not repress a slight shiver as she remembered the sideways looks and the cold, unwelcoming stares. "I haven't done anything."

"I know." Myles's jaw was rigid, and his eyes were colder than she had ever seen them. "They've made it up whole cloth, it seems."

"What did it say?" Dread filled her chest.

"Lady Looksby intimated that Dursbury broke off your engagement not just because of what happened in the library but also because he learned you had been having an affair with another man."

Genevieve felt as if the breath had been knocked out of her. She stopped abruptly and stared at Myles, unable to speak. He turned to look at her, his face so grim that an icy fear clutched her heart. "Myles—you do not think—you don't believe it, do you?"

"God, no! Genevieve." His face cleared and he pulled her into his arms. "I am not such a clunch as Dursbury. I would never believe such a thing of you."

She sagged against him in relief, drawing in the comfort of his warmth, his solidity. Tears stung her eyes, though she blinked them away. However angry Myles was with her, she at least had this to hold on to: Myles trusted her. And however storm-tossed she felt with him right now, she could rely on him. She straightened and gave him a small smile. "You just looked so—"

"Angry?" His eyes flashed. "I am. I am furious. I'd like to throttle someone." He took her arm and they started forward again. "What is so damnably frustrating is, I haven't any target for my anger. The article was very careful not to mention any names. Indeed, they couched it so that one could not prove they were referring to you. It was along the lines of 'It's said that a certain lady's being caught *en flagrante* in the library was merely the last straw for her much-tried fiancé.' Everyone knows of whom they're speaking, but to confront them for writing such lies about you only confirms that their description fits you. And of course they don't say who this elusive fellow is that you were supposedly seeing; I would have guessed they meant to implicate me, but they called him a married man."

"But why?" Genevieve's voice wavered a bit on the word, and she had to swallow hard to continue in a normal voice. "Why would this newspaper want to blacken my name? They don't even know me."

"Because it sells the repugnant little sheets. You can bet that everyone went rushing out to purchase it as soon as they heard the gossip."

They continued to walk in silence for a few minutes before Genevieve revealed her thoughts, "But why did they choose me?"

"I don't know." Myles frowned. "Their sales doubtless must have multiplied with the first bits of gossip and rumor they published about you. Perhaps they thought it would make more of a splash if they involved you again. Still, some lesser bit would have kept the interest going. Why create such a blatant, outrageous lie? It does seem oddly personal and malevolent."

"I can only think that they must have overheard that rumor somewhere. And how did the paper know so quickly about my running through the East End after that maid? Grandmama says they probably pay servants to provide them with gossip. But gossip would scarcely have had time to work its way around to the people at the newspaper."

He nodded. "I think they are getting the rumors directly from someone in the *ton*."

"So it was someone I *know* who told them that lie? Someone in the *ton* is trying to . . . to ruin my life?" Genevieve asked, appalled. "But who? Why?"

"Langdon? We know he is more of a scoundrel than we first imagined since he lured you into the library with that note."

"But how would this benefit him?"

Myles shrugged. "He fled London. He knows what would happen to him if Alec or I found him. Perhaps he realizes that I've sent a man searching for him. And there is always the possibility that you might reveal what he did, how thorough a cad the man is, and he would not be received."

"So if he could first make it so that *I* was not received, perhaps I wouldn't have the opportunity to tell anyone that he purposely lured me to the library—or, at least, people would not believe me since they have read that I'm immoral."

"That might impel a man without honor to wage this campaign against your reputation."

Genevieve mulled this over as they approached their house. "But that would indicate that Mr. Langdon is in London. He would have to be able to communicate quickly with whoever writes this Lady Looksby thing. And he would have had to hear about my pursuit of that maid. He could not do that from the Continent or wherever he's gone."

"True. It would indicate that he's still here somewhere,

and I just haven't managed to find him." Myles scowled, opening the front door and following Genevieve inside.

They settled in his study, where Myles poured a brandy for each of them and put one in Genevieve's hand. "Here. Drink this. Things will look better."

She did as he said, taking a sip of the drink and grimacing as it roared like fire down her throat. She sighed and leaned back against the chair, relaxation beginning to creep through her.

"I should have searched London more thoroughly," Myles said. "I talked to his friends and poked about his usual places. But I was sure he would have had the sense to flee the city. I should have combed through all the gambling hells and brothels for him."

"It can't be undone," Genevieve said. The thought of Myles's searching the brothels for Langdon set her teeth on edge.

"No, but I can stop him from doing anything else."

"The real question is what *we* should do."

"My first thought was to break a few heads at *The Onlooker*," Myles responded.

"I fear that would only cause more scandal."

"Perhaps. But it would certainly provide me some satisfaction."

"It would me, as well," Genevieve agreed. "But confronting them would make the situation even worse. Just think what this Lady Looksby would say about 'a certain gentleman so angry over the revelation of his wife's indiscretions that he attacked the editor.'"

"Do you wish to go back to the country?"

"It sounds delightful, but I cannot. I refuse to let whoever is doing this chase me out of town."

"I thought that would be your answer."

"I must go about my business as usual," Genevieve said, taking another sip. Despite how awful this evening had been, it was pleasant indeed to sit talking with Myles like this, as if everything were as it used to be between them, to know he was concerned for her and would help her through the ordeal. "This is a sore trial for my grandmother, but she will support me, as will Damaris and Thea." It stiffened her spine a little to think of the friends who would help her. "I have to continue to make calls—Grandmama will know whom best to call on without fear of being rebuffed. I should go about my normal life as best I can. Thea wanted me to go to Hatchards with her."

"To buy books?"

"Yes. You needn't look so surprised. I'm not illiterate, you know." Then she laughed. "Though I must admit I barely know where the shop is. We could do that tomorrow afternoon, if she's willing. We might even go to Gunter's for an ice afterward. And I must put in an appearance at the theater and opera and even some parties. If I still receive any invitations, that is."

"You will," he said with great certainty. "I shall write to my mother. I am sure she will come to help us."

"Your mother will come here?" Genevieve looked at him, astonished. "But I thought she hated London."

"She does, but she will agree that we need to marshal all our forces."

"You make it sound as if it is a campaign."

"It will be. Mother may not mingle in society much, but she is not without friends. Her bosom bow from girlhood is Lady Penbarrow."

"The Duchess of Terwyck's niece?"

"Yes. My mother does not see her often, but Lady Penbarrow is the one who keeps her informed of all the latest London news. If my family is seen to close ranks around you, it will put paid to unfounded gossip. It is one thing for your own grandmother to support you, but if your husband's family makes it clear they don't believe the nonsense, it will weigh more heavily."

"Oh, Myles . . ." Genevieve's voice faltered.

He looked at her, startled. "What? Do you not wish her to come?"

"No! No, of course not. I am happy for her to visit; I am honored. It is . . . it is just so good of her to do so. Your mother has been much kinder to me than I would ever have expected her to be." Genevieve stopped, afraid that if she went on, tears would sound in her voice.

"You are my wife," Myles replied simply. "She regards you as a daughter now. For all my mother's sweet nature, she is as fierce as any lioness when one of her cubs is in danger."

That was it, of course. Any slur on Genevieve was now a slur on the Thorwood name. She told herself she must not assume Myles had come to her rescue because he cared for her. Her honor was now his honor, and of course he would protect it. That was reassuring, naturally, but she could not help but feel a little let down.

"I am a bit tired," she said, setting her drink aside, weariness coming over her in a rush.

"Of course." Myles quickly set down his brandy, as well, and came over to give her his hand as she stood. He walked with her down the hall and stopped at the foot of the stairs. "Sleep well." He took her hand and raised it to his lips, then released it. "Don't worry. We shall get to the bottom of this."

"You are leaving?" Genevieve asked as he started toward the front door.

He turned back. "Yes. If Langdon is still in London, I intend to find him."

He strode away, leaving Genevieve standing at the foot of the stairs. She remained for a moment after the front door closed, the quiet of the house settling around her. With a sigh, she turned and started up the stairs toward her empty bed. It was wonderful, of course, that Myles was determined to right the wrong done to her, to find the villain who had started this horrid lie.

But she could not help but wish that instead of that, he were coming upstairs with her and that she would be spending this lonely night in his arms.

Twenty

Genevieve's *stomach danced with nerves* as she walked toward Gunter's. It had been easy enough to go into Hatchards with Thea. It was far less likely that she would meet anyone she knew in the bookstore. But here, in the popular confectioner's, she might well run into a lady of the *ton*. She let out a little sigh of relief when they walked inside and she saw no one she knew. It would do little good, of course, to show her face to the *ton* if no one of the *ton* was there to see it, but she could not help but be glad that she had escaped that ordeal today.

She and Thea were almost done with their ices, and Genevieve was laughing at Thea's tale of Matthew's latest misadventure, when three women walked into the confectioner's and stopped, their gazes falling on Genevieve. Genevieve's smile died, and she drew herself up.

Thea, watching her, dropped her story and turned toward the door. "Do you know them?"

"Yes," Genevieve replied, her eyes still on the three women. The oldest one, after a moment of stunned silence, turned her head away sharply, not acknowledging her. Genevieve kept her face expressionless. "That is Mrs. Farnham who just refused to acknowledge me, and one girl is her daughter Lilian. The other young lady is Iona Halford. You probably don't recognize her, as for the first time since I have known her, she is not tagging along after Lady Dursbury."

Mrs. Farnham said something to the two young women and marched over to a table as far away from Genevieve and Thea as she could get. Her daughter trailed along after her, but Miss Halford stood for another moment, regarding Genevieve with fury in her eyes. She started to turn and join her friends, but then she swung back around and marched over to Genevieve's table.

"How dare you?" Iona hissed. When Genevieve said nothing, merely raised her eyebrows coolly, she rushed on, "You should be hiding in shame after what you did! And to as good and—and upstanding a man as Lord Dursbury."

Out of the corner of her eye, Genevieve could see other patrons swiveling in their seats to look at them curiously. She knotted her fists in her lap, not sure whether she wanted more to stand up and slap Iona or turn and run from all the prying eyes, but she managed to say calmly, "Miss Halford, everyone is looking."

"I don't care!" Iona shot back. "I am not the one who should be ashamed. It is you who are the . . . the harlot!"

Genevieve drew in a sharp breath. Before she could even think what to do, Thea jumped to her feet and clamped her hand around Miss Halford's arm. Iona looked up at her in astonishment.

Thea said crisply, "Young lady, while you may not have any concern for your reputation and are happy to let everyone see your very poor manners, you might consider the other patrons of this establishment, who did not come here to listen to a silly young girl screeching like a harpy."

Iona's jaw dropped comically as she stared at Thea. "Ow! You're hurting me. Let go."

"I will be happy to if you have regained your senses," Thea began, but before she could go on, Mrs. Farnham rushed over.

"Iona! Iona!" She swung on Thea. "Let go of her! Who are you? Do you realize to whom you're speaking?"

"I am speaking to a very rude and impulsive young woman," Thea answered, gray eyes snapping behind her spectacles. "If this girl is in your charge, I can only say that you are doing a very poor job." As the woman began to puff up like a pouter pigeon, her face flaming red, Thea went on, "Though I can certainly see where she gets her taste for theatrics."

Genevieve stood up quickly. She would have liked to hug Thea for her swift and razor-sharp defense of her, but she could not let this scene escalate into another bit of fodder for Lady Looksby's column.

"We are leaving, Mrs. Farnham," Genevieve said shortly. "But I suggest you get Miss Halford in hand before she makes a spectacle of herself."

She expected an angry retort from the older woman, but Mrs. Farnham refused to even look at her, giving an ostentatious sniff and turning her head away, as if the very sight of Genevieve offended her. Genevieve was amazed at how the insult pierced her. She turned and walked to the door, not daring to even glance back to see if Thea followed her. Tears beat at the backs of her eyes, and her cheeks were hot with humiliation. She started blindly up the street, and Thea came up beside her to take her arm, turning her the other direction.

"The carriage is down here," Thea said, leading her to the Morecombes' glossy black vehicle. Thea climbed into the carriage after Genevieve and sank back into the seat. "What a horrid woman! Sometimes I find myself quite lacking in Christian charity."

Genevieve nodded, trying to smile, but tears were flooding her eyes, and she turned her head away quickly, gazing out the window as intently as if she had never seen Piccadilly before. Thea, after a quick glance at her companion, continued to talk, leaving the subject of the women they had just met and starting a paean to the ices they had eaten, followed by an account of the books she had purchased at Hatchards, and finally running out of anything to say as they were pulling up to her front door. Genevieve kept her hands clenched together in her lap, clamping down the sobs that threatened to burst from her, reaching up now and then to wipe away a trickle of tears that had escaped out of the corner of her eye.

"I should go," she said in a choked voice as they stepped down from the carriage.

"Nonsense." Thea wrapped an arm around Genevieve's

shoulders and pulled her into the house with her. Waving off the footman who stepped forward to take their hats, she took Genevieve into the small sitting room and closed the door firmly behind them. "Now, tell me." Thea took off her bonnet and dropped it into a chair. "What is the matter? Is it only that extremely silly young woman?"

"No. No." Genevieve shook her head, pressing her lips together. Her tears only seemed to come faster. "Oh, bother! I shouldn't cry! I'm so sorry."

"Of course you should cry." Thea reached out to undo the ribbons of Genevieve's hat and send it sailing onto the chair with hers. "Anyone would want to cry if someone attacked her in the confectioner's shop."

Genevieve let out a laugh at Thea's statement, but it turned somehow into a sob, and suddenly she could not hold back the tears any longer. She began to cry in earnest, great, tearing sobs wrenching her body, tears flooding down her face. Thea wrapped her arm around her and guided her over to the sofa to sit down, patting Genevieve's shoulder as she cried her heart out.

"I'm so sorry. So sorry." The words came out of Genevieve as if wrenched from her. "I've ruined everything."

"Nonsense," Thea said briskly. "Of course you haven't. What could you have ruined?"

"My—my life! Myles's life. Oh, Thea, you don't know! It is all such a horrible, horrible mess." Genevieve drew a shuddering breath and pulled out her handkerchief to wipe at the tears covering her face.

Thea took her arm from Genevieve's shoulder and

turned to face her squarely. "Why do you say you've ruined your life? Or Myles's?"

"Because I married him! I let him sacrifice himself. Worse, I seized upon his offer. And now he is—is tied to me forever!"

Thea frowned. "Has nothing changed since we last talked? Is Myles still angry with you?"

"No. Yes. Oh, I don't know! I am so confused. I think sometimes he must hate me."

"Genevieve! Surely not. Gabriel has said nothing to me of anything like that."

"Does he—" Genevieve looked at her almost beseechingly. "Does he know what Myles wants?"

"I don't know." Thea looked puzzled. "He has not said so to me. Genevieve . . . why do you think Myles hates you?"

"He—he wants me to submit to him," Genevieve burst out. Thea's eyebrows soared upward, and Genevieve blushed to the roots of her hair.

"Genevieve, what do you mean?" Thea's voice was filled with concern. "Is Myles—are you saying that he is cruel to you? That he . . . hurts you? Or makes you do something you don't wish to?"

"No! Oh, no, not in that way. He would never raise his hand to me; you must not think that." Genevieve blushed even harder, her face twisted in misery. "He said I was cold. I don't mean to be. I didn't—" She sighed. "I didn't think I was. But I don't know what a man wants."

"Myles, um, said he was 'dissatisfied'?" Thea asked delicately.

"No. But he told me I was cold, and he told me I could sleep alone in my bed as I wanted. And I don't. I didn't—want to, I mean. It's just—that's the way it's done. And I—I wanted to have some space that was mine alone, where I could go, you know, when I want to be by myself."

"There's nothing wrong with wanting to be by yourself sometimes. Back at the Priory, I have a room where I like to go and read or think or just . . . be alone."

"Do you—" Genevieve gazed at her hands, not looking at Thea. "Do you and Gabriel have your own bedrooms?"

"I'm not sure." Thea looked surprised. "I'd never thought. Not at the Priory. We never—I don't know, I never thought about it when we got married. But I grew up in a vicarage, you understand, and I am used to a great deal less space than you. At Gabriel's estate, now, yes, we have two bedrooms. It is easier with all the clothes and everything, but really . . ." Thea smiled, her cheeks turning pink. "He does not ever sleep in his chamber. It is, I guess, more a very large dressing room for him."

"Oh."

"Is that why Myles was angry . . . because of your bedroom?"

"I don't think so. He didn't say anything against it—well, you know Myles, he made some sort of flippant remark. But it wasn't what he was so furious about; it was . . ." Genevieve shrugged. "It was about me and the way I am."

"Did he never apologize for saying those things to you?"

"He tried, I suppose." Genevieve shrugged. "He said

he was sorry to have said them. Myles does not like to offend people; he likes for life to go along smoothly. But the words are still there; you cannot unsay them."

"But surely sometimes you say things you don't mean?"

"I did." Genevieve nodded and once again seemed to find her hands of great interest. "I told him I didn't care, that I wasn't like him and I didn't have his . . . appetite." She twisted the dangling end of a ribbon on her dress, then let it unwind. "It wasn't true," she almost whispered. "I did enjoy it. But I couldn't—I couldn't admit it after he'd said how cold I was. After I realized that he had been pretending."

"Pretending?" Thea said skeptically. "You think that Myles was pretending to—oh, blast, there is no delicate way to say this. But I don't think a man can falsify his, um, response."

"I don't mean that." Genevieve lifted her head. "But he is able to act as if he desires you when he clearly is not as moved as you are. At first after that fight, we could hardly speak, but then, suddenly, he started acting as if everything was all right. He was the way he used to be, teasing and light, and he'd . . ." She swallowed. "He would touch me or kiss me, and he would look at me in a certain way—do you know what I mean?"

"I have an idea," Thea replied drily.

"And I thought he was going to take me to bed again and everything would be all right. But then he wouldn't. After a bit, he would just stop. And I would feel such a fool. Except worse than a fool because I was so . . .

twitchy. He's purposely tormenting me, using what I feel for him against me, so, yes, he is being cruel. He has hurt me."

"But why? I don't understand."

"Because he wants me to grovel!" Genevieve surged to her feet. "He told me the other night he wanted me to come to his bed. He wants me to beg, to give up my—"

"Your what? He wants you to give up your . . . ?"

"Myself!" Genevieve cried out. "He said I didn't want to just be his wife, that I wanted to still be Genevieve Stafford. But I can't not be me."

"Of course not. No more than Myles cannot be Myles."

"Yes! Exactly. He wants me to capitulate entirely. And he is driving me mad! He won't stop. I know he won't stop until I either go insane or I'm driven to his bed. I cannot be like that. I won't be under a man's power." Genevieve stopped and faced Thea almost defiantly.

Thea regarded her for a moment. Finally she said, "You say you are proud. But it seems to me that you are being far too humble."

Genevieve looked at her blankly.

"You don't seem to realize that it isn't only Myles who has power over you. You have power over him."

"No. I don't," Genevieve said sadly. "He does not care about me."

"Now there I know you are wrong. Gabriel was with Myles last night when he received that message about you and the rumor. Gabriel saw his face when he realized what sort of trouble you were in, and it was not that of a man who doesn't care. He ran; he came to your side as fast as he could. Because he knew you were hurt, that you needed him. He flew to you the way I would fly to Gabriel or Matthew if they were in danger."

"I am his wife. It is his name under siege, as well."

"Those were not the actions of a man concerned about his name," Thea told her flatly.

"Then how can he kiss me until I'm quivering and then he just walks away?" Genevieve cried.

"He may walk away, but I'll warrant you it is at no small cost to him, Genevieve. You are a beautiful woman. And Myles is a man. A man, you just said, who has 'appetites.'"

"He seemed to," Genevieve admitted a little sadly.

"I cannot know what happens in your bedroom, but I have seen you and Myles together. He looks at you the way a man looks at a woman he wants. A woman he cares for. It may be that Myles is good at pretending, but I think the pretense is his walking away from you."

"Do you really think so?" Genevieve asked, unable to hide the green shoot of hope in her voice.

"Yes, I do. I am not sure just what he wants from you or why he is acting this way, but you don't have to surrender everything. There is bound to be somewhere in the middle you can meet. Have you never seen your cook haggle with a vendor?"

"You want me to negotiate with him?" Genevieve gaped at her.

"Not with words. But you can affect him just as much

as he affects you. You have to remember, men always carry a traitor in their ranks. And that is how you can end this war."

"Is my husband at home?" Genevieve asked the footman as she took off her bonnet and handed it to him.

"He's in his study, my lady."

Genevieve walked across the entry and paused in front of the large mirror that graced the opposite wall. The signs of her crying bout were still on her face, but though her eyelids remained a bit swollen, much of the redness had receded from her eyes, and her cheeks had an attractive flush. The starry points the tears had made of her lashes, the soft vulnerability of her mouth, were appealing—especially, she thought, to a man such as Myles, who could never resist a plea for help. Her hair was a bit of mess, and she reached up to tame a wayward strand, then stopped. With a small smile, she left the bit of hair free of its pins and trailing down the smooth, long line of her neck, and she started down the corridor to Myles's study.

Her fingers clenched and unclenched with nerves. She was not an actress, but surely she could manage the part of a seductress. She had, after all, the sweet, sensual days of their honeymoon to draw from. Thea was right; Myles could not have been entirely unmoved by their lovemaking. He had participated in it far too enthusiastically for that—and she could remember the things that had sparked a certain look in his eyes.

Genevieve paused at the doorway, waiting until Myles, sensing her presence, looked up. He smiled, rising to his feet. "Genevieve. I was wondering where you were. Did you go out with Thea today?"

"Yes, it was quite pleasant." She decided to leave out the scene at Gunter's. Genevieve strolled toward him, raising her hand and beginning to tug her glove from her hand, removing it bit by bit.

"I am glad." Myles's gaze was on her hand, seemingly riveted by the slow, languid movements.

She came to a stop in front of him as she finished taking off her gloves and tossed them onto his desk. Gazing into his eyes, she said, "I came to ask for your help."

"Indeed?" he murmured, reaching up to touch the lock of hair clinging to her throat.

"Yes. I thought I would take the carriage to *The Onlooker* tomorrow."

"Genevieve . . ." He looked somewhat alarmed. "I thought we agreed it would cause more scandal to confront them."

"Oh, I don't plan to go inside." She smiled up at him, taking the lapels of his jacket in her fingers and sliding them down to his stomach. "I am going to sit in the carriage and watch. I might see someone of interest going into their shop."

"Like Langdon, you mean?" His voice came out a bit rusty, and he cleared his throat.

"Exactly." She slipped her hands inside his jacket and rested them against his front. Her forefinger casually traced the pattern of his waistcoat. "But it would not do, would it, for me to go there alone?"

"No, indeed not." His chest rose and fell a trifle more rapidly, and a faint flush was rising on his cheeks.

"So I thought that as my husband, you might wish to accompany me tomorrow afternoon."

"I would." His eyes were bright and intense on hers, and Genevieve wanted quite badly to lean forward into him, to raise her lips to his. But she made herself step back, trailing her fingers down and off his waistcoat. She started toward the door, but turned back at the sound of his voice.

"Genevieve . . . what the devil are you doing?"

Her eyes glinted as she smiled slowly. "Oh, I think you know."

Genevieve turned and sauntered from the room.

Twenty-one

Genevieve went upstairs and set about renovating her wardrobe. Under the watchful gaze of her cat, who lay atop the elegant mahogany highboy, she and Penelope sifted through her gowns, deciding which ones could be altered. Genevieve had never realized before how many of her dresses were high-necked. A large number of them would look far better without a lace fichu tacked onto the neckline, and on one or two Penelope could lower the neckline.

It also occurred to Genevieve that her nightgowns were remarkably dull. Did she really need each and every one to be high-necked and long-sleeved? A bit of lace here and there would not be amiss, either. All her undergarments, from petticoats on down, could do with a sprucing up. She would have enough time to do some shopping the next day after they went to *The Onlooker*.

For supper that evening, she wore a deep plum satin gown, so rich in texture and color that it almost drew one's hand to touch it. With its lace fichu removed, the dark color and wide, square neckline showed off the white expanse of her chest to best advantage. Such a dress called for a hairstyle other than her usual rather subdued one, and she had Penelope add a few loosely corkscrewed, feathery, pale strands that brushed against her neck and face. Her success was measured in the way Myles's eyes widened in appreciation when she came into the room.

As they ate, she flirted lightly with her husband, seizing any opportunity to lightly touch his arm or hand. She could see the signs of desire soften his features and darken his eyes, and though he did not respond to her subtle overtures, she was confident he was not immune to them. Her suspicion was confirmed when after supper, Myles immediately bolted to his club.

The next morning, wearing her dressing gown and with her hair hanging loose down her back, she intercepted Myles on his way to breakfast. His eyes flew to her hair, then to the neckline of her dressing gown, where the lapels joined, revealing the white cotton of her nightgown above it.

"I had Bouldin set up a breakfast room in here," she told Myles cheerfully, taking his arm and sweeping him into the anteroom off the dining room. "'Tis so much cozier."

She indicated the small room, now furnished with a round table set for two and a sideboard on which chafing dishes of food were lined up. "I hope you do not mind that I did not dress yet. It seemed all right since it would be just the two of us. I told Bouldin we would simply serve ourselves."

He sank down into his chair without replying. Genevieve fussed around him, laying his napkin across his lap, pouring his tea, then insisting on taking his plate and filling it with food. Setting the plate down in front of him, she leaned over, letting the loosely tied dressing gown gape open a bit, revealing a further glimpse of her nightgown and the shadowy valley between her breasts.

Myles remained unusually quiet throughout the meal, but Genevieve took up the slack, chatting away about her grandmother's plans to marshal her forces over the next few days, calling on all her old friends and decrying the horrible wrong that had been done to "poor Genevieve."

"I am so relieved that she feels I should not make calls just yet. It will give us plenty of time to keep watch over that newspaper. And this afternoon, I am going by the linen drapers to pick up some lawn and lace to have some nightshirts and chemises made. I scarcely had time to buy a trousseau before our wedding, you know."

A glazed look came into Myles's eyes, which Genevieve pretended not to notice, just as she made no comment when her leg accidentally brushed his beneath the small table, although she did have to look down to hide a little smile when he shifted restlessly in his chair for the third time that morning. Taking a final sip of her tea, she popped up and came around the table to lean down and kiss his temple lightly.

"Pray excuse me. I must run and dress so that we can go to *The Onlooker.*" She paused and turned back at the door. "I quite like this room, don't you? I think we should breakfast here every morning. So much more ... intimate."

Genevieve continued her bombardment of Myles's defenses when they rode to the shop where *The Onlooker* was printed. In the close confines of the carriage, it was difficult for Myles to avoid looking at her, and the scent of her perfume subtly twined around him.

When the carriage came to a stop, Genevieve leaned across him to look out the window. "Which one is it?"

"That one with the gray door." Myles edged closer to the wall of the carriage. "You can see they have the sheets posted on the window."

"Oh, yes, I see it." Genevieve casually put her hand on his thigh to balance herself. She felt his leg twitch beneath her hand, and a moment later he moved to the opposite side of the vehicle, leaving her the seat for herself. "You needn't leave, Myles. There is plenty of room here." She smiled at him, casually twining a lock of her hair around her finger.

"I am fine here," he responded somewhat grimly. "I know how much you like to be alone."

"Not always." Genevieve gave him a long, slow smile before she turned away to watch the door across the street.

They stayed until close to noon, but no one they recognized came in or out. Finally Myles, who had been fidgeting on his seat off and on throughout their stay and had even once gotten out to take a brief walk, said, "I fear we are accomplishing little here. We might as well leave."

"No doubt you're right," Genevieve replied agreeably. "Perhaps we'll see something tomorrow."

"Genevieve . . . I think this is a futile effort."

"Still, we should give it a few more times. We've little else to go on. Do say you will come again."

With something close to a groan, Myles nodded. "Yes, very well. We shall come again tomorrow."

For the rest of the week, Genevieve and Myles kept watch on the newspaper's office. A few people went in and out, but no one of any interest appeared, and while the close confines of the carriage provided a wealth of opportunities to seduce Myles, Genevieve was beginning to think that she was tempting herself more than her husband.

She had altered her clothes and had new seductive undergarments made. But seductive nightgowns and chemises were useless if Myles never saw her in them. She had flirted with Myles shamelessly at every meal, letting no opportunity pass to lean in close or touch his arm or straighten his lapel. But though his skin might heat or his nostrils might flare at the scent of her perfume, he did not sweep her into his arms and carry her into the bedroom.

The man seemed to have a will of iron. Or perhaps—lowering thought—she simply did not appeal enough to him to lure him from his purpose. Worse, her conduct seemed to have caused Myles to avoid spending time at home. He bolted to his club every morning and did not return until it was time to dress for supper, leaving Genevieve with far too much time to idle about the house alone. She recognized the irony that she, so intent on having a bedroom where she could be alone, now had the entire house to herself—and was miserable with it.

Late one afternoon, Genevieve drifted down the stairs, restless and bored. Myles was at his club, of course, and she had several hours to pass before the Dumbarton soiree, a social occasion so dull and sparsely attended that Genevieve's grandmother had declared that Genevieve could go to it without stirring up controversy.

Boredom finally caused her to go in search of a book to pass the time, but as she started down the hall toward the library, her attention was caught by the sound of raised voices at the rear of the house. She turned back down the hall, and as she neared the butler's pantry, she saw Bouldin in a heated conversation with a dour-looking, whipcord-thin man. The stranger was dressed in gentleman's clothing, but he had a look about him that spoke of neither servant nor gentleman.

"Bouldin?" Genevieve said.

"My lady!" Bouldin pivoted toward her, his usually expressionless face filled with chagrin. "I beg your pardon. I told this fellow that Sir Myles was not at home, but he was most insistent. I suggested he leave a note for him."

"Haven't got a note with me, now do I?" the other man sneered. "And I know Thorwood will want to hear what I have to say, soon as possible."

"Then why don't you tell me what you have to say, and

I will inform my husband," Genevieve suggested crisply. When the man stared at her suspiciously, she added, "You might start by telling me your name."

"It's Parker, ma'am. I was doing some work for your husband."

"Parker!" Genevieve straightened. That was the name of the Bow Street runner Myles had employed. "Why don't you come into Sir Myles's study and tell me your news? You are right; he will wish to hear it straightaway." As the man followed her down the hallway to the study, Genevieve added, "I believe you are acquainted with my brother, as well. Lord Rawdon."

"Yes, ma'am. I've done a bit of work for him; he's a fine gentleman."

"I agree." Genevieve sat down behind Myles's desk and gestured toward Parker to take a seat across from her. "Now, do you have word of Mr. Langdon?"

As she had hoped, the mention of her brother and her knowledge of Myles's business had put the runner's mind at ease, for he said now, "I have Langdon himself."

"What? Here? In London?"

"Yes, ma'am. I found him in Bath. Took me a bit of time 'cause I went to Brighton first, but when I couldn't find him there, I tried Bath and there he was in the pump room, talking flummery to a couple of old ladies. I reckoned he'd be gone by the time I got word to you, and since Sir Myles wanted to question him, I thought I might as well bring him with me."

"How very efficient of you." She could understand

why her brother relied on the man. "Where is Mr. Langdon now?"

"In a mews not far from here. My cousin is head groom and he let me use a spare tack room. Won't nobody notice him."

"Good. I want you to take me to him."

Parker shifted in his seat uneasily. "Now, ma'am, I don't know as I ought to do that. Sir Myles might not like it."

"I see little difference between a mews in London and the stables at Castle Cleyre, which I have been in any number of times. Is your cousin likely to accost me? Or allow his men to?"

"No!" Parker exclaimed indignantly.

"I assume the mews belongs to a respectable household."

"Yes, of course, it's not far from here. It's just . . . well, if some harm should come to you . . ."

"You will be there to protect me from Mr. Langdon, won't you?"

"Yes."

"And I assume you must have him tied up or secured in some way or else he would escape." Parker nodded. "Very well. I cannot see how I could possibly come to harm. I shall send a note round to my husband to meet us there, if you will but give me the address."

She pulled a piece of notepaper from Myles's desk and picked up a pen to write, and Parker gave in, telling her the address. Genevieve made short work of the note, giving Myles the news tersely, then rang for a footman, instructing him to track down Myles at his club.

"If he is not there, then you must hunt him down," she added. "Now." She turned to Parker. "Take me to Mr. Langdon."

"Myles? Are you listening?"

"What?" Myles looked over Gabriel blankly. "Oh. I beg your pardon. No." Gabriel rolled his eyes, and Myles sighed. "Devil take it. I fear I am no fit company today."

"Today?" Gabriel asked, amusement bubbling in his voice. "My dear fellow, you have not been fit company for the better part of a week. Nay, longer than that—since you returned to London."

It was true. Myles was distracted and fuzzy-headed, irritable and jumpy, prone to snap at everyone. It had reached the point where no one was willing to spar with him anymore. He caught the look of sympathy in Gabriel's eyes and had to bite his tongue to keep from growling at him. He knew what Gabriel thought—that Myles was regretting his hasty marriage, that Genevieve was so shrewish and cold she was making him miserable, and Myles wanted to lash out at his friend for misjudging Genevieve.

Of course, he reminded himself gloomily, it *was* Genevieve's fault . . . not that he could explain that to his friends. The bloody woman had declared war on him. There was no other word for it. For the past few days, she had seized every opportunity possible to tease and torment his senses. He was beginning to think that she hoped to drive him mad.

At the breakfast table, he found himself mesmerized, watching her bite into her toast, her teeth sinking into the golden-brown bread, and when she paused to lick a bit of marmalade from her fingers, it was all he could do not to grab her wrist and pull her over into his lap. She had made it even more unbearable by enclosing the two of them in that little breakfast room, without even a servant to distract them. But his torment extended far beyond meals. Whenever he was around her, her lavender perfume teased at his nostrils. He was aware of every movement she made, each rustle of her clothes. If he sat at a desk, she would lean down to talk to him, bracing her arm on the desk, so that he had a perfect view of her firm breasts. She had come down to the library last night to look for a book, wearing nothing but her nightgown. She had stood there, the lamplight behind her, outlining her body, and he had thought he would choke with lust for her.

Suddenly her clothes all seemed . . . barer. Her dresses fell more softly about her body, as though she wore fewer petticoats beneath them. The tiny cap sleeves barely covered her shoulders, and if she threw a light shawl around her, it soon slipped lower, exposing her arms bit by bit, until he could not tear his eyes away from its progress. The luscious curve of her breasts swelled provocatively above the neckline. It was nothing more, of course, than what one saw on practically every other woman of the *ton*, and it was, indeed, a lovely sight.

Unless, of course, one was determined not to seek out her bed. Then it was ten kinds of hell.

It was his own fault for starting the whole thing. At the time, it had seemed a good idea, the perfect way to lure Genevieve into admitting her feelings for him. He wanted her to agree that theirs was no pale, bloodless relationship, no courteous union where each enjoyed one's bed partner now and then and the rest of the time went one's separate way. If he was being perfectly honest, he would admit that his pride—and perhaps more than that—had been hurt when she had declared she could easily forgo his bed. Surely there was nothing wrong with wanting one's wife to actually be his wife. To be one with him.

He had known that his efforts to tempt her would push his own desire to the limits, but he had not been prepared for how deeply his hunger for her would gnaw at him. Nor had he foreseen that Genevieve, rather than quickly yielding, would turn the tables on him, stoking his fires with temptations of her own. It was becoming more and more difficult to remember what his original goal was. As the tension had built up explosively inside him, he could no longer maintain the importance of his position. All that kept him on his course, he suspected, was sheer bloody-mindedness.

Unfortunately, Genevieve possessed the same trait in equal measure. Perhaps more. The Staffords had, he recalled broodingly, always had been a remorseless lot.

"Sir Myles."

He glanced up from his reverie and was startled to find one of his own footmen standing hesitantly behind the club's servant. Myles jumped to his feet, his pulse speeding up and his mind going immediately to Genevieve.

"Yes? What is it, Beck?"

"Lady Thorwood, sir." The man extended the note toward him, and Myles grabbed it, breaking the seal. He read it, his eyebrows soaring, and let out an oath, then ran through it once again. The words did not improve on a second reading.

"The devil take it!"

"Myles? Is everything all right?" Gabriel asked, rising to his feet. "Can I assist you in some way?"

"No, everything is most definitely not all right." Myles crumpled the note and shoved it into his pocket. "Thank you for your offer, but I will take care of this myself." Turning, he strode rapidly away.

Twenty-two

"Well, Mr. Langdon." Genevieve looked down at the man sitting on the narrow cot. His thinning, sandy hair hung limply across his head, and he sported a day's growth of beard. He wore no jacket, only an open waistcoat over his shirt, which was stained and rather the worse for wear. A manacle secured his ankle to the bedpost. "This is certainly a sorry sight."

"My lady!" He sprang up from his seat, wiping ineffectually at his hair. "Thank goodness you are here! You must tell this madman to let me go."

"Must I?" Genevieve gazed at him levelly. "I think you are hardly in a position to demand anything."

"But you know I did nothing to you," he protested. "This fellow says Sir Myles thinks I harmed you. But you know that isn't true. I have nothing but the greatest respect and admiration for you. Perhaps my zeal exceeded my sense of propriety." He paused in the midst of his grandiloquence and added more mundanely, "Is it true that you have married Thorwood?"

"Yes. I did. And he is not happy with you."

"I did not realize that you and Thorwood—that is, it was clear you and Dursbury were no love match. Else why would you turn to me? But I did not know Sir Myles had stolen a march on me." His voice died as he looked at Genevieve's stony face. He cleared his throat. "That is, um, well, in any case, you will help me, won't you? You will tell Thorwood that I never meant any harm?"

"No harm? What else did you think would happen when you lured me into the library?"

"Lured you!" He gaped at her. "My lady! Surely you cannot mean to deny that you asked me to meet you. How was I to know what would happen?" He gazed at her in righteous indignation. "I cannot help it if your fiancé followed you. When a beautiful woman seeks one out, 'tis difficult to deny her."

"You have the audacity to say *I* asked *you*? That I told you to meet me in the library?" Genevieve's temper ratcheted up several notches.

"But you did! Please, I know no lady likes to admit to making an assignation, but you cannot condemn me so unfairly."

"Mr. Langdon. I never asked you to meet me anywhere at any time, and only a fool would believe that I had. Myles has a good deal more sense than Lord Dursbury; he will not believe the worst of me. I had meant to ask my husband to be lenient with you, but if you intend to blacken my character . . ."

"I will say whatever you wish!" he assured her. "Just tell this chap to let me out of this dreadful manacle. It is excessively cumbersome. I shall leave immediately. I will go—"

At that moment, the door to the tack room slammed open and Myles walked in. "The devil! Genevieve, what in the world possessed you to come here?" He glared first at her, then at Parker, and finally his gaze fell on Langdon. His face tightened, and he started toward him.

"No! Myles, wait." Genevieve stepped in front of him as Langdon scrambled as far away as the manacle and chain would allow. "Don't be hasty. Mr. Langdon was about to tell me about that party." She turned toward the other man. "I won't let Myles hurt you, if you will only tell us the truth. Without any sort of embellishment."

"I did tell you the truth!" Langdon said in an aggrieved tone. "You sent me a note." He twitched when Myles made a low growling noise, and Langdon cast Genevieve an imploring glance. "Lady Genevieve . . ."

"Myles, please." Genevieve held his gaze until he sighed and stepped back, crossing his arms.

"Very well. Tell us your tale."

"It's not a tale." Langdon turned his gaze back to Genevieve. "You asked me to meet you in the library. I was most astonished, I'll admit, for I never could see that you had the slightest interest in me."

"I didn't," Genevieve replied bluntly. "Nor did I send you a note."

"But, my lady, you did!"

"What did it say?" Genevieve asked.

"I don't remember!" His voice rose querulously. "I was

foxed! Drunk as a wheelbarrow. You wrote, 'I must see you,' or some such thing and put the time and the place. So I went directly to the library. I think I fell asleep." He frowned. "Because I woke up and there you were. I had thought perhaps it was a joke, you see. But then you appeared. Like an angel, as it were." He sighed. "Of course, it all fell apart."

"Mr. Langdon, do you swear that you did not send me a note telling me to meet you in the library?"

"Send you a note?" He looked perplexed. "No. Don't you understand? *You* sent *me* a note, not the other way around."

Genevieve turned to Myles. He set his jaw.

"Langdon." Myles strode forward and jerked the man up by the front of his shirt, his face more coldly furious than Genevieve had ever seen it. "If I were to hold a knife to your throat, would you tell me the same story?"

"N-not if you didn't want me to," the other man replied uncertainly.

"Oh, bloody hell!" Myles shoved him back down onto the bed. "Parker, release him. Langdon, get out of this city and don't show your face here again. If I ever hear of you speaking a word about my wife, I swear I will hunt you down, and when I'm through with you, your own mother won't recognize you. Do you understand?"

Langdon nodded mutely.

Myles swung back around and cast Genevieve a fulminating glance. "You and I are going to talk." He wrapped his hand around her wrist and started from the room.

Genevieve went with him without protest. Myles handed her up into the carriage outside and settled down across from her, his face set in stone. Genevieve gazed back at him coolly.

"Are you planning to sulk all evening?" she asked after a few moments.

"I am not sulking. I am contemplating whether I dare leave you at home alone again. Blast it, Genevieve, haven't you any sense?"

"No, I suppose I must not." Genevieve's tone was glacial. "If by *having sense* you mean never acting upon anything unless I have your consent."

"Don't. Don't try to blame me for your willful disregard for your own safety. You went charging off without a word to anyone, going God knows where, by yourself, and then you act as if *I* am an ogre for wanting to protect you."

"Charging off! I was hardly by myself. Mr. Parker, whom *you* hired, accompanied me. Mr. Langdon was manacled to the bed. It is still daylight, and we are in a respectable part of the city. Not to mention the fact that I sent you a message about where I was going." Genevieve's tone turned more acidic by the word. The carriage pulled up in front of their home, and she raised a sardonic eyebrow at Myles. "You may have noticed that we are scarcely any distance from our house. Am I supposed to wait for you to escort me everywhere?"

She opened the door and climbed down without waiting for his assistance. As they went up the stairs, she said coolly, as if anger were not churning around her insides, looking for a release, "You will remember that we have the Dumbarton soiree this evening."

"Damn the soiree! Genevieve, we are not through with this discussion."

"I am." She sailed into her room, Myles on her heels. "Ah, Penelope, you have drawn a bath for me, I see. Excellent."

Her maid bobbed her a curtsy. "Yes'm. Shall I add the hot water now?"

"Yes, do. I must hurry. I am a bit behind, I fear."

Penelope left the room. Genevieve, ignoring Myles's looming presence, crossed to her dresser and began to take out her earbobs. She glanced in the mirror at Myles. He was standing beside her bed, gazing down at the clothes her maid had laid out on the bed for Genevieve to wear tonight. Beside the pale pink dress lay her new undergarments. As she watched, Myles reached out and took the delicate, lace-edged chemise between his fingers, his face bemused.

Genevieve suppressed a smile. She could not begin to identify what she was feeling at the moment—irritation, amusement, excitement, anticipation, all welling up in her, clamoring for release. She began to remove the pins from her hair.

"What are you about, Genevieve?" Myles frowned at her. "These clothes . . ."

"Yes?" Genevieve put the hairpins in their box and turned inquiringly toward him, combing her fingers through her hair as she spoke. "What about my clothes?"

"They, um . . ." He pulled his gaze away from her, finishing lamely, "They're different."

"Yes. They are. I frequently buy new underclothes and nightgowns, Myles. Do you object to your wife's expenditures?"

"What? No. You bought nightgowns as well?"

"Yes." Genevieve opened a drawer and help up a delicate nightgown. Sleeveless and high-waisted in the style of current dresses, its bodice was made entirely of lace, gathered beneath her breasts with a satin sash, and falling into a skirt of sheer voile. "It is a mite extravagant, I admit, but I thought it a pretty confection." Feigning not to notice Myles's stunned expression, she folded up the garment and replaced it in the drawer.

"Is that all?" Myles's words came out in a croak.

"No. I have others ordered. Ought I to have presented a list of my intended purchases so you could approve it?"

"No!" He cleared his throat, turning away. "Don't be nonsensical." His fingers strayed again to the gossamer-light chemise on the bed. "I am not a demanding husband."

"I would not have thought so," Genevieve retorted lightly. "I am no longer sure what to believe. Apparently you do not approve of my leaving the house on my own or purchasing new garments without telling you or"—her eyes flickered toward the bed—"how I perform my wifely duties."

"Wifely duties! Good gad, Genny, you know I—" He broke off as Genevieve's maid bustled into the room, carrying a kettle, followed by one of the other upstairs girls, similarly burdened.

He waited impatiently while Penelope poured the steaming water into the tub, then swirled her hand in it, testing the temperature.

"I know what, Myles?" Genevieve asked, lifting her hair and turning so that Penelope could unfasten her dress.

"Genevieve, stop."

"Stop what?" Genevieve looked at him with clear, limpid eyes. "I must hurry or we shall be late for the party."

He started to retort, then cast a frustrated glance at Penelope. "Oh, to hell with it!" He stalked out the door and down the hall to his room, slamming the door shut behind him.

Genevieve let out a giggle as she stepped out of her dress. She knew she should not have allowed this scene to play out in front of her maid. She and Myles had already given their servants a wealth of things to gossip about tonight. Oddly, she could not bring herself to care.

"That is all, Penelope. I'll finish the rest."

As the door closed behind the servant, Genevieve sat down to remove her stockings. She could hear Myles stomping about in his room, opening and closing drawers with excessive force, as well as one sound that she suspected was a boot being hurled across the room. She grinned as she peeled off one stocking and started on the other.

The connecting door into Myles's room opened. "Genevieve, I—" Myles stopped, frozen in the doorway, his eyes going to Genevieve's hands poised on her leg.

"Yes?" Genevieve looked at him with bland inquiry.

He was undressing, too, boots, jacket, waistcoat, and cravat gone, his shirt hanging outside his breeches. Genevieve continued with her task, hooking her thumbs under the top of her stocking and slowly traveling down her leg. She tossed the stocking aside and stood up, her eyes on Myles's face as she grasped the bow tying the front of her chemise and slowly drew it open. Myles curled his hand around the edge of the door, his fingers digging into the wood.

With careful deliberation, she undressed, grasping the bottom of the chemise and pulling it off over her head. She continued to watch him, her eyes challenging, as she untied her petticoats and let them fall. She felt no embarrassment at her nakedness, only a fierce sensual pleasure as she watched desire settle on his features, softening his mouth and sharpening the hot hunger in his eyes. She stepped out of the last of her undergarments and sauntered over to the tub. Casually picking up the washrag on its edge, she stepped into the tub and sank down in it, leaning her head back against its rim as the warm water lapped around her body.

For a moment she thought he would not move, but then he shot across the floor, reaching down and pulling her up in one smooth motion. "I will not have it!"

His arms went around her, tight and hard as iron, and he buried his lips in hers. Genevieve melted into him, clinging, as his mouth plundered hers, turning her dizzy. Finally he broke their kiss and swooped her up in his arms to carry her into his room. Little gentleness was in his face as he laid Genevieve down and stretched out on the bed beside her. Bracing on his elbows, he took her face between his hands, and stared deeply into her eyes, his face fierce.

"You will sleep in my bed. Do you hear me? You can keep that bloody room for your clothes or to bathe or to sulk in or to just shut everyone out; I don't give a damn what you do with it. But at night you will be here, where you belong. In my bed."

Genevieve's lips curved up. "Yes, Myles." She put her hands up to his face, in mirror image of him, and pulled him down to kiss her.

The breath left him in a low groan as their lips met. His mouth was hard and desperate, driven by weeks of frustration. Genevieve answered him with equal fervor. Passion, teased and repressed for too long, flamed in her, and she could not touch him or taste him enough. Her hands slid under his shirt, eager to caress his flesh. Myles's skin was hot and smooth against her fingers, and she explored him eagerly, fingertips digging into his back as if she could meld their flesh together.

Delving downward, her hands were stymied by the waistband of his breeches, and she fumbled at the buttons. He reared up, straddling her, and ripped his shirt up and off over his head, throwing it away. Her hands went to his taut stomach, sliding over his skin. Now, looking at him, touching him, she was stunned by how much she had missed him, more than she had even realized. She came up to press her lips against his skin, softly rubbing her cheek against him.

"Myles," she whispered as her arms slid around him, and she clung to him, trembling, as tears welled in her eyes and slid down her cheeks, dampening his chest as well as her face.

"Genevieve?" Concern touched his voice even as she felt him tighten and swell against her. He moved off her, peering into her face. "Are you crying? Did I hurt you? I did not mean—"

"No, no." She smiled at him, blinking away her tears. "It's nothing. It's only—I feel so—oh, Myles! I don't know what I feel. I just want you to hold me and hold me and don't let go." She wrapped her arms around his neck and squeezed him to her. "I want you," she whispered, her hand going down to slide beneath his breeches. "I want to have you inside me."

He made a low noise and shucked off his breeches. He pulled her beneath him, sliding between her legs, and she felt him probing at her flesh. Genevieve sucked in a ragged breath, moaning his name again, and moved her hips, seeking him. With infinite slowness, he sank into her, stretching and filling her, banishing the emptiness. She wrapped her legs around him as he began to move within her, stoking her passion with each long, hard thrust. Her fingers dug into his back as his movements quickened, turning faster and harder until she was panting with eagerness, yearning toward the satisfaction she knew waited just beyond.

He jerked against her, his muscles tightening, as he poured his seed into her. Genevieve cried out, pleasure exploding within her.

They lay locked together. He started to shift his weight from her, but Genevieve tightened her grip around him, and he remained. She wanted to feel the weight of him on her, bearing her down into the soft mattress. She wanted to feel his skin pressed against hers all the way up and down, to hear the ragged rasp of his breath in her ear, to feel the gallop of his heart against her chest. She thought of his words: *In his bed. Where she belonged.*

Genevieve let out a breathy laugh and pressed her lips to his neck. She was gratified to feel the leap of his movement inside her. "Already?" she murmured, and stroked her nails lightly over the muscled curve of his buttocks.

"Mm." He kissed the point of her shoulder. "It seems I cannot get enough of you." He kissed her on the lips, his kiss slow and tender, tasting and caressing where before he had seized. "It has been an age since I've been here."

"A few weeks." She chuckled again, walking her fingertips up his body, counting his ribs.

"That is an age when a man is starving." He raised his head to smile down into her face. "Tortured. Tormented."

Genevieve laughed. "Through your own doing. 'Twas you who began it."

"Did I? I cannot remember why."

"To make me bend to your will, I believe."

His eyes widened. "No, Genny. Not that. Never that."

"I cannot be other than I am, Myles," Genevieve said

a little desperately. "I know I am proud and"—she swallowed—"and somewhat cold."

"Cold!" He grinned. "I never said that, surely." He pressed his lips softly to the side of her neck.

"Yes, you did. I know you think it; everyone does. Do you think I don't wish I were different? That I could please you and be as you like?" She put her hands on either side of his face, looking up earnestly at him. "But I am too much a Stafford. Look at my grandmother; in fifty years that is how I shall be. I will never be sweet and biddable; I cannot be just your wife. I shall always be Genevieve Stafford. And I fear that we will often be at war like this."

"If all our battles turn out like this, I shall not mind a little war." He smiled and gently kissed her lips. "Genevieve . . . I said a number of things that afternoon that I shouldn't. I was angry. I did not mean them; I was . . . hurt. All I can do is ask your forgiveness. I don't ask that you excise Genevieve Stafford from you; I merely want you to be Genevieve Stafford Thorwood." He began to rain light kisses over her face. "I don't want you to be a different person; I like you as you are. I like your will stiff and straight, exactly as it is." He grinned, his hand gliding up between them to caress her breast. "Exactly as you make me."

"Don't be crude," she said with mock severity.

"How can I not be? With you lying there so lovely." He kissed her neck. "So luscious." He kissed her collarbone. "So utterly, utterly naked." He kissed the hollow of her throat. "Ah, sweet girl, can you not feel the effect you have on me?"

"Yes." She grinned and reached up to comb her fingers through his hair, wriggling her hips to emphasize her words. "It's a very intriguing sensation."

His lips lingered on her throat, then moved downward. He took his time, loving her with long, soft kisses, arousing and tempting and pleasing her. It seemed to Genevieve that he explored every inch of her body, until she was almost writhing in anticipation, and only then did he begin to move within her. He was achingly, blissfully slow in this as well, building the heat in her with long, fluid strokes, until finally they came together in a powerful cataclysm of passion.

Later, as Genevieve lay snuggled against Myles's side, both of them sated and drowsy, Myles said in a contemplative voice, "I fear we shall miss the Dumbarton soiree tonight."

Genevieve laughed, stretching lazily. "That will be no loss, I suspect. But I do regret that my bath has gone quite cold."

"I shall have the maid bring a kettle of hot water to warm it."

"No! Myles! She will know!"

"You think she does not already?" He chuckled.

Genevieve groaned, burying her blushing face in his chest. "Oh, Myles . . . the servants will think us both lust-driven animals."

"They will think us newlyweds, I imagine." He kissed

her hair. "And since they have been witness to our bad tempers till now, I suspect that they will be well pleased that we have come to an agreement."

"I can't imagine why it's so important to you that I sleep in here," Genevieve said, sitting up and stretching.

"Can't you?" He ran a lazy finger down her spine. "'Twill be far warmer, come winter. And the company is pleasant on long, dark nights."

She looked sardonically over her shoulder at him. "And that is your reason?"

"No." He wound a strand of her hair around his forefinger. "Do you dislike it that much? The idea of being with me?"

A smile softened her face. "No." She leaned down and kissed him gently on the lips. "I don't dislike it at all."

Twenty-three

"Did you believe Langdon?" *Myles* asked as they sat in front of the fire two hours later. Genevieve's bath had, unsurprisingly, turned out to take a good deal more time than it normally would since Myles decided to join her, and after that they had shared their supper in his room, too hungry to care that the long delay had rendered it dry and somewhat tasteless.

"Yes." Genevieve sat on his lap, her head resting on his shoulder. "He is a poor excuse for a man, but I think he was genuinely confused and surprised when I accused him of luring me into the library with a note."

"I did not hear all his story since someone was too eager to wait for me to join her. But Langdon seemed willing to tell whatever story would deliver him from us."

"True." Genevieve sat up straighter to look into Myles's face. "But if you think about it, could Langdon have had the intelligence to come up with such a scheme? He scarcely seems a bright sort."

"True. And he was right in saying he was badly foxed that night. I have to admit I am inclined to believe him.

Else I would not have let him go." Myles paused, then added candidly, "Though, of course, my desire to get you alone and ring a peal over your head may have had something to do with it."

"No doubt," Genevieve agreed drily. She leaned forward and kissed his ear, nipping gently at his earlobe.

"Now, don't distract me." Myles snaked his hand beneath her dressing gown.

"Me distract you! I like that," Genevieve exclaimed indignantly, her attitude undercut by laughter.

"Do you?" He nuzzled her neck, his hand wandering farther afield.

"Stop!" She swatted at his arm. "We are having a serious talk."

"You began it," he reminded her, but his hand stilled. "The very bizarre question this raises is, if it was not Langdon, who sent you that note?"

"Someone who dislikes me, that is clear enough." Genevieve settled her head back on his shoulder.

"Or someone who wanted the result which occurred."

"For you and me to marry?" Genevieve asked, puzzled.

Myles laughed. "No, my dear, though I must say, it is balm to my wounded pride that you consider that the important thing. I meant the result of you not marrying Dursbury."

"Oh. Oh!" She sat up straight. "You are right. It *was* overly fortuitous that Dursbury and his friends walked into the library at that precise moment. Two notes to assure that Langdon and I would be in the library together at that time—and anyone who knows Langdon would guess the way he would act in that situation. Then all one would have to do is to maneuver Dursbury to the library."

"Precisely. My bet would be on Miss Halford."

Genevieve nodded. "She is the one who has benefited from the incident. There are rumors flying around that the two of them will soon be engaged. And she would have noticed that Langdon was always hanging about, making a nuisance of himself. Well, well . . ." Genevieve leaned back against him. "Interesting. One feels one should do something to retaliate."

"Mm. Particularly when one is a Stafford," Myles added, idly rubbing her arm.

"I haven't any idea what I would do to her, though. Miss Halford is welcome to Dursbury; marrying that dull fish should be punishment enough for anyone. I don't like to be the subject of gossip, but, aside from that, I have been the real beneficiary of her scheme."

"Have you?" Myles hand went still on her arm, and Genevieve felt the sudden tension in him, though she was not sure why.

"Why, yes." Genevieve kept her voice light, not wanting to make a misstep, as she slipped her hand in under his robe and glided it over his chest. "I have found out several interesting things." Her forefinger circled his nipple teasingly as she leaned closer, her lips almost touching his ear. "The first being that Grandmama was very, very wrong about the duties of the marital bed."

She felt his body relax, and he nuzzled her neck, pulling the loose knot of her sash apart and parting her dressing gown. "Then let us see what else I can teach you."

Life, Genevieve decided, had become pleasant once again. Or, really, if she thought about it, life was more pleasant than she could remember it ever being. She did not mind not attending as many parties; indeed, she looked forward to staying at home with Myles. It was a bit shocking how much she enjoyed being with Myles and how often she thought of him when he was not around. How everything inside her seemed to turn warm and liquid whenever Myles walked into a room. Now and then she told herself that she was becoming like Damaris, utterly enthralled by her husband, but she could not find it in herself to care.

A few days later, Lady Julia came to town, bringing with her not only Nell but also Myles's oldest sister, Amelia, who had decided to leave most of her brood in the care of their father and governess, taking only the youngest, along with his nurse. Amelia, Myles told Genevieve in an aside, could not bear not to be in charge of whatever was going on, but Genevieve could not help but be touched by her unexpected support. Genevieve was even more pleased to see Nell, as was Xerxes, who leapt into Nell's arms with a most unusual lack of dignity.

The girl laughed and scratched the cat behind the ears, then began to chatter to Genevieve about the trip, her first to London. She was eager to see all the sights, especially Astley's Amphitheatre and the lions at the Tower, to both of which, Genevieve assured her, Myles would be pleased to escort them.

While the three of them spent the next afternoon, as promised, visiting the Tower, Lady Julia and Amelia called on Julia's friend Lady Penbarrow. The following day Lady Penbarrow and Myles's mother whisked Genevieve off to visit Lady Penbarrow's aunt, the Duchess of Terwyck. The duchess, a rather formidable woman of advancing years, was one of the pillars of English society. Disdainful of the current fashions, she wore her snow-white hair up in an intricate and towering arrangement—though, thankfully, she left it unpowdered—and her dresses still had the lower waists and wider skirts popular fifteen years earlier.

She was in many ways the opposite of Genevieve's own grandmother, for she reveled in being considered an eccentric and cared not a whit what anyone else thought of her. However, she had a towering pride similar to the Countess of Rawdon's, and she cared for nothing as much as family. Luckily, the duchess extended her definition of family to include her niece's lifelong friend Lady Thorwood and, by extension, any member of Lady Thorwood's family. Therefore, she invited Genevieve and Lady Julia to tea and even took them along with her to an exceedingly boring lecture on the various important families of Norfolk, among which the Duke of Terwyck's family held the central place.

As intended, this sign of the duchess's favor quickly

brought a number of other ladies back to paying calls on Genevieve, and her social life picked up. It even, Genevieve found with a notable lack of pleasure, caused Lady Dursbury to pay them a visit. Genevieve would have escaped Elora's visit if she had been able, but unfortunately she was absorbed in helping Nell pick out a tangle in her embroidery thread and was not aware of the woman's arrival until Bouldin announced her.

"Lady Thorwood, I am pleased beyond words to meet you," Elora gushed to Myles's mother. "And this young lady must be Myles's sister." She patted on Nell on the head, which Genevieve was certain set Nell's back up, though Elora was blissfully unaware of that, turning to Amelia to fawn over her, as well.

No doubt Elora hoped to bring about a favorable report of her to Myles, Genevieve thought sourly. The best thing about the past few days had been not having to see Lady Dursbury flirting with Genevieve's husband.

Elora wasted no time in plunging into Genevieve's problems. "You must have been so shocked, Lady Thorwood, as was I, to hear of the rumors about Lady Genevieve. Of course, anyone who knows her, as I do, would never believe such a thing of her. I trust you will endeavor to pay them no attention whatsoever."

If Elora had hoped to be urged to expound on these problems, she had little success, for Lady Julia simply smiled. "Indeed. I do not acknowledge such unfounded nonsense. Do you live in London year-round, Lady Dursbury?"

"Yes, since the death of my dear husband. While he was alive, we spent most of our time at home on his estate. I have not had the fortitude to go back there yet because of the memories."

"Ah, of course. I have always found I am comforted by my memories of my husband."

"Indeed. Indeed." Elora nodded. "No doubt in a bit, when the pain has faded." She smiled wistfully and turned to Nell. "And you, my dear, are you enjoying your visit to London?"

"Oh, yes. We've been to the Tower, and Myles has promised to take us to a show at Astley's. One of the maids said that Bartholomew Fair is in town the next few days, and it has amazing things to see. There are wire walkers and jugglers and puppet shows, as well as a man who swallows swords. But I have not convinced Genevieve to take me," she added regretfully.

"Oh, my! I have not dared to go myself," Elora said. "No doubt you will think me a poor thing indeed, but I am certain it would be much too exciting for me. I have heard that women have fainted from the suspense in the theatricals."

"Really?" Nell looked doubtful. "I wouldn't faint."

"No, I am sure you would not. But you must not go to it alone, you know," Elora added needlessly, since Nell had not suggested that she was about to. "'Twould be most naughty. And I am sure you would find it much too shocking for one of your tender years."

Elora could not have said anything more likely to

make Nell determined to go the fair, Genevieve thought with disgust. Now Genevieve would have to wheedle Myles into taking her and Nell, for Nell would be obsessed with it. Genevieve had little interest in going, but she had to admit, with an inner smile, that she would not mind convincing Myles to escort them.

Genevieve lifted the curtain a fraction and peered out the carriage window. The street in front of the print shop was quiet today. As the days had passed with nothing to show for it, she and Myles had gradually stopped keeping an eye on the visitors to the newspaper, especially now that her social duties had picked up. But this morning, feeling restless after Myles had left the house, Genevieve decided to spend an hour or two by herself in the carriage, keeping watch.

Genevieve sat a little straighter as a woman came into view, walking toward Genevieve's vehicle. Something about her was faintly familiar. When she turned into the print shop, Genevieve's interest was piqued even more. Picking up the collapsible spyglass Myles had left in the side pocket of the carriage after their earlier expeditions, she pulled it out full length. As the door to the shop opened again, Genevieve put the glass to her eye and trained it on the door.

The woman stepped out of the shop and glanced down the street before turning away and starting back in the direction she had come. Genevieve stared after her, her heart racing. She was positive that was the woman who had run from her and Damaris and Thea. The maid who had given Genevieve the false note from Myles.

Genevieve leaned out the carriage window and called up to their driver, "Follow that woman. There, in the brown dress."

He lifted his hat in acknowledgment and called to the boy to release the team's heads, then started forward. He kept a slow pace, maintaining a distance behind the woman, though once or twice he had to pull the horses to a halt to let her get ahead again. Genevieve's mind raced, wondering what she should do when the woman reached her destination. If Genevieve got out to confront her, she might well run again, and while this time Genevieve felt sure her vehicle would not desert her, it was not always easy for a carriage and team to follow a person, particularly if they wound up in the narrow, crooked streets of some of the older parts of the city.

The woman got on an omnibus, and the carriage rolled after it. Genevieve hoped the driver would be able to maintain his view of the woman. To her surprise, the carriage headed toward Mayfair. She reasoned that the woman had probably gotten employment again in the area. The woman exited the omnibus and began to walk up the street toward a small, unenclosed park, where she turned in. The driver passed the park, pulling to a stop just beyond the entrance. Genevieve lifted the curtain a crack and peered through it. The maid walked over to a bench, where another woman sat. The woman on the bench lifted her head.

Genevieve's jaw dropped. She knew that woman. It was Miss Halford's personal maid.

So it *had* been Iona Halford who had arranged for Genevieve's problems! It made sense, and though Genevieve would once have said the girl was too meek to do something so outrageous, she had seen the fire Iona was capable of bringing up where Lord Dursbury was concerned. The young lady who had accosted her in Gunter's might well be capable of setting out to ruin Genevieve.

Genevieve waited as the two women talked briefly. Iona's maid handed the other girl a small pouch and a folded note, both of which she quickly pocketed. Then both women left the park, the woman Genevieve had followed turning to go back the way she had come, and Iona's abigail walking quickly toward Genevieve's carriage, her head down.

Genevieve opened the door and slipped out of her carriage. When the maid grew close, Genevieve stepped directly into her path. Startled, the girl raised her head and came to a halt, eyes widening. Whipping around, the girl took off at a run.

Genevieve ran after her. If this chase came to light, her grandmother would flay her alive, but Genevieve was not about to let this opportunity slip out of her fingers. Lifting her skirts almost to her knees, she pounded down the sidewalk, her much longer legs eating up the distance between them. Behind her, the coachman made a startled noise and the carriage began to rumble down the street after her.

Genevieve was afraid she would have to launch herself at the girl and send them into an undignified heap on the ground, but the maid made the mistake of glancing back at Genevieve, and she caught her foot on a paving stone and went tumbling to the ground.

Genevieve was on her in an instant, wrapping her hand around the girl's arm and yanking her to her feet. "Oh!" Genevieve exclaimed loudly, in case anyone was watching. "What a nasty fall you took. Here, let me help you."

"Let go of me!" The maid twisted and jerked, but she could not break Genevieve's hold. "Why're you chasing me? I din't do nothing wrong." Her voice settled into a whine.

"Really? Then why did you run?" Genevieve cast a glance around and saw that they were still alone on the street except for her driver, so she dropped her pretense of help and said harshly, "Don't even think of running. Now, get in the carriage. If you tell me what I want to know, I won't hurt you."

After a last desperate look up the street, the girl slumped and went to the carriage, her hands clenching together. Genevieve pushed her in and climbed in behind her.

"You are Miss Halford's maid, isn't that right?"

The other girl nodded. "Yes, miss."

"What's your name?"

The girl looked troubled, but she finally mumbled, "Tansy Mullins, miss."

"All right, Tansy. I think you know what I want to learn from you."

"I can't tell you, miss. I swear I can't. She'll turn me out without a recommendation." Tears welled in the girl's eyes.

"Miss Halford need not know I heard it from you," Genevieve told her encouragingly.

"Miss Halford!" The girl let out a harsh laugh. "I'm not talking about Miss Iona. It's her ladyship!"

Genevieve stiffened. "Do you mean Lady Dursbury? Elora?"

"Of course, miss! You don't think it'd be Miss Iona who'd do such things!"

"What things?" Genevieve asked quickly.

"No, miss, please don't ask me. I can't! You don't know what she's like!"

"I think I have a fairly good idea," Genevieve said drily. "But it is Miss Halford for whom you work. You said she's not like Elora. Surely she won't turn you out for telling me."

"Oh, no, miss, it's her ladyship as hired me, not Miss Iona. Miss Iona was his lordship's ward, and it was her ladyship set me up as Miss Iona's abigail."

"Still, I think it must be Miss Halford who pays you. She would not allow Lady Dursbury to let you go."

"She wouldn't go against her ladyship." Tansy shook her head vehemently. "She never would."

"Well, there is no need for either one of them to know." Genevieve decided to try a different tack. "I certainly won't tell them where I got the information."

"But she'll know! I know she will!"

Genevieve felt a pang of sympathy for the girl, who looked stricken with fear. However, she could not let pity get the better of her. Right now she had to be a Stafford through and through. She straightened to her full height and fixed the maid with the full force of her icy gaze. "Do you know who I am, Tansy?"

"Yes, miss." She nodded. "You're the lady what was going to marry his lordship."

"I am far more than that. I am Lady Genevieve Thorwood, and my brother is the Earl of Rawdon. We are not a pleasant lot to cross. My ancestors used to put their enemies to the sword, and I can promise you that if you do not tell me what I want to know, I will make certain you regret it for the rest of your life."

Tansy gulped, staring at her with wide eyes.

Genevieve relaxed a little and smiled, offering the maid the carrot after the stick. "Now, Tansy, I assure you that I can find you another position. My grandmother and I know a great many women who are frequently hiring new maids. If you want to leave that house, whether Lady Dursbury discovers you told me or not, I will see that you get hired somewhere else. In the meantime"—Genevieve reached into her reticule and withdrew her coin purse, holding up a bright gold coin—"I can give you something to ease your way."

Tansy's eyes grew as large as the coin in Genevieve's hand. She looked from it to Genevieve, clearly torn between hope and fear. "Oh, miss . . . do you mean it?"

"I do indeed." Genevieve held out the coin to her.

Tansy chewed at her lower lip, looking away from the lure of the gold and then back. Finally, she reached out and grabbed the coin, sticking it inside her shirt in a furtive motion.

"Did Lady Dursbury hire the other girl as well? The one you just met in the park?" Genevieve hoped that a question a bit removed from the maid herself might get her talking.

"Yes, miss." Tansy nodded. "That's Hattie, me cousin. Her ladyship asked me to find another girl, someone working at the Morecombes', so I sent Hattie to try to get hired on for the party, see. I figured she might as well make the money as anybody else."

"But why did Elora use you? Why not her own maid?"

"Her? She's a foreigner. French, now, isn't she? She don't know anybody round here. Won't even talk to the rest of us, thinks she's too good. And her ladyship knew she could get me to do it. She—she's been having me spy on Miss Iona ever since she hired me."

"Spy on Miss Halford? But why?"

"I dunno." Tansy shrugged. "She never does anything her ladyship don't already know about. Miss Iona's under that one's thumb, isn't she, just like the rest of the house. So I never had to tell her nothing that . . . that hurt Miss Iona, really. I just told her how Miss Iona moons about over his lordship and how she worries about what to do about this or that. Or what hat Miss Iona admired in the milliner's window. Like that. Then maybe her ladyship'll buy that hat for Miss Iona, make her grateful to her. Like her ladyship knows her so well and is so kind and all. And if she knows Miss Iona's scared of something, then her ladyship uses it, you know, to get Miss Iona to do something she wants."

"How diabolical!"

"How what?" Tansy looked at Genevieve blankly.

"How cruel."

"Yes'm, she is."

"So she hired you to do this thing to me because she was already using you."

Tansy snorted. Now that she had gotten started, she seemed eager to talk, the words rolling out with the force of long-held resentment. "She didn't *hire* me. Not that one. She don't pay me extra; I don't make as much as that fancy French maid of hers. She knows I won't quit—where would I go? If I don't do what she wants, she'll tell Miss Iona how I've been spying on her for years, and she'll let me go. She won't give me a recommendation. More than that, her ladyship will tell any other lady that hired me that I was wicked, that I stole from her and such. She told me she would. Whenever I balk at doing something she wants, that's what she says. I daren't not do it. Miss Iona'd be that hurt, and she'd hate me. She wouldn't keep her from tossing me out."

"We'll see about that." Genevieve's eyes were bright with a cold, hard light. "Don't worry. I think Iona might feel differently if she knew the whole of it, and even if she does not, I'll see you get hired by someone much better than Lady Dursbury."

"Wouldn't be hard to be better than her," the girl muttered.

Genevieve chuckled. "There. You've got some spirit. That's good." Genevieve smiled at the girl. "Now, tell me, why did Lady Dursbury set up the scene in the library?"

"It was to help Miss Iona get his lordship. Her ladyship didn't, well, she didn't much like you." Tansy cast a worried glance over at Genevieve.

"So Elora didn't want me marrying her stepson?"

"She liked being the queen bee. His lordship let her go on running it after his father died. Her ladyship figured he would marry Miss Iona. Only then they went to that wedding, and he wanted to marry you instead. You outshine my poor miss, you see. But her ladyship wasn't going to let that happen. If my miss married him, she'd still let her ladyship run things; that's just always been the way of it, you see. But you, now . . ."

Genevieve nodded. "Yes. It would have been quite different for Elora."

"So she decided to get rid of you."

"But why did she start up this new campaign against me? She was having you and your cousin tell *The Onlooker* things to say about me, wasn't she?"

"Yes'm, she knows the man what runs it. She's told him things ever since we came to London after the old lord died. She knew this fellow when she was younger; I think they'd been, well, you know. . . . She'd drop him little bits to put in that column, and he'd send her jewels and such. She liked the gifts, but she didn't want anybody to see her go there, so she sent me."

"But it was the other girl, your cousin, whom I saw there today."

"Yes'm." Tansy nodded. "After my cousin helped with that note and all, Lady Dursbury decided to send her to the paper instead, on account of she was afraid someone might recognize me. She's—I think her ladyship is scared of you, miss. And your grandma; she calls her 'the dragon.'"

Genevieve smiled. "I am sure that would please my grandmother."

"Hattie came and told me about your chasing her; she was scared, like, of what you'd do. And I told her ladyship, so she wrote it down and sent Hattie to that paper with it. And that thing the other day, about you having the aff—well, you know."

"Yes, I know," Genevieve said drily. "But I don't understand why Elora would continue her attacks on me. She had accomplished her goal once Dursbury broke off our engagement. Does she simply dislike me so much she wants to ruin my life?"

"I don't think she'd mind, that's for sure. But it's the man."

"What man?"

"Your man. She wants him for herself."

"Myles?" Genevieve's eyes turned so fierce that the maid edged farther away from her.

"Yes'm. She was that mad when she heard he'd married you. That wasn't what she'd wanted at all. When you came back to London, she thought she could turn his head. Win him over. She fair hated it 'cause he wouldn't stray."

In the midst of her anger, Genevieve was aware of a small smug lift of joy. "So she thought that if she ruined my reputation, he would turn away from me?"

"I guess. She said as how it'd open up his eyes about you, make him angry. And she said you'd turn tail and go back to the estate. She reckoned if he was on his own in London, she'd get him to give in. He'd be lonely, see."

"I suppose it makes sense. In some mad way." Genevieve looked over at Tansy. "Do you want to go back there, Tansy? If you'd like, you can come with me now. I'll tell the housekeeper to give you a place until we can find someone who needs a lady's maid."

"Oh, miss!" The girl's eyes widened with hope, but then she looked pensive. "I think—I think I ought to talk to Miss Iona first. Explain. She's always been nice to me. And if maybe she believed me . . ." Tansy shrugged. "And if she doesn't, I could come to you." Tansy looked at Genevieve anxiously. "If that'd be all right, I mean?"

"Of course, if that's what you'd rather. I won't forget my promise; you needn't worry."

The girl's shoulders relaxed, and she offered a tiny smile. "Thank you, miss."

The girl started to climb out of the carriage, then stopped and turned back to Genevieve, frowning. "Best watch your back, miss, her ladyship's planning something. I heard her talking to that French maid of hers; I couldn't understand it, but she looked terrible angry."

"Thank you, Tansy." Genevieve leaned across and put her hand on the maid's arm. "I won't forget this."

Tansy smiled shyly and ducked her head, then climbed out of the carriage and hurried away. Genevieve pulled back the curtain and called up to her driver, "Home, Milton. And quickly."

Twenty-four

Genevieve *found the house in* chaos. Lady Julia stood in the entry, flanked by Amelia, talking urgently with a maid in tears, and Bouldin, looking more rattled than Genevieve would have imagined the impassive man could look. When Genevieve walked in, they all swung toward her with hope on their faces, but it dropped away quickly.

"Genevieve! My dear, is Nell with you? Do you know where she is?" Lady Julia asked.

Ice formed in Genevieve's chest. "No. What is wrong? Is Nell missing?"

Tears filled Julia's eyes, and she pressed her hand to her lips.

Amelia spoke for her. "We were out shopping, Mother and I. Nell wasn't interested, of course, and she stayed here with the baby." She gestured vaguely toward the crying servant, and Genevieve realized that the girl was not one of their maids, but the nursemaid who took care of Amelia's toddler. "When we got home, Nell was gone, and no one knows where she is."

Genevieve turned toward her butler, who said, "I am

so dreadfully sorry, my lady. No one saw her leave, and we have searched the house." He took a breath, looking as if he were about to fall on his sword. "I understand if you wish me to leave your employ."

"I am sure it isn't your fault," Lady Julia said, dabbing at her eyes. "Nell is so used to going her own way. I wouldn't be alarmed if we were home; it is just that here . . ."

"Yes, London is a good deal less safe," Genevieve agreed. "Let us save the recriminations, Bouldin, and concentrate on finding Miss Nell." She crossed to the crying nurse. "Was Nell with you at any time?"

"Yes, my lady," the girl said, hiccuping and wiping away the tears streaming down her cheeks. "We was out in the garden, ma'am. It was such a nice day, you see. But Master Rupert got fussy, so I took him upstairs, like, and when he went to sleep, I come back down, but Miss Nell weren't in the garden still. I just thought she'd gone up to her room or something. I never—I never—" The girl went off into wails again.

Genevieve took the girl's arm firmly. "Hush, now. Crying isn't doing anyone any good, least of all Miss Nell's mother."

The girl's tears stopped in a gulp and she gazed back at Genevieve, wide-eyed. "Yes'm."

"When was it you saw Miss Nell last?" Genevieve went on.

"About, um, I 'spect it was an hour ago. Master Rupert was still asleep when we started looking for her."

"Did she say anything about what she was planning to do or where she might go?"

"No, miss. But when I come out with the baby, she was reading something. A note, like, but she put it in her pocket and didn't say nothing about it."

"Nell was out in the garden alone before that?"

The girl nodded, and Bouldin put in, "I believe Miss Nell went out to the garden to read soon after the other ladies left. But no one noticed when she came in."

"Did anyone come by here? Ask to speak to Nell? Or give her a letter?" Genevieve asked him.

"Not that I know of, but I will ask the staff." He bowed and left the room.

"Where do you think she could have gone?" Lady Julia asked.

"I thought perhaps that wretched cat had gotten out, and she had gone looking for it," Amelia said.

"But the cat is here," Lady Julia said. "We saw him. So it could not be that."

"What was that note? Who would have sent Nell a message?" Amelia asked. "She knows no one in London."

"Perhaps she thought it was from someone she did know," Genevieve said. When the other women looked at her, confused, she went on, "I am very sorry. I think someone may be using Nell to get back at me. The person who started all the gossip."

"You mean you found out who it is?" Lady Julia asked.

"Yes." Genevieve related quickly what Miss Halford's maid had revealed to her.

"What a wicked woman!" Julia exclaimed. "But where—how—she will not harm Nell, will she?"

"I don't believe she intends to hurt her. The thing is, who knows what might happen? So far, none of Elora's schemes have worked out as she planned."

"My lady." Bouldin returned, followed by a young girl in a rough dress, one of the lowly scullery maids, Genevieve thought, from the looks of her. "May told me someone did come by earlier today. Tell her ladyship, May."

The girl cast an awed and frightened glance at Genevieve, then ducked her head and curtsied, saying, "I dunno who it was, my lady. She just, she said she had summat to give somebody, but Cook sent her off straightaway. Cook don't hold with no Frenchies."

"French! She was French?"

"That's what Cook said when she heard her." The girl looked up, concerned. "I don't know, ma'am."

"But she left without seeing anyone? Besides you and Cook, I mean."

"I didn't see her after that. I closed the door. I 'spect she went away."

"But after you closed the door, she could have seen the garden gate there on the side, couldn't she? She could have looked into the rear garden." Genevieve turned to Bouldin.

"Yes, ma'am. No one would have noticed."

"So she could have said something to Nell when she was in the garden. Or given her the note the nursemaid saw Nell reading."

"That's important? Her being French?" Lady Julia asked.

"Yes. Lady Dursbury's abigail is French. I think Elora has lured Nell away, probably with a note purporting to be from me. That is her style, and she would want to make it appear my fault."

"But how would Nell get there? Where could she have gone?" Lady Julia paled.

"That's the question." Genevieve thought for a moment, and suddenly the plan became clear to her. "Bartholomew Fair!"

"What?"

"That place Nell was talking about the other day?" Amelia asked.

"Yes. Lady Dursbury was calling on us when Nell was talking about it, and at the time I thought she was foolish because she said exactly the sort of thing that would make Nell want to go."

"You're right." Julia's face lightened. "Then we must go there."

Genevieve wrinkled her brow in thought. "We should get Myles. Lady Julia, if you and your daughter will take our carriage and go to White's, the driver can go in and fetch Myles. If he is escorting us, it will be acceptable for Nell to be there, even at Bartholomew Fair. I'll go after Nell. It will be better to take a hackney there."

"I'll go with you," Amelia said.

"No, if Elora manages to catch us there, it will be all our reputations. Better that it's just mine."

"I don't care. She is my sister, and it's my brother whom this contemptible woman wants to steal from you, and, anyway, you might need some help."

"Absolutely right." Lady Julia nodded. "I shall go after

Myles alone. You two find Nell. And if you see that woman there, I hope you will, well, I don't know, do something dreadful to her."

They split up, one footman running for the carriage for Lady Julia, and the butler himself going out to hail a hackney and put the ladies up into it. They set off at a good pace, for Genevieve had promised the man a large tip. The great fair, begun hundreds of years earlier, was held along Cloth Fair in Smithfield, just outside the ancient city walls. It had once been set up around the graveyard of the priory and along the lane, though over the years it had grown so large that it now stretched far beyond St. Bartholomew's (both the Greater and the Lesser).

The hackney had to stop at the edge of the fairgrounds, unable to drive farther in, and the two women climbed down, gazing in awe and consternation as they took in the scene before them. Makeshift lanes, all of them swarming with people, ran off in all directions, lined with tents and booths and hastily erected wooden facades of buildings. Music came from several directions, and the air was filled with the cries of booth owners hawking their wares. In the distance, Genevieve could see three gondolas hanging from temporary scaffolding, swinging back and forth like pendulums. They, too, were filled with people, all shrieking in delight or fear, she wasn't sure which.

"Oh, my," Genevieve breathed, turning from side to side. "How will we ever find her here?"

"Should we divide up?" Amelia asked. "I had thought we would, but now . . ."

"I fear we would get lost." Genevieve nodded. "Perhaps we should stay together."

So, walking together, they started down one of the jumbled lanes, looking all around them for any sight of Nell. People called to them from the booths, and more than one rough-looking fellow ogled them. Genevieve could well understand why it was considered a disreputable place, but the colorful sights and sounds were also intriguing. Acrobats tumbled across a raised stage on one side of them. On the opposite side, a rope stretched between two tall poles across a grassy plot, and a man stood on a small platform at one end, about to embark on a walk across the rope.

It would be easy for a young girl to get lost in here, Genevieve knew. Someone could grab Nell and make off with her, and they would never have any idea what had happened to her. Genevieve wished desperately that Myles were with her, but now she worried that he and his mother would not be able to find them in this crowd.

Off to her left, she could see the tops of the gondola poles, towering above everything else, and she pointed toward them, saying to Amelia, "Let's go look for her there. I think those rides would attract Nell the most, and it is the easiest place to locate. With luck she will go there if she is lost."

Amelia agreed, and they set out toward the poles. And there, staring up at the ride high above her head, stood a familiar form.

"Nell!"

The girl turned, relief flooding her face. "Genevieve!

And Amelia!" She ran to them, a grin spreading across her face. "Isn't it amazing? I've been waiting here at the rides like you said, but I was afraid I might miss you. There are so many people."

"We're here now, so everything is all right." Genevieve cast a quick look around. "And Myles is coming, as well."

"Nell, what were you thinking?" Amelia began to scold as soon as she finished hugging her younger sister. "You shouldn't have come here! Especially not by yourself!"

Nell's face clouded. "But Genevieve said to meet her at the fair. She said that way no one would know." Nell glanced from her sister to Genevieve, and her voice trailed away. "Genevieve? You sent me a note."

"No, dear, I didn't. It was a trick. Do you have it still?"

Nell nodded, reaching into the pocket of her skirt.

At a trill of laughter behind them, Genevieve stiffened. Turning around, she saw Lady Dursbury, strolling along with her hand on the arm of one of her gentlemen admirers. Iona tagged along with them, glancing around her, frightened. Two other ladies and some men of Dursbury's set also accompanied them. Well, Genevieve thought, Elora had certainly made sure her arranged scene would be well witnessed.

"Lady Genevieve!" Elora exclaimed in shocked tones. Genevieve could see that Elora was genuinely surprised to see her, but in the next instant a calculating expression crept over Elora's face, and she went on, "Whatever are you doing here? I am so surprised to see you. And all alone." She made a great show of glancing around.

"Yes," Genevieve said acidly. "I am sure it is a great surprise to you."

"She isn't alone," Nell piped up. "We're all here." She gestured toward her sister beside her.

Lady Dursbury, registering the presence of the other Thorwood women for the first time, looked taken aback. "Oh. My. I see." She paused, then cleared her throat delicately. "My dear Genevieve, I must say . . . well, this is hardly the place to take a child. Indeed, a lady should not really be in such a place."

"And yet here you are," Genevieve retorted. She was beginning to understand what her brother meant when he said his blood was up. She could feel the unspent energy humming through her as she faced Elora, and she was suddenly sharper, brighter, more keenly aware of everything around her. She was, she realized, eager to do battle with her enemy. She smiled fiercely, and Lady Dursbury blinked, taking an unconscious step backward.

"That's entirely different," Elora replied, stammering a bit before she recovered her poise. "You are but a young woman, only newly married, whereas I am a widow and—"

"I realize that you are much older than we are," Genevieve agreed pleasantly. "Still, I think a lady's reputation is easily damaged no matter what her age. Don't you?"

Elora let out a little titter and glanced at the men on either side of her. "But, my dear, I have gentlemen escorting me, whereas you do not."

"Ah, but that is where you are wrong, Lady Dursbury," a pleasant male voice said, and everyone turned to see

Myles standing a few feet away from them. His mother was beside him, smiling sweetly, and on the other side of her was Lord Morecombe.

Elora made a strangled noise. "Sir Myles."

"Good afternoon," Myles replied, strolling over to stand by Genevieve. "Genevieve, love, I was afraid for a moment that we had lost the rest of you. It is a terrible crush, isn't it?" He looked toward Lady Dursbury and her party. "I see a great number of people had the same idea as we did today."

"Yes, quite right," one of the other men said. "Devilish crowded." He glanced around him. "Have to be sure to leave before dark, of course, not the thing for the ladies then."

"Well, if you will excuse us," Sir Myles began, looping an arm around Nell and starting to move away.

"No, not just yet," Genevieve said. "I have something to say to Lady Dursbury."

"You do?" Myles cast a wary glance at his wife.

"Yes. I do." She stepped forward, her pale blue eyes intent on the other woman's face. "I know what mischief you have been up to, Elora. I know what you thought to do today to me, not caring what might happen to an innocent young girl. And I know you arranged for that scene in the library so you could keep Dursbury from marrying me."

"Genevieve! Whatever are you saying?" Lady Dursbury's lower lip trembled artfully.

"I am saying that you are a conniving, wicked wretch of a woman. I don't care that you managed to break my engagement; it was the best thing that ever happened to me, and I thank God every day that I am married to the best man in this city and not your hidebound prig of a stepson!"

Genevieve heard a stifled laugh from Elora's group, and behind her a little grunt of surprise from Myles, but she ignored them both. She was in full sail now, and she was not about to stop until she was done with Lady Dursbury.

"But you tried to cast a taint on my reputation, which touches on my husband's name as well, by spreading vicious lies about me to *The Onlooker*. And I will not stand for that. Nor am I the only one you have harmed. You have had Miss Halford spied on for years. And you have fed that scandal sheet on-dits about the members of the *ton* for months."

Iona gasped, and one of the men exclaimed, "I say!"

"I am also aware *why* you tried to ruin my reputation. You wanted me out of the way so you could have a clear path to Sir Myles. You wanted to have an affair with him. Admittedly, one can hardly blame you for that desire. However, I can and I do blame you for all the despicable things you have done in pursuit of him."

"As if I would need tricks to take him from you!" Elora spat back, her face contorted with fury. "He may be under your spell now. But you won't have him for long. He will soon tire of a cold fish like you. He'll want someone warm, someone who knows how to treat a man."

"He won't want you," Genevieve said bluntly. "You could never give him what I can: I love Myles. And that is something you are incapable of. Let me make it clear to you, Elora." Genevieve stalked forward, her finger stabbing the air in front of her. "You will never have my husband. No matter what you do or how much you scheme or how hard you try to blacken my name. I will not go running off to the country to lick my wounds and leave you in possession of the field. Myles is mine!" She stopped inches away from Lady Dursbury, looming over her, her eyes shooting pale fire. "And you know what they say about Staffords, don't you? We never give up what is ours."

For a long moment, the two women stared at each other, silence reverberating in the air.

Then Gabriel said, "Good gad, Thea will be furious she missed this."

Myles began to laugh, and Nell and his mother joined in, and even Amelia's eyes were dancing with amusement. Elora let out a strangled cry and leapt at Genevieve, her fingers raking out like claws at Genevieve's face. Genevieve flung up her left arm, deflecting the attack, and her right fist lashed out, hitting the other woman squarely on the cheek.

Elora stumbled back with a shriek, clutching at her face, and one of the men in her party caught her, and the others formed a circle around her, hustling her away. For a moment, Iona stood gazing after Lady Dursbury and the others. She looked at Genevieve, then gave her a slight nod and hurried after her group.

"A flush hit," Myles remarked, grinning, as he came up and curled his arm around Genevieve. "Now you have defeated all the Dursburys."

Genevieve grimaced at him. "You needn't look so pleased with yourself."

"How can I not?" He laughed and turned toward the others. "As we are already here, shall we look around a bit?"

The others readily agreed, and Lord Morecombe offered his arm to Lady Julia. They set off, with Genevieve and Myles lagging behind the rest.

"Well, my dear, that was interesting entertainment you provided," he said, taking her hand and raising it to his lips, then tucking it into his arm.

"I may have gotten a bit carried away," Genevieve admitted somewhat shamefacedly. "Did I embarrass you?"

He laughed. "How could I be embarrassed by that defense? I shall not have to worry about fending off unwanted advances now." He was silent for a moment, then said, his voice lower and suddenly serious, "Did you mean it?"

"Of course." Genevieve glanced at him.

"I mean, the part where you said you loved me."

Genevieve was surprised to see the faint look of trepidation in his eyes. "Yes," she said quietly, and glanced away, her stomach fluttering. "You needn't worry; I shan't make a cake of myself. I know you married me because of your sense of honor and duty. Because of your loyalty to my brother."

"Genevieve." Myles stopped and turned her to face him. "I did not marry you because of Alec. And I certainly did not do it because I'm a gentleman. I did it because . . . when I looked at you, I knew I would do anything to take that sad look from your face. A man doesn't do that out of pity or loyalty or anything else. I love you, Genevieve. I think I have deep down for years. Why else would I have kept hanging about? Why else would I have put up with that damn cat?"

Laughter gurgled up out of her throat. "Myles . . . be serious."

"I have never been more serious." He took her hands in his. "I hated it every time you talked about us not being tied to each other. I couldn't bear it that you didn't want me in your bed every night. Why do you think I waged that damned silly war with you? I wanted—so badly—to have you *choose* me. To believe that it wasn't merely desperation that brought you to marry me. I wanted you to tell me that you didn't want some cold, loveless marriage of convenience any more than I did. I wanted to know . . . that you loved me."

"I do. Oh, Myles, I do love you. And I have never been more grateful for anything than I am for that awful debacle at the Morecombes' party. Because without it, I wouldn't have you." She wound her arms around his neck, gazing up at him.

"You'd best have a care," he warned her, smiling. "Everyone is looking at us."

"Then let's give them something to see." Genevieve stretched up on tiptoe and kissed him.